NEW YORK TIMES BESTSELLING AUTHOR

DIANA PALMER

A CATTLEMAN'S HONOR

Previously published as
Nelson's Brand and *The Wedding in White*

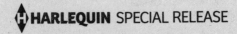

HARLEQUIN SPECIAL RELEASE

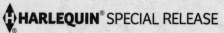

HARLEQUIN® SPECIAL RELEASE

ISBN-13: 978-1-335-14162-0

A Cattleman's Honor

Copyright © 2020 by Harlequin Books S.A.

Nelson's Brand
First published in 1991. This edition published in 2020.
Copyright © 1991 by Diana Palmer

The Wedding in White
First published in 2000. This edition published in 2020.
Copyright © 2000 by Diana Palmer

Recycling programs
for this product may
not exist in your area.

This edition published by arrangement with Harlequin Books S.A.

For questions and comments about the quality of this book, please contact us at CustomerService@Harlequin.com.

Harlequin Enterprises ULC
22 Adelaide St. West, 40th Floor
Toronto, Ontario M5H 4E3, Canada
www.Harlequin.com

Printed in U.S.A.

A prolific author of more than one hundred books, **Diana Palmer** got her start as a newspaper reporter. A *New York Times* bestselling author and voted one of the top ten romance writers in America, she has a gift for telling the most sensual tales with charm and humor. Diana lives with her family in Cornelia, Georgia. Visit her website at dianapalmer.com.

Books by Diana Palmer

Long, Tall Texans

Fearless
Heartless
Dangerous
Merciless
Courageous
Protector
Invincible
Untamed
Defender
Undaunted

The Wyoming Men

Wyoming Tough
Wyoming Fierce
Wyoming Bold
Wyoming Strong
Wyoming Rugged
Wyoming Brave

The Morcai Battalion

The Morcai Battalion
The Morcai Battalion: The Recruit
The Morcai Battalion: Invictus
The Morcai Battalion: The Rescue

Visit the Author Profile page
at Harlequin.com for more titles.

CONTENTS

NELSON'S BRAND

For Kathryn Falk and Melinda Helfer
of *RT Book Reviews* with love.

a corner table, a little away from it on one side, with his half brother Dwight, and Dwight's fiancée, Winnie. He didn't know her name, but he was pretty sure that she was Winnie's out-of-town houseguest. Pryor, Wyoming, was a small town, and news traveled fast when anyone had company.

He took another sip of his whiskey and stared at the small shot glass contemplatively. He drank far too much lately. When he started staying out late at night and couldn't remember anything about it the next morning, he needed to take another look at his life, he thought bitterly. Dale Branigan had caught him in a weak moment and now she was hounding him for dates. Not that she was bad-looking, but she reminded him of the excesses that were taking him straight to hell, according to Dwight.

He glanced toward Dwight's disapproving face, so unlike his, and deliberately raised the shot glass to his thin lips with a mocking smile. He drained it, but when the bartender asked if he wanted another, he said no. It wasn't Dwight who stopped him. It was the expression on that woman's face who was sitting with Dwight and Winnie. There was something quiet and calming about her face, about the oddly compassionate way she was looking at him. What he'd thought was a flirting stare didn't seem to be one. As he met her eyes across the room, he felt a jolt of pure emotion run through him. Odd. He hadn't felt that before. Maybe it was the liquor.

He looked around. The bar was crowded, and there weren't many women around. Thank God Dale wasn't here to pester him. Frequently on a Friday night, he drove up to Billings for a little entertainment. Tonight, he wasn't in the mood. He'd overheard a chance remark from one of his men and his quick temper had cost him a good mechanic. It was his nature to strike out when he was angry. With a soft, cold laugh he considered that he'd probably inherited that trait from his father. From his *real* father, not the man who'd been married to his mother for more than twenty years. Until six months ago, his name had been Gene Nelson and he was accepted by everyone as Hank Nelson's son. But six months ago, Hank Nelson had died—ten years after Gene's mother—and he'd left a will that was as much a confession as a bequeath. It had contained the shocking news that he'd adopted Gene at the age of four.

Gene realized that he was idly sliding the shot glass around on the bar and stopped. He paid for the drink and turned toward the door.

Dwight called to him and he hesitated. His younger half brother was the head honcho at the Triple N Ranch now. That was the biggest blow to his pride. He'd been the eldest son. Now he was the outsider, and Dwight was the rightful heir. That took a lot of getting used to after thirty years.

He cocked his hat over one eye and strode toward Dwight's table, his lean, dark face rigid, his pale green eyes like wet peridots under lashes as thick and black as the straight hair under the gray Stetson.

"You haven't met Gene, have you, Allison?" Winnie asked, smiling. She was blond and petite and very pretty. Her fairness matched Dwight's, who also had blond hair and blue eyes, a fact that had often puzzled

Gene. Their sister Marie was equally fair. Only Gene
was dark, and he alone had green eyes. His mother had
been a blue-eyed blonde, like Hank Nelson. Why had
he never connected those stray facts? Perhaps he'd been
dodging the issue all along.

"No, we haven't met," Allison said softly. She looked
up at Gene with hazel eyes that were his instant undoing. He'd never seen eyes like that. There was something in them that made him feel warm inside. "How
do you do, Mr. Nelson?" she asked, and she smiled. It
was like sunshine on a cloudy day.

He caught his breath silently. She'd called him Mr.
Nelson, but he wasn't a Nelson. He straightened. What
the hell, it was the only name he'd ever known. He nodded curtly. "Miss…?"

"Hathoway," she replied.

"Are you on your way back to the ranch?" Dwight
asked, his tone reconciliatory, hesitant.

"Yes."

"I'll see you there, then."

Gene let his eyes fall to the woman again, to her gentle oval face. Her eyes and mouth were her best features.
She wasn't really pretty, but she had a glow about her.
It grew as he looked at her unsmilingly, and he finally
realized that she was blushing. Strange response, for a
woman her age. She was out of her teens; probably in
her mid-twenties.

"Gene, are you coming to the barbecue tomorrow
night?" Winnie asked.

He was still staring at Allison. "Maybe." His head
moved a little to the side as he looked down at Allison.

"Are you Winnie's houseguest?" he asked her, his voice slow and deep, without a noticeable accent.

"Yes," she said. "Just for a couple of weeks, I mean," she stammered. He made her nervous. She'd never felt such an instant attraction to anyone.

Unbeknownst to her, neither had Gene. He was having a hard time trying to drag himself away. This woman made him feel as if he'd suddenly come out of a daze, and he didn't understand why. "I've got to get home," he said, forcing the words out. He nodded curtly and left them, his booted feet heavy on the wood floor, his back arrow-straight.

Allison Hathoway watched him go. She'd never seen anyone quite as fascinating as the departing Mr. Nelson. He looked like a cowboy she'd seen in a movie once, tall and lean and lithe, with wide shoulders and narrow hips and long, powerful legs. She, who had little if anything to do with men, was so affected by him that she was still flushed and shaking inside from the brief encounter.

"I didn't think he was going to stop," Dwight said with a rueful smile. "He avoids me a lot these days. Marie, too. Except to start fights."

"It isn't getting any easier at home, is it?" Winnie asked her fiancé, laying a small hand on his.

Dwight shook his head as he curled his fingers around hers. "Gene won't talk about it. He just goes on as if nothing has happened. Marie's at the end of her rope, and so am I. We love him, but he's convinced himself that he's no longer part of our family."

Allison listened without understanding what they were talking about.

"Is he much older than you, Dwight?" she asked.

He lifted an eyebrow, smiling at her interest. "About six years. He's thirty-four."

"But he's not a man to risk your heart on," Winnie said softly. "Gene's just gone through a bad time. He's hurt and he's ready to lash out at anybody who gets too close."

"I hate to agree, but she's right," Dwight replied quietly. "Gene's gone from bad to worse in the past few months. Women, liquor, fights. He threw a punch at our mechanic and fired him this morning."

"The man deserved it," Winnie said quietly. "You know what he called Gene."

"He wouldn't have called Gene anything if my brother hadn't started acting like one of the hands instead of the boss," Dwight said angrily. "He hates the routine of working cattle every day. He had the business head and he was good at organization. I'm not. I was better at working cattle and taking care of the shipping and receiving. The will reversed our duties. Now we're both miserable. I can't handle the men, and Gene won't. The ranch is going to pot because he won't buckle down. He drinks on the weekends and the men's morale is at rock bottom. They're looking for excuses to quit or get fired."

"But...he only had one drink at the bar," Allison said softly, puzzled, because one drink surely wasn't that bad.

Dwight lifted a blond eyebrow. "So he did. He kept

glancing at you, and then he put down the glass. I was watching. It seemed to bother him. That's the first time I've known him to stop at one drink."

"He always used to," Winnie recalled. "In fact, he hardly ever touched the stuff."

"He's so damned brittle," Dwight sighed. "He can't bend. God, I feel for him! I can imagine how it would be if I were in his shoes. He's so alone."

"Most people are, really," Allison said, her hazel eyes soft and quiet. "And when they hurt, they do bad things sometimes."

Winnie smiled at her warmly. "You'd find excuses for hardened criminals, wouldn't you?" she asked gently. "I suppose that's why you're so good at what you do."

"At what I *did*," Allison corrected. Her eyes fell worriedly to the table. "I don't know that I'll ever be able to do it again."

"You need time," Winnie replied sympathetically. "That's all, Allie. You just need time."

"Something I have in common with your future brother-in-law, I gather," came the reply. Allison sighed and sipped her ginger ale. "I hope you're right."

But that night, alone in bed, the nightmares came again and she woke, as she always did these days, in a cold sweat, trying not to hear the sound of guns, the sound of screams.

She wrapped her white chenille bathrobe around her worn white gown and made her way to the kitchen. Winnie was already there. Her mother was still in bed. Mrs. Manley was no early bird, even if her daughter was.

Allison's long black hair was around her shoulders in

a wavy tangle, her hazel eyes bloodshot, her face pale. She felt dragged out.

"Bad dreams again, I'll bet," Winnie said gently.

Allison managed a wan smile. She accepted the cup of hot black coffee Winnie handed her as they sat down at the kitchen table. "It's better than it was," she said.

"I'm just glad that you came to us," Winnie replied. She was wearing an expensive pink silk ensemble. The Manleys were much better off financially than the Hathoways had ever been, but Mrs. Manley and Allison's late mother had been best friends. As they grew up, Winnie and Allison became best friends, too.

They'd all lived near Bisbee, Arizona, when the girls were young and in school. Then the Manleys had moved to Pryor, Wyoming, when Mr. Manley took another job with an international mining concern. The Hathoways had been reassigned and Allison had gone with them to Central America.

The last few weeks could have been just a bad memory except that Allison was alone now. She'd called Winnie the minute she'd landed in the States again, and Winnie had flown down to Tucson to pick her up. It had been days before Allison could stop crying. Now, at last, she was beginning to heal. Yesterday was the first time Winnie had been able to coax her out among people. Allison was running from the news media that had followed her to Tucson, and she didn't want any attention drawn to her. She'd successfully covered her tracks, but she didn't know for how long.

"The barbecue is tonight. You have to come," Winnie told Allison. "Don't worry," she added quickly when the taller girl froze. "They're all rodeo people that Dwight's introducing me to. Nobody will bother you."

"Dwight's brother said he might be there," Allison murmured.

Winnie groaned. "For God's sake, don't tempt fate by getting too close to Gene. You've just come through one trauma; you don't need another one."

"I know." Allison cupped her cold hands around her coffee cup and closed her eyes. "I suppose I'm pretty vulnerable right now. It's just the aloneness. I've never been really alone before." She looked up and there was faint panic in her face.

"You'll never be alone as long as the Manleys are alive," Winnie said firmly. She laid a warm hand over Allison's forearm. "We all love you very much."

"Yes, I know. Do you know how much I care for all of you, and how grateful I am for a place to stay?" Allison replied sincerely. "I couldn't even go back to the house in Bisbee. Mom and Dad rented it out... Well, before we went to Central America." She faltered. "I was afraid to go near it even for possessions, in case somebody from the press was watching."

"All the furor will die down once the fighting stops," Winnie assured her. "You're being hunted because you have firsthand information about what really happened there. With the occupation forces in control, not much word is getting out. Once the government is well in power, it will become old news and they'll leave you alone. In the meantime, you can stay with us as long as you like."

"I'm in the way. Your marriage..."

"My marriage isn't for six months," Winnie reminded her with a warm smile. "You'll be my maid of honor. By then, all this will just be a sad memory. You'll have started to live again."

"I hope so," Allison replied huskily. "Oh, I hope so!"

Back at the Nelson place, Gene had just gone into the house to find his half sister, Marie, glaring at him from the living room. She looked like Dwight, except that she was petite and sharp-tongued.

"Dale's been calling again," she said irritably. "She seems to have the idea that she's engaged to you."

"I don't marry one-night stands," he said with deliberate cruelty.

"Then you should make that clear at the beginning," she returned.

His broad shoulders rose and fell. "I was too drunk."

Marie got up and went to him, her expression concerned. "Look at what you're doing to yourself," she said miserably. "This is your home. Dwight and I don't think of you as an outsider, Gene."

"Don't start," he said curtly, his pale green eyes flashing at her.

She threw up her hands with an angry sigh. "You won't listen! You drink, you carouse, you won't even pay attention to the lax discipline that's letting the men goof off half the time. I saw Rance with a bottle in broad daylight the other day!"

"If I see him, I'll do something about him," he said, striding toward the staircase.

"And when will that be? You're too busy having a good time to notice!"

He didn't answer her and he didn't look back. He went upstairs, his booted feet making soft thuds on the carpet.

"What about Dale? What do I tell her if she calls again?" she called after him.

"Tell her I joined a monastery and took vows of chastity," he drawled.

She chuckled. "That'll be the day," she murmured as she went back into the living room. At least he had been sober when he got home last night, she thought. And then she frowned. Not his usual style on a Friday night, she pondered.

It wasn't until later in the morning, when Dwight told her about his meeting with Allison, that his behavior registered.

"You mean, he looked at her and put the shot glass down?" Marie asked, all eyes.

"He certainly did," Dwight replied. Gene had gone out to check on the branding. Considering the size of the ranch and the number of new calves, it was much more than a couple of days' work. "He couldn't seem to keep his eyes off her."

"Is she pretty?" Marie asked.

He shook his head. "Nice. Very sweet. And a passable figure. But no, she's no beauty. Odd, isn't it, for Gene to even notice a woman like that? His tastes run to those brassy, experienced women he meets at rodeos. But Allison seemed to captivate him."

"If she influenced him enough to keep him sober on

a Friday night, I take my hat off to her," Marie said with genuine feeling. "He was like his old self last night. It was nice, seeing him that way. He's been so different for the past few months."

"Yes. I know it's hurt him. I never realized how much until I saw him coming apart in front of my eyes. Knowing about his real father has driven him half-mad."

"We can't help who our parents are," Marie said. "And Gene wouldn't be like that man in a million years. Surely he knows it?"

"He mumbled something about never having kids of his own because of his bad blood, one night when he was drinking," Dwight confided. He sighed and finished his coffee. "I wish we could find some way to cope with it. He has no peace."

Marie fingered her coffee cup thoughtfully. "Maybe he can find it with our Miss Hathoway," she mused, her eyes twinkling as they met his. "If she had that effect from a distance, imagine what it could be like at close range?"

"Except that she isn't Gene's kind of woman," he replied, and began to tell her all about the quiet Miss Hathoway.

Marie whistled. "My gosh. Poor kid."

"She's an amazing lady," he said, smiling. "Winnie's very fond of her. So fond that she'll discourage her from even looking at Gene, much less anything else."

"I can see why. The angel and the outlaw," she murmured, and smiled gently. "I guess I was daydreaming."

"Nothing wrong with dreams," he told her as he got up from the table. "But they won't run a ranch."

"Or organize a barbecue," Marie said, smiling. "Good luck with the books."

He groaned. "I'll have us in the poorhouse in another few months. If Gene was more approachable, I'd ask him to switch duties with me."

"Could you do that?"

"No reason why not," he said. "But he hasn't been in a listening mood."

"Don't give up. There's always tomorrow."

He laughed. "Tell him." He left her sitting there, still looking thoughtful.

Chapter Two

"Are you sure this looks all right on me?" Allison asked worriedly as she stared into the mirror at the low neckline of the strapless sundress Winnie had loaned her for the barbecue. They'd spent a lazy day at home, and now it was almost time to leave for the Nelsons' Triple N Ranch.

"Will you stop fussing? You look fine," Winnie assured her. "You've been out of touch with fashion for a while. Don't worry, it's perfectly proper. Even for Pryor, Wyoming," she added with a mischievous grin.

Allison sighed at her reflection in the full-length mirror. The young woman staring back at her looked like a stranger. Her long, dark hair was loose and wavy, framing her lovely oval face to its best advantage. She'd used mascara to emphasize her hazel eyes and she'd applied foundation and lipstick much more liberally than usual. Too, the off-the-shoulder sundress with its form-fitting bodice certainly did make her appear sophisticated. Its daring green, white and black pattern was exotic and somehow suited her tall, full-figured body. The strappy white sandals Winnie had loaned her completed the outfit.

Winnie modeled dresses for a local department store, so she was able to buy clothes at a considerable discount. She knew all sorts of beauty secrets, ways of making the most of her assets and downplaying the minor flaws of face and figure. She'd used them to advantage on her houseguest. Allison hardly recognized herself.

"I always knew you'd be a knockout if you were dressed and made up properly." Winnie nodded, approving her handiwork. "I'm glad you finally gave in and let me do my thing. You'll have the bachelors flitting around you like bees around clover. Dwight has a friend who'd be perfect for you, if he just shows up. He'll be bowled over."

"That'll be the day." Allison laughed softly, but she was secretly hoping that one particular bachelor named Gene might give her at least a second glance. She didn't know what kind of problems he had, but knowing that he'd been hurt, too, gave her a fellow feeling for him. It wasn't good to be alone when you were in pain.

"You're a late bloomer. Trust me." Winnie dragged her out of the bedroom and down the hall to the living room, where her mother was waiting. "Mom, look what I did to Allie," she called.

Mrs. Manley, a tall, graying woman, smiled as she turned to greet the two young women. "My, what a change," she said. "You look lovely, Allie. I wish your parents could see you."

Allie sobered. "Yes. So do I, Mrs. Manley."

"Forgive me," the older woman said. "Your mother and I were best friends for thirty years. But as hard as it is for me, I know it must be ten times harder for you."

"Life goes on," Allie said. She sighed, spreading her long, elegant fingers over the full skirt of the dress. "Isn't this a dream? I don't know how to thank you and Winnie for letting me stay with you. I really had nowhere else to go."

"I'm sure you have plenty of friends besides us, even if they are spread around the world a bit," Winnie chided. She hugged Allison. "But I'm still your best one. Remember when we were in seventh grade together back in Bisbee and we had to climb the mountain every day after school to get to our houses?"

"I miss Arizona sometimes," Allison said absently.

"I don't," Mrs. Manley said, shaking her head. "I used to have nightmares about falling into the Lavender Pit." She shuddered delicately. "It suited me when Winnie's father changed jobs and we moved here. Of course, if I'd known he was going to have to travel all over the world, I might have had second thoughts. He's gone almost all the time lately."

"He'll retire next year," Winnie reminded her.

"Yes, so he will." Mrs. Manley smiled and changed the subject. "You two had better get going, or you'll be late. The barbecue's at the Nelsons'?"

"Yes. Dwight invited us." Winnie grinned. "I'll have to make sure he doesn't toss me into the corral with those wild horses and ride off with Allie."

"Small chance when you're engaged." Allison grinned.

Winnie drove them to the Nelson place in her small Japanese car, a sporty model that suited her. Allison could drive, but she didn't have a current license. Where she'd been for the past two years, she hadn't needed one.

"Before we get there," Winnie said with a worried glance at Allison, "remember what I said and don't get too close to Gene. I don't think he'd let you get near him anyway—he's pretty standoffish around shy little innocents. But I wasn't kidding when I told you he was a dangerous customer. Even his brother and sister walk wide around him lately."

"He can't be that bad," Allison said gently and smiled.

"Don't you believe it." Winnie wasn't convinced. She scowled. "You watch yourself."

"All right. I will," she promised, but she had her fingers crossed beside her. "Is he by chance a jilted man, embittered by the faithlessness of some jaded woman, or was he treated horribly by his mother?" she added dryly.

"Gene doesn't get jilted by women, and his mother was a saint, according to Dwight," Winnie recalled. "A really wonderful woman who was loved by the whole community. She died about ten years ago. His father was a small-time rancher with a big heart. They were happily married. His…father died about six months ago."

Allison wondered at the hesitation in Winnie's voice when she talked about the late Mr. Nelson. "Do you know what's wrong with Gene, then?" she persisted.

"Yes. But I can't tell you," was the quiet reply. "It's not really any of my business, and Dwight's already been asked too many questions by the whole community. I don't mean to sound rude, and I trust you with my life," Winnie added, "but it's Gene's business."

"I understand."

"No, you don't, but Dwight may tell you one day. Or Marie."

"Is Marie like Gene or Dwight?"

"In coloring, she's like Dwight, blond and blue-eyed. Gene's...different. More hardheaded. Fiery."

"I gathered that. Doesn't he ever smile?"

"Sometimes," Winnie said. "Usually when he's about to hit somebody. He isn't an easygoing man. He's arrogant and proud and just a little too quick on the trigger to be good company. You'll find all that out. I just don't want you to find it out at close range, the hard way."

"I can take care of myself, you know," Allison mused. "I've been doing it in some pretty rough places for a long time."

"I know. But there's a big difference in what you've been doing and a man-woman relationship." She glanced at Allison as she turned into a long, graveled driveway. "Honestly, for a twenty-five-year-old woman, you're just hopelessly backward, and I mean that in the nicest possible way. It isn't as if you've had the opportunity to lead a wild life. But you've been criminally exposed in some ways and criminally sheltered in others. I don't think your parents ever really considered you when they made their plans."

Allison laughed gently. "Yes, they did. I'm just like

them, Winnie. I loved every minute of what we all did together, and I'll miss it terribly, even now." Her eyes clouded. "Things happen as God means them to. I can cope."

"It was such a waste, though...."

"Oh, no," Allison said, remembering the glowing faces she'd seen, the purpose and peace in the dark eyes. "No, it was never a waste. They're still alive, in the work they did, in the lives they changed."

"I won't argue with you," Winnie said gently. "We've kept in touch and remained friends all these long years since we were in school together in Bisbee. You're still the sister I never had. You'll have a home as long as I'm alive."

Tears sprang to Allison's big eyes. She hurriedly dashed them away. "If the circumstances were reversed, I hope you know that I'd do the same thing for you."

"I know," Winnie said. She wiped away a tear of her own.

There was a crowd of cars in the front driveway at the Nelsons' after they'd wound their way up past the towering lodgepole pines and aspen trees to the big stone house, backed by jagged high mountains.

"Isn't it just heaven?" Allison sighed involuntarily. "Wyoming is beautiful."

"Yes, it certainly is. I can happily spend the rest of my life here. Now, Allie, you aren't planning to sit behind bushes all night, are you?" she muttered. "The whole idea of this party is to meet people."

"For *you* to meet people," Allison emphasized. "You're the one who's getting married, not me."

"You can take advantage of it, all the same. These are interesting people, too. Most of them are rodeo folks, and the rest are cattlemen or horse breeders."

"You're making me nervous," Allison said, fidgeting in her seat as Winnie parked the car behind a silver-gray Lincoln. "I don't know anything about rodeo or horses or cattle."

"No time like the present to learn," Winnie said easily. "Come on. Out of there."

"Is this trip really necessary?" Allison murmured, swinging her long, elegant legs out of the car. "I could stay in the car and make sure it doesn't roll down the hill."

"Not a chance, my friend. After all the work I've put in on you today, I want to show you off."

"Gloating over your artistry, I gather?" Allison primped. "Well, let's spread me among the peasants, then."

"I'd forgotten your Auntie Mame impersonation," Winnie winced. "You really have to stop watching those old movies. Don't lay it on too thick, now."

"Cross my heart and hope to die," Allison agreed. She drew an imaginary line across her stomach.

"Your heart isn't down there," Winnie said worriedly.

"Yes, it is. The only thing I really love is food, so that's where my heart is. Right?"

"I give up."

Allison followed her friend up the wide stone steps to where Dwight Nelson waited on the porch, his blond hair gleaming in the fading sunlight.

"There you are!" he chuckled, and swung a beaming Winnie up in his arms to kiss her soundly. "Hello, Allie, glad you could come," he told the other woman and suddenly stopped, his eyes widening as he stared at her. "Allie? That is you, isn't it?"

Allison sent a dry look in her friend's direction. "Go ahead. Gloat," she dared.

"I did it all," Winnie said, smiling haughtily. "Just look. Isn't she hot?"

"Indeed she is, and if I hadn't seen you first…" Dwight began.

Winnie stomped on his big foot through his boot. "Hold it right there, buster, before you talk yourself into a broken leg. You're all mine, and don't you forget it."

"As if I could." Dwight winced, flexing his booted foot. "You look gorgeous, Allie, now will you tell her I was kidding?"

"He was kidding," Allie told Winnie.

"All right. You're safe, this time." Winnie slid her arm around Dwight's lean waist. "Where's Marie?"

"Around back," he said, grimacing as he glanced toward the sound of a local band beyond the arch in the surrounding wall. "Gene's out there."

"Gene and Marie don't get along," Winnie told Allison.

"That's like saying old-time cowboys and old-time Indians don't get along." Dwight sighed. "Fortunately the guests will keep them from killing each other in public. Mother used to spend her life separating them. It was fine while Gene was abroad for a year on a selling trip. We actually had peaceful meals. Now we have indigestion and a new cook every month." He pursed his lips. "Speaking of food, let's go see if there's any left." Dwight glanced over their heads toward the driveway. "I think you two are the last people we expected."

"The best always are, darling," Winnie said, smiling up at him with sparkling affection.

Allison had to fight her inclination to be jealous, but if anyone ever deserved happiness, Winnie did. She had a heart as big as the whole world.

She followed the engaged couple through the stone arch to the tents that had been set up with tables and chairs positioned underneath it to seat guests. A huge steer carcass was roasting over an open fire while a man basted it with sauce, smiling and nodding as two women, one of whom Winnie whispered was Marie Nelson, carried off platters of it to the tables.

Other pots contained baked beans and Brunswick stew, which were being served as well, along with what had to be homemade rolls.

"It smells heavenly," Allison sighed, closing her eyes to inhale the sweet aroma.

"It tastes heavenly, too," Dwight said. "I grabbed a sample on my way around the house. Here, sit down and dig in."

He herded them toward the first tent, where there were several vacant seats, but he and Winnie were waylaid by a couple they knew and Allison was left to make her own way to the long table.

She took a plate and utensils from the end of the table, along with a glass of iced tea, and sat down. Platters of barbecue and rolls, and bowls of baked beans and Brunswick stew, were strategically placed all along the table. Allison filled her plate with small portions. It had been a long time since she'd felt comfortable eating her fill, and she had difficulty now with the sheer volume of food facing her.

Gene Nelson was standing nearby talking to a visiting cattleman when he saw Allison sit down alone at the table. His eyes had found her instantly, as if he'd known the second she'd arrived. He didn't understand his fierce attraction to her, even if she did look good enough to eat tonight. Her dress was blatantly sexy, and she seemed much more sophisticated than she had in the bar with Dwight and Winnie. Winnie was a model, and he knew she had some liberated friends. He'd even dated Winnie once, which was why Dwight's fiancée had such a bad opinion of him. Not that he'd gotten very far. Dwight had cut him out about the second date, and women were so thick on the ground that he'd never given Dwight's appropriation of his date a second thought. That might have added to Winnie's disapproval, he mused, the fact that he hadn't wanted her enough to fight for her. It was nothing personal. He'd simply never wanted any woman enough to fight for her. They were all alike. Well, most all alike, he thought, staring helplessly at Allison, with her long, dark hair almost down to her narrow waist.

He sighed heavily as he watched her. It had been a while since he'd had a woman. His body ached for sensual oblivion, for something to ease the emotional pain he'd been through. Not that he remembered much about that supposedly wild night with Dale Branigan that had kept her hounding him. In fact, he hardly remembered it at all. Maybe that was why his body ached so when he looked at Allison. These dry spells were hell on the nerves.

Allison felt his gaze and lifted her hazel eyes to seek his across the space that separated them. Oh, but he was handsome, she thought dizzily. He was dressed in designer jeans and a neat white Western shirt with pearl snaps instead of buttons. He wore a burgundy bandanna around his neck and hand-tooled leather boots. His head was bare, his hair almost black and faintly damp, as if he'd just come from a shower. He was more masculine and threatening than any man Allison had ever known, and the way he looked at her made her tingle all over.

She shouldn't encourage him; she knew she shouldn't. But she couldn't stop looking at him. Her life had been barren of eligible men. It was inevitable that she might be attracted to the first nice-looking bachelor she met, she told herself.

If that look in her eyes wasn't an invitation, he was blind, Gene thought, giving in to it with hardly a struggle. He excused himself, leaving the cattleman with another associate, and picked up a glass of beer and a plate and utensils before he joined Allison. He threw a long leg over the wooden bench at the table and sat down, glancing at the tiny portions on her plate.

"Don't you like barbecue?" he asked coolly, and he didn't smile.

She looked up into pale green eyes in a lean face with a deeply tanned complexion. Her eyes were a nice medium hazel flecked with green and gold, but his were like peridot—as pale as green ice under thick black lashes. His black hair was straight and conventionally cut, parted on the left side and pulled back from a broad forehead. He had high cheekbones and a square chin with a hint of a cleft in it. His mouth was as perfectly formed as the mouth on a Greek statue—wide and firm and faintly chiseled, with a thin upper lip and an only slightly fuller lower one. He wasn't smiling, and he studied Allison with a blatantly familiar kind of scrutiny. It wasn't the first time a man had undressed her with his eyes, but it was the first time it had affected her so completely. She wanted to pull the tablecloth off the table and wrap herself in it.

But that wouldn't do, she told herself. Hadn't she learned that the only way to confront a predator was with steady courage? Her sense of humor came to her rescue, and she warmed to the part she was playing.

"I said, don't you like barbecue?" he repeated. His voice was like velvet, and very deep. The kind of voice that would sound best, she imagined, in intimacy. She started at her own thoughts. She must be in need of rest, to be thinking such things about a total stranger, even if he was lithe and lean and attractive.

"Oh, I like barbecue," she answered with a demure smile. "I'm just not used to having it cut off the cow in front of me."

He smiled faintly, a quirk of his mouth that matched the arrogant set of his head. "Do tell."

"Do tell what?" she asked with what she hoped was a provocative glance from under the thick lashes that mascara had lengthened.

He was a little disappointed at her easy flirting. He'd rather expected her to be shy and maidenly. But it certainly wouldn't be the first time he'd been mistaken about a woman. He lifted a thick eyebrow. "Give me time. I'll think up something."

"A reason to stay alive," she sighed, touching a hand to her chest. "I do hope you aren't married with six children, Mr. Nelson. I would hate to spoil the barbecue by throwing myself off the roof."

His eyes registered mild humor. "I'm not married."

"You must wear a disguise in public," she mused.

He studied her with pursed lips for a minute before he picked up his plate and glass and came around the table. Her heart skipped when he sat down beside her— very close. He smelled of soap and cologne, potent to a woman who wasn't used to men in any form.

"You didn't come alone, I suppose," he mused, watching her closely. "Let me get a few bites of this under my belt so that I'll have enough strength to beat your escort to his knees."

"Oh, I don't have one of those," she assured him, hiding her nervousness in humor, as she always had. "I came with Winnie."

"That spares my knuckles." He was flirting, too, but she appealed to him.

"Have you known Winnie a long time?" he asked pleasantly.

"Yes," she said. "We've been friends since we were kids, back in Arizona."

Winnie had never mentioned her, but then, he hadn't been around Winnie that much since she'd become engaged to Dwight. And these days, he had very little to say to Dwight.

"You said at the bar that you'd only be here a couple of weeks. How long have you been in Pryor?"

She smiled faintly. "Just a few days. I'm looking forward to a nice visit with Winnie. It's been years since we spent any time together." She couldn't very well tell him that the length of her stay depended on whether or not she could keep anybody in Pryor from knowing who she was and why she was here. She'd successfully ducked the media since her arrival. She didn't want them after her again.

"Have you done much sightseeing?" he asked, letting his eyes fall to her bare shoulders with bold interest.

"Not yet. But I'm enjoying myself. It's nice to have a vacation from work."

That sounded odd, as if she'd forced the words out and didn't mean them. One pale eye narrowed even more. His gaze slid over her curiously, lingering on the thrust of her breasts under the low neckline. "What do you normally do—when you aren't visiting old friends?" he asked.

"I'm a vamp," she murmured dryly, enjoying herself as she registered his mild surprise. It was like being an actress, playing a part. It took her mind off the horror of the past months.

"No, I won't buy that," he said after a minute. "What do you really do?" he persisted, fingering his glass.

She lifted her own glass to her lips, to give her time to think. He didn't look stupid. She couldn't say anything that might give her away to Winnie's neighbors, especially her future brother-in-law.

"I'm in the salvage business," she said finally.

He stared at her.

She laughed. "Oh, no, I didn't mean used cars and scrap metal and such. I'm in the human salvage business. I'm..." she hesitated, searching for something that wouldn't be a total lie.

"You're what?" he asked.

He was dangerously inquisitive, and almost too quick for her. She had to throw him off the track before he tripped her up and got at the truth. She lifted her eyebrows. "Are you by any chance the reincarnation of the Spanish Inquisition?"

"I don't even speak Spanish," he said. He smiled slowly, interested despite his suspicions. "How old are you?"

"Sir, you take my breath away!" she exclaimed.

His eyes fell to her mouth. "Is that a request?" he murmured, and there was suddenly a world of experience in the pale eyes that skimmed her mouth, in the deepness of his soft voice.

Her hand trembled as she put down the glass. He was out of her league and she was getting nervous. It didn't take a college degree to understand what he meant. "You're going too fast," she blurted out.

He leaned back, studying her through narrow eyes. She was a puzzle, a little mass of contradictions. But in spite of that, she appealed to him as no one else had in recent years.

"Okay, honey," he said after a minute, and smiled faintly. "I'll put on the brakes." He took another bite of barbecue and washed it down with what looked and smelled like beer.

"How old are you?" she asked without meaning to, her eyes on the hard lines of his face. She imagined that he had a poker face when he wanted to, that he could hide what he was feeling with ease. She knew his age, because Dwight had told her, but it wouldn't do to let him know that she'd been asking questions about him from the very first time she saw him.

He glanced at her, searching her wide, curious eyes. "I'm thirty-four."

She dropped her eyes to his chin and farther down, to his broad chest.

"Too old for you, cupcake?" he asked carelessly.

"I'm twenty-five," she said.

His dark brows drew together. He'd thought she was younger than that. Yes, she had a few lines in her face, and even a thread or two of gray in her dark hair. Nine years his junior. Not much difference in years, and at her age, she couldn't possibly be innocent. His heart accelerated as he studied what he could see of her body in the revealing dress and wondered what she'd look like without it. She was nicely shaped, and if that beautiful bow of a mouth was anything to go by, she was probably going to be a delicious little morsel. If only she wasn't best friends with Winnie.

He studied her again. She really was a puzzle. Young, and then, suddenly, not young. There had been a fleeting expression in her eyes when he'd asked her about her profession—an expression that confused him. He had a feeling that she wasn't at all what she seemed. But, like him, she seemed to hide her emotions.

"Twenty-five. You're no baby, are you?" he murmured.

Her eyes came up and that expression was in them again, before she erased it and smiled. Fascinating, he thought, like watching an actress put on her stage makeup.

"No. I'm no baby," she agreed softly, her mind on the ordeal she'd been through and not really on the question. She didn't realize what she was saying to him with her words, that she was admitting to experience that she didn't have.

He felt his body reacting to the look in her eyes and he stiffened with surprise. It usually took longer for a woman to affect him so physically. He wouldn't let her look away. The electricity began to flow between them and his eyes narrowed as he saw her mouth part helplessly. She was close, and she smelled of floral cologne that drifted up, mingling with the spicy scent of barbecue and the malt smell of his beer.

His gaze dropped to the cleft between her breasts and lingered there, on skin as smooth and pink as a sun-ripened peach. His chest rose and fell roughly as he tried to imagine how her breasts would feel under his open mouth...

The sudden shock of voices made the glass of beer jerk in his lean hand.

"Did you think we'd deserted you?" Dwight asked Allison, echoing Winnie's greeting. "I see you've found Gene," he added, patting the older man on the shoulder as he paused beside him. "Be careful that he doesn't try to drag you under the table."

"Watch it," the older man returned humorously. But his eyes were glinting, and he knew that Dwight wouldn't mistake the warning even if it flew right past his new acquaintance.

Dwight understood, all right, but he didn't do the expected thing and go away.

"You don't mind if we join you, do you?"

"Of course not," Allison said, frowning slightly at Gene's antagonism. She glanced from him to Dwight. "You two don't favor each other a lot."

There was an embarrassed silence and Winnie actually grimaced.

"No, we don't, do we?" Gene's eyes narrowed as they glanced off Dwight's apologetic ones. "We all share the same mother, but not the same father." He leaned back and laughed coldly. "Isn't that right, Dwight?"

Dwight went red. "Allison didn't know," he said curtly. "You're always on the defensive lately, Gene."

The past few months came back to torment him. He stared at his half brother with eyes as cold and unfeeling as green stone. "I can't forget. Why should you be expected to?"

"You're family," Dwight said, almost apologetically. "Or you would be if you'd stop lashing out at everybody. You're always giving Marie hell."

"She gives it back." Gene swallowed his drink and put the glass on the table. His eyes went to a silent, curious Allison. "You don't understand, do you, cupcake?" he asked with a smile that was mocking and cruel. "I had a different father than Dwight and Marie. I was adopted. Something my mother and stepfather apparently didn't think I needed to know until my stepfather died six months ago."

She watched him get up, and her eyes were soft and compassionate as they searched his. "I'm sorry," she said gently. "It must have been very hard to find it out so suddenly."

He hated that softness in her eyes, that warmth. He didn't want compassion from her. The only thing he might ever want from her was that silky body, but this was hardly the time to be thinking about it. He glared at her. "I don't want pity, thanks."

"Gene, for God's sake," Dwight ground out.

"Don't worry. I won't spoil your party." He caught a strand of Allison's dark hair and tugged it. "Stay away from me. I'm bad medicine. Ask anybody."

He grabbed his beer and walked away without another word.

Allison's eyes followed him, and she almost felt his pain. Poor, tormented man....

"Don't make the mistake of feeling sorry for him," Dwight told her when Gene was out of earshot. "Pity is the last thing he wants or needs. He has to come to grips with it himself."

"Where is his real father?" Allison asked quietly.

He started to speak, but before he could, a smaller, female version of Dwight slammed down into a chair beside Winnie.

"So he's gone," Marie Nelson muttered. "Dwight, he's just impossible. I can't even talk to him...." She colored, looking at Allison. "Sorry," she said. "You must be Allison. Winnie's been hiding you for days, I thought she'd never introduce us!" she said with a smile.

"I didn't mean to start airing the family linen in public. You'll have to excuse me. Gene always sets me off."

"What's he done now?" Dwight groaned.

"He seduced my best friend," she muttered.

"Dale Branigan is not your best friend," Dwight reminded her. "She's a divorcée with claws two inches long, and if anybody got seduced it was Gene, not her. It's not his fault that she won't realize it was a one-shot fling for him."

"I don't mean Dale," she sighed. "I meant Jessie."

"Gene's never been near Jessie," Dwight said shortly.

"She says he has. She says—"

"Marie," he said, calling her by name for the first time and confirming Allison's suspicions, "Jessie couldn't tell the truth if her life depended on it. She's been crazy about Gene for years and it's gotten her nowhere. This is just a last-ditch effort to get him to marry her. I'm telling you, it won't work. She can't blackmail him to the altar."

"She might not be lying," Marie said, although not with as much conviction as before. "You know how Gene is with women."

"I don't think you do," Dwight said. "Jessie isn't even his type. He likes sophisticated, worldly women."

Marie leaned back in her chair with a sigh. "Poor Jessie."

"Poor Jessie," Dwight agreed. "Now say hello to Winnie."

"Hi, Winnie," Marie greeted belatedly, and smiled. "It's nice to see you again. And I'm glad Allison could come," she added, smiling. She didn't add what Dwight had said about the effect she had on Gene. Now that she'd seen it for herself, she was intrigued. There was indeed something very special about Miss Hathoway, and apparently Gene had noticed it.

"Thank you for inviting me," Allison replied sincerely. "I wouldn't want to impose."

"You aren't. How do you like Wyoming?"

"Very much. It's beautiful."

"We think so." Marie studied her curiously. "Winnie's very secretive about you. You aren't a fugitive Hell's Angel or anything, are you?" she teased, trying not to give away what Dwight had told her about the other woman.

"I don't think so," Allison said, leaning forward to add, "but what if I have memory failure and I've got a motorcycle stashed somewhere?"

"As long as it's a Harley-Davidson, it's okay." Marie grinned. "I've always wanted to ride one."

"Horses, okay. Motorcycles, never." Her brother grinned. "She's a former rodeo champion, or did I mention it?" he added.

"Are you, really?" Allison asked, all eyes.

"Gene, too," Marie said, sighing. "He was world champion roper one year, before he hurt his hand. He doesn't compete anymore. He's bitter about so many things. I wish he could stop blaming Dwight and me. We love him, you know. But he won't believe any of us do."

"Maybe he'll come around someday. It's a blessing that he has so much to do that he doesn't have time to brood," Dwight added. "We supply broncs and bulls for rodeos," he told Allison. "It's a full-time job, especially since we're always shipping or receiving livestock. The paperwork alone is a nightmare."

"It sounds complicated. And dangerous," she added, thinking about the wildness of the animals involved. She wasn't a rodeo fan, but she'd seen the kind of animals cowboys had to ride in competition when she and Winnie had lived in Arizona.

"Working around livestock is always dangerous," Dwight agreed. "But it goes with the territory."

"And we have a good safety record," Marie chimed in. "Have you ever seen a real rodeo, Allison?"

"Yes," Allison nodded. "Once, when Winnie and I were little."

"I remember the candy better than I remember the rodeo," Winnie laughed. "I imagine Allie does, too."

"I'm afraid you're right," Allison agreed.

"We'll make a fan of you, if you stay here long enough," Dwight promised. "How about some music, Marie? We might as well drag the band out of the barbecue and make them work."

"I'll get them started."

The dancing was fun, but by the time Allison and Winnie went home, Gene Nelson hadn't made another appearance and Allison was disappointed. She was fascinated by him, despite what she'd heard about his reputation. He liked sophisticated women, and tonight she'd pretended to be one. But he'd walked away and left her. She sighed miserably. Even when she was pretending to be a siren, she was still just plain old Allison, she thought dully. It was too much to hope for, that a man like Gene would give her a second glance.

With determination, she smiled and danced and socialized. But her heart wasn't in it. Without the elusive Mr. Nelson, everything had gone flat.

The elusive Mr. Nelson was, in fact, feeling the same way. He'd had to force himself to leave the barbecue, because he'd wanted to dance with Allison. But getting involved with her would only create more problems and he'd had enough. He thought about going into town to the bar, but that felt flat, too. He was losing his taste for liquor and wild women. Maybe he'd caught a virus or something.

He strolled past the bunkhouse, hearing loud laughter, led by the redheaded Rance. It was Saturday night, and he couldn't forbid the men liquor on their own time. But one of these days, he was going to have to confront that venomous rider. He'd been needling Gene for days. The man was sweet on Dale Branigan, and fiercely jealous of Gene. He could have told him there was no need, but it wouldn't have done any good.

He kept walking, his mind still on the way Allison had looked in that sundress. He paused to check two of the sick calves in the barn, marveling at how much he'd changed in just one day and one night. Maybe it was his age, he thought. Then a picture of Allison Hathoway's soft hazel eyes burned into his brain and he groaned. With a muttered curse, he saddled a horse and went out to check on the night herders—something he hadn't done in months.

Chapter Three

Allison wasn't comfortable talking to Winnie about Gene Nelson, but she was too curious about him not to ask questions. He'd warned her away himself, telling her that he was bad medicine. But she was attracted despite the warnings. Secretly she wondered if it could be because of them. She'd led a conventional life all the way, never putting a step wrong. A renegade was bound to appeal to her.

"You can't get involved with him," Winnie said quietly when Allison couldn't resist questioning her the next day.

"He didn't seem like a bad man," Allison protested.

"I didn't say he was," Winnie replied, and her expression was sympathetic. "In fact, there isn't a nicer man than Gene. But he's gone wild since he found out about his father. You heard what Marie accused him of yesterday. She wasn't kidding. Gene makes no secret that he has only one use for a woman, and he's done a lot of hard drinking and hard living in the past few months. Because everybody around Pryor knows it, just being seen with him could ruin your reputation. That's why I don't want you to go out with him. I'd never begrudge you a little happiness, but Gene could cost you your respectability. And that's something you can't afford to lose, my friend, in your chosen vocation."

"Yes, I know," Allison murmured. Her heart sank. Winnie was drowning all her dreams. "You said that Gene didn't know about his real father?"

"No. He was just four when his mother divorced his father and married Hank Nelson," Winnie said, startling her. "Until six months ago, when his stepfather died, he never knew that he wasn't a blood Nelson."

Allison's tender heart ached for him. "Poor man," she said huskily. "How terrible, to find out like that!"

"It's been terrible for all of them," Winnie said honestly. "Don't get me wrong. Dwight and Marie don't feel any differently now than they ever did about Gene, but it's changed everything for him. He worshiped Hank."

"No wonder he's embittered," Allison said softly.

"None of that," Winnie murmured dryly. "Your soft heart will be your undoing yet. Now let's talk about something besides Gene. I don't think he's got a soft spot anymore, but he could hurt you if you tried to find it, even for the best of reasons."

"Yes, I know," Allison replied. "I sensed that, too. But you don't need to worry," she added with a sad smile. "I'm not the type of woman who could appeal to a man like him. He's very handsome and suave. I'm just…me."

"You weren't yourself at the barbecue," her friend murmured tongue in cheek. "You were light and flirtatious and carefree. Gene has no idea who and what you really are, and that kind of secret is dangerous to keep."

"Any kind of secret is dangerous to keep," she replied with a gentle smile.

"Amen. Just trust me and keep your distance." She patted Allison's hand gently. "Don't underestimate your own attractions, my friend. You're a knockout when you dress up, and that warm heart of yours attracts everyone, including men like Gene."

"It never has before," Allison sighed. "Well, not the right kind of men, anyway."

"One of these days the right man is going to come along. If anybody deserves him, you do."

Allison smiled. "Thanks. I could return the compliment. I like your Dwight very much."

"So do I."

"Will you live with his family when you marry?"

"No," Winnie returned, grateful for the change of subject. "There's another house on the ranch, where Dwight's grandfather used to live. It's being remodeled, and we'll live there. I'll take you to see it one day, if you like."

"I would."

Winnie smiled. "You're so much better than you were when you first came here," she said gently. "Is it easing off a little?"

Allison nodded. "Every day, thanks to you and your mother."

"That's what we both hoped. Dad will be home soon, and then we can do some sightseeing. You know I'm hopeless at finding things, and mother hates to drive distances. There's a lot of history around here."

"I know. I read all the books I could find about northern Wyoming before I ever dreamed I might actually come here." She lowered her eyes. "I had hoped it would be for a happier reason, though."

"So did I." Winnie sipped coffee. "What do you want to see?"

"The nightly rodeo in Cody," came the immediate reply. "Not to mention the historical center there. And there's a place called Shoshone Canyon just outside it, on the way to Yellowstone…"

"Shoshone Canyon gives me the cold willies," Winnie said, shivering. "It's eerie, especially when you have to come across the dam to Cody, through the mountain tunnel. I only have to go that way when we're coming back from Yellowstone National Park, thank God. Cody is northwest of here, so we can avoid the canyon altogether."

"You chicken, you," Allison gasped. "I'd love it!"

"I imagine you would. Well, we'll go when Dad gets back, but I'll wear a blindfold."

"I'll make sure you have one," Allison laughed.

There was no more mention of Gene Nelson, even if he did seem to haunt Allison's dreams.

Then, all at once, she seemed to run into him everywhere. She waved to him in town as he drove by in his big Jeep, and he waved back with a smile. She saw him on his horse occasionally as she drove past the ranch with Winnie, and he seemed to watch for her. When she and Winnie visited Dwight, he sometimes paused in the doorway to talk, and his green eyes ran over her with frank curiosity as he joined in the conversation. It always seemed to be about cattle or horses or rodeo, and Allison never understood it, but then it didn't matter. She just loved looking at Gene.

He noticed that rapt stare of hers and was amused by it. Women had always chased him, but there was something different about this one. She was interested in him, but too shy to flirt or play up to him. Ironically that interested him more than a blatant invitation would have.

He began to look for her after that, despite his misgivings about getting involved. She stirred something inside him that he didn't even know he possessed. It was irritating, but he felt as if he'd been caught in an avalanche, and he couldn't stop it.

A few days after the barbecue he noticed Winnie's car going past the ranch, with a passenger, on the way in to Pryor. And he'd found an excuse to go into town himself. To get a new rope, he said. The ranch had enough ropes to furnish Pancho Villa's army already, but it was an excuse if he really needed one to appease his conscience.

That was how Allison came upon him, seemingly accidentally, in Pryor that afternoon while she was picking up some crocheting thread for Mrs. Manley and Winnie was having a fitting for her wedding gown.

He was coming out of the feed store with what looked like a new rope in one lean hand. He'd been working. He was wearing stained jeans with muddy boots and dusty bat-wing chaps. A worn and battered tan Stetson was cocked over one pale green eye, and he needed another shave, even though it was midafternoon. He looked totally out of sorts.

In fact, he was, and Allison was the reason for his bad humor. All the reasons why he should snub her came falling into his brain. It didn't do any good, of course, to tell himself that she was the last complication he needed right now. Miss Chic Society there wasn't cut out for ranch life or anything more than a wild fling, and he was beginning to feel his age. Instead of running around with wild women, he needed to be thinking about a wife and kids. Except that kids might be out of the question, considering the character of his real father. His expression hardened. Besides that, considering his reputation with women, it was going to be hard to find a decent woman who'd be willing to marry him. This wouldn't be a bad time to work on improving his image, and he couldn't do that by linking himself with another sophisticated party girl. Which Miss Hathoway seemed to be, given her performance at the barbecue.

Of course, it wasn't that easy to put the brakes on his interest. Now here she stood, looking at him with those big hazel eyes and making his body ache. And he'd initiated the confrontation.

"Hello, Mr. Nelson," she said, smiling at him. "Out looking for a lost cow?" she added, nodding toward the rope in his hand.

His eyebrows arched. "I came in to buy some new rope, Miss Hathoway." He was irritated at having told a blatant lie.

"Oh." She stared at it. "Can you spin a loop and jump through it?"

He glared at her. "This," he said, hefting it irritably, "is nylon rope. It isn't worth a damn until you tie it between the back bumper of a truck and a fence-post and stretch it."

"You're kidding," she said.

"I am not." He moved closer, looking down at her. She was at least average height, but he still had to look down. She seemed very fragile somehow. Perhaps her lifestyle made her brittle.

He searched her soft eyes. "Did you drive in?" he asked so that she wouldn't know he'd followed her to town.

"Yes. With Winnie," she said. "She's trying on her wedding gown."

His thick eyebrow jerked. "The wedding will be Pryor's social event of the season," he said with faint sarcasm. The thought of the wedding stung him. Dwight was a Nelson, truly his father's son. Dwight had inherited the lion's share of the business, even though Gene couldn't complain about his own inheritance. It was just that he'd been the eldest son all his life. He'd belonged. Now he didn't. Dwight and Winnie's wedding was a potent, stinging reminder of that.

"It hurts you, doesn't it?"

The gentle question brought a silent gasp from his lips. He stared down at her, caught completely off guard by her unexpected remark. The compassion in those eyes was like a body blow. She almost seemed to glow with it. He couldn't have imagined anyone looking at him like that a week ago, and he wasn't sure he liked it even now.

"Haven't you got someplace to go, Miss Hathoway?" he asked irritably.

"I suppose that means you wish I did. Why are you wearing bat-wing chaps in the northwest?" she asked pleasantly. "And Mexican rowels?"

His eyes widened. "I used to work down in Texas," he said hesitantly. "What do you know about chaps?"

"Lots." She grinned. "I grew up reading Zane Grey."

"No better teacher, except Louis L'Amour," he murmured. His pale eyes slid down her body. She was wearing jeans and a white shirt, short sleeved, because it was June and warm.

"No hat," he observed, narrow-eyed. "You know better, or you should, having lived in Arizona. June is a hot month, even here."

She grimaced. "Yes, but I hate hats. It isn't usually this warm, surely, this far north?"

Those hazel eyes were casting spells. He had to drag his away. "We get hot summers. Winters are the problem," he said, nodding toward the distant peaks, snow covered even in the summer. "We get three and four feet of snow at a time. Trying to find calving cows in that can be a headache."

"I expect so." Her eyes went to his thin mouth. "But isn't summer a busier time?"

He looked down at her. "Not as much so as April and September. That's when we round up cattle."

"I guess that keeps you busy," she said softly.

"No more than anything else does," he said shortly. He had to get away from her. She disturbed him. "I've got to go."

"That's it, reject me," she said with a theatrical sigh, hiding her shyness in humor. "Push me aside—I can take it."

He smiled without meaning to. "Can you?" he murmured absently.

"Probably not," she confessed dryly. She searched his eyes. "Winnie warned me to stay away from you. She says you're a womanizer."

He stared down at her. "So? She's right," he said without pulling his punches. "I've never made any secret of it." His eyes narrowed on her face. "Did you expect a different answer?"

She shook her head. "I'm glad I didn't get one. I don't mind the truth."

"Neither do I, but we're pretty much in the minority. I find that most people prefer lies, however blatant."

She felt momentarily guilty, because she was trying to behave like someone she wasn't. But she knew that her real self wasn't likely to appeal to him. She couldn't help herself.

Gene saw that expression come and go on her face and was puzzled by it. He glanced past her, watching Winnie in the doorway of a shop, talking to another woman.

"You'd better go," he said abruptly. "Your watchdog's about to spot you talking to me." He smiled with pure sarcasm. "She'll give you hell all day if she sees us together."

"Would you mind?" she asked.

He nodded. "For Dwight's sake, yes, I would. I don't want to alienate Winnie before the wedding." He laughed curtly. "Plenty of time for that afterward."

"You aren't half as bad as you pretend to be," she remarked.

He sobered instantly. "Don't you believe it, cupcake," he replied. "You'd better go."

"All right." She sighed, clutching the bag of thread against her breasts. "See you."

"Sure." He walked past her to his black Jeep and he didn't allow himself to look back. Pursuing her had been a big mistake. She was Winnie's best friend, and Winnie was obviously determined not to let her become one of his casual interludes. He had to keep his head. He had more than enough problems already, and alienating his future sister-in-law wasn't going to solve any of them. That being the case, it might be wise, he told himself sarcastically, if he stopped following her around!

Allison was calm by the time Winnie finally joined her. "My dress is coming along beautifully," she said. "Did I see you talking to someone?"

"Just passing conversation. I got your mother's thread," Allison said, evading the curious question gracefully. By the time they got back to the car, Winnie had forgotten all about it.

But Allison couldn't forget about Gene. When she was invited, along with Winnie, to supper at the Nelson home two days later, it was almost as if Fate was working in her favor.

She wore a plain gray dress with a high neckline and straight skirt, gently gathered at the waist with a belt. It wasn't a sexy dress, but when she wore it, it became one. She did her hair in a neat French plait and put on makeup as Winnie had taught her. When she finished, she looked much less sophisticated than she had at the barbecue—a puzzling outcome.

"I don't look the way I did before," she told Winnie after they'd said good-night to Mrs. Manley and were on the way to the Nelsons'.

"You look great," Winnie corrected. "And tonight, will you please be yourself?"

"Why? Are you hoping that Gene Nelson might keep his distance if he sees what a frump I really am?" she murmured dryly.

"He seems to be doing that all by himself," Winnie reminded her. "I'm not trying to be difficult, honestly I'm not." She sighed worriedly. "I just don't want to see you hurt. Gene…isn't himself these days."

"What was he like before?" Allison asked softly.

Winnie laughed. "Full of fun. He always had his eye on the ladies, but he was less blatant with it. Now, he's reckless and apparently without conscience when it comes to women. He doesn't really care whom he hurts."

"I don't think he'd hurt me, though, Winnie," she said.

"Don't bet on it," the other woman replied. "You put too much faith in people's better instincts. Some people don't have any."

"I'll never believe that," Allison said firmly. "Not after what I've seen. Beauty often hides in the most horrible places."

Winnie's eyes were gentle as they glanced toward her friend. She didn't know what to say to Allison. Probably nothing would do much good. She'd just have to hope that Gene was out, or that, if he was home, he wasn't interested in Allison.

It was late afternoon, and still light. A gentle flutter of rain greeted them as they arrived in front of the Nelson house and darted up the steps to the front door.

"You're early," Marie stammered, flustered and wild-eyed when she opened the door for them. She swept back her blond hair. "Oh, gosh, do either of you know anything about first aid? Dwight had to run to town for some wine, and Gene's ripped open his arm. I'm just hopeless…!"

"Where is he?" Allison asked, her voice cool and professional-sounding. "I know what to do."

"Thank God!" Marie motioned them along behind her, down the long hall toward the bedrooms.

"I think I'll wait in the living room, if you don't mind." Winnie hesitated, grimacing. "I'm as hopeless as Marie is."

"You won't be alone long," Marie promised her. "I can't stand the sight of blood, either! He's in there, Allison," she added, nodding toward an open bedroom door. "You can hear him from out in the hall."

"I'll look after him," Allison assured her, leaving Marie to keep Winnie company while she ventured into the room.

Muttered curses were coming from the bathroom. Allison moved hesitantly past the antique furniture in the cream and brown confines of the room, certain that it was Gene's. The bed was king-size. There was a desk and chair in one corner and two chairs and a floor lamp in the other, beside a fireplace. The earth tones and Native American accent pieces suited what she knew of Gene Nelson.

But she didn't have time to study his taste in furnishings. She pushed open the bathroom door, which was already ajar, and walked in. The bathroom, like the bedroom, was done in beige and brown with a tile floor and a huge glass-fronted shower with gold fittings. There was a Jacuzzi, too. But it was the vanity sink that caught her eye. Gene was standing in front of it, in clothes similar to those he'd been wearing in town. His shirt was off and one brown, hair-roughened forearm was cut from elbow to wrist and dripping bright red blood into the marble sink.

"That needs stitching," she said.

He turned, his green eyes darker with pain, his lean face hard and without a smile. "What the hell do you want?" he asked, irritated because he'd been thinking of her when he'd gone too close to one of his few horned cows and had his arm ripped for his pains.

"A Ferrari and a house on the Riviera," she said. She moved close, trying not to stare blatantly at the broad, bronzed chest with its thick wedge of hair that ran down his flat stomach and under the heavy brass belt buckle that secured his jeans. He was beautifully male, so striking that she had to drag her eyes away.

"You know what I mean," he returned shortly.

"Marie and your future sister-in-law are squeamish. I'm not. Let me see, please." She scanned the things he'd dragged out of the medicine cabinet and proceeded to gently bathe the long gash with soap and water before she used a strong disinfectant and then an antibiotic cream. "I guess you'll scream if I suggest the local hospital emergency room?" she asked as she worked.

He stared down at her bent dark head with mingled emotions. He'd hoped to be gone before she and Winnie arrived, but he hadn't counted on letting his mind wander and getting himself gored. "I've had worse than this," he replied.

She looked up into his searching eyes, trying to ignore the beat of her pulse and the difficulty she was having with getting her breath. She was too involved with hiding her own reactions to notice his racing pulse and quick breathing. "At least it's stopped bleeding. I don't suppose you have any butterfly bandages?"

"What?" he murmured, lost in her eyes.

"B...butterfly bandages," she stammered. She dragged her eyes down to his forearm. "Never mind. I'll make do with these."

Her hands felt cool on his hot skin. He watched her work, marveling at the ease and confidence with which she put the dressing in place.

"You've done this before, haven't you?" he asked.

"Oh, yes," she said, smiling reminiscently. "Many times. I'm used to patching up people." She didn't add anything to that. It was too soon to talk about her past yet.

"You're good at it. That feels better."

"How did it happen?"

He chuckled softly. "I zigged when I should have zagged, cupcake. Now that you've gotten that one under control, care to have a go at this one?"

She put the last piece of adhesive in place and lifted her eyes. "Which one?" she asked.

He pointed to a smaller gash on his chest that was still bleeding.

"I guess your shirt was a total loss," she murmured dryly, trying to stop the trembling of her hands as she began to bathe the scratch. His chest was warm under her fingers, and she loved the feel of that thick hair as she worked through it to the cut. Her lips parted on quick, jerky breaths. He was hurt. She had to keep that in mind, and not let herself lose control like this.

"My shirt and the denim jacket I was wearing over it," he murmured. The feel of her hands on him was giving him problems. His body began to tense slowly as he watched her clean the cut. "If you try to put a bandage on that, I'm leaving," he added when she'd stopped the bleeding.

"I... I guess adhesive tape would hurt when it had to come off, with all that...hair," she faltered, her eyes helplessly tracing the muscular lines of his torso with involuntary delight.

The way she said it was faintly arousing. He ran a hand over the thick mass of it, nodding absently. "Just put some antiseptic on it, honey, and we'll let it go, okay?"

"Okay." *Honey.* No man had ever called her that in such a deep, sexy way, so that her toes curled inside her shoes. She took the antibiotic cream and put a little on her fingers. But when she began to rub it gently over the cut, he flinched and her fingers paused on his body.

"Did it hurt?" she whispered, puzzled by the heavy beat of his heart under her hand and by the sudden fierce glitter of his eyes.

"Not the way you mean," he said curtly. He felt hot all over, and when she lifted her face, he could see the same awareness there. He couldn't let this happen, he told himself firmly. He had to stop it now.

But she smelled of flowers, and he loved the touch of those gentle hands on his bare skin. Involuntarily he traced her long, elegant fingers, simultaneously pressing them deeper into the hair on his chest so that they caressed the hard muscle. His eyes lifted to hers, holding them in a silence that was suddenly tense and hot with promise.

She looked younger tonight, in that gray dress with her hair in a braid at her back. Despite the makeup she'd used, she looked country fresh. He liked her better this way than in that sexy dress she'd worn at the barbecue. He almost said so, but he managed to bite back the comment in time.

"It's...stopped bleeding," she whispered. But she was looking into his eyes, not at the cut.

"So it has," he replied.

The hand that was caressing the back of hers moved her fingers slowly over a taut, flat male nipple, letting her feel the effect her touch was having on him. He pressed it close and hard, his whole hand covering hers as the silence continued.

She smelled leather and a faint breath of hay on him, pleasant scents that mingled with the after-shave he wore. Her heart was beating madly, and under her fingers she could feel the fierce pulsation of his own.

"Gene," she whispered unsteadily.

The sound of his name on her lips was his undoing. He couldn't help himself. He bent slowly, his eyes on her soft mouth, no other thought in his mind except possession.

His hands moved up to frame her face, warm and strong on her cheeks as he tilted her head to give him total access to her parted lips.

She didn't make even a pretense of resisting. Her hands rested lightly, with fascination, on the hard, warm contours of his chest, spearing into the thick mat of hair that covered it. She could taste his breath, warm on her mouth, and she wanted him to kiss her with an almost feverish desperation. There had never been a man she'd felt this kind of attraction to. Just once she wanted to taste him. Just…once…

Her eyes closed. She stood on her tiptoes to coax his mouth the rest of the way while the world vanished around her. She heard the sharp intake of his breath and felt his hands contract and his mouth almost touched hers.

And just then a sharp, feminine voice broke into the tense silence with all the subtlety of an explosion.

Chapter Four

"Allison, is he all right?"

Winnie's voice hit Gene with the impact of a sledgehammer. He jerked back from Allison even as his hard mouth touched hers, his face going as rigid as the arousal he barely kept her from feeling.

He whirled away, grabbing his shirt and jacket. "Yes, he's all right," he called, irritated. He didn't know which bothered him the most—the interruption or his weakness.

"Oh. Sorry!" Winnie stammered.

There were fading footsteps. "My God, does she think I'm in any condition to ravish you?" he asked angrily, running a restless hand through his thick, straight hair.

Allison was still getting her breath back. She leaned against the vanity sink, her trembling hands behind her. "You don't understand," she said softly, wondering if she could find the right words to explain Winnie's protectiveness.

He turned, glancing at her irritably until his searching gaze fell to the taut nipples pressing against the soft fabric of her dress. His breath sighed out heavily. "Are you what you seem to be, Allison?" he asked unexpectedly, resignation in his tone. His eyes lifted back to capture hers. "Are you modern and sophisticated?"

"Why do you want to know?" She sidestepped the question.

His eyes narrowed and stabbed into hers. "Because there's no way on earth I'm getting involved with you if you aren't."

Her heart ran wild. "Do you want to get involved with me?" she asked huskily.

"My God, can't you tell?" he demanded. His chest rose and fell roughly. "I've barely touched you, and I'm on fire!"

That made two of them, but she didn't imagine he could tell how she felt. She wanted to get close to him. If she told him the truth, he wouldn't come near her. If she kept her secret, there was a slight chance that he might drop his guard, that she might get to see the real man, the hurting one. As for anything more, perhaps they could agree to some ground rules that would protect her until she could tell him the truth.

"I'm not modern enough to jump into bed with any man who asks," she said simply, and met his eyes bravely. "I like to know what I'm getting into first."

His chin lifted with faint arrogance. "You're cautious, then. So am I. I won't rush you. But I don't want a platonic relationship."

"Neither do I," she said, but with her eyes averted.

He hesitated. Something didn't ring true about what she was saying, but he couldn't quite put his finger on it. He wondered if this wasn't lunacy. A woman was the last complication he needed right now, and he hadn't forgotten that her best friend was marrying his brother. There were at least ten good reasons for keeping his distance, but none of them mattered when he was around Allison. He seemed to have been alone for a very long time. When he was with her, the aching loneliness vanished.

"Suppose we go to a movie tomorrow night?" he asked.

"Winnie won't like it."

"I'm not asking Winnie," he replied easily. "Or anyone else. Just you and me."

"Could we go to Cody? Isn't there a rodeo there every night?"

He smiled slowly. "Every night during the summer," he corrected. "We'll save that for another time. But we can detour through Cody, if you like. The nearest movie house is in Billings."

"Montana?" she exclaimed. "But that's over a hundred miles away!"

"No distance at all out here, cupcake."

"I suppose not. It's like that in Arizona, too, but I'd forgotten." She stared at him quietly, her heart still beating wildly. "I guess you supply animals to the rodeo in Cody, too?"

He nodded. "That one and any number of others." He studied her for a long moment. "You'd better get out of here. I need a shower before we eat."

"All right."

"Unless you'd like to stay and scrub my back?" he mused, a wicked gleam in his eyes.

"It's much too early for that sort of thing," she told him and left with a demure glance from under her lashes.

He was smiling when she left the room, but she wasn't. She wondered what she was letting herself in for, and how she thought she was going to keep a man like that at bay. If he really was the womanizer everyone said he was, she'd be in over her head in no time.

"He's as good as new," Allison assured the two women when she joined them in the living room. "Almost, anyway. The cut on his arm really needed stitching, but he won't go to a doctor."

"That's Gene," Marie said wearily. "It's been so hard for him. I wish Dad had never left that letter. It would have been so much kinder not to have told him after such a long time. Let's go on into the dining room. Gene won't be long, I'm sure, and we can drink coffee while we talk."

She led them into the dining room, where a cherry table was set under an elegant crystal chandelier. The floor was oak, highly polished, and the walls were wood paneled. It was the most elegant room Allison had seen in years. They sat down and busied themselves with coffee for several minutes before Allison finally voiced the question that had been nagging her.

"Why did your father leave a note for Gene?" she asked curiously.

Marie shook her head. "Nobody knows. Dad was honest to a fault, and he was a deep thinker. Maybe he thought Gene had the right to know. His real father is still alive, even if Gene would rather die than go to see him. Heritage, health, so many things depend on knowing who your real parents are. I think that he planned to tell Gene before he died. That would have been Dad's way. He certainly wouldn't have wanted him to find out the way he did. It's hurt Gene so badly."

"I suppose it's been difficult for you and Dwight, too," Allison said gently.

"You can't imagine. We don't care who Gene's real dad is. Gene is our brother and we love him. But he can't accept that," Marie said. "He's still trying to come to grips with it. I wonder sometimes if he ever will. Meanwhile, he's just hell to live with."

"Is he staying for supper?" Winnie asked with a worried glance at Allison.

"Yes," Allison said. "At least he said he was."

"Don't look so worried," Marie told Winnie, grinning at her expression. "He'll be nice because Allison's here. I think he likes her."

"God forbid!" Winnie said. "You know how he is with women!"

"He won't hurt Allison," Marie said. "Don't be such a worrywart."

"I hope you're right. Anyway," Winnie sighed, "he's involved with Dale, isn't he?"

"No, he isn't," Gene said from the doorway. He lifted

an eyebrow at Winnie's shocked face as he joined them, freshly showered and shaved, dressed in a white shirt and dark slacks. He looked wickedly handsome, and Allison's heart raced at the sight of him.

"Sorry," Winnie began.

Gene lifted a careless hand, stopping her before she got started. "I'm not going to gobble up your house-guest," he said quietly. "But she'll be safer with me than some of the other yahoos around here, especially at night," he added with a meaningful stare. "I'll take care of her."

"Okay. I suppose you're right." Winnie sighed softly. "It's just that…" She glanced toward Allison, grimacing. "Well…"

"She's your best friend," Gene finished for her with a faint smile. "No problem. I won't hurt her, Winnie."

"Will you stop?" Allison asked Winnie on an exasperated laugh. "I'm twenty-five."

"Yes, but…"

"What are we having for dinner?" Allison interrupted, arching her eyebrows at an amused Marie.

"Duck," Marie returned. "And if I don't take the orange sauce out of the microwave, we'll be having it without sauce! Excuse me."

Before Winnie could say anything else to Gene and Allison, Dwight was back with the wine. But all through dinner, Gene's eyes kept darting to Allison's, as hers did to him. Whatever there was between them, it was explosive and mutual. She hoped she wouldn't have cause to regret giving it a chance.

Over dinner, she learned that Gene was a wizard

with figures and that his taste in books ran to mysteries and biographies, while he took a conservative stand on politics and a radical one on ecology. She discovered that he enjoyed a lot of the same things she did, like winter sports and the Winter Olympics, not to mention science fiction movies. He was droll and faintly sarcastic, but underneath there had to be a sensitive caring man. Allison wanted to flush him out.

He pulled her aside while Winnie was saying goodnight to Dwight and Marie.

"I'll pick you up at five tomorrow afternoon," he said. "We'll need to get an early start. It's a long drive."

"You're sure you want to?"

"No," he said curtly, and meant it. He'd never wanted involvement with her, but things seemed to be out of his hands for once. Out of control, like his life. He shifted his stance, putting the past away from him. "We'll have dinner in Billings," he continued, searching her eyes slowly, "before the movie starts. There's a nice restaurant in one of the hotels."

"Okay." She smiled shyly. "I'll look forward to it."

He only nodded. He didn't want to admit how easily he could echo that sentiment. In the past, being a loner had had distinct advantages. He didn't want to have to account for his time or have restraints put on his freedom. Dale had tried that tack, and Jessie, God bless her, was as thick as a plank. One smile and Jessie was hearing wedding bells.

Allison's soft voice caught his attention again and he glanced to where she and Winnie were laughing with

Marie over some television program they'd apparently all seen as they said good-night at the front door.

He waved in their general direction and went up to his room. He wondered if Winnie was going to talk Allison out of tomorrow's date. If she did, it might be the best thing for both of them, he decided.

But Winnie didn't manage that, despite the fact that she coaxed and pleaded all the way home that night.

"Your reputation...!" she concluded finally, using one last desperate argument.

"It will survive one or two dates," Allison said firmly. "Oh, Winnie, he's so alone! Can't you see it? Can't you see the pain in his eyes, the emptiness?"

Winnie pulled up in front of her house, turned off the engine and the lights with a long sigh. "No. I don't suppose I'm blessed with your particular kind of empathy. But you don't know what it's like with an experienced man. You've hardly even dated, and Gene has been around. If you drop your guard for a minute, he'll seduce you, you crazy little trusting idiot!"

"It takes two," Allison reminded her.

"Yes, and I can see sparks flying between the two of you the minute you're together! Allie, it's an explosive chemistry and you don't have the faintest idea how helpless you'd be if he turned up the heat!"

"Aren't you forgetting how my parents brought me up?" Allison asked gently.

"No, I'm not," Winnie replied tersely. "But I'm telling you that ideals and principles have a breaking point. Sexual attraction is physical, and the mind doesn't have a lot of control over it."

"I can say no," Allison replied. "Now let's go and watch some television. Okay?"

Winnie started to speak, but she realized it was going to be futile. It was like trying to explain surfing to an Eskimo. She could only hope that Allie's resolve was equal to Gene Nelson's ardor when it was put to the test.

Gene pulled up in the yard at exactly five o'clock the next afternoon. He was wearing gray slacks with a Western shirt and a bola tie, a matching gray Stetson atop his head and hand-tooled gray boots on his feet. He looked elegant, and Allison's heart skipped when he came in the front door behind Winnie.

She looked good, he mused. She had on a pretty lilac vintage shirtwaist dress with a flowery scarf, and her hair was loose, hanging down her back like a wavy dark curtain almost to her waist. The dress clung gently to her slender body in just the right places, enhancing her firm, high breasts and narrow waist. She had it buttoned up right to her throat, but it only made the fit more sexy to Gene, who assumed that the prim fashion statement was a calculated one. He smiled gently, liking her subtle gesture.

Allison, unaware of his thoughts, smiled back. "Is this dressy enough, or should I wear something else?" she asked. "I'm not used to fancy restaurants."

"You look fine," Gene assured her.

"Indeed you do. Have fun," Winnie said gently. She glanced at Gene. "Take care of her," she said worriedly.

"No sweat." He linked Allison's soft hand in his and

led her out the door, leaving an unconvinced Winnie behind.

"Why is she so protective of you?" Gene asked when they were out on the main highway in his sleek black Jeep.

Allison studied him from the comparative safety of her deep bucket seat. "She thinks you're too experienced for me."

He raised an eloquent eyebrow. "Am I, cupcake?" he asked with cynical mockery.

She laughed softly. "Probably. But you don't scare me."

"Give me time." He draped his hand over the wheel casually. "You haven't asked which movie I'm taking you to."

"No, I haven't. Is it a good one?"

"I don't know. I don't see movies too much these days. This one is supposed to be about the cattle business. But if it follows the trend, it'll be about people taking their clothes off to discuss gene splicing and cloning of pedigree cattle."

She laughed involuntarily at the disgust in his voice. "You don't think much of 'modern' films, I gather?"

"No. Too much skin, not enough substance. Sex," he replied with a glance in her direction, "should not be a spectator sport."

"You're right," she said, averting her eyes to the darkening skyline. She was glad of the dimly lit interior of the Jeep, so that he couldn't see the slight embarrassment the remark caused her.

They drove in silence for a few minutes. He took a

detour to let her see a bit more of Wyoming, going north and west several miles out of the way so that she could see one of the area's most fascinating sights.

When he mentioned that they were traveling through Shoshone Canyon, Allison didn't need to be told that, because the eerie sound of the wind and the gnarled outcroppings of rock in their desert colors gave her cold chills. She remembered what Winnie had said about the area, and she almost asked Gene about it, but the tunnel through the mountain came into view ahead and her curiosity vanished in sheer fascination at the engineering job it must have been to put that long tunnel through solid rock.

Once they were through the tunnel, it was just a little way into Cody. Gene pointed out the famous Buffalo Bill Cody museum and the rodeo grounds on the way through the small city, adding that one of the first water systems in the West had been funded by Bill Cody with labour provided by the Mormons.

"Why, this looks like southern Arizona!" Allison exclaimed as she looked out the window when they were driving north out of Cody.

"Yes, it does," he said. "But when we go through the Pryor Mountains and head into Montana you'll see the difference in the terrain. Wyoming is mostly jagged mountains, and southern Montana is mostly buttes and rolling grassland." He smiled at her. "I love both. I could happily spend the rest of my life in Billings, but I suppose I've gotten too used to Wyoming."

"Where were you born?" she asked.

His face hardened and his lean hands gripped the

wheel convulsively. "My birth certificate says Billings, Montana," he replied tersely. "I suppose that's where my mother and her...husband lived at the time." He didn't add that he'd never had occasion to look at his birth certificate in all those years—even when he'd joined the service, his mother had provided records to the authorities. Why hadn't he ever questioned it? It wasn't until after Hank Nelson died that he'd seen all the paperwork—the birth certificate with the name he was born under and the adoption papers. God, it hurt to realize how easily he'd accepted the lies....

Allison hesitated. She could tell that it was like putting a knife into him to answer the question. But his own avoidance of the subject had surely added to his discomfort.

"You don't like to talk about it, do you?" she asked quietly.

"No," he said honestly.

"When a splinter gets under the skin," she began carefully, "pulling it out at once prevents it from doing too much damage. But when it's left inside, it festers and causes infection."

His eyes sliced through her. "And that's what my past is, do you think? A splinter that's embedded?"

"In a manner of speaking," she replied. Her eyes fell to the firm set of his lips. "I imagine it was the shock of your life to find out who your father was in such a way. But I agree with Marie. I think your stepfather meant to tell you and kept putting it off until it was too late."

His pale green eyes flashed. He didn't like being reminded of it, but what she said made sense. It was just the newness of discussing it, he supposed. He wouldn't let Marie or Dwight talk about it around him. He couldn't really understand why he hadn't already cut Allison dead. He knew instinctively that she was sensitive enough that one hard word would stop her. He just couldn't seem to speak that one hard word. The idea of hurting her didn't appeal to him at all.

They drove into Billings, along the wide streets, and Gene pointed out the landmarks.

"The airport sits on the Rimrocks," he added, nodding toward his left as they turned toward the hotel. "Yellowstone Kelly's buried up there, and the old graveyard is down the hill from the grave."

"I'll bet I could spend a whole day just looking around Billings," she remarked.

"Billings is big, all right," he agreed, his eyes on a traffic light up ahead. "And the surrounding area is full of history."

"Yes, I know," she said excitedly. "The Custer Battlefield is somewhere nearby, isn't it?"

"Over near Hardin," he said. "I'll take you there one day if you like."

Her heart jumped. He made it sound as if they were headed for a real relationship, not just a quick flirtation. She stared at his profile with a feeling of slow warmth building inside her.

"I'd like that very much, Gene," she said softly.

He was grateful that the traffic light changed in time to distract him, because the expression on her face could have hypnotized him. He'd never seen such warmth in a woman's eyes. It drew him like a blazing fire on a snowy night.

"You shouldn't look at me that way when I'm trying to drive," he said curtly.

"I beg your pardon?"

He glanced at her as he pulled into the hotel parking lot, mentally praying for an empty spot. She looked blank, as if the remark didn't register.

"Never mind," he murmured, his keen eyes on the last space, where a car was backing out. "The answer to a prayer," he chuckled.

"The parking spot?"

"You bet," he agreed. "The food here is something special, as you'll see, so it's usually crowded on weekends."

He pulled into the vacated parking spot and parked. The night air was warm and the city smelled of anything but exhaust fumes. Perhaps it was its very spaciousness.

"This doesn't look like Arizona, but it's just as spread out," she remarked, staring around her with interest.

"Most Western cities are," he said. He escorted her into the lobby and then into the elevator. They rode up to the restaurant near the top of the building and were seated by a window overlooking the Yellowstone River and the railroad tracks. A freight train was barreling through the darkness and Allison's eyes followed it wistfully.

"Do you like trains?" he asked, glancing down at the passing train.

"Oh, yes," she said with a sigh. "I used to dream about having an electric train set of my very own, when

I was little. But I was taught that there were many things more important than toys."

He smiled gently. "Such as?"

She returned the smile. "A pair of shoes for a neighbor's little girl who didn't have any. Glasses for a seamstress who was the sole support of three children. Insulin for a diabetic who could barely afford to pay rent."

He had to search for words. He hadn't expected that reply. "Taught by whom? Your parents?"

She nodded. She looked down, toying with her utensils. "They were…very special people." She had to bite down hard to keep the tears back. Nightmare memories flashed through her mind.

Gene didn't miss the sudden look of panic on her face. His lean hand crossed the table and caught hers, enveloping it tightly. "You can tell me about it later," he said quietly.

His compassion startled her. Her lips parted as she met his pale green eyes and searched them, while her fingers curled trustingly into his. "It's still fresh, you see," she whispered huskily.

"You lost them recently?"

She nodded. Words couldn't get past the lump in her throat.

"So that's why you're here," he said, thinking aloud. "And why Winnie's so protective of you."

She didn't disagree. There was so much more to it than that, but she couldn't talk about it just yet. Instead her fingers curled against the firm, comforting strength of his.

"If it helps, I know what you're going through," he said. His voice was as comforting as his clasp. "You'll get past it. Take it one day at a time and give yourself room to grieve. Don't shut it inside."

She took a steadying breath and forced a smile. "Look who's telling whom not to shut it inside," she said, meeting his gaze.

He laughed softly. "Okay. Point taken." The smile faded and he frowned with real concern as he studied her wan face. "Want to give this a miss and go back to Winnie's?"

Her lips parted. "Oh, no, please," she faltered. "I'm okay. It was just…sometimes I think about them and it hurts. I'm sorry. I didn't mean to spoil your evening."

"What makes you think you have?" he asked quietly. "I know how it feels to hurt inside. You don't have to hide it from me."

She took a steadying breath and smiled. "Thank you."

He shrugged. "No sweat. Are you hungry?"

She laughed. "Yes."

"Good. So am I."

Their waitress made an appearance, almost running to keep up with the demands on her, apologetic as she deposited a menu and then took their order. Gene found that Allison shared his taste in food, because she ordered a steak and salad and coffee, just as he had. He grinned.

"Coffee will poison you," he reminded her after the waitress had left it and gone off to the kitchen.

She put cream and sugar into hers. "As long as it

doesn't cripple me, I'll be okay," she said. "You're drinking it, too," she pointed out.

"Of course. I didn't say it would poison *me*."

Her face beamed as she studied him. "I noticed."

He grinned at her. "I hope you also noticed that I'm not drinking."

"It's hard to miss," she confided. "You're turning purple."

"I'll survive," he replied.

Just then, the waitress brought their orders and then they were too busy eating to talk. Allison hadn't realized how hungry she was. She ate, but, with every bite, her eyes were helplessly on Gene Nelson's dark face.

Chapter Five

The theater wasn't crowded, so Gene and Allison had a whole row to themselves, away from the few other people in the audience. Gene put his Stetson atop one folded seat and stretched his long legs, crossing one over the other while the previews ran. Allison munched the popcorn he'd bought her and tried to pay attention to the screen.

It had been a long time since she'd seen a movie, because there hadn't even been a television set where she and her parents had spent the past few years. She was behind the times in a lot of ways, and the fact was really brought home to her as the story unfolded. As Gene had predicted, despite the fact that the story was supposed to deal with cattle ranching, most of it seemed to take place in bedrooms. She watched, red-faced, during one particular scene replete with heavy breathing and explicit material.

Gene glanced at her expression with faint curiosity. That wide-eyed gape couldn't be for real. Nobody who had a television set could be shocked these days. Of course, it could be seeing a scene like this with him, a comparative stranger, that made her nervous. She might not be all that experienced, even if she'd been with one or two men. Funny how it disturbed him to think of her being with any man at all except himself.

He reached for her hand and drew it gently into his, resting it on his muscular thigh. She resisted for a few seconds, until the contact began to weaken her and she gave in.

His long fingers played with hers, teasing between them while things heated up on the screen. He lifted them to his lips and began to nibble at her fingertips with slow, sensual intent.

Allison had never been exposed to this kind of thing. She felt his lips against her fingers and almost gasped at the sensations she felt when he nibbled them.

She tried to draw back her hand, but he held it in a firm, gentle grasp. What was happening now on the screen had her rigid with disbelief.

Gene glanced down at Allison, watching her reaction to the screen. Her expression was one of astonished awe, and something scratched at the back of his mind, only to be gone before he could let it in. Her fingers clenched around his unconsciously and he returned the pressure.

"Amazing what they can get away with, isn't it?" he murmured deeply, keeping his voice low. The nearest people were three rows away, so there was little danger of being overheard. His thumb rubbed slowly across her damp palm, pressing the back of her hand into the powerful muscle of his thigh. The sensation rocked him, because it was such an innocent contact. He looked back at the screen, all too aware of her warm touch. His chest rose and fell heavily as he watched the couple on the screen. "Does it embarrass you?" he asked quietly.

"Yes," she moaned, giving in to honesty.

"I thought you said you were a modern girl," he murmured, and he smiled, but it was a kind smile.

"I thought you said sex shouldn't be a spectator sport," she returned.

He chuckled at the riposte. "Touché." The screen suddenly drew their attention as the sounds grew louder and more frantic and finally ended in breathless cries of simulated ecstasy.

Allison was almost trembling by now. Gene felt stirred himself. It had been a while between women. He looked down at Allison with fascination as he felt the shiver go through her. She had to be very sensitive to react so fiercely to a love scene.

His hand absently moved hers up his thigh, until he realized what he was doing and felt the almost frantic restraint of her hand.

"Sorry," he murmured dryly as he released her fingers and watched them retreat to her lap. "I guess it got to me more than I realized."

"They shouldn't show things like that," she faltered, still red-faced and unsteady.

"I couldn't agree more. I didn't realize it would be

this explicit." He stood and tugged her along with him, ignoring the curious glances of much younger couples.

"They think we're crazy to leave, don't they?" she asked as they walked through the lobby to gain the street.

"No doubt. But they're a different generation. Come to think of it," he added as they reached the dark sidewalk, "so are you."

"I'm only nine years younger than you are," she protested.

He smiled down at her, the coolness of the night air calming his heated blood. "Almost a generation, these days," he observed. He slid his hand into hers and clasped it gently, his head lifting as he heard the first strains of Mozart in the distance. "If you don't care for explicit sex, how about soft music and ice cream?"

"Soft music?"

"There's an ice-cream social, complete with orchestra concert, in the park on summer nights," he explained. "Come on. I'll show you."

He helped her into the car and drove down to the enormous city park she'd seen earlier, with its ancient towering cottonwood trees and lush grass. Tables and chairs were set up for visitors, although plenty of the guests were sprawled on blankets or quilts on the dry grass. It was like something out of a fantasy, and Allison was enchanted.

"How delightful!" she exclaimed.

Gene lifted an eyebrow and smiled as he led her from the car into the throng, past where the symphony orchestra played magnificently. This was very much his kind of affair, and it touched him that Allison should find it so enjoyable, which she very obviously did.

"I have to admit that this is much more my scene than risqué movies," he mused. "Doing it is one thing, but watching other people do it—or pretend to—doesn't really appeal to me."

She averted her eyes, clinging to his strong lean hand as he led her to one of the tables where homemade ice cream was being dished up.

"I guess you know enough about it already, if what people say about your reputation is true," she said quietly when they were standing in line.

He turned to look down at her, worldly knowledge in his pale eyes. "Are you fishing for a denial?" he asked in a voice that sent goose bumps down her spine. "What they say about me is true. I've never made any secret of it. I've just been a little less discreet in the past few months."

She felt nervous. He'd never looked more like a predator, and she was feeling more threatened by the minute.

He moved closer to her as the line caught up and surged forward. His reputation had never bothered him before. It bothered him when Allison looked at him in that threatened way. "What about you?" he asked just above her ear. "You don't talk about your private life very much."

"There's not a lot to tell," she confessed.

His lean hand traced her shoulder lazily, an action calculated to disturb her. It didn't fail. Her breath caught audibly, and he felt a surge of desire for her that made his knees go weak.

"I don't believe that." He caught her waist with both hands and held her lightly in front of him while the queue moved ever closer to the ice cream. "What flavor do you like?"

"Vanilla," she said at once, because whenever that rare treat had been available, vanilla was invariably all that was offered.

"I like chocolate myself."

"Most men do, I think," she recalled with a smile, remembering how her charges, even the oldest of them, grumbled about the lack of that flavor.

His fingers tightened. "Something you know from experience?"

She put her hands over his to support them. "I suppose, in a way," she agreed.

"How experienced are you?" he asked.

"That's a question a gentleman doesn't ask," she chided, trying to make a joke out of it. And fortunately, before he could pursue the matter, they reached the ice cream.

The orchestra played many familiar pieces, and Allison found herself sitting beside Gene on the grass on a quilt they'd borrowed from a younger couple nearby.

Gene had mentioned that they'd come up from Wyoming, and the young man—much thinner and fairer than Gene—had grinned and asked, "Came up especially for the music, did you?"

"To tell you the truth, we came up for a movie," Gene replied ruefully. "But we left."

The young woman, a vivid redhead, put her hands

over her mouth and giggled with a shy glance at her companion. "The one about cattle ranching?" she asked.

"That's right," Gene agreed.

"We left, too," she said in a very country-sounding drawl. "My daddy would skin me alive if he knew I'd been to such a film, so I made Johnny leave. He liked it," she added with another meaningful look.

"It's life," the boy replied. "We're getting married in two months, after all, Gertie."

"Johnny!" She went scarlet and jumped up. "I'll get us some more ice cream!"

"Virgins," Johnny sighed and then smiled with pure joy.

That smile bothered Gene. He'd never known a virgin, not in all his life. He'd certainly never dated one. But part of him envied that young boy, to be going into a marriage with a woman who'd saved such a precious part of her life for him. He'd never have to wonder about his wife's ex-lovers or how he compared, because there hadn't been any. He'd be the only one, at first anyway, and all her first times would be with him.

He looked down at Allison with speculation. How would it be, he wondered, if she were that fresh and untouched? His eyes ran slowly down her body and he tried to picture himself with her in bed, slowly teaching her things he'd learned. Would she be shocked? Or would it all be old hat to her? He'd found that experienced women tended to be inventive in bed, and uninhibited. That was a definite plus. But it must have been special, too, to be able to teach those responses to a woman, to touch her and hear her cry out with pleasure and know that no other man had ever seen or heard her in ecstasy.

The thoughts bothered him. Surely Allison was experienced, at her age, and she could certainly flirt with the best of them. He sighed. Anyway, what could he expect from a casual interlude like she was going to be? It was just going to be sex, nothing more, and daydreams had no part in this.

As the music built and the last of the ice cream began to disappear, Gene suddenly became aware of time. It was almost a three-hour drive back to Pryor at night, and they were going to be later than he'd expected.

"I hate this, but we have to go," he told Allison after checking his watch. "We've got a long drive back."

"We saw your Jeep," Johnny remarked. He smiled. "Nice wheels. We're starting out in an ancient pickup. But it's tough," he added, "and that's what you need on a ranch."

"Tell me about it." Gene grinned. "We've got a twenty-year-old Ford pickup that I still use to haul calves. Nothing wrong with a classic vehicle."

Johnny beamed. "You bet!"

Gene shrugged. "Starting out is fun. Everybody does it."

"You two married?" Gertie asked.

"No chance," Gene chuckled. "She'd run a mile if I asked her."

"Too bad. You look good together." Gertie leaned against Johnny with love beaming out of her face as she looked up at him.

"So do you two," Allison said gently. "God bless."

"You, too."

"Thanks for the loan of the quilt," Gene added, neatly folding it before handing it back. He didn't want to think about how he and Allison looked together, and marriage was the last thing on his mind. He was glad Allison hadn't made an issue of his reply to Johnny's question. She seemed almost relieved that he'd made a joke of it. Maybe she was marriage-shy, too. That would make things easier.

"Our pleasure. Drive carefully."

Gene nodded. He took Allison's hand and walked her back to the Jeep.

"That was fun," she said. "Thank you."

He looked down at her. "We'll do it again sometime," he said noncommittally.

He opened the passenger door for her, but as she moved into the space he'd made, he turned unexpectedly so that his body was touching hers, one hand holding the door, the other on the cab, so that she was trapped.

"I like the dress," he said. "Lilac suits you."

"Thank you," she replied. His proximity was working on her like a drug. She felt her breath catch as she drank in the clean, cologne-scented warmth of his tall, fit body close to hers.

He bent one leg, so that his knee brushed past her thigh to rest against the seat. The contact brought him even closer, his body shielding her from onlookers in the park.

His breath was warm as his head bent, his glittery eyes meeting hers in the light from the park. "I'll be too busy for a few days, but on the weekend we could go sightseeing up around the Custer Battlefield. And next Tuesday night, we'll go up to Cody for the rodeo if you like."

"Yes," she said without hesitation. She searched his lean, dark face with pure pleasure. "I'd like that very much." Allison was surprised at the effect he had on her. He wasn't even touching her and her body was tingling.

He smiled, because he could read her expression very well indeed. He bent a little closer, so that she could feel his breath on her mouth. She could almost taste him.

"So would I, cupcake," he said softly. He let his eyes drop deliberately to her mouth and stared at it until he heard her breath catch and saw her lips part in helpless response. He leaned just a little closer. "We'd better go," he whispered, letting his breath brush her mouth. It was exciting to tease her; she responded to it so deliciously. She made him feel like the first man who'd done this with her, and his ego soared.

Just as she was beginning to tremble with anticipation, he drew back slowly, still smiling, and gently handed her into the cab. As he went around to the driver's side, his eyes gleamed with unholy delight. The one advantage of experience was that it could recognize capitulation. He was going to stay away from her for a few days and build the tension between them before he made another move. Calculation, surely, but it would be for her benefit, too. Their first time would be explosive.

He got in and started the Jeep. "It'll warm up in a minute," he said, watching her wrap her arms around her breasts.

She smiled thankfully, trying to hide her nervousness. "I didn't think it would get chilly at night."

"Now you know."

"I sure do!" she agreed with a laugh, and shivered until the heater began to blow warm air.

She leaned her head back against the seat and Gene turned on a country-and-western radio station. The drive back to Pryor was very pleasant, despite the fact that they talked very little. She felt safe with him. Comfortable and safe, even through the excitement he generated in her. She wondered if earlier he'd wanted to kiss her and had drawn back because of the crowd. Or was he playing with her? She didn't know. She sighed silently, wishing she had just a little more experience of men to draw on.

They pulled up at the Manley house. It was dark, except for the porch light, and when Allison glanced at the Jeep's clock, she was amazed to find it was three o'clock in the morning.

"I told you we'd be late getting home," Gene mused, watching her catch her breath as she looked toward the dash. "At least they don't seem to be worried about you," he added, nodding toward the darkened windows.

"Don't you believe it," she replied with a gentle smile. "The lights may be off, but I'll bet Winnie isn't asleep. She's like a mother hen sometimes."

He turned in his seat and unfastened her seat belt and then his, leaning back as one dark hand went out to tease the hair at her throat lazily. "Do you need one?" he laughed softly.

She felt her body tingle. All evening it had been a

war of nerves with him, from the way he'd played with her hand in the theater to the way he'd looked at her in the park and that almost-kiss as he'd helped her into the Jeep to come home. Now she was at fever pitch, and she wanted his mouth more than she'd ever imagined she could want anything.

"No, I...don't think so," she said unsteadily. Her eyes fell to his mouth hungrily.

He saw that rapt stare and his heart jumped. She was easy to read for a sophisticated woman. Perhaps it was the first time she'd reacted so strongly to a prospective lover, and that made him proud. It was one thing to turn a virgin's head, but quite another to make an experienced woman nervous and unsure of herself.

His fingers moved to her cheek and traced it lightly and then settled at her jaw while his thumb dragged across her soft mouth in a savagely arousing motion.

She actually gasped, her eyes widening as they met his in the dim light from the dash.

"You don't wear much makeup, do you?" he asked deeply. The feel of her mouth was exciting to him. His thumb rubbed more insistently at her lips, parting them against the pearly white of her teeth. "I'm glad. I don't like layers of lipstick on a woman's mouth when I kiss it."

She felt hot all over. Winnie had warned her about Gene Nelson's expertise and she hadn't understood. Now, suddenly, she began to. She wanted to pull his fingers away from her mouth, she wanted to pull them closer, she wanted to run!

He saw and felt that reaction, registering it with a

little curiosity and a lot of pride. He smiled softly as he caught a handful of her long hair with his other hand and pulled her face under his with easy mastery.

"Bite me," he breathed as his mouth dragged against hers in brief, arousing kisses. She tasted mint and coffee and ice cream and pure man as he played on her attraction to him in the smouldering silence that followed. She couldn't breathe properly. Her fingers bit into his broad shoulders, feeling the steely tautness of the warm muscle as his teeth nibbled at her lower lip.

He lifted his head a fraction and looked into her dazed hazel eyes, his own pale green ones bright with arousal. "Bite me," he repeated gruffly, his fingers contracting in her hair to force her face back up to his. "I like it rough," he breathed into her open mouth. "Don't you?"

She didn't know how she liked it or what he expected of her. She could barely think at all and the words didn't really register. She moved closer, not needing the impetus of his strong hand in her hair to force the movement. She felt him stiffen a little as she slid her arms around his neck with a helpless moan and pushed her mouth hard against his.

The kiss was sweet and heady. His lips parted hungrily and he pressed her head back into his shoulder with the sheer force of his ardor. He made a sound deep in his throat. The taste of her was making him drunk. He couldn't remember the last time he'd felt like this in a woman's arms. Her soft, eager response tested his control to the limits. For an experienced woman, she was

purely lacking in seductive skills, unless this rapt submission to his mouth was some kind of feminine tactic.

At any rate, he was too involved to care. He shifted
her, bringing her across his hard thighs to lie in his arms
while his mouth began to invade hers.

She struggled faintly and he drew away, his breath
shuddering out against her moist, swollen lips.

"What is it?" he asked, his voice almost betraying
him with its deep, drowsy huskiness.

She swallowed, trembling at the feel of his hard
thighs under her. Something had happened to him while
they were kissing, something masculine that was totally out of her experience, and she was shy and a little
frightened.

When she tried to shift away, he understood, but he
only smiled mockingly. "Is this a problem?" he murmured, one steely hand pressing at the base of her spine
to hold her against his raging arousal.

She gasped and stiffened in his arms.

"Too much too soon, Allison?" he murmured, his
pale green eyes narrowing as they met hers. "At any
rate, I can't help it."

"Please," she said, flustered, and tried again to move
away. He held her, firmly but gently. She knew she probably sounded like an outraged virgin—but that was
what she was.

"You're twenty-five," he said solemnly. "Too old for
little-girl games." His hand contracted again, deliberately, and he watched her face flush, her eyes widen.
Odd, that reaction, because it actually seemed genuine.
Not that it could be. He refused to believe that.

"Gene," she protested breathlessly, because incredibly the evidence of his need kindled something comparable in her. She'd never felt that knotting in her lower belly, the rush of warmth, the weak trembling that made her helpless.

He bent toward her, his lips poised just above hers, tempting them. He whispered something then, something so explicit and softly threatening that she actually gasped. When her lips parted, his moved sensuously between them, his tongue probing tenderly past her teeth as if to emphasize what he'd just said to her.

The combination of seductive whisper and equally seductive action tore a shocked moan from her throat. What he was doing to her mouth was…outrageous! Crude, and suggestive and…

She shivered. Her eyes opened to find him watching her while his tongue probed and withdrew in a soft, gentle, subtly arousing rhythm that she was utterly helpless to resist.

And while his tongue touched and tasted, one lean hand was riding up her rib cage to tease around a swollen breast. Even through three layers of fabric, the sensation was devastating. He held her gaze the whole while, intoxicated with the way she responded to it, with the look on her face, the shocked, almost terrified fascination in her misty, dilated eyes. When his thumb suddenly stroked her taut nipple she shuddered and moaned sharply.

He lifted his head, because he liked that. He wanted to see if he could make it happen again. And he did. Again and again, the sound of his fingers faintly abrasive against the fabric of her bodice unnaturally loud in the cab of the Jeep. His hand became more insistent on her soft body, openly caressing now as she gasped for breath and stiffened in his arms, lying helplessly against him and without resistance.

"Yes, it feels good, doesn't it?" he breathed, pride and faint arrogance in the way he was watching her. "You're very, very aroused, little Allison," he said softly, turning his attention to the hard tip of her breast, so very visible through her thin dress. "And just so you won't forget until I see you again…"

Before she realized what he meant to do, he bent and put his lips over the hard nipple and suddenly closed his teeth on it.

She gasped and pushed at him frantically, shocked and frightened by the intimacy.

He lifted his head, frowning, because her reaction puzzled him.

"My God," he breathed. "You don't surely think I meant to hurt you?"

"Di…didn't you?" she whispered shakily, all eyes.

He touched her gently, soothing the place his teeth had been, noticing that she flinched at even that light caress. "I'm sorry if I frightened you," he said tenderly. "Evidently you're used to gentler men altogether."

"Well, yes, I am," she faltered. It was true, too, but not in the way he meant it. She was still shivering from the force of what he'd made her feel.

"I'm not a gentle lover," he said quietly, searching her eyes. "I've never had to be. My kind of woman can match my passion move for move, and it's always been rough and wild because I like it that way." He drew in a slow breath, and his hand flattened over her breast suddenly, in an almost protective gesture. "It never occurred to me before that some women might find that kind of ardor intimidating."

"I'm sorry," she said softly. "I didn't quite know what to expect."

Why in God's name he should feel guilty, he didn't know. But he did. He bent and kissed her with noticeable restraint, almost with tenderness. "Next time," he whispered at her lips, "I'll be a little less wild with you, and a hell of a lot gentler. The last thing I want is to make you afraid of me."

She searched his dark face with wonder. He seemed as surprised by what they'd shared as she did. But he wasn't inexperienced. Shouldn't it have been routine to him to make love to a woman and experience those feelings? She wished she could ask him, but that would mean admitting her naïveté. And once he knew how innocent she really was, he'd never come near her again. He'd said so.

She tried to relax, to carry on the fiction of sophistication. But the blatant masculinity of his body against her made her uneasy.

"I'm not afraid," she said.

He moved his hand away from her breast and lightly touched her mouth, liking the way she lay so softly in his arms, her long hair draping around her shoulders, her eyes gentle and trusting now. She was a woman who needed tenderness, and he was angry with himself for the way he'd treated her. What had been natural with other women seemed out of place and crude with her. He remembered what he'd whispered to her, and winced now, wishing he could take it back.

"What is it?" she asked, having seen that change of expression.

"I said something pretty crude to you a few minutes ago," he said with quiet honesty. "I'm sorry. I suppose I'd forgotten that a woman with some experience can still be a lady, and deserves to be treated like one. The next time I make love to you, it won't be like this."

He moved her gently out of his arms while she was still absorbing the shock of what he'd said.

He went around the cab and helped her out, holding her arm protectively as he escorted her onto the well-lit porch. He looked down at her and his eyes fell suddenly to her dress. He smiled ruefully.

"Good thing Winnie's not up," he murmured.

She followed his gaze and flushed. There was a very obvious dampness on her dress around the nipple that no engaged woman would mistake the reason for.

He cupped her face in his hands and held it up to his eyes, smiling indulgently at her. "Don't worry, no one will see it. Next time," he breathed, bending to her mouth with agonizing slowness, "we'll make sure the fabric is out of the way before I put my lips on you."

She gasped and he smiled against her mouth as he kissed it. His body went rigid instantly, drawing a shocked gasp from his own mouth.

"God, you excite me!" he said roughly, drawing back. "I'd better get out of here before I shock us both. I'll call in a day or so and we'll set a time for that trip to

Hardin. By the way, you can tell your mother hen that I won't keep you out this late again."

"I will." She was holding his arms for support. It wasn't easy to let go. She didn't want to be away from him for a minute, much less two days. "Well, good night. I enjoyed the dinner and the concert."

"Not the movie?" he murmured dryly, smiling at her faint flush. His smile faded as he looked down into her eyes. "Never mind. I think I'm getting too old for careless passion." He touched her mouth with a long forefinger. "I would be tender with you," he said huskily. "I know enough to give you heaven. And when the time comes, I will. That's a promise."

Before she could get her breath or her wits back, he'd turned and was on his way back to the Jeep, his lean-hipped stride holding her eyes against her will. He was so good to look at, and what she felt with him was terrifying. She knew then, hopelessly, that she'd give him anything he asked for. She couldn't even run. The pull of attraction was too strong to fight. She watched him drive away without looking back and wondered sadly if this was how it would be when it was over, and he was going out of her life for good.

Gene knew she was still standing on the porch, but he didn't wave. He was teeming with new and confusing emotions that he really didn't want to explore too fully. His planned seduction was going sadly awry. His conscience was getting in the way.

Allison unlocked the door and went inside, half afraid that Winnie was going to see her. Impulsively she grabbed up a sweater from the clothes tree in the hall and slipped it on, pulling it over her breasts. And in the nick of time, too, because Winnie appeared in the hall as she was on the way to her room.

"About time, too," Winnie said worriedly. "Where have you been?"

Allison told her, making light of the date and raving over the symphony.

"So that's all it was," Winnie relaxed. She smiled ruefully. "I'm sorry. I know I'm overreacting. But he's so potent, Allie. So much a man…"

A sudden, horrible suspicion grew in the back of Allison's mind. "Is he?" she probed.

Winnie grimaced. "I guess you'd better know. I dated Gene before Dwight cut him out. It was innocent; I never slept with him," she emphasized. "The thing is, I would have," she confessed miserably. "And he knew it. That's why I warned you. Gene takes what he wants, but he has nothing to give in return. You're playing a very dangerous game. I'm no Snow White, and I could have survived an affair with him—if I hadn't fallen so hopelessly in love with Dwight. But you're very innocent, Allie. I don't think you could live with yourself. Especially after your upbringing."

"I'm not sure I could, either," she confessed on a hard sigh. "He's…very potent."

"So I see."

The amused drawl brought her eyes down and she noticed then that the sweater had fallen open. She went scarlet, wrapping it protectively over her breasts.

"Don't look so haunted," Winnie said gently. "I understand. A man like that is too hard to resist. You can't be blamed for being human. But to keep seeing him is asking for trouble."

"I know." Allison looked down at the floor. "I...think I'm falling in love."

Winnie bit her lower lip. "He can't help being the way he is. But he isn't a man who knows how to love. Or commit himself to a long-term relationship."

Allison looked up with haunted, sad eyes. "There's still a chance."

"And you're too hooked to listen to warnings, aren't you?" her friend replied gently. She hugged Allison to her with a sigh. "Try to keep your head, at least."

"I'll do that. Complications are the last thing I need."

"At least you know about precautions," Winnie sighed, smiling at Allison's flush. "Your training may come in handy before you're through. Okay, no more lectures. Go to bed. Is the wild man coming back?"

"Yes. Sometime in the middle of the week. He's taking me to see the Custer Battlefield. Then next week, we're going to the rodeo in Cody," she said.

Winnie just shook her head.

Allison changed into her nightgown, awed and frightened by the way it had been. Her first intimacy with a man, and she couldn't even admit it to him. She wondered if he'd have been different with her, had he known how naïve she was. Probably he'd have done what he swore at the beginning—he'd have left her strictly alone. He'd been honest about his opinion of innocence; that he wanted no part of it. She felt guilty about hiding hers, but she was falling in love. Even if he got angry at her later, she had to have a chance. He might fall in love with her, too, and then it would be all right.

Except that in the meantime he might seduce her, she thought worriedly. His ardor was unexpected and so was her helplessness. She'd never experienced those sensations, and they were addictive.

She tried to push it out of her mind when she went to bed. But she felt as if her body had scorched the sheets by morning. She'd never had such erotic dreams in all her life, and they were full of Gene.

Chapter Six

Gene was surprised by the force of his attraction to Allison. He'd meant to wait a few days before he saw her again, to give her time to miss him, to enhance her response to him. But he found himself thinking about her all too much. By the second day, the tables had suddenly turned on him and *he* was missing *her*.

He gunned the Jeep into the Manley driveway, smiling when he saw Allison out digging in Mrs. Manley's small flower garden near the porch steps. She was wearing Bermuda shorts and a pink tank top, her long black hair in a ponytail, and she looked charming. He cut off the engine and climbed out of the big vehicle, his bat-wing chaps making a leathery rustling sound as he walked toward her.

"They've put you to work, I see," he drawled.

Allison flushed and smiled shyly, getting to her feet. She'd just been daydreaming about him, and here he was! "Hi!" she said, her whole face radiant with the greeting.

His heart jumped a little. "Hi, yourself," he murmured, moving closer. His eyes fell from her firm breasts down her narrow waist to softly flaring hips and long, elegant legs. She even had pretty feet, encased in brown leather thongs. "Nice legs," he murmured with a wicked glance.

"Thank you," she stammered. "Are you looking for Winnie and Mrs. Manley? They had to run to the store...."

"I came to see you, cupcake," he said softly, his wide-brimmed hat shadowing his eyes as they searched hers. "But I hardly dared hope I'd find you alone."

She felt her heart race. "Did you?" she whispered.

He tipped her chin up and bent his head unexpectedly, brushing his mouth with lazy expertise over her parted lips. "No, that won't do," he breathed, his voice deep and slow as he reached for her. "Come close, little one."

He enveloped her in his muscular arms and drew her against his body as he bent again. This time the kiss was longer, harder, but so different from the way he'd kissed her two nights ago. This one was gentle, full of respect and warmth. She reacted to it with all her heart, sliding her arms under his and around his lean waist, loving the way his mouth played with hers and teased around it between kisses.

"Very nice," he mused when he lifted his head. It

was much better like this, gentle and sweet, so that she responded and didn't fight or draw away. He liked it when she wasn't frightened. "Dessert, in the middle of the day," he added, teasing. "You taste sweet."

She laughed softly, her hazel eyes adoring him. "I just ate a cinnamon bun."

"And that wasn't what I meant," he murmured. "Does tomorrow suit you to drive up to Hardin? We can leave about nine, if you like."

"Oh, yes," she said, already excited.

"Good. I'll make sure I'm free. Wear jeans and boots. There are rattlers in that area. I don't want you hurt."

Her smile widened. "I will," she promised, surprised and pleased that he was concerned about her. Being with him shot her through and through with pleasure.

He drew his forefinger down her nose. "Don't get sunstroke out here. What are you doing?"

"Weeding Mrs. Manley's flowers," she said. "I hate just sitting around. I hate talk shows and I can't do handicrafts. I like working."

The women he usually escorted liked to preen and put themselves on display. He scowled as he thought about it. Not one of them would like getting her hands dirty digging in a garden. His eyes slid over Allison's soft face and lingered there. His mother had been an enthusiastic gardener, too.

"Do you have a garden where you live?" he asked suddenly.

Her smile faded and she averted her eyes to the spade she was using. "Yes, I had a vegetable garden," she said. "But it...was ruined."

"I'm sorry. I don't think Winnie's mother grows vegetables."

"No, she's a flower enthusiast," Allison replied. She looked up at him again, smiling as she studied the way he looked in his working clothes, very lean and lithe and Western. Very masculine, too, as he stood with his hands on his hips, his Stetson low over his eyes. "You look like an ad for a Western vacation," she said involuntarily. "Very, very handsome."

He chuckled. "That's it, hit me in my weak spot."

She laughed, too. "You could have phoned. About Hardin, I mean."

"I know." He touched her soft mouth lightly. "I wanted to see you. Don't overdo. I'll pick you up at nine."

"Okay," she said, her voice low and gentle.

He winked at her, but he didn't touch her again. He pulled his hat lower over one eye and strode back to the Jeep. He didn't look back as he drove away. She had a feeling that he never did, and it just vaguely disturbed her. It was a reminder that he wasn't a committing man. And he was used to walking away from women without looking back.

But by the time he picked her up the next morning, she'd convinced herself that she was going to be the one exception to his rule. He did at least seem to be different with her since the other night, when she'd drawn back from his overwhelming ardor. Maybe he sensed her innocence and wasn't put off by it. She laughed silently. More likely, he'd decided that roughness might put her off him, and he was soft pedaling his raging desire until he could coax her into satisfying it. She had to be realistic, but it was difficult when she was so vulnerable to him. That had to be mutual, though, she told herself. Otherwise, why would he have come all the way to the Manleys' to see her, when he could have phoned? She tingled with the delicious possibilities.

He was dressed in jeans and boots and a brown-and-white patterned Western shirt, the familiar Stetson cocked over one eye. Allison had dressed similarly, with a beige tank top under a blue-and-brown striped shirt. She laughed at the way they matched.

So did Gene. He helped her into the truck, jamming a Caterpillar bibbed cap down over her hair, which she'd pulled up in a soft bun. The cap came down to her eyebrows. "You can fix that. There's an adjustable strap in the back," he told her as he drove. "I figured you'd forget your hat."

She beamed. He was taking such good care of her. She looked at him, her heart overflowing with warm feelings. "Thanks," she said softly, and adjusted the plastic strip.

"I have to take care of my best girl," he said softly. The strange thing was that he meant it. She was the best girl he'd ever taken out. She wasn't demanding or petulant or sulky. She reminded him of bright summer sunshine, always cheerful.

She became radiant as she heard the words, blushing. It got worse when he reached out and tangled her fingers in his as he drove.

"Miss me?" he asked gently.

"Oh, yes," she said, not bothering with subterfuge. He glanced at her, his eyes lingering on her rosy cheeks and soft, parted mouth before he forced his gaze back to his driving. "That goes double for me." His fingers clenched in hers. "You're good medicine, sunshine."

"Medicine?" she teased.

"Up in this part of the world, medicine means more than drugs. The Plains Indians used to 'make medicine' before battle, to protect them and help their spirits find the way to the hereafter. There was good medicine and bad, equally potent. They filled small rawhide bags with special talismans to protect their bodies from their enemies. Good medicine," he added, smiling as he glanced at her. "But I'd have hell stuffing you into a rawhide pouch."

She laughed. "I expect it would be uncomfortable, at that." Her eyes adored him. "Thank you for taking me to the battlefield. I've wanted to see it all my life."

"My pleasure. I don't think you'll be disappointed."

She wasn't. There was a museum and guided tours were available. She noticed that Gene avoided the groups of tourists as they meandered along the paved walkway up to the graves in their wrought-iron square and the tall monument on which was carved the names of the soldiers who died at the spot.

"We're standing on Crow land," he explained, nodding down the ridge to the small stream that cut a deep ravine through the green grass. Beyond it was a large stand of trees and an even larger body of water. "Through there was the encampment. Several Native American tribes came together to form an army of several thousand. This fenced area is where the last stand was made. Custer died here, so they say, along with his brother and brother-in-law and nephew. He was shot through the left breast and the temple."

"I read somewhere that he committed suicide."

He shook his head. "I think that's unlikely. If you read his book, *My Life on the Plains*, you get a picture of a man who is definitely not the type for suicide. One authority on him thinks he was shot down in that ravine, through the left breast, and brought up here to the last stand position by his men. A bullet wound was found in his left temple. The Indians usually shot their enemies at close range to make sure they were dead. It was reported that after a buckskinned soldier was wounded in the ravine, the soldiers lost heart and seemed not to fight so hard. If it was Custer who got shot, then it would explain that near rout. His men were young and mostly inexperienced. Few of them had ever seen Indians on the warpath."

"I guess it would be scary," she said, looking up at him with fascination.

"You don't know the half of it, cupcake. Plains Indians in full regalia were painted—faces, surely, and bodies. Even the horses were painted. Add to that the death cry they all yelled as they went into battle, and the eagle bone whistles they blew, and you've got a vision of death terrifying enough to make a seasoned trooper nervous."

He stopped and looked out over the rolling buttes and high ridges and vast stretch of horizon. "My God," he breathed, "no wonder they fought so hard to keep it.

Look. Virgin land, untouched, unpoisoned by civilization. God's country."

"Yes. It really is beautiful," she said.

The wind was blowing hard and he slid an arm around her, drawing her close. "Want to walk down to the ravine?" he asked.

"Could we?"

"Surely. There's a trail. Watch for snakes, now."

He led her down the deceptively long path to the ravine, stopping at each place that marked where men had fallen in battle. He seemed familiar with all of them, and the history. He stopped for a long moment beside one marker.

"My great-great-uncle," he said, smiling at her expression. "Surprised? Now you know how I knew so much about the battle. His wife kept a journal, and I have it. The last entry was the night before he set out with Custer's 7th for the Little Bighorn. He probably kept a journal all the way here, too, but the Native tribes scoured the battlefield after the fight, and took everything they thought they could use. Watches, pistols, clothing, even saddles and boots were carried off. They threw away the soles of the boots and used the leather to make other things out of."

"Tell me about your great-great-uncle," she said, and listened attentively while they walked back up from the steep banks of the ravine. He held her hand tightly, speaking at length about the battle and its historical controversies.

He took her to the museum when they were through. She wandered through the souvenir shop afterward, oohing and aahing over the exquisite beadwork on the crafts. She paused by a full-length warbonnet and sighed over a war lance. It was amazing to consider how terrifying these same things would have been to a woman only a hundred years before. Gene insisted on buying her a pair of beaded earrings for her pierced ears. On the way home, he explained the wearing of earrings by the various Plains tribes and how you could tell warriors of each tribe apart by their hairstyles and earrings.

"It's just fascinating," she said.

Gene glowed with pride. None of his dates had ever liked to hear him hold forth about the battle. Allison not only listened, but she seemed to be really interested. He learned as they drove back that she was a student of Native cultures herself, and she seemed to have a wealth of knowledge about the Mayans. He listened to her on the way back, absorbing little-known facts about the Mayans.

"You're good," he said when he drove up in front of the Manley house just after dark. "Damned good. Where did you learn all that?"

She smiled wistfully. "I just read a lot and kept my ears open, I guess," she said, neglecting to add that she'd climbed over Mayan temples where she and her parents had been assigned. The smile faded as the memories came back. "I had a good time, Gene. A really good time. Thank you."

He drew her to him. "So did I." He searched her eyes in the dim light from the dash. "We'll say our good-nights here," he said softly, letting his eyes drop to her mouth. "The way we kiss might shock them."

As he whispered the words, his lips slowly parted hers. They didn't take, they coaxed this time. Moist, aching pressure teased her mouth open in a silence that grew with strained breathing. He moved, so that her head fell back against the seat, and his face followed hers, his mouth still teasing, provoking, tantalizing until she was trembling.

"You set me on fire," he groaned as the need finally broke through. The pressure of the kiss pushed her head hard into the back of the seat, and she felt him shiver as his tongue slowly thrust past her teeth. He groaned again, one lean hand sliding down her throat to her breast under the shirt, over the thin tank top. "Stop wearing bras," he managed unsteadily. "They just get in my way."

She opened her mouth to speak, but no words came out. He was kissing her again, and this time his hand slid boldly right under the fabric. His thumb rubbed tenderly over her hard nipple, his moist palm cupping the firm underside of her breast. She moaned and he lifted his head.

"Satin and velvet," he said, his eyes glittery as they met hers. He deliberately pulled her tank top and bra out, so that he could look down at her taut, bare breast. "Yes," he said huskily, but without touching her this time. "You look as I knew you would. Pretty breasts. Tip-tilted and exquisitely pretty."

Her lips parted, but she was beyond shock. She shivered and actually arched toward him, so aroused that she wanted his mouth on her, there.

But he saw what she didn't—the curtains moving at the window. He released her reluctantly and lifted his head. "I can't touch you there," he said quietly. "Not now. We have an audience."

"Oh," she stammered, all at sea.

He lifted his invading hand back to her cheek and searched her eyes for a long moment. "We'll be good together," he said quietly. "You know it, too, don't you?"

She should tell him, she thought. She should… "Yes," she replied instead.

He nodded. "I won't rush you," he said. "But I won't wait a great deal longer, either. It's been too long for me."

She didn't know what to say. She shifted a little, still on fire in the aftermath of his ardor.

"Good night, sweet thing," he murmured, kissing her closed eyelids. "You're very special."

He drew back then and helped her out of the Jeep, keeping his arm around her as they walked back to the porch.

"Your guardian angel is hanging back," he mused, smiling down at her. "Is she giving up?"

Her heart leaped. "Sort of. She's engaged, you know."

He cocked an eyebrow. "So she is." He tapped her cheek. "I'll never be," he said suddenly. "You know that, don't you? I enjoy being with you, and physically, we burn each other up. But I won't lie and promise you happy ever after. I'm a confirmed bachelor."

Her heart didn't want to hear that. She forced a smile to her mouth. "Yes, I know."

He nodded slowly, searching her eyes. He couldn't let her get her hopes up. Marriage was definitely not on his agenda. He was still having hell coping with his past. And there was one very good reason why he didn't want to procreate. Bad genes could be passed on. He shifted. "Good girl. I'll pick you up tomorrow night and we'll go to the rodeo. I know I said next week, but I don't want to wait that long. Do you?"

She shook her head. "No. Not really," she confessed.

"Then I'll come for you at six." He nuzzled her face and kissed her softly. "Good night, pretty thing."

She smiled up at him a little wanly. "Good night. Thanks for the trip, and my earrings."

He twitched them, watching them dangle. "They suit you. See you tomorrow."

He was gone at once, without another kiss and still without looking back. She went into the house, smiling as Winnie came to meet her.

"We're just putting supper on the table," Winnie said. "Have fun?"

"Oh, yes. He knows a lot about the Custer Battlefield, doesn't he?" she asked.

"Indeed he does. Did he bore you with it? Marie says he drives them crazy spouting history."

"But I love it!" Allison said, surprised. "History is one of my hobbies. I found it fascinating."

Winnie's eyebrows went up. "My, my, imagine that." She grinned. "Way to go, tiger. You may land that feisty fish yet. Come on. I'll feed you."

The remark gave Allison hope, and she needed it. Her conscience was bothering her. She really should tell Gene the truth. If only she could be sure that he wouldn't turn around and walk away from her for good.

The next day, Allison decided that the best thing to wear to a rodeo—since her one pair of jeans was in the wash—was a blue denim skirt with sporty pull-on pink sneakers and a pink T-shirt. But she wore a lightweight rose-patterned sweater with it, because she hadn't forgotten how cool it had been in Billings after dark. She pulled her hair into a ponytail and tied it with a pink scarf. Then she sat down to wait for Gene, because she'd dressed two hours early for their date. Every few minutes she involuntarily checked her watch. The instrument was so much part of her uniform when she worked that she felt naked without it. Despite the innovations in modern medicine, a watch with a sweep second hand was about the most advanced equipment for pulse monitoring available in the primitive areas where she and her parents had worked.

Winnie's mother had been invited to a baby shower for a friend's daughter, and Winnie was going out with Dwight. They left just a few minutes before Gene arrived. True to her word, Winnie didn't make a single remark about the date. She just hugged Allison and smiled sympathetically. That was no surprise. Winnie was in love herself, so she certainly understood how it felt.

Gene arrived exactly on time. He was dressed for a casual evening, in jeans and hand-tooled black leather boots with a blue Western shirt and a turquoise-and-silver bola. He wore a new black Stetson tonight with a moccasin headband, and he was freshly shaved and showered.

He smiled down appreciatively at the way she looked in her skirt and T-shirt with her silky black hair in a ponytail. His body had given him no peace for the past few days, going over and over the sweetness of Allison's response to him and the joy he'd felt in her company. They shared so many common interests that he actually enjoyed talking to her. Not that the way they exploded when they touched was any less potent. Not for worlds would he have admitted how much he'd looked forward to tonight. Looking at her made him feel good. Being with her was satisfying and sweet. And, unfortunately, addictive. He was going to have to do something about it; the sooner the better. She couldn't be staying much longer, and she was beginning to interfere with not only his work, but his sleep. He found himself thinking of her constantly, wanting to be with her. He was acting like a lovesick boy and he didn't want to disgrace himself by letting anyone know. The sooner he got her out of his system physically, the sooner he could get back to normal and deal with his worst problems.

The odd thing was that since Allison had been around, he hadn't worried so much about his parentage or that will that had changed his life. In fact, he was more at peace than he'd ever been. She gave him the first peace he'd had in weeks. Months. He felt as if there was no problem he couldn't overcome when he was with her. And that was disturbing. Really disturbing.

He pushed the thoughts to the back of his mind. "You look cute," he murmured dryly. "I like the T-shirt."

It read Women's Revolutionary Sewing Society. She'd found it in an out-of-the-way shop, and she loved it. She grinned up at him, her eyes warm in her oval face with its exquisite peaches-and-cream complexion. "It appealed to my sense of the ridiculous. Do you really like it?"

"I like the way you fill it out better," he said quietly, his eyes admiring her breasts and darkening with memory. "Is that skirt going to fall off without a belt?" he added, frowning at the way it fit in the waist—very loosely.

"I've lost a little weight in the past few weeks," she said noncommittally. "But it will stay up. I couldn't find my belt."

Of course not. It was still in Central America, along with most of her other belongings. That brought back vivid memories of how she'd left foreign surroundings, and how the media had followed her. Being seen in public could put her in jeopardy, but it was unlikely that Gene would introduce her to anybody from the press. She relaxed, shifting restlessly as she pushed the worries to the back of her mind.

He glanced around. "Where's Winnie?"

"Out with Dwight. Didn't you know?"

He laughed curtly, and without any real humor, his lean face full of mockery, his pale green eyes narrow and cool. "Dwight doesn't discuss his social life with me these days."

She moved closer to him, and because of the heels

on his boots and the lack of them on her sneakers, she had to look up a lot farther than usual. He smelled of spicy cologne, a fragrance that made her pulse race almost as much as being close to him did. "He might, if you didn't make it so difficult for him," she said gently, and with a smile that took the sting out of the words.

He'd have thrown a punch at any man who dared say something like that to his face. But somehow it didn't offend him when Allison said it. One corner of his thin, disciplined mouth twitched and his eyes sparkled with faint amusement as he looked down at her.

"You standing in a ditch?" he asked unexpectedly. "Or did you get wet and shrink overnight?"

She laughed, her whole body on fire with life and love and his company. "I'm wearing sneakers."

"Is that it?" He looked down at her feet in pink tennis shoes. "Dainty little things," he mused.

"Nobody could ever describe *your* feet that way," she replied with a meaningful glance at his long boots.

"I throw away the boots and wear the shoe boxes," he agreed pleasantly. "Mrs. Manley isn't here, either?" he added, glancing around.

"She went to a baby shower."

He drew a slow breath, feeling a contentment he could hardly remember in his life stealing over him as he stared at her. "No lectures from your mother hen before she left with Dwight?"

She shook her head.

He chuckled. "She really has given up!"

"Yes." She searched his face quietly, loving every

strong, lean line of it, its darkness, its masculinity. She could have stood looking at him all day.

His eyebrow jerked. Her delight was evident, and it made him bristle with pride. "We'd better go," he said after a minute.

"Yes."

But he didn't move, and neither did she. His eyes fell to her mouth, its pale pink owing nothing to lipstick. He caught her by the waist and drew her lazily against him, bending to brush his lips softly over hers in a delicate kiss that aroused but didn't satisfy. She tasted of mint and he smiled against her soft mouth, liking the hungry, instant response he got. Her arms moved up to hold him and he half lifted her against him in an embrace that made her think inexplicably of Christmas and mistletoe and falling snow, because she was warm and safe.

He wasn't thinking at all. The feel of her in his arms had stopped his mind dead. Everything was sensation now. Warm, soft breasts flattened against him, the floral scent of her body, the trembling eagerness of the soft lips parting under his rough mouth. His body stiffened as the first wave of desire hit him.

He forced himself to lift his head. He had to catch his breath, and she seemed similarly occupied. He searched her wide, stunned eyes for a long moment, until his heartbeat echoed in his ears like a throbbing drum.

Her face was beautiful. Her exquisite complexion was softly flushed, her lips were swollen and moist from the long, hard contact with his mouth. Wisps of black hair trailed around her rosy cheeks, and her hazel eyes looked totally helpless.

"It might be a good idea if we go, while we still have a choice," he murmured ruefully. He put her back on her feet and let her arms slide away from his neck. God, she was potent!

"Yes, it might," she agreed gently, equally affected and having a hard time dealing with it.

He waited while she locked the door and escorted her to the Jeep. "If you stick around long enough, I'll buy a car," he murmured when they were driving off.

"I like the Jeep," she protested. "And it must come in handy on the ranch."

"It does," he had to agree. He glanced at her, frowning. So many secrets, he thought. She was mysterious, and he had a terrible secret of his own, about his real father. It would be better for both of them if he took her back to Winnie's and didn't see her again. But he couldn't seem to force himself to do that. Whatever happened, he had to have her, even if it was only one time. He knew instinctively that it would be different with her than it ever had been before; that it would be a kind of ecstasy he'd never known. He ached for her now. It was too late to stop it.

He'd been having more trouble sleeping lately than he ever had in his life—and more cold showers. He opened the window, needing air, and glanced at Allison.

"Do you mind?" he asked.

She leaned her head against the seat and studied his face warmly. "No."

"It'll keep me awake. I haven't been sleeping well. Too many things on my mind."

"What things?" she asked gently.

"Life, Allison."

The sound of her name on his lips made her tingle. She liked the way he said it.

"It's been difficult for you, I know," she replied. "The important thing is that you'll get through it. Nothing lasts forever. Not even pain."

He scowled, darting a glance in her direction. "Don't bet on it," he replied.

Her eyes fell to his firm jaw, to the cut of his lips. She liked his profile. It was strong, like the man himself. "It's early days yet, though," she reminded him. "You can't expect to have your life torn apart and put back together overnight. I don't imagine that waiting comes easily to you."

He smiled in spite of himself. "No. It doesn't." He was quiet for a minute before he spoke again. "But in this case, I don't have a lot of choice. Are you impatient, Allison? Or do you find it easy to wait for the things you want?"

"I was always taught that patience was among the greatest virtues," she said simply. "But sometimes it's very difficult to stand back and not try to force things into place. Accepting things isn't much easier," she added, thinking of her parents.

He nodded. "I guess we're all human, aren't we, cupcake?" he asked quietly. "And there are times when it seems that we can't manage any control over our own destiny."

"You don't go to church, I guess," she asked softly.

He shook his head. "No." His face hardened. "I can't believe in a God who torments people."

"He doesn't," she said. "We do that to ourselves. He watches and helps when we ask Him, but I think we're somewhat responsible for our own destinies. When we have choices, we make them. Life takes care of the rest."

"And where does God enter into it?"

"He gave us free will," she said, smiling. "Otherwise, Eve would never have handed Adam that delicious, succulent juicy apple."

He burst out laughing. "Do tell?" he chuckled.

"Besides, there are other forces at work in the world. Balance means evil exists with good. Sometimes it's hard to win against the darker forces." Her eyes clouded. "That doesn't mean you quit trying. You just work harder."

"You sound like a minister we used to have," he mused without looking at her, which was a shame. The expression on her face would have fascinated him. "He wasn't a bad sort. I used to enjoy listening to him."

"What stopped you from going to services?" she asked, curious.

"I don't know," he shrugged. "I guess it was because it didn't seem to make any difference. Going to church didn't solve my problems."

"It doesn't solve them. It helps you cope with them," she said with a gentle smile. "Being religious doesn't automatically make you immune to hard times and hurt."

"That's what I discovered for myself. I expected miracles."

"Miracles are all around," she said. "They happen every day."

"Do they really?" he asked, unconvinced.

"Oh, yes." She could have told him that she was one. That she was alive was truly through divine intervention. She glanced out the window. "We aren't going through Shoshone Canyon again, are we?" she asked, changing the subject delicately.

"No. I took you on a wide Western detour to show you the canyon and the tunnel. We're going northwest straight into Cody this time. Have you ever been to a rodeo?"

"Once or twice, down in Arizona. It's very dangerous, isn't it?"

"More than one cowboy has lost his life in a rodeo arena," he agreed. "All it takes is one small lapse of concentration, or carelessness. You can be gored by a bull, kicked by a horse, trampled, bitten, thrown so hard you break a bone... It's no game for city cowboys."

"Have any tried?" she asked, curious now.

He chuckled softly. "We had this guy from back East at one of the Cody rodeos last year," he began. "He'd been riding those mechanical bulls in bars and figured he was plenty good enough for a hick rodeo. He signed up and paid his entrance money. They put him up on one of the bulls we'd supplied. Old Scratch, by name." He grinned at her. "There he sat, waiting for the buzzer and for the gate to open, when the announcer gave Old Scratch's history and mentioned that in seventy-eight rides, not one cowboy had stayed on him until the horn sounded. The look on that dude's face was worth money."

"What happened?" she prompted.

"He and the bull parted company two seconds out of

the chute. He broke his arm and one rib. Last I heard, he'd given up bull riding in favor of his old job—selling shoes at a department store back home."

She gasped. "Oh, the poor man!"

"Poor man, hell. Anybody who thinks riding almost a ton of bucking beef is a picnic ought to have his rear end busted. It's no game for shoe wranglers."

She studied Gene's lean, hard face and let her eyes fall to his tall, fit body. "Do you ride; in rodeos, I mean?" she asked.

A smile touched his thin lips as he shot a quick glance her way. "Do you think I'm too old, cupcake?"

She smiled back. "No. I was just curious. I guess what you do at the ranch takes up most of your time."

"It used to," he recalled bitterly. "Until control of it passed to Dwight."

"Dwight doesn't seem like the kind of person who'd take over everything," she said slowly, not wanting to offend him. "I'm sure he was as upset as you were by what came out."

He scowled. She hit nerves. "I guess he was, at that," he said in a slow, even tone. "He inherited the business side of the ranch, which he hates, and I wound up with the day-to-day operation of it, which I hate. I don't mind physical labor, you understand, but while I'm helping load cattle into trailers, Dwight's committing financial suicide with the accounts."

"Haven't the two of you talked about that?" she probed.

He tilted his hat across his brow. "There's Cody up ahead," he said, discouraging any further comment.

When he parked the Jeep and helped her out, it occurred to him that he'd told her more about himself than he'd shared with anyone in recent years. And in return, he'd learned nothing—not one damned thing—about her. He looked down at her steadily as they waited in line for tickets.

"You don't talk about yourself, do you?" he asked suddenly.

She lifted both eyebrows, startled by a question she hadn't expected. "Well, no, not a lot," she admitted.

"Is it deliberate?"

She shrugged. "I can't learn very much about other people if I spend my time talking about myself."

He tugged at her long ponytail mischievously. "I'll dig it out of you before I'm through."

"I'm shaking in my boots," she assured him.

"You aren't wearing boots."

"Picky, picky," she said, and laughed up at him. He was easily the most physically impressive man in the line, and the handsomest, to her at least.

"Well, hello, Gene," a soft, feminine voice drawled beside them, and a striking raven-haired beauty with flashing blue eyes attached on to his arm.

"Hello, Dale," he replied with a stiff nod.

"It's been months. Why haven't you called me?" the woman asked. She was dressed in rodeo clothes, with a white Stetson and matching boots. She was beautiful and younger than Allison by about three years.

"If I'd had anything to say, I would have," Gene replied curtly, irritated by Dale's possessive manner and the blatant way she was leaning against him.

Dale's blue eyes glared at Allison. "Is she the reason?" she demanded, giving the older woman a hard appraisal. "She's hardly a beauty, is she?"

Gene took her arm roughly and moved her aside, his eyes as threatening as his cold tone. "Get lost. Now."

Dale tore away from him, glaring back. "You weren't so unfriendly once."

He gave her a mocking, icy smile. "I wasn't sober, either, was I?"

She all but gasped. Realizing that they were attracting attention, she turned and stormed off toward the back of the arena.

"I'm sorry about that," Gene told Allison, angry that she'd been embarrassed and hurt by Dale's harsh remarks.

Allison only nodded. So his conquests weren't in far-flung cities. She had a glimpse of how it might be if she married someone like him, and had to be constantly reminded of his wildness. Only a few months ago, the woman had said, and he was already resentful at having to see her again. Allison shuddered, thinking that she might have just seen herself in the future. She couldn't look up at Gene again. She was afraid of what she might give away.

But he sensed her discomfort. When they were seated in the bleachers waiting for the first event to start, he stared at her until she looked up.

"I'm sorry," he said curtly. His pale green eyes searched her wan face quietly. "That couldn't have come at a worse time, could it?"

"She's very pretty," she voiced involuntarily.

"Yes. I was drunk and she was willing, and I thought

that would be the end of it. But she's tenacious. I'd forgotten that she was entered in the barrel-racing competition tonight."

"Is she good?" Allison asked.

He glared at her. "In the saddle, or in bed?" he asked, taking the question at face value.

She averted her eyes. "In the saddle, of course."

His face hardened. "You take some getting used to," he said after a minute. "I always expect sarcasm from a woman. It's hard to acclimate to honesty."

"Maybe it's your choice of women that's at fault," she replied, trying to smile. Hearing him talk so casually about one of his conquests made her uncomfortable.

He had to admit that Allison wasn't like any of his other women. She appealed to a lot more than his senses. He scowled, because that bothered him. He clenched his hands togther as he stared toward the chutes. "Okay, honey, here we go," he said, nodding toward the announcer, who'd just started speaking.

It was the best rodeo Allison had ever seen. Gene knew most of the contestants and most of the livestock, so he pointed out the strongest riders in each competition and the worst bulls and broncs.

"Now that son of a mustang leaped flat-footed into the backseat of a convertible on a neighboring ranch," he informed her as one of the worst bareback broncs trotted away after unseating his would-be rider. "He doesn't belong to us, and I'm glad. He's a really bad customer. All but unridable and bad-tempered to boot. I've been kicked by him a time or two myself."

"You said you didn't ride," she remarked.

"Not often," he corrected. "Now and again when I've had a beer too many, I get the old urge to try to break my neck in the arena," he chuckled.

That didn't sound encouraging, either, as if he liked to go on binges. Allison knew so little about men and their habits. She really had led a sheltered life.

"Look, here comes one of ours," he said, nudging her. "That's Rocky Road. He can outbuck most of the others hands down."

Sure enough, the bronc unseated his rider in jig time and sashayed off without a care in the world. The cowboy he'd unseated slammed his hat down in the dirt and jumped on it repeatedly while the audience laughed at the unexpected entertainment.

Allison laughed with him. She really couldn't help it.

"Oh, the poor man," she choked.

"You pay your money and take your chances," he said without much real sympathy. "It happens to all of us. The name of the game is to keep down the number of winners. A rodeo exists to make money, not to give it away, you know."

"I guess I didn't think. But I still feel sorry for the men who lose."

"So do I, actually."

The next man stayed on and Allison thought he'd done extremely well, but he didn't score at all.

"He didn't get thrown!" Allison protested on the man's behalf.

"The horse didn't buck enough, honey," Gene explained patiently, and then went on to point out that a cowboy was judged on much more than just staying on the horse's back.

"It's so complicated." She shook her head.

"That's the name of the game," he replied. He smiled down at her. "If you watch rodeo enough, you'll get the hang of seeing how it's judged. That's an art in itself."

She smiled back at him, tingling from head to toe at the warm, intimate look in his eyes before they averted back to the action down in the arena. She couldn't remember when she'd felt happier or more alive. Especially when Gene appropriated her hand and clasped it warmly in his while they watched the rest of the competition.

The last of the bareback bronc riding finished, with the winner and second and third places announced. Then came barrel racing, and the woman named Dale was competing. Allison noticed that Gene didn't applaud or pay much attention to the pretty young woman in the arena. He didn't even react when his ex-lover won the race. Dale Branigan, they announced, and Allison stared down at the younger woman with envy. She was pretty and young and full of the joy of life as she reacted to her win by jumping in the air and giving out a loud, laughing yell. So that was the kind of woman who attracted the taciturn man at her side: young, aggressive, eager for intimacy and fancy-free. She didn't really have much of a chance. That might be a good thing, considering how he seemed to treat women he'd slept with. She felt suddenly sad. She was daydreaming, and it was no good. He might be wonderful to kiss, and delightful as a companion, but it was all just means to an end, she was sure of it. The thought depressed her terribly, although Gene didn't seem to notice. He was quiet after the barrel racing.

He felt Allison's gaze, but he didn't meet it. Seeing Dale again had disturbed him. He remembered very little of the night he'd spent with her, and now he was ashamed of his part in it. The old Gene wouldn't have had any qualms at spending the night in the arms of a pretty, willing woman. But since he'd been taking Allison places, the ease of his old conquest disturbed him. He couldn't sort out the confused feelings he was entertaining for Allison, or the guilt she aroused in him sometimes. She seemed to look for the best in everyone and everything, as if she wouldn't even admit the existence of evil in people. She was caring and kind and gentle, and sensuous in a strange, reserved way. He was surprised at her inhibitions when he kissed and held her intimately, and he wondered why her own conquests hadn't taught her more. Perhaps she'd been sleeping with the wrong men. He thought about sleeping with her himself, and his body vibrated with excitement. It would be like having a virgin, he thought, and his heartbeat increased fiercely. He didn't dare look at her until he got himself under control again.

Unaware of his thoughts, Allison concentrated on the arena. But there seemed to be a distance between Gene and herself, and she didn't understand why.

In no time, the competition was over, the prizes awarded and it was time to go home. Allison followed Gene down from the bleachers, noting his dark scowl as he saw Dale coming toward them with her award.

"Going to congratulate me?" she asked Gene, apparently having recovered from her bad humor, because she was smiling seductively.

"Sure. Congratulations." He slid an arm around Allison's shoulders and drew her close, glancing down at her possessively. "We thought you were great, didn't we, cupcake?" he added, his voice low and caressing for Allison.

She smiled with difficulty, going along with the pretense. "Yes." She looked at the younger woman with kind eyes. "You were very good."

Dale shifted restlessly under that warm, easy smile, which showed no trace of antagonism or hostility. She didn't know how to react to a woman who didn't behave like a spitting cat. "Thanks," she said uneasily. "Going to the dance?" she added.

"We might," he said.

"Going to introduce me?" she persisted, nodding toward Allison.

"This is Allison Hathoway," he said, glancing down at her. "She's an old friend of Winnie's. You know Winnie—she's engaged to Dwight."

"I know her. Nice to meet you. I'm Dale Branigan." She extended a hand and shook Allison's firmly, her blue eyes unwavering. "Are you just visiting?"

Allison nodded. "For another week or so," she said, hating to put into words how little time she had left. But she couldn't impose much longer on the Manleys, and she had to go to Arizona and finish tying up the loose ends of her parents' lives. It was a task she didn't anticipate with pleasure.

Gene stiffened. He hadn't realized how soon she planned to leave. It disturbed him to think of her going away, and he didn't understand why.

Allison felt the sudden stiffening and looked up at Gene just as he glanced down at her. The tension exploded between them so that it was almost visible. Dale said something and left and neither of them noticed her departure. Allison's lips parted under the force of the shared look, the impact like lightning striking. Her heart raced.

"Do you want to go to a dance with me?" he asked huskily, his body suddenly on fire. "It would mean going home very, very late."

"Yes." She spoke without hesitation. She didn't want to go home yet; she didn't want to say good-night to him. She wasn't considering the dangers of being seen in public or giving the media any clues to her whereabouts. She wanted to be held in his arms, for as long as possible. She was too much in love to care about the consequences anymore.

Gene was feeling the same thing. His world had just narrowed to the woman beside him. "All right," he said curtly. "To hell with the consequences. Come on."

patterns on the back of her hand while his eyes held hers. "I like beer. I'll taste of it when we leave here." His gaze fell to her mouth. "If you taste of it, too, it won't bother you when we make love."

Her lips parted and her heart jumped. "Tonight?" she stammered, because he looked as if he meant business this time.

"Tonight, Allison," he said huskily. He caught her eyes again and held them, his whole body throbbing with anticipation. She was staring back at him just as intently and he felt his body react fiercely. He leaned closer, his lips almost touching hers as he spoke. "There's a line cabin between here and the house," he breathed. He caught her chin and tilted it tenderly so that his thin lips could brush lightly over hers in a whisper of rough persuasion. "I promise you, I'll be gentle. It will be exactly the way you want it, all the way."

She tried to speak, but his teeth closed on her lower lip, tugging, and before she could get a word out, the moist warmth of his mouth buried itself in hers. She was so sweet. He could hardly breathe for his need of her. He hadn't meant to let it go this far, but once he felt her mouth under his, he didn't want to stop.

He wasn't the only one. Allison shivered with reaction. Her mouth answered his, blind to where they were, deaf to the people and music around them, hopelessly lost in him. Nothing mattered except being in his arms. She'd been alone so long, been through so much. Surely she could be given this one, sweet night! To lie in the arms of the man she loved and be cherished, just one time. The temptation was overwhelming. And he'd said he'd be gentle. That had to mean he cared. Hadn't he told her at the beginning that he was always rough because that was the way he liked it—and now here he was putting her wants before his. He had to care, a little.

When he lifted his head, they were both breathing roughly. He had to force himself to draw away. With a jerky movement, he reached for his mug of beer and all but drained it.

"I didn't mean to do that, yet," he said unsteadily. He stared at her solemnly, his eyes lingering on her delicately flushed face with its exquisite complexion. Her eyes were misty, a little dazed, and her mouth was swollen and parted from the long, hard kiss. Just the sight of her knocked the breath out of him.

"It's all right," she said huskily.

He averted his gaze and found himself looking at Dale, who was dancing stiffly with a plain, lanky man wearing a red shirt. She gave him a pouting, accusing look before she turned her attention back to her partner.

Allison followed the cold stare of his eyes. "She's very pretty," she remarked quietly.

He turned, his gaze glittering. "Yes. But she wanted more than I could give her."

Was she like that, too, Allison wondered, wanting more than he had to give? It didn't seem to matter. She was too hopelessly in love with him to let it matter tonight. Soon she'd be alone again, for the rest of her life. Just this one night, she prayed silently. And then the thought bored into her mind—be careful what you ask for…you might get it.

She quickly lowered her gaze to her own beer. She

cupped her hands around the frosty mug and lifted it to her lips, making a face when she tasted it.

She looked over at Gene. They came from different worlds. He wouldn't understand her hang-ups any more than she could understand his lack of scruples with women. She'd told a lie and now it was catching up with her. Despite the fact that he'd opened up to her, that they were getting along well together, she was still afraid to tell him the truth about herself. But would it matter—if he were gentle? She flushed.

Her eyes searched his stern expression. There was a different man that he kept hidden from the world. She caught glimpses of him from time to time, behind the sarcasm and tough facade. She wanted a glimpse of the lonely, wounded man he was hiding.

A sudden cry split the noise of people and music, and suddenly everything around them abruptly stopped.

"What is it?" Allison asked, frowning as she looked toward the bar.

He turned in his seat and stood. "Oh, boy," he murmured. "Somebody broke a beer bottle and cut his hand half off. Dale's new beau, Ben, no less."

Allison got up without a word and went to the hurt man. She smiled at Dale and then at the cowboy, who was holding his hand and shivering with pain while Dale tried ineffectually to stem the flow of blood.

"Let me," she said gently, taking the cloth from Dale's shaking hands. "I know what to do."

She did, too. Gene watched her with fascination, remembering how efficiently she'd patched him up. He wondered where and why she'd gotten her first-aid training. She was good at it, calm and collected and quietly reassuring. Even Dale relaxed, color coming back into her white face.

"That should do it," she said after a few minutes of applied pressure. "Fortunately it was a vein and not an artery. But it will need stitches," she added gently, cleaning her hands with a basin and cloth the bartender had provided after she'd put a temporary bandage over the cut. "Can you drive him to the hospital?"

"Yes," Dale said. She hesitated. "Thanks."

"That goes double for me," the cowboy said with a quiet smile of his own, although he was still in a lot of pain. "I could have bled to death."

"Not likely, but you're welcome. Good night."

They left, and Allison noticed that Dale gave Gene a long, hurting look even as she went out the door with her wounded cowboy. Poor thing, she thought miserably. Maybe she'd look like that one day, when Gene didn't want her anymore.

Without sparing her a glance, Gene led Allison out onto the dance floor. "Full of surprises, aren't you?" he mused. "Where did you learn so much about first aid?"

"I had a good teacher," she said noncommittally, smiling up at him.

He scowled down at her. "I can't dig anything out of you, can I?" he asked quietly. "You're very mysterious, cupcake."

"There's nothing out of the ordinary about me," she laughed. "I'm just a working girl."

"When are you leaving the Manleys'?" he asked suddenly.

She lowered her eyes to his broad chest. "Next week. I don't want to, but I need to," she said. "I've got a lot to do."

"Where?"

"In Arizona," she said.

"Is that where you work?"

She hesitated. "I guess it's where I'll be working now," she replied. She didn't want to think about it. Life was suddenly very complicated, and the worst of it was going to be leaving here and not seeing Gene Nelson again.

He sighed half angrily. One lean arm pulled her closer and he turned her sharply to the music, so that his powerful leg insinuated itself intimately close to hers.

She stiffened a little and he slowed, pausing to look down at her.

"Don't fight it," he said huskily. "Life's too short as it is, and what we've got together is magic." And with that, he caught both her arms and eased them under his and around him while his circled her, bringing her totally against him.

"Gene," she protested weakly.

"This is the way everyone else is doing it, if you want to look around us. Put your cheek on my chest and give in."

She knew it was suicide, but she couldn't help her own weakness. She moved close to him with a long sigh and laid her cheek against his hard chest. Under his blue shirt she could feel the warmth of his body and the rough beat of his heart. He smelled of soap and cologne and starch, and the slow caress of his hands on her back was drugging.

They moved lazily around the floor as the lights dimmed and the music became sultry. Everyone was relaxed now, a little high from the beer and revelry, and when Gene's hands slid down to her lower spine and pulled her intimately to him, she didn't protest.

His lean, fit body began to react to that closeness almost at once. He felt himself going rigid against her, but he didn't try to shield her from it. It was too late, anyway.

He lifted his head and looked down into her eyes while they danced. She looked a little nervous and uncertain, but she wasn't protesting.

His eyes fell to her breasts, lingering on them. With a low murmur, he drew his hands up her back to her rib cage and slowly, torturously moved her toward him so that her breasts brushed sensuously against his hard chest, making the tips suddenly hard and swollen. He could feel them even through the fabric, and when she trembled, he felt that, too.

His eyes lifted to hers, and held them as his hands moved again, down, down, until they reached her hips. He lifted her gently and her thighs brushed his, hard.

Her breath caught. She flushed, because even an innocent couldn't mistake what he was feeling and what he wanted now. But the worst of it was that she wanted it just as much. She was caught in a sensual daze and her body ached. She wanted him to kiss her. She wanted his hands on her body to soothe the burning ache he'd created. She wanted…him.

He stopped dancing and stood with her in the middle of the dance floor, his pale eyes glittery as they searched hers. "I want to take you out of here," he said huskily. "I can't stand much more of this."

"Yes," she whispered. She knew what he was saying, and part of her was ashamed and frightened and reluctant. But she cared too much to refuse him.

"All right." He let her move slowly away from him, but he didn't let her go. "I need a minute, cupcake," he said softly. He pulled her back into his arms, but so that their legs didn't touch. He drew in deep breaths until he could get his body back in control so that what he felt wouldn't be on public display. Then, gently, he led her off the dance floor and out the door to the Jeep, ignoring the sandwiches he'd already paid for that had just been placed on their table. Food was the very last thing on his mind right now.

"Did you enjoy the rodeo?" he asked on the way home. He hadn't touched her or said anything vaguely romantic since they'd left the bar. Allison was still in a daze, and her body was on fire to be held close to his. But she tried to keep that to herself.

"I enjoyed it very much," she said. "I never realized the events were so complicated."

"It helps when you know a bit about it," he said. He was nervous. Imagine that, he thought with graveyard humor, and with his reputation. But Allison wasn't like other women he'd made love to. She was very, very special, and he wanted this to be like no other time for her. He wanted to give her everything.

He pulled off the main road and drove toward the

ranch, but there was a dirt track that led into a grove of trees by the creek, and he took that one instead of the ranch road that led home.

Allison felt herself tensing, because she knew instinctively what was in that grove of trees down the road. But she didn't say a word. She'd committed herself back in Cody. It would be cowardly and cruel to back down now. Of course, that was only an excuse to appease her conscience, and she knew it. She looked at the man beside her and knew that she'd do anything he asked of her. No one had ever been so gentle and kind to her, no man had ever made her feel so special. He'd rescued her from a kind of limbo that she'd been in ever since her parents' death.

"The line cabin is down there," he said, trying not to show how desperately he needed her or how nervous he was. "It's old. Probably the oldest building still in use on the place. The men stay here during the winter when they have to keep up with the outlying herds."

"I see."

He pulled up in front of a small, darkened cabin that looked like something out of a history journal and cut the engine and the lights. "It doesn't look like much, but it's pretty well kept."

He got out and helped her out, then led her up the porch to the front door and inside. She felt oddly light-headed, probably, she thought dizzily, the result of the beer and no food.

"See, we even have electricity," he mused, turning on a small lamp.

The cabin was only one room, with a small kitchen,

a fireplace and two chairs, and a neatly made bed with a blue-beige-and-red-patterned quilted coverlet over it. Just the thing, Allison thought, for a cowboy on his own in the winter.

"The bed linen is washed weekly, even if nobody stays here, and we keep a supply of food in the kitchen," he told her. He turned, his gaze slow and warm on her face as he took off his Stetson and tossed it onto a chair. She looked so young, he thought, watching her. So sweet and vulnerable and hungry for him. His heart raced.

Without another word, he unfastened his bola and unsnapped the buttons down the front of his shirt with a dark, lean hand.

Her breath caught in her throat as he pulled the shirt out of his jeans and opened it. His chest was darkly tanned and thick with curling black hair. He moved toward her with a faintly arrogant expression, as if he knew how exciting and sensuous he was without the trembling of her body and the sudden parting of her lips to tell him.

He caught her cool hands and brought them under the lapels of the open shirt, pressing them palm down on his warm, rough chest. The sensation was incredible. He shivered. "Feel me," he said huskily, moving her hands around. He drew her to him and bent to her lips, pausing just above them to tease them, torment them, while he let her hands learn the contours of his torso. It was sheer heaven, the feel of those soft, warm fingers on his taut body. He felt himself going rigid all at once and didn't even try to hold back.

"Allison," he groaned as he bent to her mouth. "Oh, God, I've never wanted anyone so much!"

The wording weakened her, because she knew how he felt. Odd, with his reputation that he could be so vulnerable to an innocent like her. Of course, she thought uneasily, he didn't know she was innocent. His hands were moving over her back and she hesitated for just one second with maidenly fear of the unknown. Then she relaxed as the kiss began to work on her, his exploring lips making her mouth soft and eager for its moist, warm touch.

All at once, the wanting broke through his control. His tongue shot into the dark softness of her mouth in a rhythm that was staggeringly sensual and arousing. She gasped in shocked pleasure. But there was more to come.

His lean hands caught the backs of her thighs and lifted her up to his aroused body in a sharp, quick rhythm that made her knees go weak and shaky. Sensations of hot pleasure rippled through her lower belly like the tide itself. She shuddered all over and grabbed his arms to keep from toppling over at the feverish need she felt. She cried out under his mouth, and he made a deep, satisfied sound in his throat.

He bent, lifting her totally against him, her feet dangling as his hands suddenly brought his hard thighs between her legs and pressed her intimately to him.

She moaned harshly, clinging, almost in tears from the sudden fury of her desire of him. She knew in the back of her mind that this was wrong, that she was letting him go too far, but she was helpless from the hot surge of passion he'd kindled in her. She'd never known such pleasure.

Her mouth answered his, giving him back the deep kiss as hungrily as he offered it. He felt his own body begin to tremble and he knew there was no way he could stop now. It had gone too far.

He fell onto the bed with her, shivering with need, his hands trembling as they slipped her out of her sweater and T-shirt and the filmy bra she wore under them. He didn't stop there, either. While he was at it, he un-snapped the skirt and kissed his way down to her thighs while he smoothed the rest of her clothing down her body and tossed it aside with her shoes.

She lay nude under the slow, insistent brush of his hard mouth. His hands explored while his mouth learned every soft curve of her in a silence that grew hotter with her soft cries of pleasure and the helpless movements of her body on the springy mattress.

He lifted his head while his fingers brushed expertly over the hard crests of her breasts and he looked into her eyes with pure masculine need. She was shivering, her eyes wide and glazed, her lips parted under hopelessly gasping breaths. Her long legs were moving helplessly on the bed in little jerky motions. Yes, he thought feverishly, and he touched her gently where she was most a woman, deliberately adding to her helplessness as shocks of pleasure lifted her hips and closed her eyes.

He didn't question why she should be so easily and quickly aroused, or why her eyes opened in something like faint shock when he threw off his shirt and boots and socks and started unzipping his jeans with quick, economical movements. He didn't question why she lifted up suddenly on her elbows and gasped when he turned, his blatant arousal the crowning glory of a body that some women had called perfection itself. His mind was buried in the desire for her that had made him shudder at just the sight of that creamy pink body with its firm, soft breasts and exquisite figure, lying there waiting for him, trembling.

He straddled her hips arrogantly, watching her watch him with wide, almost frightened eyes.

"You can take me, if that's what you're frightened of," he said gently, levering down so that his body slowly overwhelmed hers, his elbows catching his weight. "A woman's body is a miracle," he whispered at her lips. "Elastic and soft and vibrant with life." His mouth brushed hers in tender little contacts that aroused like wildfire while his hands smoothed down her body; his thumbs hard on her belly, rough, making some unbelievable sensations kindle with each long pass of his hands. She shivered under his warm mouth, her nudity and his maleness almost forgotten until his knee began to ease between her long legs.

"Shhh," he whispered when she tensed. "Don't do that. I want you just as badly, but if you tense up, it's going to hurt."

She swallowed. It would hurt anyway, but it was too late to tell him that, because his hips were already probing delicately at hers.

He kissed her face with trembling, aching tenderness, while his lean hands gently positioned her hips. "One, long, sweet joining," he whispered into her open mouth. "That's what I want first, before I even begin to love you." His thumbs pressed into her belly again, making her shiver. He smiled tenderly against her lips. "Now lift up against me, very, very slowly," he whispered. He lifted his eyes to watch. He'd never wanted to watch before, but this was like no other time in his life. Her eyes were wide, almost frightened. "Shhh," he breathed, achingly tender as he began the slow, downward movement of his body. "Shhh. Be one with me, now," he whispered. She tensed and he smiled, sliding one hand between them to gently caress her flat belly. "Yes, just relax and let it happen. Don't close your eyes," he said huskily. "Watch me. Let me watch you. I want… to see you…take me!"

His teeth ground together and Allison was so shocked by what he was saying and doing that she forgot to be afraid. His powerful body was tanned all over, except for that pale strip across his lean hips, and she saw his eyes dilate, his teeth clench, his face contort with wonder. She could feel the shudder that went through him, she could actually see him lose control.

It was what made it bearable when he suddenly cried out and pushed into her body with helpless, driving urgency. The pain was scalding, like being torn with a hot knife, and she both stiffened and dug her fingers into his arms, weeping suddenly as he hurt her.

But she was too ready for him for it to last long. Gene felt the barrier give, somewhere in the back of his mind, although it didn't register through the blinding throb of pleasure that ran down his backbone and sent him wild in her arms. He buffeted her with a total, absolute loss of control, borne of too many months of abstinence and his raging hunger for her.

Allison wept silently for her lack of resistance. He was going to hate her. He couldn't not know what she was, now.

Seconds later, he stiffened and cried out, and Allison watched his corded torso lift as his hips enforced their mastery of her, watched his face contort in the unmistakable mask of fulfillment. His voice throbbed hoarsely as he cried her name once, twice, and then like a prayer, his body convulsed in a red fever of blinding ecstasy.

It hadn't hurt as much as she thought it would. He was lying on her heavily now, his body drenched in sweat, his mouth against her bare shoulder. Still flushing from what she'd seen, she stroked his damp, black hair absently, her eyes wide and shocked as she stared at the rough wood of the ceiling. Despite everything it was so sweet to lie and hold him like this, so close that they were still one person. The embarrassment and pain and shame would follow, she knew, and would be almost unbearable. But for these few seconds, he was helpless and in need of comfort, and she held him to her with tender generosity, her eyes closing as she whispered her love for him silently, without a sound.

Gene got his breath back and lifted his head to look at Allison. Her eyes opened slowly and she blushed. There was something in those soft hazel eyes that hurt him. He'd failed her all the way around.

He accepted the knowledge with shame and a kind of helpless pleasure as his eyes slid down to her breasts, still hard-tipped because he hadn't satisfied her. He would have been more than willing to do that, because she'd given him heaven. But it would be too soon for her, after the ordeal of her first time. First time. He shivered. A virgin. He was her first man.

The thought humbled him. He bent and started to kiss her soft mouth, but she turned her head, and then he saw it. The shame. The fear. He took a sharp breath and rolled away from her, standing up to dress quietly, with cold efficiency. It had never been like that, he thought bitterly; it had never been so urgent that he couldn't wait for his partner. He couldn't even blame the beer, because he hadn't had that much. And he knew damned well he hadn't satisfied Allison. There hadn't been time. Besides that, he thought, horrified as he turned to look at her, she'd been unnaturally tight and afraid and now he knew that he must have hurt her terribly. They said no man could tell, but even without glancing at that faint stain on the coverlet, he knew. Somehow, he thought he'd known from the beginning. And if his own guilt wasn't enough, she wouldn't even look at him. She made him feel like less than a man.

He looked away while she put on her own clothes with trembling hands. When he turned again, she was sitting on the edge of the bed with her hands folded on her thighs, her eyes downcast, her thin body trembling.

The most beautiful experience of his life, and he'd cost her not only her chastity but any pleasure she might have had, all because he'd been selfish. She looked as if what she'd done was some unforgivable sin to boot. Her downcast, defeated expression made him hurt. His guilt and self-contempt spurred his temper, and he exploded with rage.

He reached out and grabbed her arms, jerking her roughly to her feet. "Damn you," he said icily, shaking her none too gently. His blazing eyes made her flinch. "You lied to me! You told me you were experienced, when all the time you were a virgin!"

She all but cringed, closing her eyes. Neither of them saw or heard the shadowy figure on horseback who'd heard that furious accusation. The rider moved a little closer and spotted them through the window, a sarcastic smile on his mouth. He didn't hesitate. He abruptly turned his mount and stealthily rode away.

"Why did you do it?" Gene was demanding.

"I wanted to get to know you," she said dully.

"Well, you did, didn't you?" he asked with deliberate cruelty, and a meaningful glance at the stain on the coverlet.

Her eyes dropped on a hurting moan. Tears were rolling down her cheeks without a sound. She stared at his throat, watching the pulse throb there. She deserved the anger, so she didn't fight it. He was right. She'd lied and let him think she was experienced and because of it, he hadn't felt any need to hold back physically. Now he'd seduced her and she only had herself to blame. Worse than that, she hadn't taken any precautions or asked him to. One time might not be anything to worry about, of course, but there were no guarantees. And she still had to live with her guilt and shame, with her conscience.

He let go of her abruptly, savagely ashamed of his

own uncharacteristic behavior. He didn't think he'd ever be able to look at her again without hating himself.

Allison, of course, didn't realize that his anger was directed at himself, not at her. She thought he surely must hate her now, and she couldn't bear to meet his eyes.

He noticed, with bitter pain. "We'd better go," he said coldly.

He turned out the light and jerked open the door, helping her inside the Jeep with icy courtesy before he went back to lock the cabin. He got into the Jeep without a single word, and that was how he drove home.

When he pulled up at the Manleys' house, she got out without assistance, clutching her purse, and she didn't say anything or look back as she went up onto the porch. Shades of Gene Nelson himself, she thought with almost hysterical humor. Wasn't he the one who never looked back?

But apparently he wasn't going to let her get away with it that easily. He went with her, staying her hand as she started to unlock the door.

"Are you all right?" he asked tersely, forcing the words out.

"Yes." She didn't look up. Her soul was tarnished.

He took off his Stetson and ran a hand through his hair. "Allison," he began hesitantly. "What I said back there…"

"It doesn't matter," she replied numbly. "I have to go in now. I'm sorry about…about what happened. I've never had alcohol before."

"And that was why?" he asked with a mocking laugh.

"You were drunk?" Deny it, he was thinking. For God's sake, tell me it was because you loved me!

But the silent plea passed into the night. She unlocked the door. "Goodbye, Gene," she said gently, even now unable to blame him for something she'd encouraged to happen.

"Isn't that a little premature?" he asked hesitantly.

"I'll be leaving in the morning," she said without looking at him. "You won't have to worry that I'll…be like Dale and hound you…" Her voice broke and she got inside fast, closing and locking the door behind her.

Gene stood staring at the closed door for a long moment. He felt empty and alone and deeply ashamed. What had possessed him to attack her, as if the whole thing was her fault? She was a gentle woman, with a soft heart and a heavy conscience, and it bothered him that she'd looked so torn when he let her go. She talked about religion a lot and church, and he wondered if she believed sleeping around was a mortal sin. It amazed him that he hadn't seen through the act, that he'd really believed she was experienced, when everything pointed the other way. If he'd kept his head, he'd have known in time that she was innocent, and he could have stopped. But he didn't know, and he hadn't been rational enough to control his raging desire. A desire that he still felt, to a frightening degree. Allison. He felt her loss to his very soul. In a few days she'd become an integral part of his life, his thoughts. He wasn't sure if he could go on living when she left Pryor. Could half a man live?

He turned and went back to the Jeep, cursing himself all the way. She'd leave and he'd never have the opportunity to apologize. Not that she was completely blameless, he told himself. It hadn't been all his fault. But what had motivated her? Had it been desire? Loneliness? Curiosity? Or had there been some feeling in her for him? She was a virgin and she'd given herself. Would she really have done that, being the kind of person she was, unless she cared deeply? His heart leaped at the thought of Allison loving him.

Of course, she was twenty-five and modern, he reminded himself grimly. Maybe she was just tired of being a virgin. He didn't like to consider that last possibility. And even if she had begun to care about him, she surely wouldn't now. His cruelty would have shown her how fruitless that would be. He climbed into the Jeep, started the engine, threw the car in gear and pulled out of the yard. This time he stopped the car, and he looked back. It was the first time in his life that he ever had. But darkened windows were all that met his hungry gaze. After a moment, he pulled the Jeep back onto the road and drove home.

Inside the house, Allison had made it to her room without being seen by Winnie. She took a shower, with water as hot as she could stand it, to wash away the scent and feel of Gene Nelson. She washed her hair as well. Her body felt bruised and torn, but she couldn't bring herself to tell Winnie what had happened. She was going to have to invent an argument or something to explain her sudden departure. But whatever happened, she couldn't stay here any longer. Even the horror of the past few weeks and the fear of being hounded by the media were preferable to ever having to see Gene again. He hated her. She'd made him hate her by lying to him. He must feel terrible now, too, knowing the truth about her. He'd said he didn't play around with virgins, and she'd made a liar out of him.

She lay down, but she didn't sleep. Her mind went over and over that painful episode in the line cabin until she was utterly sick. The worst of it was that Gene was right. It was her fault. She'd ignored Winnie's warnings about Gene and the danger of physical attraction. Now she understood, too late, what it was all about. She'd never dreamed that she could be so hungry for a man that principles and morals could be totally forgotten. Now she knew. She wondered if she'd ever be able to forget what she'd done. Loving him didn't seem to excuse her behavior, or justify her submission anymore.

She got up before daylight and packed. The phone rang long before she dressed and went downstairs, but apparently it wasn't for her, because she wasn't disturbed.

She put her hair up in a bun and dressed in her sedate gray dress with matching high heels for the trip to Arizona. With a glance at her too-pale face in the mirror, she went in to breakfast and pasted a smile on her lips.

But there was no one there. She searched the house and found a scribbled note from Winnie. "Gone to hospital," she read. "Dwight hurt in wreck."

She caught her breath. Poor Winnie! And poor Dwight! She picked up the phone and called the hospital immediately, having found the number in the telephone directory.

She got the floor nurse on Dwight's ward and talked

to her. After introducing herself, she explained about Dwight and Winnie and the nurse was sympathetic enough to tell her what had happened. When she hung up, she knew it was going to be impossible for her to leave. Dwight was in intensive care and he might die. She was trapped. She couldn't leave Winnie at a time like this, even if it meant having to endure Gene's hatred in the process.

Chapter Eight

Winne came home at lunch, red-eyed and wilted, supported by her worried mother.

"Oh, Winnie, I'm so sorry," Allison said, hugging her friend warmly. "Is there any change?"

"Not yet." Winnie wept. "Allie, I can't bear to lose him! I can't!"

"Head injuries are tricky," Allison said quietly. "He's in a coma, but that doesn't mean he won't come out of it. I've seen some near-fatal injuries that recovered fully. Give it time."

"I'll go mad!" the blonde wailed.

Allison hugged her again. "No, you won't. Come on, I've made lunch. I'll bet you're both starved."

"I certainly am," Mrs. Manley said gently. She smiled at Allison. "Bless you for thinking of food. We really hadn't."

"I can understand why. What happened?"

"Nobody knows. The car he was driving went down a ravine. They only found him early this morning. Gene and Marie are at the hospital. Gene looks really bad," Winnie said.

Allison averted her face before anyone could see that she did, too, and make any embarrassing connections. "I'll pour the coffee," she said.

She didn't want to go to the hospital with them, but Winnie pleaded, so she did.

When they walked into the waiting room, only Marie was there, and Allison thanked her lucky stars. She hugged Marie and murmured all the comforting things she could think of. Then she went in search of the floor nurse she'd talked to on the phone, while Winnie and Mrs. Manley sat with Marie.

Tina Gates was in charge of the intensive care unit, a twenty-two-year veteran of nursing arts. She welcomed Allison and showed her through the ward, pausing at Dwight's bed.

"He's bad," she told Allison. "But he's a fighter, like the rest of his family, and strong-willed. I think he'll come out of it."

"I hope so," Allison said gently, staring at Dwight's unnaturally pale face. "My best friend loves him very much."

"Sometimes love is what it takes." She continued the tour, and they came back to Dwight's cubicle when they finished. "If you ever want a job, we've got a place for you," she told Allison. "Help is hard to get out here, and you're more qualified than even I am. I never had the opportunity to go on and get my degree in nursing arts."

"I was lucky," Allison said. "My parents sacrificed a lot for my education. It's important work, and I love it. I don't know that I could get used to the routine in a hospital. I'm too accustomed to primitive conditions. But I appreciate the offer, all the same."

"I'll repeat it at intervals, if you promise to consider it," Tina promised, smiling. "This is pretty country, and there are some nice folks here. You might like it."

"I already do. But I made a promise to my parents that I'd carry on the work they did," Allison said finally. "I don't like to break promises."

"Actually, neither do…look!"

Tina went quickly to Dwight's side and watched him move restlessly. His eyes opened and he groaned.

"Head…hurts," he mumbled.

"Hallelujah!" Tina grinned. "If your head hurts, Mr. Nelson, it means you're alive. I'll get Dr. Jackson right now!"

"I'll go and tell Winnie. Dwight, I'm glad you're back with us," she said gently, touching his arm where the IV was attached. "They'll give you something for the pain. Just try to relax and don't move around too much."

He looked up at her, licking dry lips. "Gene?" he whispered.

Her face closed up. "Do you want to see him?"

"Yes."

"I'll try to find him. Rest, now." She patted his hand and walked out, all nerves.

Gene was in the waiting room when she came out. He stiffened as she approached, but Allison pretended not to notice. After the night before, it was all she could

do to stay in the same room with him without breaking
down and crying.

"He's out of the coma," she said, talking to Winnie
and Marie. "They're getting the doctor. I think he'll
be all right."

"Oh, thank God!" Winnie burst out, and Marie
laughed and cried as the two women hugged each other.

"Your first-aid training qualifies you to make prog-
noses, does it?" Gene drawled suddenly with cold mockery. Having her deliberately ignore him had hurt him
terribly.

"First-aid training?" Winnie asked, frowning. "Gene,
she's a registered nurse, didn't she tell you?"

Gene scowled. "A nurse!"

"A graduate nurse, with a college degree," Winnie
said. "You didn't tell him?" she asked Allison.

Allison's eyes warned her not to give anything
else away. "There was no need to," she said simply.
She didn't want him to know about the life she'd led.
"Dwight is asking for you," she said.

"He wants to talk business," Winnie muttered. "Well,
that can wait. I want to see him first. Marie, come on,
we'll go together."

"But the doctor..." Allison began.

"We'll ask first," Winnie promised, dragging a smiling Marie along with her.

Allison was left alone with Gene, who shoved his
hands into his pockets.

"A nurse. No wonder you were so good at patching people up," he said absently. Even Dwight's mi-
raculous return to consciousness didn't quite register

through the shock. He glared at her. "How many other secrets are you keeping?" he asked bitterly. She hadn't trusted him at all. Did everyone know things about her that he didn't?

"Enough, I suppose," she said, folding her hands in front of her. She turned away from him and stared out the window.

"I thought you were leaving today."

"So did I. Don't worry. This is just a temporary setback. The minute Dwight's off the critical list, I'll be on the next plane out."

His eyes narrowed. Was that what she thought? That he couldn't wait to get rid of her? Seeing her did play havoc with his conscience, but probably it was worse for her. Why hadn't she told him she was a qualified nurse? And what were those other secrets she was keeping? She hadn't shared anything with him, except her body, and she hadn't enjoyed that. It would haunt him forever that he'd taken his pleasure at her expense. Poor little thing, all she'd given him since they met was tenderness and concern and compassion. And for that, he'd given her a nightmare experience that would scar her.

Guilt was riding him hard. It was the first time in memory that he'd ever hurt a woman in bed, and he didn't like the feeling. His teeth ground together. If only she'd told him! He'd have made her glory in that sweet sacrifice. Of course, he had to admit that it could have been worse. He'd aroused her totally, and he'd treated her like a virgin, as if maybe subconsciously he had known. A man without scruples could have done her a lot more damage. He frowned, thinking about Allison in bed with some other man. It made him livid with jealousy.

"A nurse, of all things," he said curtly, glaring at her. "It's a miracle that you reached your present age intact. Don't they teach you anything about sex in nurses' training?"

She went scarlet and wouldn't look at him. "It isn't the same as reading about it," she said stiffly.

His jaw clenched. "No doubt. You little fool, if I'd known, I could have made you faint with the pleasure! God knows, I had the experience to give you that. I hurt you. My conscience is giving me hell. Damn it, Allison, if I'd known, I could have stopped!"

She turned, her eyes shy but knowing. "Could you, Gene?" she asked sadly.

He averted his eyes to the wall. No, of course he couldn't have. But it made him feel better to think so. "Dwight will have to have around-the-clock nursing when he comes home. He's got some internal injuries and a busted rib besides the concussion."

"It shouldn't be too difficult finding someone," she said slowly, although she had her doubts after what Tina Gates had said about the shortage of nurses around here.

He whirled and stared at her. "He likes you." Was he out of his mind, he wondered? The very last thing she'd agree to was a job that put her near him. But the thought was intriguing. Having her in his home, near him, being able to look at her whenever he liked would be so sweet. He caught his breath at the very thought of it.

Allison was catching her own breath. She didn't want

to be near him, not at any price. "No," she said hastily. "No, I can't do it. I have to go back to Arizona."

He moved toward her, and she backed up a step, afraid to be close to him again. What had happened once was never going to be allowed to happen again.

Gene stopped. He understood that timid retreat. He'd hurt her, mentally and physically. She had every right to be intimidated by him.

"Dwight needs you," he said softly. Charm had never meant much to him before, but if he could lure her home with him, he might have a chance that she'd begin to trust him. "Winnie would be grateful," he coaxed. "And so would Marie and I."

"You needn't pretend that you want me around, Gene," she replied miserably. "You can find someone else to sit with Dwight."

"He has nothing to do with you and me," he said after a minute, his eyes narrow and steady on her face. "He's my brother, honey. I love him."

That got to her when nothing else had. She clasped her hands tightly together. "I thought you'd decided you weren't part of his family anymore," she murmured.

He sighed. "So I had. Until I heard he'd been hurt. Strange how nothing else seems to matter when someone's near death. I thought of all the good times we had as kids, all the games we played together, all the mischief we got into." A faint smile came to his thin lips. "Even if there wasn't much blood tying us together, we were the best of friends. Marie and I fight, but we'd die for each other. I guess I've been living inside myself without a thought to how it affected them." He looked straight at her. "It's still hard for me. But I think we can work it out now, if I don't have to worry about somebody to take care of Dwight. The hospital is short staffed."

"Tina told me," she said. She wrapped her arms around her breasts and turned away, head bent.

He moved closer, keeping some distance between them so that she wouldn't feel uncomfortable. "You can't regret what happened any more than I do, sweetheart," he said unexpectedly, and in a tone that made her legs tremble. "I'm sorry."

Her eyes closed. "It was my fault, too," she replied huskily, shaken by his compassion and the soft endearment. "Can we...not talk about it anymore, please?"

"Can I assume that since you've had medical training, you knew how to take care of yourself after what we did?" he persisted, holding his breath while he waited for her reply. He knew he hadn't taken any precautions, and he was pretty sure she hadn't. But he wanted to know.

She didn't look at him. "It wasn't a dangerous time of the month, if that's what you're asking," she said, coloring.

He let out a heavy sigh. "Allison," he said softly, "that wasn't what I asked."

She bit her lower lip. "I think it's too late to do anything now," she said, averting her gaze to the window.

"I see." He moved again, towering over her. "A few weeks, then...until we know for certain?" he asked quietly.

She didn't look up, but she nodded.

He started to speak, but anything he said would be the wrong thing now. His shoulders lifted and fell in a strangely impotent gesture and he moved back to the chairs.

The thought of a child scared him to death. He couldn't imagine what they'd do if they'd created a life together during that frenzied coupling. He didn't want a child to suffer for his lapse. He was terrified because of his father's character, sick at the thought of passing those genes onto a child. It wasn't rational, but it was how he felt. God, there couldn't be a child!

But even as he dreaded that thought, his eyes sought Allison and he scowled thoughtfully. She had a built-in maternal instinct. He could imagine her with a baby in her arms, suckling at her breast…

The sudden, fierce arousal of his body made him gasp audibly. God, what a thing to trigger it! But the more he thought about Allison's slim body growing big with a child, the worse it got. He got up from the chair and left the room without another word, leaving Allison to stare after him with sad curiosity. He couldn't imagine what was wrong with him!

Dwight was glad to see him, and Gene was relieved that his baby brother wasn't going to meet his maker just yet. He looked at the face so like his, and yet so unalike, and smiled indulgently as he held the other man's hand tightly for a minute.

"Need anything you haven't got?" he asked.

Dwight smiled through a drugged haze. "Not really, thanks. You handle things for us while I'm here, okay? I think I've made a real mess of the books."

"You don't know what I've done to the daily routine with the livestock," Gene confessed with a grin.

"Dad sure fouled us up, didn't he?" Dwight groaned. "I know he never meant it to wind up this way. He knew I couldn't handle finances. Why saddle me with it?"

"We'll never know," Gene replied. "We just have to make the best of it."

"No, we don't. We can go back to the way we were doing things before Dad died. If we both agree to it, we can have a contract drawn up and the will won't be binding. I've already asked our attorneys."

"You didn't mention that to me," Gene reminded him.

Dwight shifted. "You weren't ready to listen. I know it hit you hard, finding out about the past. But I figured when you were ready, we could talk about it." He winced. "Head hurts real bad, Gene."

"I know." He patted the younger man's shoulder. "I'm trying to talk Allison into nursing you at home. Would you like that?"

He smiled weakly. "Yes. They'd let me go home earlier if I had my own nurse."

"Did you know she was one?" Gene asked, scowling.

"Sure. Winnie told me. And about her parents. Incredible, that she got out at all, isn't it...? Gene, I need a shot real bad."

"I'll go and ask for you," Gene replied, puzzled about what Dwight had started to say. What about Allison's parents? Had there been anything unusual about the way they died? And what was that about it being incredible that Allison got out? Out of where? What? He glowered with frustration. Well, he was going to find out one way or the other. He was tired of being kept in the dark.

Winnie asked, and so did Marie, if Allison would

nurse Dwight. It had been hard enough to refuse Gene, but there was no way she could refuse Winnie. What she didn't know was how she was going to survive a week or more under Gene's roof when Dwight went home.

"You've been different lately," Winnie said several days later, when Allison had put some things into a small bag to take to the Nelson home.

"Different, how?" she hedged.

"Quieter. Less interested in the world. Have you and Gene had a fight? Is that it?"

"Yes," Allison said, because it was easier to admit that than to tell the truth. "A very bad falling out. I was going to leave the morning that Dwight got hurt."

"Oh, Allie." Winnie sat down on the bed where Allison was folding clothes. "I'm sorry. But if Gene wants you to stay with Dwight—and Marie said it was his idea—he can't be holding a grudge."

"He has a lot of reasons to hold one," Allison confessed. She lowered her eyes to the floor. "It's better that I don't see too much of him, that's all."

Marie's eyes narrowed. "Would this have anything to do with Dale Branigan?"

Allison lifted her head. "How did you know about her?"

"Everybody knows about her." Winnie grimaced. "She's been after Gene for a long time—just like most of the single women around here. But she was more blatant with it, and she's a very modern girl. Gene wasn't the first or the last, but she's persistent."

"Yes, I noticed."

"I gave you a bad impression of Gene at the start," Winnie began. "I just wanted to protect you, but I wasn't quite fair to him. Gene can't help being attractive, and I hear he's just plain dynamite in bed. Women chase him. They always have. But since he met you, he's not as wild as he was—he's calmed down a good bit. It's just that he can't shake his old reputation, and I didn't want yours damaged by it."

"Thanks," Allison said quietly. "I know you meant well." She managed not to blush at Winnie's remark about how Gene was in bed. She knew all too well that he was dynamite, and if she hadn't been a virgin, maybe it would have gone on feeling as sweet as it had when he was just kissing and stroking her body.

But maybe that really was all sex was supposed to feel like, for a woman. Maybe it was the preliminary part that made women give in. She sighed. If that was what sex felt like, she wasn't in any rush to experience it again, despite the brief pleasure that had led to it.

Winnie drove her over to the Nelson house, where Dwight was tucked up in bed with every conceivable amusement scattered around him. He had his own TV, DVDs, all the latest movies and a veritable library of the latest bestsellers.

"Talk about the man who has everything," Allison said, smiling at him.

"Not quite everything," Dwight said with weak humor. "My head could use a replacement."

"You'll get better day by day. Don't be too impatient. I'll take very good care of you."

"Thanks." He hesitated, staring up at her with his vivid blue eyes. "I get the feeling that you and Gene are having some problems. In view of that, I really appreciate the sacrifice you're making for me," he added.

She smiled wanly. "Gene and I had a difference of opinion, that's all," she said, trying to downplay it.

"In other words, he tried to get you into bed and you said no." He chuckled when she went scarlet. "Good for you. It will do him good to have the wind knocked out of him."

She didn't say anything. Let him think what he liked. She couldn't bear having anyone find out what had really caused her difference of opinion with Gene. It was a godsend that he was out with the cattle, and she didn't have to see him until she'd settled in.

Winnie was there for supper, visiting with Marie while Allison got Dwight up and ready for the meal that would be served on a tray in his room.

"Gene won't be in until late," Marie said as she helped Winnie and Allison fix a tray. "I'm sorry this had to happen to Dwight, but it's a good thing, in a way. It's brought Gene to the realization that he's still part of this family. I wouldn't take a million dollars for that. He's actually being civil to me, and he's been wonderful to Dwight."

"Sometimes it takes a near tragedy to make us appreciate what we have," she agreed. "You two have a nice supper. I'll come down and get something later. I'm not really hungry right now."

"Okay," Marie said, and smiled. "There's plenty of stuff in the fridge, and if there's anything you need in your room, let us know."

"I'll do that. Thank you, Marie."

"No. Thank *you*," the other woman replied, impulsively hugging her. "You don't know what a load you've taken off our minds."

"Yes, she does," Winnie said warmly, smiling at Allison. "She's very special."

"I'm leaving." Allison laughed. "See you later."

She arranged Dwight's tray and sat down by the bed while he maneuvered his utensils through a pained fog.

"Isn't Gene home yet?" he asked.

She shook her head. "Marie said he'd be late," she replied, hating to talk about him at all.

Dwight caught that note in her voice. He studied her curiously. "You haven't told Gene anything about yourself. Why?"

She couldn't answer that. In the beginning it had been because she didn't want to scare him off. Now, she didn't see any logic in it. She'd be gone soon and Gene wanted no more of her.

"I don't know," she told Dwight. "I suppose the way I've lived has taught me to keep things to myself. My parents were the kind of people who didn't like whiners. They believed in honor and hard work and love." She smiled sadly. "I'll miss them all my life."

"I miss my father that way," he replied. "So do the others. Gene, too. Dad was the only father he really knew."

"What about Gene's real father?" she asked softly.

He started to speak and hesitated. "You'd better ask Gene that," he said. "He and I are getting along better than we have in a long time. I don't want to interfere in his business."

"I can understand that. Can I get you anything?" she asked.

He shook his head. "Thanks. I think I could sleep a little now."

She straightened his pillow with a smile. "I'll get something to read and be nearby if you need me. You've got medicine for the pain. Please don't be nervous about asking for it if you need it. Your body can't heal itself and fight off the pain all at once in your weakened condition. All right?"

"You make it sound simple."

"Most things are. It's people that complicate it all. Sleep well."

Winnie came up later to check on him, and volunteered to sit with Dwight while Allison went down to get herself a sandwich.

Marie had gone to a movie with one of her friends since Allison and Winnie were staying with Dwight. She had, she told them, needed the diversion. It had been a traumatic few days.

Allison understood that. She'd had a pretty traumatic few days herself.

She went downstairs and fixed herself a sandwich in the kitchen. She ate at the kitchen table, liking the cozy atmosphere, with all Marie's green plants giving the yellow and white decor of the room the feel of a conservatory. She was just starting on her second cup of hot black tea when the back door opened and Gene came in.

He looked tired, his face under his wide-brimmed hat hard with new lines. He was wearing dusty boots and jeans and bat-wing chaps, as he had been that day

Allison had met him in town, but despite the dust, he was still the most physically devastating man Allison had ever met.

He paused at the table, absently unfastening his chaps while he studied her. She was wearing the gray dress he'd seen her in several times, with her hair up and no makeup, and she looked as tired as he felt.

"Worn-out, little one?" he asked gently.

His unexpected compassion all but made her cry. She took a sip of hot tea to steady herself. "I'm okay." She glanced at him and away, shyly. He was incredibly handsome, with that lean dark face and black hair and glittering peridot eyes. "You look pretty worn-out yourself."

He tossed his Stetson onto the sideboard and smoothed back his black hair. "I've been helping brand cattle." He straddled a chair and folded his arms over the back. "Got another cup?"

"Of course." She poured him a cup of steaming tea. "Want anything in it?" she asked.

He shook his head. "Thanks." He took it from her, noticing how she avoided letting her hand come into contact with his. But he caught her free hand lightly, clasping it in his as he searched her face. "Can't you look at me, sweetheart?" he asked when she kept her eyes downcast.

The endearment went through her like lightning. She didn't dare let him see her eyes. "Let me go, please," she said, and tugged gently at her hand.

He released her with reluctance, watching her as she went back to her own chair and sat down. He no longer had any doubts about her reaction to him. He wrapped his lean hands around his cup and flexed his shoulders, strained from hours in the saddle and back-breaking work as they threw calves to brand them.

"How's Dwight?" he asked after a minute.

"He's doing very well," she replied. "He's still in a lot of pain, of course. Winnie's sitting with him right now. Marie's gone to a movie."

"I haven't said it, but I appreciate having you stay with him. Especially under the circumstances."

She sipped her tea quietly, darting a quick glance up at him. He was watching her with steady, narrow, unblinking eyes. She averted her gaze to her cup again.

"I'm doing it for Winnie," she said finally.

"That goes without saying." He put his cup down and folded his arms over his chest. "How long will it take, do you think, before he's on his feet again?"

"I don't know," she said. "You'd have to ask the doctor about that."

He watched the steam rise from his mug, not really seeing it. He'd driven himself hard today, trying not to think about Allison and what he'd done. But it hadn't worked. Here she was, and sitting with her was the first peace he'd known all day. She had a calming effect on him. She made him feel at ease with himself and the world around him. It was a feeling he'd never known before. His emotions had gone wild with Hank Nelson's death and the subsequent revelations about his past.

He thought about his real father and the shame it would bring on him to have people know what kind of parent he'd had. But the sting of that knowledge seemed to have lessened. Now he could look at Allison and none of the anguish he'd known seemed to matter anymore. All he could think about was how it had been with her during the time they'd spent together, her softness in his arms, her gentle voice full of compassion and warmth. But he'd killed all that. He'd reduced what they were building together into a feverish sexual fling, without meaning or purpose. That was how she was bound to see it, and it wasn't true. He'd used women before, of course he had, but Allison wasn't an interlude. She was…everything.

He looked at her with soft wonder. She couldn't know how she'd changed him. She probably wouldn't care, even if she knew it. The more he saw of her, the more he realized how genuinely kind she was. He'd never met a woman like her. He knew he never would again.

"I've been a fool about my family, Allison," he said suddenly, his dark brows knitted together as he stared at her. "I think I went mad when I found out how I'd been lied to all these years. Hurt pride, arrogance, I don't know. Whatever it was, I've just come to my senses."

"I'm glad about that," she replied. "You have a nice family. They shouldn't have to pay for things they never did."

"I've come to that conclusion myself." He picked up the cup, but didn't drink from it. "Are you going to be able to forgive what I've done to you?" he asked suddenly.

Her heart jumped at the question. But in all fairness, she couldn't let him take all the blame. Nobody held a gun on her and made her do it, she knew. That one lapse could have cost her her career as a missionary if anyone had found out about it, but she couldn't have blamed him totally even then. She was pretty lucky that they hadn't been seen at that line cabin, she supposed. "You didn't do anything that I didn't invite," she said dully. "It doesn't matter."

Her reply caught him on the raw. "You might have my child inside your body, and it doesn't matter?" he asked icily.

She flushed. "It isn't likely," she said stubbornly.

He set the mug down again and his chest rose and fell roughly. Even now she wouldn't put all the blame on him. His lean hand speared across the table and gently slid into hers, holding it warmly. "I'm sorry I made it into something you'd rather not remember," he said solemnly. "It shouldn't have been like that, your first time. The least a man owes a virgin is satisfaction. All I gave you was pain."

She colored furiously and drew back her hand. "I have to get back to Dwight," she said huskily. "Good night, Gene."

She stood, but so did he, moving around the table so fast that she didn't see him coming until he had her gently by the shoulders, his tall, fit body looming over her.

"Do you hate me?" he asked abruptly. "No subterfuge, no half-truths. I need to know."

She swallowed. "No. I...don't hate you."

He let out a heavy sigh. "Thank God." He bent and brushed his mouth over her eyelids, closing them with aching tenderness. His hands held her, but not in any confining way, and he didn't move a fraction of an inch closer or threaten her mouth with his lips.

"Good night, little one," he said softly, lifting his head. There was something new in his eyes, in his voice, in the way he touched her. He knew it and was stunned by it. Women came and went in his life, but this one spun a cocoon of love around him and made him whole. He wanted her as he'd never wanted anything else. But it wasn't going to be easy. His eyes fell to her stomach and darkened. A child. He found the thought of a child not nearly as frightening as he had. He could almost picture a little boy with dark hair and green eyes, following him around. A miniature of himself in small blue jeans and little sneakers. His heart lurched. Allison would be wonderful with a child. And maybe genes weren't so important. Maybe it wouldn't matter about his father. But the manner of the child's possible conception bothered him and he frowned.

His hands contracted. "A baby shouldn't be made like that," he said huskily. "Not as a consequence. It should be planned. Wanted. God in heaven, why didn't I stop?"

He let go of her all at once, and turned, leaving the kitchen like a wild man. He sounded bitter and furiously angry. Probably he hated her. She couldn't blame him for that. He might even think she'd deliberately done without precautions to trap him into a marriage he didn't want. Tears stung her eyes. All the same, he'd been worried that she might hate him, and that gave her a little solace. She finished her tea, emptied the pot and cleaned it, washed the few dishes and went back up to sit with Dwight.

Chapter Nine

The next day, Allison went outside for the first time since she'd been in residence, to clear her head while Marie spent a few minutes with her brother.

It was a beautiful day, warm and sultry, and there was so much to see. Puppies and kittens, ducks and chickens were everywhere, not to mention the bulls and cows and steers and horses. Corrals were spaced beyond the house and its small kitchen garden, down a dirt road. She strolled along in her jeans and yellow T-shirt with her long hair drifting on the breeze. Even with all that had happened, she loved it here. But she knew her stay was limited—she had to think about leaving.

She'd been given some time off to cope with her parents' death, and avoid the press, but soon she'd have to go back to work. It was a good thing that she'd face that problem in Arizona and not here, because there was a morals clause in her contract. But nobody knew, she reminded herself. Nobody knew except Gene and herself.

She was worrying about Gene's sudden avoidance of her today when a voice hailed her from the corral.

She turned, frowning, to find a lean, wickedly smiling redheaded cowhand leaning against the fence. His eyes gave her a lazy appraisal and there was something vaguely insulting about the blatant way he sized her up.

"Miss Hathoway, isn't it?" he drawled. "Thought I recognized you."

She started. *Recognized her?* "Were you at the barbecue?" she asked, trying to be polite.

The man laughed, weaving a little as he pushed himself away from the fence. He approached her and she could smell the whiskey on his breath. "No, I don't get invited to that sort of socializing. I meant, I recognized you from the other night. In the line cabin. You were there with the boss."

Her face went stark white. She was quite literally at a loss for words.

He laughed unsteadily, moving closer, but she backed away before he could reach for her. That had obviously been his intention, because he looked surprised that she avoided his outstretched hands.

"No stomach for a common ranch hand, is that it?" he jeered. "You were hot enough for the boss. Of course, he's got money."

"Please!" she cried huskily, scarlet in the face that she and Gene should have been seen—like that!

"The boss won't have much to do with you these

days, though, will he, Miss High and Mighty?" he taunted. "I heard what he said. Mad as hell that you were a virgin, wasn't he? Not his usual kind of woman, for sure, he likes 'em worldly. Now me," he said, stalking her again, smiling, "I like innocents. I'd take my sweet time with you, pretty thing, and you wouldn't be looking like the end of the world afterward. He must have been in one hell of a rush. You weren't in there ten minutes."

Allison put her hand to her mouth and turned, running wildly for the house with tears in her eyes. She didn't know what to do. It terrified her that the cowboy might tell someone else what he knew. At least he hadn't seen them, or she knew he'd have taunted her with that, too. But he knew! He'd overheard what Gene said! And now he'd spread that horrible gossip around. She could imagine having her name bandied around the bunkhouse all night. And that wasn't the worst of it. What if it got around the community? Her reputation would be lost forever and her job along with it. The least breath of scandal attached to her name would cost her everything. She hadn't considered the potential for disaster, but now all her mistakes were coming home to roost.

She went back into the house and stayed there, taking a few minutes in her room to wash her face and get her nerves back together before she went to Dwight's room to check on him. It was almost time for his medicine.

If she'd hoped nobody would notice her turmoil, she was doomed to failure.

"What's wrong?" Winnie asked, concerned. "Allie, you're so pale!"

The temptation to tell her friend was great, but it wouldn't be fair to share the burden now. Winnie had enough to worry about with Dwight. She forced a smile. "I feel a little queasy," she said. "I think it was the sausage I had for breakfast. I love it, but sometimes it upsets my stomach."

"Tomorrow, you'll have steak," Dwight said with a weak smile. "I promise. Tell Gene to shoot you a cow."

She started just at the mention of Gene's name. How could she face him, ever, after what that terrible man had said? How would he react if he knew one of his men was making crude remarks to her? She sighed. After the way he'd walked away from her so angrily that night in the kitchen, he probably wouldn't say anything. He might think she deserved it. After all, he'd been very vocal about Dale Branigan and his contempt for her after he'd slept with her.

She gave Dwight his medicine and put on a fairly convincing act from then on. But when she was alone in her room, she cried until she thought her heart would break. She was paying a very high price for the one indiscretion of her life, and learning a hard lesson about how easy it was to tarnish a heretofore spotless reputation. She thought about how hard her parents had worked to invest her with a sense of morality, and she'd let them down so badly. Maybe it was as well that they'd never have to know about her downfall. But she could have talked to her mother about it, and there would have been no censure, no condemnation. Her mother was a loving, gentle woman who always looked for the best in everyone. She cried all the harder, missing her.

For the next few days, she didn't go outside at all. But inevitably, Winnie noticed it and asked why. Allison made up a story about not wanting to be out of earshot of Dwight. But Winnie told Marie. And Marie told Gene.

He alone knew that Allison might simply be avoiding him. But he'd been away from the ranch for a couple of days on business, and that wouldn't explain why she was staying inside while he was gone. He almost said something to her about it. Her abrupt departure from any room he entered stopped him. She obviously wanted no part of his company, so he forced himself not to invade her privacy. All the while, he was cursing himself for what he'd done to her. Even he, a relative stranger, could see the change in her since that night in the line cabin. She was almost a different person, so quiet and shy that she might have been a mouse. She never entered into conversations with the rest of the family, or laughed, or did anything except be professional as she charted Dwight's progress and talked to the doctor who checked on him several times a week. She didn't look at Gene or speak to him, and when he tried to make conversation with her, she found a reason to go somewhere else. His pride and ego took a hard blow from her attitude, even if he understood it. Women had never avoided him. Quite the contrary. Of course, he'd never hurt anyone the way he'd hurt Allison.

Winnie and Marie finally browbeat her into going into Pryor with them to shop. She felt fairly safe about going there, sure that she wouldn't run into anyone who knew her.

She was wrong. Dale Branigan was shopping, too, in the boutique where Marie and Winnie took Allison. She caught sight of the older woman and with a purely cattish smile, Dale maneuvered closer.

"Nice to see you again, Miss Hathoway," she said. "Ben's doing nicely, thanks to your quick thinking at the bar that night."

"I'm glad to hear it," Allison said pleasantly.

Dale gave the other woman's gray dress a demeaning scrutiny, shrugging when she realized how much prettier she was in a pink sundress that flattered her figure.

"I hear Gene's gone off you after that one night," she said out of the blue.

"I beg your pardon?" Allison asked reluctantly.

"After he slept with you in the line cabin," she said carelessly, smiling at Allison's gasped shock. "Didn't you know? It's all over town. You can't expect a man like Danny Rance to keep his mouth shut. He's a bigger gossip than most women. He really laid it on thick about you and Gene. Too bad. You should have held out for a wedding ring." She sighed theatrically. "By the way, there's a reporter in town. He's looking for some woman missionary who escaped from Central America in a hail of bullets. Someone said she'd left a trail that led here."

"Really?" Allison's hands were shaking. "Well, it could hardly be me, could it?" she asked huskily.

Dale laughed. "Not if you're giving out with Gene, it couldn't," she said mockingly. "Hardly a missionary's nature, is it?"

"Hardly. Excuse me." Allison went out the door and got into the car without a word to Marie or Winnie. She sat in shock, her body shaking, her face paper white as she tried to cope with what that malicious woman had said to her. She was branded. Really branded. She'd never get her job back. She'd have no place to go. Her family was dead, and now she was almost certainly going to lose the only work she'd ever wanted to do. It was inevitable that the reporter would track her to the Nelson place, inevitable that Dale or someone like her would relate the whole sordid story of her one-night stand with Gene. She'd given in to temptation and lost everything. If she'd had a lesser will, she'd probably have gone right off a cliff. She didn't know what she was going to do. Oh, please, God, she prayed silently. Please forgive me. Please help me!

Winnie and Marie belatedly noticed her absence and came looking for her.

"Are you all right?" Winnie frowned. "I saw Dale Branigan talking to you. What did she say?"

"Something about Gene, no doubt," Marie said heavily as they started the drive home. "She's so jealous it's sick. I'm sorry, Allison, I should have hustled you out of there the minute I saw her."

"It's all right. She was just…telling me something I already knew."

"There's a reporter in town," Winnie said uneasily. "That was what she said, wasn't it?"

"Yes. I may have a few days before he finds me," she said with defeat in her whole look. "It doesn't matter anymore. I don't have anything left to lose."

"What are you talking about?" Winnie demanded. "You've got your job, your future…!"

"I don't have anything." Allison pushed back wisps of hair with shaking hands. "I've ruined my life."

"How?"

Allison just shook her head and stared out the window. She was too hurt and upset to even talk.

When they got back to the ranch she went to her room and locked the door. She couldn't face anyone just yet.

"What's wrong with her?" Marie asked quietly when she and Winnie were drinking coffee while Dwight slept. "Something's upset her terribly. I wonder what Dale said to her? Could it just be the reporter who's got her upset?"

"I don't know." Winnie sipped coffee, aware of the front door opening and closing. "Surely, Gene won't let him come here, will he?"

"I won't let who come here?" Gene asked abruptly, taking off his work gloves as he paused in the doorway.

"That reporter," Marie said. "The one who's looking for Allison."

He scowled. "What reporter? And why is he looking for our houseguest?"

Winnie hesitated. She exchanged glances with Marie and grimaced. "I guess you'd better hear it all. Allison isn't going to tell you, but someone needs to. You'd better sit down."

He sprawled in the armchair next to the sofa and crossed his arms over his chest. "All right," he said, his green eyes solemn. It would be almost a relief to know it all. He'd had a feeling from the very first that Allison wasn't what she seemed, although he had one strong premonition that he wasn't going to like what he found out.

"Allison and her parents were sent to Central America to set up a small clinic in one of the rural provinces," Winnie began. "It was a war zone, and inevitably, two opposing factions threatened the village."

"What were they doing in Central America?" Gene interrupted.

Winnie blinked. "Why, they were missionaries."

Gene's face went several shades paler and his jaw clenched. "All of them?" he asked in a choked tone. "Allison, too?"

"Yes," Winnie replied, confirming his worst fears.

He ran a hand through his hair, his eyes blank. Now it all made sense. No wonder she'd been so naïve, so trusting. He closed his eyes. If the guilt had been there before, it was almost unbearable now. A missionary. He'd seduced a missionary! "Finish it," he said stiffly, opening his eyes to glare at her.

"They were taken prisoner," Winnie said slowly. "Allison's parents were shot to death right beside her, and the firing squad had taken aim at her when the opposing force marched in and spared her. She was smuggled out of the country by international peacekeepers. She has information that nobody else has, and that's why the media's been after her. She came here to heal, Gene."

He'd gone rigid during that revelation. When Winnie finished, he got up out of his chair without a word and went out the front door. He didn't want anyone to see what he felt at the thought of bullets tearing into that gentle, loving woman. He felt something wet in his eyes and kept walking while stark terror ran over his body like fire. Incredible, Dwight had said. No. Not incredible. A miracle. Allison believed in miracles, she'd told him once, and now he knew why. She was alive because of one.

The sound of approaching voices disturbed his thoughts. He wasn't really listening, it was just some of the hands heading into the bunkhouse for lunch. But then one loud, slurred voice caught his attention.

Rance, he thought angrily, drinking again. He'd warned the man once. Now he was going to have to do something about it. The hands knew he wouldn't tolerate alcohol during working hours.

Just as he started around the barn toward the bunkhouse, he heard what Rance was saying.

"She wouldn't give me the time of day," the man snarled. "Can you imagine that? She didn't mind rolling around in that line cabin with the boss, but she was too good to let me touch her. Dale hates her guts, and I can see why. Well, it's all over town about the high and mighty Miss Hathoway and Nelson, and before I'm through…"

His voice trailed off as the object of his venom walked into the bunkhouse with an expression on his face that made the rest of the men scatter.

"Now, boss," Rance began hesitantly, because he knew the set of the older man's lean body and the glitter of those green eyes from long experience.

"You son of a…!" The last word was muffled by a huge fist as Gene knocked the cowboy to the floor and dived after him. They demolished chairs in the struggle, but it was no contest. Gene was quicker and more muscular than the young cowboy, and he had the advantage of murderous anger.

He pulled Rance up from the floor and knocked him through the open bunkhouse door and out into the dirt, and was going after him again when one of the older hands stepped in front of him.

"He's had enough, boss," the man said gently, keeping his voice low and calm. "You got the point across. No need to tear his arms off. None of us listened to his venom. A blind man would know that Miss Hathoway's a lady."

Gene was breathing heavily. He looked from the half-conscious man on the ground to the one who was speaking, his green eyes hot and wild. He took a deep breath to steady himself. "If anyone else asks, Miss Hathoway is my *fiancée*," he emphasized the word, looking at each cowboy's face individually with an expression that was calm and dangerous all at once. "I may deserve that kind of malicious gossip, but she doesn't. She's a missionary. A man who *is* a man doesn't belittle a woman of her sort!"

The men looked shamefaced. They stood uncomfortably congregated with downcast eyes.

"Rance told some reporter she was here," one of them said. "We did try to reason with him, Mr. Nelson, but he was half lit and out for blood. Dale Branigan fed him a lot of bull about you and he's sweet on her; not to mention him drinking like a fish half the time when you didn't see him."

"He can be sweet on her from a closer distance from

now on," Gene said, trying to cope with all the new developments at once. He'd been lax on the job a lot. It was just coming home to him how much time he'd spent wallowing in self-pity over his parentage while he let his stepfather's ranch go to hell. Well, there wouldn't be any more of that. He stood over Rance, watching the man open a swollen eye to stare up at him with evident fear.

"Get off my land," Gene said coldly, and without raising his voice. "If I see you again, I'll break your neck. I'll send your check along in care of Dale Branigan. But if you're counting on a little romance with her, you'll have to get past Ben Hardy. He's all but engaged to her, in case you didn't know."

Rance looked shocked. "Ben...?"

"She played you for a fool, didn't she?" Gene asked with a mocking smile. "You poor stupid fish, that will be all over town by tomorrow, too. I promise you it will, along with the news of my engagement to Allison and the damage you tried to do to her reputation."

Rance dragged himself to his feet, considerably more sober now. He wiped blood away from a cut lip and shivered a little with reaction and muscle strain as he reached for his hat and put it back on.

"No need to beat a man half to death over some woman," Rance said angrily.

"No need to make her out to be a tramp because she won't let you touch her, either," Gene said dangerously, his temper kindling again. "You're finished in Pryor, Rance. I'll see to it, no matter what it takes."

Rance straightened. "I've had my fill of Wyoming, anyway," he said shortly. "You can have it."

He hobbled into the bunkhouse to pack. Gene turned on his heel and walked away, ignoring the murmurs of comment from his men as he stalked toward the house with blood in his eye.

He went straight up the staircase without a word to Marie and Winnie, who'd been standing speechless at the window, watching the byplay.

Dwight was asleep when he peeped in the door, so he went straight along to Allison's room.

He knocked and waited for her to answer. It only took a minute. She was surprised to see him, and he wondered absently if she'd have opened it if she'd known it was him. She looked terrible.

He rubbed his fist against the corner of his mouth, feeling the cut there as he stared down at her furiously. "Why didn't you tell me what Rance was saying about you?" he demanded without preamble. "Why didn't you tell me what you'd gone through in Central America, and what you and your parents were doing there?"

She was looking at his bruised, cut face, hardly hearing the words. "You're hurt," she said worriedly. "What happened to you?"

"I've been out in the backyard beating the hell out of Rance before I fired him," he said icily. "And I enjoyed it. Does that shock you? I wish I'd hit him twice as damned hard!"

"You know...all of it?" she asked hesitantly.

"All of it," he assured her. His broad chest rose and fell jerkily. "Oh, God, why didn't you trust me?" he asked huskily. "Why didn't you tell me the truth?"

Her eyes fell to his shirt buttons. "I couldn't. It hurt

too much to talk about it, at first. And then I knew you'd take off like a shot if you knew, well, what I did for a living. I lied because I wanted to be alive, just for a little while. I wanted to be someone else, I wanted to be like other women, to be…loved." She almost choked on the word and her eyes closed. "But I had no right."

"Do you think I did?" he groaned. He stepped into the room and slammed the door, jerking her hungrily into his arms. He held her against him, rocking her gently, folding her to his heart in a silence that was broken only by the sound of her soft weeping.

"The worst of it is that I was so wrapped up in my own problems that I was blind to your character," he said bitterly. "I deliberately overlooked all the telltale signs of your innocence because I wanted you so badly. I deserve to be shot!"

"But, I wanted you, too," she whispered at his ear, feeling his cheek warm and rough against hers as he held her. "It's not all your fault. You were hurting. I understood."

"That doesn't excuse it. And to have that redheaded vermin gossiping about you in town!" he groaned. "I'm sorry."

"I won't be here much longer," she reminded him miserably. "And if that reporter just doesn't find me…"

His arms tightened. "It won't matter if he does," he said curtly. "I've just told the men that we're engaged. I'll make sure that gets around town. Dale will wind up with egg on her face from her damned gossiping."

"Engaged?" she gasped. "But I can't!"

He drew back, scowling. "Why can't you? You're a missionary, not a nun. Marriage is permissible."

"But not like this, Gene," she said quietly, her hazel eyes sad and regretful. "Not to spare my reputation. It will be all right. I'm a qualified nurse. I can still get a job."

His eyes searched her face, down to her soft mouth. "Marriage is a job, isn't it? Dwight and I are switching responsibilities, and we'll both be happier. That means I'll be home more. I can spend time with you and the kids."

She flushed. "There aren't any kids."

His lean hands smoothed down her hips and one of them lightly touched her belly. "Yet."

She shivered and tried to pull away.

But he held her, gently, firmly. "I know. I hurt you, didn't I? Your first time was a nightmare that you don't want to repeat, especially with me."

She nodded slowly, without looking at him.

He bent and suddenly lifted her in his hard arms, his eyes searching her frightened ones as he carried her toward the bed.

"If I can make you want me, in spite of what happened before, will you agree to marry me?" he asked softly.

"But, I don't…!" she protested.

He covered the frantic words with his mouth, gently this time, using every shred of skill he possessed to coax her set lips into a shy response.

He laid her down on the coverlet and stretched out beside her, his lips teasing hers in a gentle, exquisite kind of exploration. His fingers traced her cheeks, pushing back the wispy strands of long black hair that had escaped from her bun while the seconds lengthened into minutes.

"I like your hair long and loose," he breathed against her yielding mouth, one lean hand disposing of pins and combs before he arranged her loosened mane of hair around her flushed face.

She looked up at him nervously, her body already taut from the threat of his, her memory all too vivid of the last time.

"There's a barrier," he whispered deeply, holding her eyes while he traced a long forefinger around the swollen contours of her mouth. "It's called a maidenhead. It protects a woman's chastity. The first time, it has to be disposed of, and that's why I hurt you. It won't ever be like that again. Now that I know how innocent you really are, I'll make a meal of you, Miss Hathoway. When I've finished, fear is the last thing you'll feel when you look at me."

She colored. "I'm a nurse," she reminded him, trying to sound worldly. "I do know something about my own anatomy."

He brushed her open mouth with his. "I was in too much of a hurry to wait for you. I lost my head. I won't lose it with you again until I've satisfied you."

"Please," she moaned, "you mustn't talk to me like this!"

"You're my woman," he said, lifting his head to hold her eyes. "We're lovers, Allison. We're going to be mar-

ried. You'll have to face the implications of that, sooner
or later."

"I won't marry you!"

"Like hell you won't marry me," he said with quiet
determination. He searched her eyes. "I'm sorry," he
said as he bent. "But this is the only way, now."

She didn't understand what he meant at first. He
covered her mouth with his and his hands smoothed
down her body while he built the kiss from a slow caress to a blazing, raging statement of intent. She shivered as the heat exploded in her body when his mouth
suddenly went down hard over her breast and began
to suckle it through the fabric of her dress. She arched
and gasped, at the same time that one lean hand found
the fastening of her jeans and slipped expertly inside
against warm flesh.

"Gene, you can't!" she whimpered.

But he touched her intimately then, and his mouth
became as insistent and rhythmic as the hand invading
her privacy with such slow, sweet mastery. She began
to shiver. Her eyes closed. She couldn't fight this sweet
tide of pleasure, she couldn't! She heard her breath shuddering out in little gasps, felt her body lifting, yielding
itself to whatever he wanted. His face nuzzled under the
fabric of her blouse and nudged her bra aside so that he
could find the hard, aching tip of her swelling breast,
hot and moist against the silky bare flesh.

"Gene," she whispered, her voice breaking on his
name as he quickened the rhythm and increased the
insistence of his mouth on her body. "Gene! Oh, Gene,
please—!"

Her voice broke and he gave her what she begged for, feeling her release with pride and indulgent pleasure. He lifted his head and watched her convulse, her face a study in rigid ecstasy, her body completely his. She wept afterward, and he comforted her, kissing away the tears, lightly caressing her trembling body until she was completely still in his arms.

"That's what it feels like, Allison," he said softly, holding her shocked eyes. "That's what it was like for me, that night in the cabin. I wanted you to know, because next time, I'll give you this same pleasure with my body. Only it will be an agony of a climax, I promise you. This will be nothing by comparison."

She blushed as she met his eyes. "Why?"

He kissed her nose. "I told you. I want you to marry me."

"You don't have to go that far to spare my reputation, or salve your own guilt. I told you, I don't blame you... Gene!" she gasped sharply.

His body had levered over hers in midsentence and he'd coaxed his way between her long legs, so that she felt him in blatant intimacy, became shockingly aware of the power and need of his body.

He moved deliberately, balancing himself above her on his forearms, smiling down at her with the slow, deliberate shifting of his lean hips.

"Say, yes, I'll marry you, Gene," he instructed very slowly, "or I'll peel you out of those jeans right now and make you scream like a banshee under me. If you think your reputation's in shreds already, wait until that unholy crew in the bunkhouse hears the noises I drag out of you now."

She shivered, because she was vulnerable and he knew it. Worse, the window was open, she glanced at it and saw the curtains moving.

"Better say it quick, cupcake, before I get too involved to roll away," he said huskily and pressed his lips down hard over hers. "It's getting worse."

Yes, it was, and her face registered her knowledge of it. She swallowed, sensations in her lower belly making her hot and weak all at once. Her legs trembled under his. "You can't do that…to me," she protested. "Marie and Winnie—"

"Are downstairs," he said, "and the door is closed. Neither of them is likely to walk in without an invitation since they know I'm up here with you," he said in a deep, husky tone. "Open your legs, Allison," he whispered, his mouth poising over hers to brush at it with soft, sensual intent. His own long, powerful legs began to edge out and she felt him against her in a hot daze. She gasped softly and looked up into his glittering green eyes, feeling a kindred recklessness. With a faint moan, she let him shift her legs, let him fit his lean body intimately to hers while he watched her face with unblinking intensity. His jaw tautened and she felt his body swell even more in the stark closeness. She shivered.

His hand went between them and ripped open his shirt and pushed hers up, easily unclipping her bra and moving it out of the way. He looked down as he brushed his hair-roughened chest blatantly over the hard tips of her breasts and watched her shiver with reaction. His hips began to move upward over hers, throbbing with building passion as his eyes bit into hers.

"Tell me you don't want to be filled," he whispered at her lips. "Filled hard, and deep."

She made a helpless sound and shivered again, totally helpless.

His hands went to her jeans, and then to his own, and seconds later, she felt his muscular, hair-roughened nudity against her softness with a sense of wonder. His body echoed the soft shiver of hers.

"Are you going to let me?" he whispered, drawing his hips against hers.

"We shouldn't… Gene," she choked.

"Yes, we should," he whispered tenderly. His hands smoothed down her silky hips, under her thighs, and he lifted them, eased them apart with such gentleness that she couldn't find a single protest.

He moved then, fitting himself to her in a silence that smoldered with promise.

She looked straight into his eyes and gasped softly as he began to possess her, with exquisitely gentle movements.

"Yes," he whispered tenderly. "You see? It doesn't hurt. No, don't tense up. That's it," he coaxed. He took her mouth under his and cherished it. "That's it, little one. I'm only going to love you. Isn't that what you said you wanted? To be loved?"

She'd meant another kind of love entirely, but this was heaven. She wondered if he'd ever been so tender with anyone else, but he moved then, and she couldn't think anymore.

He probed her body softly. "Yes, watch my eyes, Allison. You watched me, that night. Now I want to watch you."

As he spoke, he moved, slow and easy movements that brought them first into stark intimacy, and then into contact, and then totally together. She gasped as she felt her body absorbing his, stunned with the ease of his passage, the readiness of her own body. She stared into his eyes with wonder, trying to feel guilt and shame, but she couldn't. She couldn't have imagined the expression on his lean face in her wildest dreams. His eyes were soft and warm, full of secret knowledge and tenderness and excitement.

He moved lazily against her, smiling as he settled on her body in a soft rhythm that lifted her very slowly to an ecstasy she'd never dreamed possible.

She cried out and pushed at his chest, frightened, but he continued the steady rhythm, increasing it now, his breathing suddenly changing as he watched her eyes.

"Don't look away," he said huskily. "I'm going to watch. Now, Allison. Now, little one. Now. Now!"

She made sounds she'd never made in her life as the sensations gathered and suddenly exploded. She wept in what sounded like anguished pain, her breath trapped in her throat, her face contorted like her convulsing body. He went with her every step of the way, only giving in when she was almost exhausted. He laughed even as his body corded over hers, laughed through the vicious ecstasy that suspended him above her in a shuddering anguish of satisfaction.

He ground out something and went rigid before he collapsed on her body, his heartbeat shaking both of them. He trembled, as she did, long afterward.

"I really should have closed the window," he murmured dryly, feeling the heat in her cheeks. "Don't curl up. We're too far from the bunkhouse and the living room for anyone to hear you, and Dwight's asleep. Did it hurt this time?" he asked, smiling as he lifted his head to search her eyes, knowing the answer already.

She swallowed. "Oh, no," she whispered. She was still trembling a little, and so was he. They were both drenched with sweat, but her body felt deliciously boneless, although it still tingled with pleasure. "No, it was..." She searched for the right word as she looked into his soft eyes. "It was beautiful."

"That's how it should be," he breathed at her ear, gathering her legs in the muscular cage of his as he kissed her tenderly. He lifted his head. "I hope you weren't disappointed this time."

"You were...watching," she whispered, coloring. "Couldn't you, well, see?"

"I saw, all right." His face hardened with the memory and he kissed her roughly. "I've never watched before. I've never been satisfied like that before, either. If you don't marry me, so help me, I'll move in here with you until I shame you into saying yes."

She swallowed. "Gene..."

He brushed back her damp hair. "Your conscience will beat you to death over this," he said quietly, drawing her gaze along their bodies until she flushed and averted her eyes. "I didn't force you or coerce you. It was mutual. We've got a lot going for us. I want to live with you, cupcake."

"Sex wouldn't be enough for you," she whispered sadly. "And you'd have a long time to regret it."

"I won't regret it." He brushed his mouth over her eyes. And he knew he wouldn't. He was awash with new feelings, with a tenderness he'd never experienced before. He studied her quietly. "You'll be everything I ever needed, or wanted. I'll take care of you until I die. And someday, somehow, I'll make you glad you said yes."

Those words echoed in her mind long after they'd dressed and gone downstairs to announce their engagement. Allison couldn't decide if she believed him or not; if she dared to believe him. Because it sounded very much as if more than physical need was the basis for the proposal. About that, only time would tell.

Chapter Ten

"I just can't believe it," Marie said later, smiling at Allison. "I never thought I'd live long enough to see Gene married. Imagine that, my footloose, fancy-free brother not only willing, but anxious to tie the knot! And to someone I really like!"

"I'm glad of that," Allison said, but her eyes were troubled.

Winnie was upstairs with Dwight, and Gene had gone back out to work after a brief lunch. Marie was still getting over the shock of what Gene had announced so matter-of-factly.

Marie stared at her for a moment. "There's something more, isn't there?" she asked gently. "Forgive me for prying, but I know my brother very well and I've learned quite a bit about you. Something happened that night that Rance gossiped about, and you think Gene is only marrying you to appease his conscience. That's it, isn't it?"

Allison started to deny it, but there really wasn't any point. She stared down at her hands folded in her lap. "Yes."

"Gene has a conscience," Marie continued. "But nothing could make him marry a woman in cold blood, not even that. You'd better believe that it isn't guilt on his part."

"There could be a baby," Allison said painfully, amazed that she could talk to Marie this way when she couldn't bring herself to tell Winnie about it.

Marie smiled. "Gene loves children," she said simply. "So do all the rest of us. A baby would be the sweetest kind of surprise."

Allison fought tears and lost. She put her head in her hands and wept bitterly. "I've trapped him, all because I got in over my head," she moaned. "Whatever his motives, inevitably he'll hate me!"

Marie hugged her warmly. "No, I don't think so. Not the way he's been acting since you've been around. You've changed him. All the bitterness and mockery are gone. He's gentler, less volatile."

"Mr. Rance wouldn't agree with you," Allison said with a watery smile.

"Mr. Rance deserved what he got," Marie said shortly. "I don't feel sorry for him. Now you cheer up," she told Allison. "No more regrets. You're the first sister-in-law prospect Gene's ever presented me with, and I'm not letting you escape!"

Marie's enthusiasm was catching. Allison went back up to sit with Dwight in a brighter mood altogether. If she had doubts, she kept them to herself.

Gene led her off into the study later that night, after they'd had supper, and closed the door.

She was nervous, and he smiled gently at the expression on her face.

"Don't look so threatened," he said, his green eyes twinkling at her. "The couch is too short, and the desk would be hell on your back."

She blushed, her eyes like saucers as they met his.

He moved toward her, indulgent and smiling. "How can you still blush?" he asked, drawing her gently to him. "You wide-eyed little innocent."

"Not so innocent now," she said quietly.

He bent and kissed her softly. "It won't do much good to ask you not to beat your conscience to death. But try not to go overboard. God made us human, little one," he said, his voice deep and caressing as he searched her eyes. "He gave us physical pleasure to ensure the perpetuation of the species."

"And He gave us responsibility not to make a mockery of it, or twist it into something bad," she replied miserably.

He framed her wan face in his lean hands and studied her. "You believed in me when no one else did," he said. "You weren't put off by my reputation or intimidated by my temper. You gave yourself to me more than any other reason because you knew how desperately I needed you." He sighed heavily. "Allison, what we did, that night at the cabin and today, was as natural as breathing. It isn't hateful to want someone, especially when it goes beyond a physical need."

"Did it, though?" she asked sadly.

He nodded. "Yes. This afternoon, it most certainly went beyond desire."

"You were…so tender," she whispered.

He drew her against him and enveloped her in his arms, resting his cheek on her dark hair. "It's going to be that way every time, from now on," he said. His arms tightened as he felt her warmth and softness so close to him. His body reacted predictably and he laughed. "My God, feel that," he whispered at her ear.

"Stop," she protested in a flutter.

"You're a nurse. You should know that I can't stop it."

"That wasn't what I meant." She buried her face in his chest and felt him suddenly go stiff and catch his breath.

His hands moved slowly into her hair. He drew her mouth against him, through the shirt, and his breathing became ragged. "Allison," he whispered huskily. His eyes closed. He'd never felt so vulnerable, or minded it so little.

"You like that?" she whispered hesitantly.

"I like it a lot." He eased a lean hand between them. "But I'd like it on my bare skin more, sweetheart," he said, unfastening buttons as he spoke. "Push my shirt out of the way and put your mouth on me," he whispered sensuously.

"We shouldn't," she protested weakly. "What if…"

"We're going to be married," he said at her forehead. "A piece of paper and the right words aren't going to bind us any closer than our bodies already have. You're mine now. I love being part of you, feeling you share my pleasure. Is it really so frightening to let me love you now?"

"It isn't…frightening," she confessed. She rubbed her hands flat against his hair-laden chest, up and down in a sensual pattern.

He drew her mouth to his warm skin, feeling her lips search through the mat of hair to the hard muscles of his chest and he caught his breath, tautening involuntarily.

It was intoxicating, she thought dazedly, smoothing her hands over him while her mouth lifted and touched. He smelled of spicy cologne and the touch of his body was all of heaven.

Her hands smoothed down to his belt and his lips brushed her closed eyelids. "Lower," he whispered. "I want you to touch me."

She hesitated. She was curious, but all her inhibitions were protesting.

"I belong to you as surely as you belong to me," he said quietly. "Aren't you curious about the differences between your body and mine?"

"Well, yes," she confessed hesitantly.

His lips parted against her eyebrows. "Then find them out for yourself."

She lay her cheek on his chest and slowly let her cool, nervous hands trespass past the wide belt. He jerked a little at the unfamiliar touch, and she hesitated, but his hands trapped hers when she tried to pull them away.

"It's all right," he whispered against her temple. "I'm no more used to this than you are."

"You're experienced…" she protested.

"Not in this, I'm not," he replied, surprisingly. "What we've done together is totally new for me, up to and including this. Haven't you realized that I'm not playing some sophisticated game with you?" he asked. "Allison, I'm as helpless as you are when we make love. Your touch is just as exciting and potent to me as mine seems to be to you."

"I didn't realize that," she whispered. Under her softly questing hands, his body was powerfully male and very, very responsive. He gasped and she felt his body shudder. "Did I hurt you?" she breathed.

"No," he said, his voice faintly choked. "I'm sensitive there."

"Oh."

"Don't stop," he whispered, searching for her lips with his mouth. He opened it to a slow, deep kiss that seemed to have no end, glorying in her tender exploration of him. He guided her hand to the zipper and groaned helplessly when she touched him under the fabric. They wound up on the couch in a tangle of arms and legs, fighting their way into each other's arms through a sea of uncooperative clothing.

She shivered, her breasts flattened in the thicket of hair on his warm chest, swelling as he traced them with his thumbs while they kissed.

"When are you going to marry me?" he whispered into her open mouth.

"Whenever…you like," she managed unsteadily.

"Friday?"

"That's only three days away," she said huskily.

He smiled against her mouth. "I know." He lifted his head and looked down where her body was lying across his lap, her torso bare against his. "And not a minute too soon." He tugged at her lower lip with his teeth, in a sensual throbbing fantasy that made him dizzy. "Make a baby with me, Allison," he whispered, easing her down onto the sofa as he lifted his head to hold her hazel eyes in thrall. "Here. Now."

"Gene…!" she exclaimed when he moved.

But it was already too late for second thoughts, because he joined them with a minimum of fuss and smiled gently into her shocked eyes as he began to move sensually and with expert knowledge of her body.

"Yes, that's it," he whispered when she ground her teeth together and gasped. "Only don't cry out when I satisfy you," he added with a slow, sensual smile, "because the walls aren't that thick and the door isn't locked. Do you hear me? Bite my chest or kiss me when it happens, so that the sound doesn't penetrate the walls. God, you're noisy," he whispered as she began to bite back the sounds. "One day I'll make love to you deep in the woods and you can scream for me. Yes. Yes. That's it, lift up to me." His hands gripped her hips and pulled her to him in a ragged, rough rhythm. "Yes. Yes!" His eyes closed and he began to shudder, then they opened straight into hers and his body impaled her fiercely. She felt the spiraling rhythm explode into ecstasy and rocked her slender body.

"I want a son!" he bit off in her ear, and his hands clenched on her hips and ground her into him as he shuddered against her.

It was the most unbelievable pleasure she'd ever shared with him. He collapsed against her and she clung to him, trembling in the aftermath.

"God, that was good," he whispered hoarsely at her ear. His arms contracted, riveting her to him. "Did you hear what I said, just at the last?"

"Yes." She drew him closer. "You whispered that you wanted a son," she said, shivering.

"I meant it. A son. A daughter. Our child." He lifted his head and searched her eyes, his sweaty hair hanging down onto his broad forehead, his green eyes glittery with spent pleasure. "It's exciting to make love like this. I never wanted children before. But it's all I think about when I'm with you."

She reached up and touched his mouth. "I can never say no to you," she whispered. "It's…frightening."

"It's your inhibitions," he corrected. He kissed her softly and moved away, smiling indulgently at her embarrassment as she rearranged her clothing while he fastened his own. "Feverish, isn't it?" he asked wickedly. "Hot and wild and out of control. You're every dream I ever dreamed. I don't know how I lived this long without you."

"Are you sure it isn't just physical?" she asked after a minute, really worried.

He brought her face up to his and kissed her gently. "If it was only physical, why would I want to make babies with you?" he whispered tenderly.

She smiled, her heart in her eyes, and laid her head against his chest. "Then I'll marry you whenever you say, Gene."

He hesitated. "There's something I have to tell you, before you commit yourself," he told her a minute later. "A secret I've held back. I should have told you before we ever got involved. I can't ask you to live with me unless you know it."

She lifted her head. "It won't matter. What is it?"

"My father," he began slowly, watching her face closely, "my real father, I mean…is in prison."

Her eyes didn't waver. She smiled up at him. "I'm sorry about that. But what does it have to do with my marrying you?"

He let out the breath he'd been holding. "My God," he ground out. He caught her up roughly and held her close enough to bruise her, his eyes closed as he rocked her against him. "My God, I was scared to death to tell you…!"

"But why?" she asked gently.

"You might be afraid of our children inheriting bad blood," he said curtly. "My father is a thief. From what I've been able to find out, he's been in trouble with the law all his life."

She nuzzled her face against him, feeling warm and safe and secure. "Environment plays a big part in shaping a person's character," she said drowsily. "I get sleepy when you love me. Is that natural?"

His breath caught. "When I love you," he repeated in a slow whisper, feeling the words to his bones. His eyes closed and he held her closer, shivering. Love her. Love her. It *was* loving. Why hadn't he realized it? "My God."

"Is something wrong?" she asked, her voice puzzled.

"No. Not a single thing." He drew back and searched

her eyes, holding them while he looked for more secrets, hoping that he'd hit on the right one. "How do you feel about me, sweetheart?" he asked gently.

"I... I want you," she stammered, embarrassed.

He shook his head slowly. "Sex wouldn't be enough for you. Even good sex. Not with your background. Try again."

She hesitated. It was hard to lay her heart down in front of him, but clearly that was what he wanted.

He brushed his thumb over her soft lips. "It takes a lot of trust, doesn't it? But I trusted you enough to tell you the most painful secret I have."

That was true. He had. She was the one lacking in trust, not him. She drew a slow, steadying breath and looked up at him. "I love you, Gene," she said simply.

"Do you?" he asked huskily.

The expression on his lean, hard face made her confident. "With all my heart," she whispered.

He traced the soft contours of her mouth with fingers that were faintly unsteady. "Forever, little one," he breathed, bending to her mouth.

Tears stung her eyes as she closed them. "Forever!"

He kissed her with aching tenderness and picked her up in his arms, sitting down in an armchair with her in his lap. He tucked her face into his throat and sat just holding her close for a long, long time before he finally leaned back with a heavy sigh, still cradling her close.

"Now, you're going to tell me about your parents."

She shivered. "I can't."

"You can. We're part of each other now. There's nothing you can't share with me. Tell me about them."

She lay quietly for a minute. Then she began to speak. She told him about the countries where they'd lived, the conditions of unspeakable poverty they'd endured.

"They never let it get them down," she told him. "They were always sure that things would get better. If we ran out of supplies, they were confident that new ones would come in time. And they always did," she said wonderingly. "I've never known people like them. They really lived what they believed in. And then, one day, it all came down around our ears. The regimes changed so quickly." She hesitated.

He pulled her closer, sensing her feelings. "I've got you. You're safe. Tell me what happened."

"We were arrested for giving comfort to the enemy," she said, giving in to the terrifying memories. She pressed closer. "They locked us up overnight. Even then, my parents were sure that we'd be set free by the government troops when they arrived. But the next morning we were marched out of the village along with some other political prisoners and stood up against an ocotillo fence." She swallowed. "We could hear firing in the distance. I kept thinking, if we can just hold on for a few minutes, they'll come, they'll rescue us. Just as I thought it, the guns started firing. My father, and then my mother, fell beside me. I closed my eyes, waiting." She shivered and he held her close, bruisingly close. "A bullet whizzed past my head and I knew the next one was going to get me. But before it hit, gunfire erupted around the three of us who were still alive. I was taken out of the village by a priest we knew. He got me to safety, although how is still a blur. Of all the people I knew, Winnie was the only one I could trust, so I called her and she brought me here."

He thanked God that she was with him, that he was holding her, that the bullets had missed and the soldiers had saved her. "So that's why you came here."

She nodded, staring across his broad chest toward the window. She sighed heavily. "It was a nightmare. Sometimes I still wake up crying in the night."

"If you wake up crying from now on, I'll be there to hold you," he said gently. "Starting tonight."

"But, Gene…!"

He put a finger over her lips. "I'll leave you before morning. No one will know except the two of us." He searched her soft eyes. "God, honey, it's going to be hell being separated from you even while I work, much less at night, do you know that? I don't want you out of my sight!"

Her lips parted on a rush of breath.

"Are you shocked?" he asked huskily, searching her rapt face. "I thought you knew by now that I'm hopelessly in love with you, Allie."

"Oh, Gene," she whispered, shaken.

"I never knew what love was," he said softly. "I'm not sure I was even alive until you came along."

"I feel the same way," she whispered. Her fingers touched his hard mouth tenderly. "I'd die for you, Gene."

His eyes closed and he shivered. He'd never felt anything so intense, or so special.

Allison kissed him softly, again and again. He looked as if he needed comforting. Incredible, for such an independent, self-sufficient man.

"What about your career, little one?" he asked later.

"I can't go back to it," she murmured, without mentioning the blemish on her reputation from the night in the line cabin that would cost her that career. There was no need to make him feel worse than he already did. "I couldn't ask you to leave here and follow me around the world. And I couldn't go without you. Besides," she said gently, "there's every possibility that I could be pregnant now. Today was the very best time for it to happen."

"Was it?" he murmured, and smiled tenderly, laying a big, lean hand on her belly. "Kids and cattle sort of go together, you know. It takes a big family to manage these days."

"I'd like a big family," she said drowsily, curling up in his hard arms. "I hope we can have one."

"If we can't, there are plenty of kids around who'd love to be needed by someone," he murmured, smiling. "Raising them makes people parents, not just having them."

She smiled back. "I'm sleepy."

His arms contracted. "Too much loving," he whispered. "I've exhausted you."

She opened her eyes and looked up at him. "Only temporarily," she whispered. "I love how it feels with you when you love me, Gene."

His jaw tensed. "So do I." He drew in a steadying breath. "We'd better get out of here before it happens again. You make me insatiable."

"I hope to keep you that way, when we're married," she said shyly.

"I'll hold you to it," he promised. He lifted her and got up, too. "I have something for you. In the heat of things, I forgot to give it to you." He opened his desk drawer and removed a felt-covered box. He opened it and slid a marquise diamond onto her engagement finger, leaving the companion wedding band in the box.

"Do you want me to wear a ring when we're married?" he asked seriously.

"Of course," she replied. "If I wear your brand," she said with a mischievous smile, "you have to wear mine."

He chuckled. "Nelson's brand, is that it? I like the sound of it. No trespassing allowed."

"And don't you forget it," she said.

She clung to his hand, wonderingly, astonished that her life could have changed so much in such a short period of time. All her nightmares were going to fade away now, she was sure of it.

Gene was equally sure of it. He'd laid his own ghosts to rest, including his worst one. Allison had said that environment played a big part in shaping a man's character. Perhaps it did. Maybe his real father had had a hard time of it and couldn't cope. Whatever the reason, it didn't have to affect his own life unless he let it. He could live with being an adopted Nelson. Marie and Dwight loved him, there was no doubt about that, and he and Dwight were going to work out the rest of the problems. He'd never been so certain of anything. He looked down at Allison and felt as if he were floating.

Dwight was able to go to the wedding the following week. He and Marie and Winnie witnessed at the small, quiet ceremony where Allison Hathoway became Mrs. Gene Nelson. She wore a simple white dress and carried a bouquet of daisies, and Gene thought he'd never seen anyone so beautiful. He said so, several times after they arrived at the hotel in Yellowstone National Park where they were spending part of their honeymoon.

"The most amazing thing is that nobody discovered we were sharing a bed until we got married," Allison said with a shy smile.

"Sharing it was all we did," he murmured ruefully, "because of your conscience. Not to mention my own. But it was sweet, honey. I never dreamed anything could be as sweet as holding you all night in my arms, even if we didn't make love."

"And now we never have to be apart again," she whispered, lifting into his arms as he began to kiss her very softly.

"Did you notice the reporter?" he asked against her mouth.

"The one you sent sprawling into the mud puddle?" she whispered, laughing involuntarily when she remembered the astonishment on the journalist's face. "Amazing that he finally found me, and by the time he did, it didn't matter anymore. They've started releasing all sorts of information through the international forces. I'm old news now."

"Thank God. He won't be hounding us anymore."

"I just wish my parents could have gotten out with me," she said, allowing herself that one regret.

"So do I, little one," he replied gently. "I'm just glad that you did."

She pressed close to him, drawing strength from his lean, powerful body.

"Make love to me this time," he whispered at her ear.

"But I don't know how," she said softly.

"No problem. I'll teach you."

And he did. He guided her, smiled at her reticence, laughed at her fumbling efforts to undress him. But when they were finally together on the big bed, softness to hardness, dark to light, the laughing stopped and they loved as they never had before. From tenderness to rough passion, to lazy sweetness and sharp demand, they didn't sleep all night long. By morning they lay exhausted in each other's arms, too tired to even move.

It was lunchtime before they stirred. Allison opened her eyes to find Gene sitting on the bed beside her, watching her as he toweled his hair dry.

"Good morning, Mrs. Nelson," he said softly.

She opened her arms, smiling as she dislodged the sheet and felt him lift her against his bare chest while he kissed her tenderly.

"Was it good?" he whispered.

"I thought I was going to die," she replied huskily.

"So did I. And I still may." He groaned, sitting upright, and then he laughed. "I think my back's broken."

"Married twenty-four hours, and you're already complaining," she moaned.

"That wasn't a complaint," he chuckled. He kissed her again and pulled her out of bed, his eyes sliding possessively over her soft pink nudity. "God, you're beautiful. Inside and out. You're my world, Allison."

She pressed close against him. "You're mine. I'll never live long enough to tell you how much I love you."

"Yes, you will." He smoothed her hair. "Now get dressed. I don't know about you, but I'm starved!"

"Come to think of it, so am I," she said, blinking. "Gene, we never had supper! Not to mention breakfast or lunch!"

He chuckled. "We didn't, did we?"

"No wonder we're hungry!"

"Amen. So get moving, woman."

She got dressed, with his dubious assistance, which took twice as long. They had a leisurely supper and then went out to see Old Faithful erupt. Later they drove up to the mud volcano, past the fishing bridge, and sat beside a little stream that cut through towering lodgepole pines with the jagged Rocky Mountains rising majestically in the distance and Yellowstone Lake in the other direction.

"Tomorrow's Sunday," he said when they were back in the hotel room, curled up together in bed.

"So it is," she replied.

He sighed softly and pressed her cheek to his bare chest. "They have church services nearby," he said. "I asked. Suppose we go?"

Her breath caught. She sat up, looking at him in the light from outside the room. "Do you mean it? You really want to?"

"I mean it," he said quietly.

She had to fight tears. "Oh, Gene," she whispered, because she knew what a giant step it was for him to make.

He brushed away the moistness from her eyes. "I

love you," he said. "From now on, we go together—
wherever we go."

"Yes." She laughed, so full of happiness that it was
all but overflowing. "Oh, yes!"

He pulled her close and rested his cheek on her soft
hair. Minutes later, he heard her breathing change as
she fell asleep. He watched her sleeping face with quiet
wonder for a few minutes before he pulled the covers
over them and settled down beside her, with her cheek
resting on his broad, warm shoulder.

Outside, a bird was making sofÁt night noises, and
his eyes closed as he relaxed into the mattress. He'd
been looking for a place in life, somewhere he belonged,
somewhere he fit. Now he'd found it. He fit very nicely
into Allison's warm, soft arms—and even better in her
gentle heart. She made him complete. He closed his
eyes with a slow smile. He'd have to remember to tell
her that in the morning.

* * * * *

THE WEDDING IN WHITE

For Irene Sullivan, my friend

Chapter One

"I'll never get married!" Vivian wailed. "He won't let me have Whit here at all. I only wanted him to come for supper, and now I have to call him and say it's off! Mack's just hateful!"

"There, there," Natalie Brock soothed, hugging the younger girl. "He's not hateful. He just doesn't understand how you feel about Whit. And you have to remember, he's been totally responsible for you since you were fifteen."

"But he's my brother, not my father," came the sniffling reply. Vivian dashed tears off on the back of her hand. "I'm twenty-two," she added in a plaintive tone. "He can't tell me what to do anymore, anyway!"

"He can, on Medicine Ridge Ranch," Natalie reminded her wryly. Medicine Ridge Ranch was the largest spread in this part of Montana—even the town was named after it. "He's the big boss."

"Humph!" Vivian dabbed at her red eyes with a handkerchief. "Only because Daddy left it to him."

"That isn't quite true," came the amused rejoinder. "Your father left him a ranch that was almost bankrupt, on land the bank was trying to repossess." She waved her hand around the expensive Victorian furnishings of the living room. "All this came from his hard work, not a will."

"And so whatever McKinzey Donald Killain wants, he gets," Vivian raged.

It was odd to hear him called by his complete name. For years, everyone around Medicine Ridge, Montana, which had grown up around the Killain ranch, had called him Mack. It was an abbreviation of his first name, which few of his childhood friends could pronounce.

"He only wants you to be happy," Natalie said softly, kissing the flushed cheek of the blond girl. "I'll go talk to him."

"Would you?" Bright blue eyes looked up hopefully. "I will."

"You're just the nicest friend anybody ever had, Nat," Vivian said fervently. "Nobody else around here has the guts to say anything to him," she added.

"Bob and Charles don't feel comfortable telling him what to do." Natalie defended the younger brothers of the household. Mack had been responsible for all three of his siblings from his early twenties. He was twenty-eight now, crusty and impatient, a real hell-raiser whom most people found intimidating. Natalie had teased him and picked at him from her teens, and she still did. She adored him, despite his fiery temper and legendary impatience. A lot of that ill humor came from having one eye, and she knew it.

Soon after the accident that could as easily have killed him as blinded him, she told him that the rakish patch over his left eye made him look like a sexy pirate. He'd told her to go home and mind her own damned business. She ignored him and continued to help Vivian nurse him, even when he'd come home from the hospital. That hadn't been easy. Natalie was a senior in high school at the time. She'd just gone from the orphanage where she'd spent most of her life to her maiden aunt's house the year before the accident occurred. Her aunt, old Mrs. Barnes, didn't approve of Mack Killain, although she respected him. Natalie had had to beg to get her aunt to drive her first to the hospital and then to the Killain ranch every day to look after Mack. Her aunt had felt it was Vivian's job—not Natalie's—but Vivian couldn't do a thing with her elder brother. Left alone, Mack would have been out on the northern border with his men helping to brand calves.

At first, the doctors feared that he'd lost the sight in both eyes. But later, it had become evident that the right one still functioned. During that time of uncertainty, Natalie had attached herself to him and refused to go away, teasing him when he became despondent, cheering him up when he wanted to quit. She wouldn't let him give up, and soon there had been visible progress in his recovery.

Of course, he'd tossed her out the minute he was back on his feet, and she hadn't protested. She knew him right down to his bones, and he realized it and resented it. He didn't want her for a friend and made it obvious. She didn't push. As an orphan, she was used to rejection. Her aunt hadn't taken her in until the dignified lady was diagnosed with heart failure and needed someone to take care of her. Natalie had gone willingly, not only because she was tired of the orphanage, but also because her aunt lived on Killain's southern border. Natalie visited her new friend Vivian most every day after that. It wasn't until her aunt had died unexpectedly and left her a sizeable nest egg that she'd been able to put herself through college and keep up the payments on the little house she and her aunt had occupied together.

She lived frugally, and she'd managed all by herself. The money was almost gone now, but she'd made good grades and she had the promise of a teaching position at the local elementary school when she graduated. Life at the age of twenty-two looked much better than life at age six, when a grieving child had been taken from her family home and placed in the orphanage after a fire had killed both her parents. Like Mack, she'd had her share of tragedy and grief.

But teaching was wonderful. She loved first graders, so open and loving and curious. That was going to be her future. She and Dave Markham, a sixth-grade teacher at the school, had been dating for several weeks. No one knew that they were more friends than a romantic couple. Dave was sweet on the clerk at the local insurance agency, who was mooning over one of the men she worked with. Natalie wasn't interested in marriage anytime soon. Her only taste of love had been a crush on an older teenager when she was in her senior year. He'd just started noticing her when he was killed in a wreck while driving home from an out-of-town weekend fishing trip with his cousin. Losing her parents, then the one love of her short life, had taught her the danger of loving. She wanted to be safe. She wanted to be alone.

Besides that, she was far too fastidious for the impulsive leap-into-bed relationships that seemed the goal of many modern young women. She had no interest in falling in love, or in a purely physical affair. So until Dave came along, she hadn't dated at all. Well, that wasn't quite true, she conceded.

There was the dance she'd coaxed Mack into taking her to, but he'd been far older than the boys at the local community college who had attended. Nevertheless, he'd made Natalie the belle of the ball just by escorting her. Mack was a dish, by anybody's standards, even if he did lack social graces. By the time they left, he'd put more backs up than a debating team. She hadn't asked him to take her anywhere else, though. He seemed to dislike everybody these days. Especially Natalie.

Natalie hadn't really minded his abrasive company. She admired his penchant for telling the truth even when it wasn't welcome, and for saying what he thought, not what was socially acceptable. She tended to speak her own mind, too. She'd learned that from Mack. He'd forced her to fight back soon after she became friends with his sister. He put her back up and kept it up, refusing to let her rush off and cry. He taught her to stand her ground, to have the courage of her convictions. He made her strong enough to bear up under almost anything.

She remembered that they had an argument the night she'd coaxed him to the dance. He'd left her at her front door with one poisonous remark too many, his black eye narrow and no smile to ease the hard, lean contours of his face. There was too much between them to let a disagreement keep them apart, though.

Mack looked much older than twenty-eight. He'd had so much responsibility on his broad shoulders that he'd been robbed of a real childhood. His mother had died young, and his father had succumbed to drink, and then became abusive to the kids. Mack had stood up to him, many times taking blows meant for the other three. In the end, their father had suffered a stroke and been placed in a nursing home while Mack kept the younger Killains together and supported them by working as a mechanic in town. When Mack was twenty-one, his father had died, leaving Mack with three teenagers to raise.

Meanwhile, he'd invested carefully, bought good stock and started breeding his own strain of Red Angus. He was successful at everything he touched. His only run of real bad luck had been when he'd been thrown from his horse in the pasture with a big Angus bull. When the bull had charged him and he'd tried to catch it by the horns to save himself, he'd been gored in the face. He'd lost his sight, but fortunately only in one eye. The rest of him was still pure, splendid male, and women found him very appealing physically. He was every woman's secret desire, until he opened his mouth. His lack of diplomacy kept him single.

Natalie left Vivian crying in the living room and went to find Mack. He was on one knee in a stall on the cobblestones of the spacious, clean barn, ruffling the fur of one of his border collies. He was a kind man, for the most part, and he did love animals. Every stray in Baker County made a beeline for the Killain place, and there were always furry friends around to pet. The border collies were working dogs, of course, and used to help herd cattle on the vast plains. But Mack adored them, and it was mutual.

Natalie leaned against the doorway of the barn with her arms folded and smiled at the picture he made with the pup.

As if he sensed her presence, his head rose. She couldn't see his eyes under the shadow of his wide-brimmed hat, but she knew he was probably glaring at her. He didn't like letting people see how very human he was.

"Slumming, Miss Educator?" he drawled, rising gracefully to his feet.

She only smiled, used to his remarks. "Seeing how the other half lives, Mr. Cattle Rancher," she shot back. "Vivian says you won't let the love of her life through the front door."

"So what are you, a virgin sacrifice to appease me?" he asked, approaching her with that quick, menacing stride that made her heart jump.

"You aren't supposed to know that I'm a virgin," she pointed out when he stopped just an arm's length away.

He let out a nasty word and smiled mockingly, waiting to see what she'd say.

She ignored the bad language, refusing to rise to the bait. She grinned at him instead.

That disconcerted him, apparently. He pushed his hat over his jet black hair and stared at her. He had Lakota blood two generations back. He could speak that language as fluently as French and German. He took classes from far-flung colleges on the internet. He was a great student; everything fascinated him.

His bold gaze roamed down her slender body in the neat, fairly loose jeans and soft yellow V-neck sweater she wore. She had short dark hair, very wavy, and emerald green eyes. She wasn't pretty, but her eyes and her soft bow mouth were. Her figure drew far more attention than she was comfortable with, especially from Mack.

"Viv's would-be boyfriend got the Henry girl pregnant last year," he said abruptly.

Her gasp made his eye narrow.

"You didn't have a clue, did you?" he mused. "You and Viv are just alike."

"I beg your pardon?"

"Pitiful taste in men," he added.

She gave him a look of mock indignation. "And I was just going to say how very sexy you were!"

"Pull the other one," he said with amazing coldness.

Her eyebrows arched. "My, we're touchy today!"

He glared at her. "What do you want? If it's an invitation to supper for Viv's heartthrob, he can't come unless you do."

That surprised her. He usually couldn't wait to shoo her off the place. "Three's a crowd?" she murmured dryly.

"Four. I live here," he pointed out. He frowned. "More than four," he continued. "Vivian, Bob and Charles and me. You and the would-be Romeo make six."

"That's splitting hairs," she pointed out. "You're suggesting that I come over to make the numbers even, of course," she chided.

His face didn't betray any emotion at all. "Wear a dress."

That really surprised her. "Listen, you aren't planning any pagan sacrificial rites at a volcano?" she asked, rubbing in the virgin sacrifice notion.

"Nothing low-cut," he persisted, his gaze narrow and faintly sensual on her pert breasts under the sweater.

"Stop staring at my breasts!" she burst out indignantly, crossing her arms over them.

"Wear a bra," he returned imperturbably.

Her face flamed. "I am wearing a bra!"

His black eye twinkled. "Wear a thicker bra."

She glared at him. "I don't know what's gotten into you!"

He lifted an eyebrow and his eye slid down her body appraisingly. "Lust," he said matter-of-factly. "I haven't had sex for so long, I'm not even sure I remember how."

She couldn't handle a remark like that. They shared such intimate memories for two old sparring partners. She couldn't fence with him verbally when he let his voice drop like that, an octave lower than normal. It was so sensuous that it made her knees weak. So was the memory of that one unforgettable night they'd shared. Warning signals shot to her brain.

He sighed theatrically when her cheeks turned pink. "So much for all that sophistication you pretend to have," he mused.

She cleared her throat. "I wish you wouldn't say things like that to me," she said worriedly.

"Maybe I shouldn't," he conceded. His hand went out and pushed a strand of hair behind her small ear. She jerked at his touch, and he moved a step closer. "I'd never hurt you, Natalie," he said quietly.

She managed a nervous smile. "I'd like that in writing," she said, trying to move away without making it look as if she was intimidated, even though she was.

The barn door was at her back, though, and there was no way to escape. He knew that. She could see it on his face as he slid one long arm beside her head and rested his hand by her ear.

Her heart jumped into her throat. She looked at him with all her darkest fears reflecting in her emerald eyes.

He searched them without speaking for a long moment. "Carl would never have made you happy," he said suddenly. "His people had money. They wouldn't have let him marry an orphan with no assets."

Her eyes darkened with pain. "You don't know that."

"I *do* know that," he returned sharply. "They said as much at the funeral, when someone mentioned how devastated you were. You couldn't even go to the funeral."

She remembered that. She remembered, too, that Mack had come looking for her in her aunt's home the night Carl had died. Her aunt was out of town shopping over the weekend, and she'd been all alone. Mack found her in a very sexy pink satin gown and robe, crying her eyes out. He'd picked her up, carried her to the old easy chair by the bed, and he'd held her in his lap until she couldn't cry anymore. After a close call that still made her knees weak, even in memory, he'd stayed with her that whole long, anguished night, sitting in the chair beside the bed, watching her sleep. It was a mark of the respect he commanded in the community that even Natalie's aunt hadn't said a word about his presence there when she found out about it on her return. Natalie inspired defense in the strangest quarters. Her tenderness made even the toughest people oddly vulnerable around her.

"You held me," she recalled softly.

"Yes." His face seemed to tauten as he looked at her. "I held you."

She felt him so close that it was like being lifted and carried away. Little twinges of pleasure shot through her when she met his searching gaze. The sensation was so intense as they looked at each other, she could almost feel his bare chest against hers. Five years had passed since that night, but it seemed like yesterday. It was like stepping into space.

"And when I lost my sight," he continued, "you held me."

She bit her lower lip hard to stop it from trembling. "I wasn't the only one who tried to nurse you," she recalled.

"Vivian cried when I snapped at her, and the boys hid

under their beds. You didn't. You snapped right back. You made me want to go on living."

She lowered her eyes to his chest. He had the build of a rodeo cowboy, broad-shouldered and lean-hipped. His checked shirt was open at the neck, and she saw the thick, curling hair that covered him from his chest to his belt. He wasn't a hairy man, but he was devastating without a shirt. She'd seen him like that more often than she was comfortable remembering. He was beautiful under his clothing, like a sculpture she'd seen in pictures of museum exhibits. She even knew how he felt, there where the hair was thick over his breastbone....

"You were kind to me when Carl died," she returned.

There was a new tension between them after she spoke. She sensed a steely anger in him.

"Since we're on the subject of your poor taste in men, what do you see in that Markham man?" he asked curtly. "He's as prissy as someone's maiden aunt, and in a stand-up fight, he'd go out in seconds."

She lifted her face. "Dave's my friend," she said shortly. "And certainly he's no worse than that refugee from the witch trials that you go around with!"

His firm lips pursed. "Glenna's not a witch."

"She's not a saint, either," she assured him. "And if you're going without sex, I can guarantee it's not *her* fault!" she added without thinking. But once the words left her stupid mouth, and she saw the unholy light in the eye that wasn't covered by the black eye patch, she could have bitten her tongue in two.

"Will you two keep your voices down?" young Bob Killain groaned, as he peered around the barn door to stare at them. "If Sadie Marshall hears you all the way in the kitchen, she'll tell everybody in her Sunday school class that you two are living in sin out here!" he exclaimed, naming the Killain housekeeper.

Natalie looked at him indignantly, both hands on her slender hips. "It's Glenna you'd better worry about, if he gets involved with her!" she assured Mack's youngest brother, a redhead. "Her name is written in so many phone booths, she could qualify as a tourist attraction!"

Mack tried not to laugh, but he couldn't help himself. He pulled his hat across his eyes at a slant and turned into the barn. "Oh, hell, I'm going to work. Haven't you got something to do?" he asked his brother.

Bob cleared his throat and tried desperately not to laugh, either. "I'm just going over to Mary Burns's house to help her with her trigonometry."

"Carry protection," Mack's droll voice came back to him.

Bob turned as red as his hair. "Well, we don't all stand around talking about sex all day!" he muttered.

"No," Natalie agreed facetiously. She looked at Mack deliberately. "Some of us go looking for names in phone booths and call them up for dates!"

"Can it, Nat," Mack said as he opened a stall and led a horse out. He proceeded to saddle it, ignoring Natalie and Bob.

"I'll be back by midnight!" Bob called, seeing an opportunity to escape.

"You heard what I said," Mack called after him.

Bob made an indignant sound and stomped out of the barn.

"He's just sixteen, Mack," she said, regaining her composure enough to join him as he fastened the cinch tight.

He glanced at her. "You were just seventeen when you were dating the football hero," he reminded her.

She stared at him curiously. "Yes, but except for a few very chaste kisses, there wasn't much going on."

He gave her an amused glance before he went back to his chore. He tested the cinch, found it properly tight and adjusted the stirrups.

"What does that look mean?" Natalie asked curiously.

"I had a long talk with him when I found out you'd accepted a date for the Christmas dance from him."

Her lips fell open. "You what?"

He slid a booted foot into the stirrup and vaulted into the saddle with easy grace. He leaned over the pommel and looked at Natalie. "I told him that if he seduced you, he'd have me to contend with. I told his parents the same thing."

She was horrified. She could hardly breathe. "Of all the interfering, presumptuous—"

"You were raised in an orphanage by spinster women, and then you lived with your aunt, who couldn't even talk about kissing without going into a swoon," he said, and he didn't smile. "You knew nothing about men or sex or hormones. Someone had to protect you, and there wasn't anybody else to do it."

"You had no right!"

His dark eye slid over her with something like possession. "I had more right than I'll ever tell you," he said quietly. "And that's all I'll say on the subject."

He turned the horse, deaf to her fury.

"Mack!" she raged.

He paused and looked at her. "Tell Viv she can have her friend over for supper Saturday night, on the condition that you come, too."

"I don't want to come!"

He hesitated for a minute, then turned the horse and came back to her. "You and I will always disagree on some things," he said. "But we're closer than you realize. I know you," he added in a tone that made her knees wobble. "And you know me."

She couldn't fight the emotions that made her more confused, more stirred, than she'd ever been before. She looked at him with eyes that betrayed her longing for him.

He drew in a long, slow breath, and his face seemed to lose its rigor. "I won't apologize for looking out for you."

"I'm not part of your family, Mack," she said huskily. "You can tell Viv and Bob and Charles what to do, but you can't tell me!"

He studied her angry face and smiled gently, in a way that he rarely smiled at anyone. "Oh, I'm not telling, baby," he replied softly.

"And don't call me baby, either!"

"All that fire and fury," he mused, watching her. "What a waste."

She was so confused that she could hardly think. "I don't understand you at all today!"

"No," he agreed, the smile fading. He looked straight into her eyes, unblinking. "You work hard at it, too."

He turned the horse, and this time he kept riding.

She wanted to throw things. She couldn't believe that he'd said such things to her, that he'd come so close in the barn that for an instant she'd thought that he meant to kiss her. And not a chaste brush on the cheek, like at Christmas parties under the mistletoe, either. But a kiss like ones she'd seen in movies, where the hero crushed the heroine against the length of his body and put his mouth so hard against hers that she couldn't breathe at all.

She tried to picture Mack's hard, beautiful mouth on her lips, and she shivered. It was bad enough remembering how it had been that rainy night that Carl had died, when one thin strap on her nightgown had slid down her arm and…

Oh, no, she told herself firmly. Oh, no, none of that! She wasn't going to start daydreaming about Mack again. She'd gone down that road once already, and the consequences had been horrible.

She went back into the house to tell Viv the bad news.

"But that's wonderful!" her friend exclaimed, all smiles instead of tears. "You'll come, won't you?"

"He's trying to manipulate me," Natalie said irritably. "I won't let him do that!"

"But if you don't come, Whit can't come," came the miserable reply. "You just have to, Nat, if I'm your friend at all."

Natalie grumbled, but in the end, she gave in.

Vivian hugged her tight. "I knew you would," she said happily. "I can hardly wait until Saturday! You'll like him, and so will Mack. He's such a sweet guy."

Natalie hesitated, but if she didn't tell her friend, Mack certainly would, and less kindly. "Viv, did you know that he got a girl in trouble?"

"Well, yes," she said. "But it was her fault," she pointed out. "She chased him and then when they did it, she wouldn't let him use anything. He told me."

Natalie blushed for the second time that day, terribly uncomfortable around people who seemed content to speak about the most embarrassing things openly.

"Sorry," Viv said with a kind smile. "You're very unworldly, you know."

"That's just what your brother said," Natalie muttered.

Vivian studied her curiously for a long time. "He may not like the idea of Whit, but he likes the idea of your friend Dave Markham even less," she confided.

"He's one to criticize *my* social life, while he runs around with the likes of Glenna the Bimbo. Stop laughing, it isn't funny!"

Vivian cleared her throat. "Sorry. But she's really very nice," she told her friend. "She just likes men."

"One after the other," Natalie agreed, "and even simultaneously, from what people say. Your brother is going to catch some god-awful disease and it will be his own fault. Why are you still laughing?"

"You're jealous," Vivian said.

"That'll be the day!" Natalie said harshly. "I'm going home."

"He's only gone out with her twice," her best friend continued, unabashed, "and he didn't even have lipstick on his shirt when he came home. They just went to a movie together."

"I'm sure your brother didn't get to his present age without learning how to get around lipstick stains," she said belligerently.

"The ladies seem to like him," Vivian said.

"Until he speaks and ruins his image," Natalie added. "His idea of diplomacy is a gun and a smile. If Glenna likes him, it's only because she's taped his mouth shut!"

Vivian laughed helplessly. "I guess that could be true," she confessed. "But he is a refreshing change from all the politically correct people who are afraid to open their mouths at all."

"I suppose so."

Vivian stood up. "Natalie?"

"What?"

She stared at her friend quietly. "You're still in love with him, aren't you?"

Natalie turned quickly toward the door. She wasn't going to answer. "I really have got to go. I have exams next week, and I'd better hit the books hard. It wouldn't do to flub my exams and not graduate," she added.

Vivian wanted to tell Natalie that she had a pretty good idea of what had happened between her and Mack so long ago, but it would embarrass Natalie if she came right out with it. Her friend was so repressed.

"I don't know what happened," she lied, "but you have to remember, you were just seventeen. He was twenty-three."

Natalie turned, her face pale and shocked. "He… told you?"

"He didn't tell me anything," Vivian said softly and honestly. She hadn't needed to be told. Her brother and her best friend had given it away themselves without a word. She smiled. "But you walked around in a constant state of misery and wouldn't come near the place when he was home. He wouldn't be at home if he knew you were coming over to see me. I figured he'd probably said something really harsh and you'd had a terrible fight."

Natalie's face closed up. "The past is best left buried," she said curtly.

"I'm not prying. I'm just making an observation."

"I'll come Saturday night, but only because he won't let Whit come if I don't," Natalie said a little stiffly.

"I'll never mention it again," Vivian said, and Natalie knew what she meant. "I'm sorry. I didn't mean to dredge up something painful."

"No harm done. I'd long since forgotten." The lie slid glibly from her tongue, and she smiled one last time at Vivian before she went out the door. Pretending it didn't matter was the hardest thing she'd done in years.

Chapter Two

Natalie sat in the elementary-school classroom the next morning, bleary-eyed from having been up so late the night before studying for her final exams. It was imperative that she read over her notes in all her classes every night so that when the exam schedule was posted, she'd be ready. She'd barely had time to think, and she didn't want to. She never wanted to remember again how it had been that night when she was seventeen and Mack had held her in the darkness.

Mrs. Ringgold's gentle voice, reminding her that it was time to start handwriting practice, brought her to the present. She apologized and organized the class into small groups around the two large class tables. Mrs. Ringgold took one and she the other as they guided the children through the cursive alphabet, taking time to study each effort and offer praise and corrections where they were necessary.

It was during lunch that she met Dave Markham in the line.

"You look smug today," he said with a smile. He was tall and slender, but not in the same way that Mack was. Dave was an intellectual who liked classical music and literature. He couldn't ride or rope and he knew next to nothing about agriculture. But he was sweet, and at least he was someone Natalie could date without having to worry about fighting him off after dessert.

"Mrs. Ringgold says I'm doing great in the classroom," she advised. "Professor Bailey comes to observe me tomorrow. Then, next week, finals." She made a mock shiver.

"You'll pass," he said, smiling. "Everybody's terrified of exams, but if you read your notes once a day, you won't have any trouble with them."

"I wish I *could* read my notes," she confided in a low tone. "If Professor Bailey could flunk me on handwriting, I'd already be out on my ear."

"And you're teaching children how to write?" Dave asked in mock horror.

She glared at him. "Listen, I can tell people how to do things I can't do. It's all a matter of using authority in your voice."

"You do that pretty well," he had to admit. "I hear you had a good tutor."

"What?"

"McKinzey Killain," he offered.

"Mack," she corrected. "Nobody calls him McKinzey."

"Everybody calls him Mr. Killain, except you," he corrected. "And from what I hear, most people around here try not to call him at all."

"He's not so bad," she said. "He just has a little problem with diplomacy."

"Yes. He doesn't know what it is."

"In his tax bracket, you don't have to." She chuckled. "Are you really going to eat liver and onions?" she asked, glancing at his plate and making a face.

"Organ meats are healthy. Lots healthier than that," he returned, making a face at her taco. "Your stomach will dissolve from jalapeño peppers."

"My stomach is made of cast iron, thanks."

"How about a movie Saturday night?" he asked. "That new science fiction movie is on at the Grand."

"I'd love to…oh, I'm sorry, I can't," she corrected, grimacing. "I promised Vivian I'd come to supper that night."

"Is that a regular thing?" he wanted to know.

"Only when Vivian wants to bring a special man home," she said with a rueful smile. "Mack says if I don't come, her boyfriend can't come."

He gave her an odd look. "Why?"

She hesitated with her tray, looking for a place to sit. "Why? I don't know. He just made it a condition. Maybe he thought I wouldn't show up and he could put Viv off. He doesn't like the boy at all."

"Oh, I see."

"Where did all these people come from?" she asked, curious because there were hardly any seats vacant at the teachers' table.

"Visiting committee from the board of education.

They're here to study the space problem," he added amusedly.

"They should be able to see that there isn't any space, especially now."

"We're hoping they may agree to budget an addition for us, so that we can get rid of the trailers we're presently using for classrooms."

"I wonder if we'll get it."

He shrugged. "Anybody's guess. Every time they talk about adding to the millage rate, there's a groundswell of protest from property owners who don't have children."

"I remember."

He found them two seats at the very end of the teachers' table and they sat down to the meal. She smiled at the visiting committee and spent the rest of her lunch hour discussing the new playground equipment the board of education had already promised them. She was grateful to have something to think about other than Mack Killain.

Natalie's little house was just on the outskirts of the Killain ranch, and she often complained that her yard was an afterthought. There was so little grass that she could use a Weed Eater for her yard work. One thing she did have was a fenced-in back yard with climbing roses everywhere. She loved to sit on the tiny patio and watch birds come and go at the small bird feeders hanging from every limb of her one tree—a tall cottonwood. Beyond her boundary, she could catch occasional glimpses of the red-coated Red Angus purebred cattle the Killains raised. The view outside was wonderful.

The view inside was another story. The kitchen had a stove and a refrigerator and a sink, not much else. The living-room-dining-room combination had a sofa and an easy chair—both second-hand—and a used Persian rug with holes. The bedroom had a single bed and a dresser, an old armchair and a straight chair. The porches were small and needed general repair. As homes went, it was hardly the American dream. But to Natalie, whose life had been spent in an orphanage, it was luxury to have her own space. Until her junior year, when she moved into her aunt's house to become a companion/nurse/housekeeper for the two years until her aunt died suddenly, she'd never been by herself much.

She had one framed portrait of her parents and another of Vivian and Mack and Bob and Charles—a group shot of the four Killains that she'd taken herself at a barbecue Vivian had invited her to on the ranch. She picked up the picture frame and stared hard at the tallest man in the group. He was glaring at the camera, and she recalled amusedly that he'd been so busy giving her instructions on how to take the picture that she'd caught him with his mouth open.

He was like that everywhere. He knew how to do a lot of things very well, and he wasn't shy with his advice. He'd walked right into the kitchen of a restaurant one memorable day and taught the haughty French chef how to make a proper barbecue sauce. Fortunately, the two of them had gone into the back alley before anything got broken.

She put the picture down and went to make herself a sandwich. Mack said she didn't eat right, and she had to agree. She could cook, but it seemed such a waste of time to go to all that trouble just for herself. Besides, she was usually so tired when she got home from her student teaching that she didn't have the energy to prepare a meal.

Ham, lettuce, cheese and mayonnaise on bread. All the essentials, she thought. She approved her latest effort before she ate it. Not bad for a single woman.

She turned on the small color television the Killains had given her last Christmas—a luxury she'd protested, for all the good it did her. The news was on, and as usual, it was all bad. She turned on an afternoon cartoon show instead. Marvin the Martian was much better company than anything going on in Washington, D.C.

When she finished her sandwich, she kicked off her shoes and curled up on the sofa with a cup of black coffee. There was nothing like having a real home, she thought, smiling as her eyes danced around the room. And today was Friday. She'd traded days with another checkout girl, so she had Friday and Saturday off from the grocery store she worked at part-time. The market was open on Sunday, but with a skeleton crew, and Natalie wasn't scheduled for that day, either. It would be a dream of a weekend if she didn't have to dress up and go over to the Killains' for supper the following night. She hoped Vivian wasn't serious about the young man she'd invited over. When Mack didn't approve of people, they didn't usually come back.

Natalie only had one good dress, a black crepe one with spaghetti straps, that fell in a straight line to her

ankles. There was a lacy shawl she'd bought to go with
it, and a plain little pair of sling-back pumps for her
small feet. She used more makeup than usual and grimaced at her reflection. She still didn't look her age.
She could have passed for eighteen.

She got into her small used car and drove to the
Killain ranch, approving the new paint job Mack's
men had given the fences around the sprawling Victorian home with its exquisite gingerbread woodwork
and latticed porches. It could have slept ten visitors
comfortably even before Mack added another wing to
accommodate his young brothers' desire for privacy.
There was a matching garage out back where Mack
kept his Lincoln and the big double-cabbed Dodge Ram
truck he used on the ranch. There was a modern barn
where the tractors and combine and other ranch equipment were kept, and an even bigger stable where Mack
lodged his prize bulls. A separate stable housed the saddle horses. There was a tennis court, which was rarely
used, and an Olympic-size indoor swimming pool and
conservatory. The conservatory was Natalie's favorite
place when she visited. Mack grew many species of or-
chids there, and Natalie loved them as much as he did.

She expected Vivian to meet her at the foot of the
steps, but Mack came himself. He was wearing a dark
suit and he looked elegant and perturbed with his hands
deep in his pockets as he waited for her to mount the
staircase.

"Don't you have another dress?" he asked irritably.
"Every time you come over here, you wear that one."

She lifted her chin haughtily. "I work six days a week

to put myself through college, pay for gas and utilities and groceries. What's left over wouldn't buy a new piece of material for a mouse suit."

"Excuses, excuses," he murmured. His eyes narrowed on the low cleavage. "And I still don't like that neckline," he said shortly. "It shows too much of your breasts."

She threw up both hands, almost flinging her small evening bag against the ceiling. "Listen, what's this hang-up you have about my breasts lately?" she demanded.

He was frowning as he stared at her bodice. "You're flaunting them."

"I am *not!*"

"It's all right to do it around me," he continued flatly, "but I don't want Vivian's sex maniac boyfriend to start drooling over you at my supper table."

"I don't attract that sort of attention," she muttered.

"With a body like that, you'd attract attention from a dead man," he said shortly. "Just looking at you makes me ache."

She didn't have a comeback. He'd taken the sense right out of her head with that typically blunt remark.

"No sassy reply?" he taunted.

Her eyes ran over him in the becoming suit. "You don't look like a man with an ache."

"How would you know?" he asked. "You don't even understand what an ache is."

She frowned. "You're very difficult to understand."

"It wouldn't take an experienced woman five seconds to know what I meant," he told her. "You're not only repressed, you're blind."

Both eyebrows lifted. "I beg your pardon?"

He let out an angry breath. "Oh, hell, forget it." He turned on his heel. "Are you coming in or not?"

"You're testy as all get out tonight," she murmured dryly, following him. "What's wrong with you? Can't Glenna get rid of that...ache?"

He stopped and she cannoned into his back, almost tripping in the process. He spun around and caught her by the waist, jerking her right against him. He held her there, and one lean hand went to the small of her back and ground her hips deliberately into his.

He held her gaze while his body tautened and swelled blatantly against her stomach. "Glenna can't get rid of it because she doesn't cause it," he said with undeniable mockery.

"McKinzey Donald Killain!" she gasped, outraged.

"Are you shocked?" he asked quietly.

She tried to move back, but his hand contracted and he groaned sharply, so she stood very still in the sensual embrace.

"Does it hurt you?" she whispered huskily.

His breathing was ragged. "When you move," he agreed, a ripple running through his powerful frame.

She stared at him curiously, her body relaxing into the hard curve of him as both his hands went to her hips and held her there very gently.

He returned her quiet stare with his good eye narrowed, intent, searching her face. "I've never let you feel that before," he said huskily.

She was fascinated, not only with the intimacy of their position, but also with the strange sense of belonging it gave her to know that she could arouse him so easily. It didn't embarrass her, really. She felt possessive about him. She always had.

"Do you have this effect on Markham?" he asked, and he didn't smile.

"Dave is my friend," she replied. "It would never occur to him to hold me...like this."

"Would you let him, if he wanted to?"

She thought about that for a few seconds and she frowned again, worried. "Well, no," she confessed reluctantly.

"Why not?"

Her eyes searched his good one. "It would be...repulsive with him."

She felt his heartbeat skip. "Would it?" he asked. "Why?"

"It just would."

His lean hands spread blatantly over her hips and drew her completely against him. He shivered a little at the pleasure it sent careening through his body. His teeth ground together, and he closed his eyes as he bent to rest his forehead against hers.

Natalie felt her breasts go hard at the tips. Her arms were under his now, her hands flat against the rough fabric of his jacket. Her small evening bag lay somewhere on the wooden floor of the porch, completely forgotten. She felt, saw, heard nothing except Mack. Her whole body pulsated with delight at the feel of him so close to her. She could feel his minty breath on her lips while the sounds of the night dimmed to insignificance in her ears.

"Natalie," he whispered huskily, and his hands began to move her hips in a slow, sweet rotation against him. He groaned harshly.

She shivered with the pleasure. Her body rippled with delicious, dangerous sensations.

"Mack?" she whispered, lifting involuntarily toward him in a sensuous little rhythm.

His hands slid to her hips, her waist and blatantly over the thin fabric that covered her breasts in the lacy little long-line bra she wore under the dress. As she met his searching gaze, his hands went inside the deep V neckline and down over the silky skin of her breasts. She caught her breath at the bold caress.

"This," he said softly, "is a very bad idea."

"Of course it is," she agreed unsteadily. Her body was showing a will of its own, lifting and shifting to tease his lean hands closer to the hard tips that wanted so desperately to be caressed.

"Don't," he murmured quietly.

"Mack?"

His forehead moved softly against hers as he tried to catch his breath. "If I touch you the way you want me to, I won't be able to stop. There are four people right inside the house, and three of them would pass out if they saw us like this."

"Do you really think they would?" she asked in a breathless tone.

His thumbs edged down toward the tiny hardnesses inside the long-line and she whimpered.

"Do you want me to touch them?" he whispered at her lips.

"Yes!" she choked.

"It won't be enough," he murmured.

"It will. It will!"

"Not nearly enough," he continued. His mouth touched her eyelids and closed them while his thumbs worked their way lazily inside the lacy cups. "You have the prettiest little breasts, Natalie," he whispered as he traced the soft skin tenderly. "I'd give almost anything right now to put my mouth over them and suckle you."

She cried out, shocked at the delicious images the words produced in her mind.

"I ache," he breathed into her lips, even as his thumbs finally, *finally,* found her and pressed hard against the little peaks.

She sobbed, pushing her face against him as she shivered in the throes of unbelievable sensation.

He made a rough sound and maneuvered her closer to the dark end of the porch, away from the door and windows. His hands cupped her, caressed her insistently while his hot mouth pressed hungrily against her throat just where her pulse throbbed.

"Yes," she choked, lifting even closer into his hands. "Yes, Mack, yes, please, oh, please!"

"You crazy little fool!" he moaned.

Seconds later, he'd unzipped the dress and his mouth was where his hands had been, hot and feverish in its urgency as it sought the soft skin of her breast and finally forced its way into the lacy cup to fasten hungrily on the hard peak.

Her nails bit into the nape of his neck like tiny blades, pulling his mouth even closer as she fed on the exquisite demands it made on her innocence. She lifted against him rhythmically while he suckled her in the warm darkness, his arms contracted to bring her as close as he could get her.

The suddenness with which he pushed her away left her staggering, so weak that she could hardly stand. He'd moved away from her to lean against the wall, where one big hand pressed hard to support him. He was breathing as if he'd been running a race, and she could see the shudders that ran through his tall body. She didn't know what to say or what to do. She was overwhelmed. She couldn't even move to pull up her dress.

After a few seconds he took a harsh, deep breath and turned to look at her. She hadn't moved a step since he'd dragged himself away from her. He smiled ruefully. She was, he thought, painfully innocent.

"Here," he said in a husky tone, moving to pull up her dress and fasten it. "You can't go inside like that."

She looked at him like a curious little cat while he dressed her, as if it was a matter of course to do it.

"Natalie," he laughed harshly, "you have to stop looking like an accident victim."

"Do you do that with her?" she asked, and her pale green eyes flashed.

He mumbled a curse as he fastened the hook at the top of the dress. "Glenna is none of your business."

"Oh, I see. You can ask me about my social life, and I can't ask you about yours, is that how it works?"

He frowned as he held her by both shoulders and looked at her. "Glenna isn't a fuzzy little peach ripening on a tree limb," he muttered. "She's a grown, sophisticated woman who doesn't equate a good time with a wedding ring."

"Mack!" Natalie exclaimed furiously.

"I don't even have to look at you to know you're blushing," he said heavily. "Twenty-two, and you haven't really aged a day since I held you in your bedroom the night of Carl's wreck."

"You looked at me," she whispered.

His hands tightened. "Lucky you, that looking was all I did."

Her eyes searched his face in the dim light. "You wanted me," she said with sudden realization.

"Yes, I did," he confessed. "But you were seventeen."

"And now I'm twenty-two."

He sighed and smiled. "There isn't much difference," he murmured. "And there still isn't any future in it."

"Not for a man who just wants to have a little fun occasionally," she said sarcastically.

"You certainly don't fall into that category," he agreed. "I've got two brothers and a sister to take care of here. There isn't room for a wife."

"Okay. Just forget that I proposed."

His fingers trailed gently across her soft, swollen mouth. "Besides the responsibilities, I'm not ready to settle down. Not for years yet."

"I'm sure they'll take back the engagement ring if I ask them nicely."

He blinked. "Are we having the same conversation?"

"I only bought you a cheap engagement ring, anyway," she continued outrageously. "It probably wouldn't have fit, so don't worry about it."

He started laughing. He couldn't help it. She really was a pain in the neck. "Damn it, Natalie!" He hugged her close and hard, an affectionate hug with bare overtones of unsatisfied lust.

She hugged him back with a long sigh, and her eyes closed. "I think it's like baby ducks," she murmured absently.

"What is?"

"Imprinting. They follow the first moving thing they see when they hatch, assuming it's their mother. Maybe it's like that with men and women. You were the first man I was ever barely intimate with, so I've imprinted on you."

His heart jumped wildly and his arms tightened around her. "The world is full of men who want to get married and have kids."

"And I'll find one someday," she finished for him. "Have it your own way. But if you really want me to find someone else to fixate on, I have to tell you that dragging me into dark corners and pulling my dress half off isn't the way to go about it."

He was really laughing now, so hard that he had to let her go. "I give up," he said helplessly.

"It's too late now," she returned, going to fetch her purse from the floor. "You've said you don't want the ring."

"Let's go inside while there's still time," he replied as he moved toward the door.

"Not yet," she said quickly. She moved into a patch of light and looked into her compact mirror, taking time to replace her lipstick and fix her hair.

He watched her calmly, his gaze narrow and intense.

She put the compact in her evening bag and moved toward him. "You'd better do some quick repairs of your own," she murmured after she examined his face. "That shade of lipstick definitely doesn't suit you."

He gave her a glare, but he pulled out his handkerchief and let her remove the stains from his cheek and neck. Fortunately, the lipstick had missed his white collar or there wouldn't be any disguising it.

"Next time, don't put on six layers of it before you come over here," he advised coolly.

"Next time, keep your hands in your pockets."

He chuckled dryly. "Fat chance, with your dress showing off your breasts like that."

She unfastened her lacy shawl and draped it across her bodice and over her shoulder. She gave him a haughty glance and waited for him to open the front door.

"The next dress I buy will have a mandarin neckline, you can bet on that," she told him under her breath.

"Make sure it doesn't have buttons, then," he whispered outrageously as he stood aside to let her pass.

"Lecher," she whispered.

"Temptress," he whispered back.

She walked past him and into the living room before he could think up any more smart remarks to throw at her. She looked calm, but inside, she was rippling with tiny fears and remnants of pleasure from his touch. It occurred to her that, over the years, she'd been more intimate with him than any other man she'd ever known, but he'd never kissed her.

Thinking about that didn't help her situation, so she smiled warmly at Bob and Charles as they rose to their feet, and then at Vivian and the tall, blond man who stood up from his seat on the sofa beside her.

"Natalie, this is Whit," Vivian introduced them. Her blue eyes looked at the blond man with total possession. Whit, in turn, looked at Natalie as if he'd just discovered oil.

Oh, boy, Natalie thought miserably as she registered the gleam in Whit's blue eyes when they shook hands. He held hers for just a few seconds too long, and she grimaced. Here was a complication she hadn't counted on.

Chapter Three

It didn't help matters that Whit was a graduate of the same community college Natalie attended and had taken classes with some of the professors who taught her. Vivian had never wanted to go to college, and was unsure what she wanted to do with her life. Just recently, Mack had put his foot down and insisted that she get either a job or a degree. Vivian had been horrified, but she'd finally agreed to try a course in computer programming at the local vocational school. That was where she'd met Whit, who taught English there.

As they ate dinner, Natalie carefully maneuvered the conversation toward the vocational school, so that Vivian could join in. Vivian was livid and getting more upset by the minute. Natalie could have kicked Mack for putting her in this position. If only he'd let Vivian invite Whit over unconditionally!

"Why didn't you go to college to study computer programming?" Whit asked Vivian, and managed to make it sound condescending.

"The classes were already full when I decided to go," Vivian said with a forced smile. "Besides, I'd never have met you if I'd gone to college instead of the vocational school."

"I suppose not." He smiled at her, but his attention went immediately back to Natalie. "What grade do you plan to teach?"

"First or second," Natalie said. "And I have to leave very soon, I'm afraid. I have exams next week, so I expect to be up very late tonight studying."

"You can't even stay for dessert?" Whit asked.

"Nope...sorry."

"What a shame," Whit said.

"Yes, what a shame." Vivian echoed the words, but the tone was totally different.

"I'll walk you out to your car," Mack said before Whit could volunteer.

Whit knew when he was beaten. He smiled sheepishly and asked Vivian if she'd pour him a second cup of coffee.

It was pitch black outside. Mack held Natalie's arm on the way down the steps, but not in any affectionate way. He was all but cutting off the circulation.

"Well, that was a disaster," he said through his teeth.

"It was your disaster," she pointed out irritably. "If you hadn't insisted that I come over, too—"

"Disaster is my middle name lately," he replied with halfhearted amusement.

"He isn't a bad man," she told him. "He's just normal. He likes anything with a passable figure. Sooner or later, Viv is going to realize that he has a wandering eye, and she'll drop him. *If,*" she added forcibly, "you don't put her back up by disapproving of him. In that case, she'll probably marry him out of spite!"

He stopped at the driver's side of her car and let her arm fall. "Not if you're around, she won't."

"I won't be around. He gives me the willies," she said flatly. "If I hadn't had this shawl on, I'd have pulled the tablecloth over my head!"

"I told you not to wear anything low-cut."

"I only did that to spite you," she admitted. "Next time, I'll wear an overcoat." She dug in her evening bag for her car keys. "And I thought you said he was a boy. He isn't. He's a teacher."

"He's a boy compared to me."

"Most men are boys compared to you," she said impatiently. "If Viv used you as a yardstick, she'd never date anybody at all!"

He glared at her. "That doesn't sound very much like a compliment."

"It isn't. You expect anything male to be just like you."

"I'm successful."

"Yes, you're successful," she conceded. "But you're a social disaster! You open your mouth, and people run for the exits!"

"Is it my fault if people can't do their jobs properly?"

he shot back. "I try not to interfere unless I see people making really big mistakes," he began.

"Waitresses who can't get the coffee strong enough," she interrupted, counting on her fingers. "Bandleaders who don't conduct with enough spirit, firemen who don't hold the hoses right, police officers who forget to give turn signals when you're following them, little children whose shoelaces aren't tied properly—"

"Maybe I interfere a little," he defended himself.

"You're a walking consumer advocate group," she countered, exasperated. "If you ever get captured by an enemy force, they'll shoot themselves!"

He started to smile. "Think so?"

She threw up her hands. "I'm going home."

"Good idea. Maybe the English expert will follow suit."

"If he doesn't, you could always correct his grammar," she suggested.

"That's the spirit."

She opened the door and got into the car.

"Don't speed," he said, leaning to the open window, and he wasn't smiling. "There's more than a little fog out here. Take your time getting home, and keep your doors locked."

"Stop nursemaiding me," she muttered.

"You do it to me all the time," he pointed out.

"You don't take care of yourself," she replied quietly.

"Why should I bother, when you're so good at doing it for me?" he queried.

She was losing the battle. It did serve to keep her mind off the way he'd held her earlier, the touch of those strong hands on her bare flesh. She had to stop thinking about it.

"Keep next Friday night open," he said unexpectedly.

She frowned. "Why?"

"I thought we might take Vivian and the professor over to Billings to have dinner and see a play."

She hesitated. "I don't know…"

"What's your exam schedule?"

"One on Monday, one on Tuesday, one on Thursday and one on Friday."

"You'll be ready to cut loose by then," he said confidently. "You can afford one new dress, surely?"

"I'll buy myself some chain mail," she promised.

He grinned. It changed him, made him look younger, more approachable. It made her tingle when he looked like that.

"We'll pick you up about five."

She smiled at him. "Okay."

He moved away from the car, waiting until she started it and put it in gear before he waved and walked toward the porch. She watched him helplessly for several seconds. There had been a shift in their relationship. Part of her was terrified of it. Another part was excited.

She drove home, forcing herself not to think about it.

That night, Natalie had passionate, hot dreams of herself and Mack in a big double bed somewhere. She woke sweating and couldn't go back to sleep. She felt guilty enough to go to church. But when she got home and fixed herself a bowl of soup for lunch, she started thinking about Mack again and couldn't quit.

The rain was coming down steadily. If the temperature had been just a little lower, it might have turned to snow, even this late in the spring. Montana weather was unpredictable at best.

She got out her biology textbook and grimaced as she tried to read her notes. This was her second course on the subject, and she was uncomfortable about the upcoming exam. No matter how hard she studied, science just went right through her head. Genetics was a nightmare, and animal anatomy was a disaster. Her professor warned them that they'd better spend a lot of time in the lab, because they were going to be expected to trace blood flow through the various arteries and veins and the lymphatic system. Despite the extra hours she'd put in with her small lab study group, she was tearing her hair out trying to remember everything she'd learned over the course of the semester.

She'd been hard at it all afternoon when there was a knock at the front door. It was almost dark, and she was hungry. She'd have to find something to eat, she supposed. Halfway expecting Vivian, she went to the door barefooted, in jeans and a loose button-up green shirt with no makeup on and her hair uncombed. She opened the door and found Mack there, dressed in jeans and a yellow knit shirt, carrying a bag of food.

"Fish and chips," he announced.

"For me?" she asked, surprised.

"For us," he countered, elbowing his way in. "I came to coach you."

"You did?" She was beginning to feel like a parrot.

"For the biology exam," he continued. "Or don't you need help?"

"I'm considering around-the-clock prayer and going to class on crutches for a sympathy concession from my professor."

"I know your professor, and he wouldn't feel sorry for a dismembered kitten if it was trying to get out of his exam," he returned. "Do I get to stay?"

She laughed softly. "Sure."

He went into the kitchen and started getting down plates.

"I'll make another pot of coffee," she volunteered. She felt a little shy of him after the night before. They had such intimate memories for two old sparring partners. She glanced at him a little nervously as she went about the ritual of making coffee. "Wasn't your science fiction show on tonight?" she asked, because she knew he only watched one, and this was the night it ran.

"It's a rerun," he said smoothly. "Have you got any ketchup?"

"You're going to put ketchup on fish?" she asked in mock surprise.

"I don't eat things I can't put ketchup on," he replied.

"That lets out ice cream."

He tossed her a grin. "It's good on vanilla."

"Yuck!"

"Where's your sense of adventure?" he taunted. "You have to experience new things to become well rounded."

"I'm not eating ketchup on ice cream, whether it rounds people out or not."

"Suit yourself." He put fish and chips onto the plates, fished out two napkins and put silverware at two places on the small kitchen table.

"I gather we're eating in here," she murmured dryly.

"If we eat in the living room, you'll want to watch television," he pointed out. "And if you can find a movie you like, the studying will be over."

"Spoilsport."

"I want you to graduate. You've worked too hard, too long to slack off at the eleventh hour."

"I guess you know all about genetics?" she sighed, seating herself while the coffee finished dripping.

"I breed cattle," he reminded her. "Of course I do."

She grimaced. "I love biology. You'd think I'd be good at it."

"You're good with children," he said, smiling gently at her. "That's what matters the most."

She shrugged. "I suppose you're right." She studied his lean, dark face with its striking black eye patch. "Are you still half buried in internet college courses?"

"Yes. It's forensic archaeology this semester. Bones," he clarified. His eye twinkled. "Want to hear all about it?"

"Not over fish and chips," she said distastefully.

"Squeamish, are you?"

"Only when I'm eating," she replied. She glanced at the coffeemaker, noted that the brewing cycle was over and got up to fill two thick white mugs with black coffee. She put his in front of him and seated herself. Neither of them took cream or sugar, so there was no sense in putting them on the table.

"How's Viv?" she asked as they started on the fish.

"Fuming. Lover boy went home without asking her for another date." He gave her a curious look. "She thought he might have phoned you."

"Not a chance," she said easily. "Besides, he's not my type."

"What is? The Markham man?" That was pure venom in his deep voice.

"Dave is nice."

"Nice." He finished a bite of fish and washed it down with coffee. "Am I nice?" he persisted.

She met his teasing glance and made a face at him. "You and a den of rattlesnakes."

"That's what I thought." He munched on a chip, leaning back in his chair to give her a long, steady scrutiny. "You're the only woman I know who improves without makeup."

"It's too much work when I'm home alone. I wasn't expecting company," she added.

He smiled. "I noticed. How old is that blouse?"

"Three years," she said with a sigh, noting the faded pattern. "But it's comfortable."

His gaze lingered on it just a little too long, narrow and vaguely disturbing.

"I am wearing a bra!" she blurted.

His eyebrows lifted. "Are you really?" he asked in mock surprise.

"Don't stare."

He only smiled and finished his fish, oblivious to her glare.

"Tell me about blood groups," he said when they were on their second cup of coffee.

She did, naming them and describing which groups were compatible and which weren't.

"Not bad," he said when she was through. "Now, let's discuss recessive genes."

She hadn't realized just how much material she'd already absorbed until she started answering questions on those topics. It was only when they came to the formulae for the various combinations and the descriptions of genetic populations and gene pools that she foundered.

They went into the living room. She handed him the book. He stretched out on the sofa, slipping off his boots so that he could sprawl while she curled up in the big armchair across from him.

He read the descriptions to her, made her recite them, then formulated questions to prompt the right answers. She couldn't remember being drilled so competently on a subject before.

Then he took her lab report and had her point out the various circulation patterns of blood through the body of a lab rat the class had dissected. He drew her onto the floor with him and put the book in front of them, so that she could see the diagram and label the various organs as well as the major arteries and veins.

"How does he do this on the exams?" he asked. "Does he lay out a diagram and have you fill in the spaces?"

"No. He usually just sticks a pin in the organ or vein or artery he wants us to identify."

"Barbarian," he muttered.

She grinned. "That's what we call him when he isn't listening," she admitted. "Actually, we have a much more thorough course of study in biology than most of the surrounding colleges, because most of our students go on to medical school or into nursing. Biology is a real headache here, but none of our students ever have to take remedial courses later on."

"That says a lot for the quality of teaching."

She smiled. "So it does."

He went over the anatomy schematic with her until she knew the answers without prompting. But it was ten o'clock when she started to yawn.

"You're tired," he said. "You need a good night's sleep, so you can feel up to the exam in the morning."

"Thanks for helping me."

He shrugged. "What are neighbors for?" he asked with a chuckle. "How about a cup of hot chocolate before I go home?"

"I'll make it."

He stretched lazily on the carpet. "I was hoping you'd offer. I can't make it unless I have something you just stir into hot milk. As I recall, you can do it from scratch."

"I can," she said smugly. "Won't take a jiffy."

She got down the ingredients, mixed them, heated the milk in her used microwave oven and took two steaming mugs into the living room. He was still sprawled on the carpet, so she sprawled with him, both of them using the sofa for a backrest while they drained the warm liquid.

"Just the thing to make me sleep," she murmured drowsily. "As if I needed help!"

"Do you think you know the material now?" he asked.

"Inside out," she agreed. "Thanks."

"You'd do the same for me."

"Yes, I would."

He finished his drink and put the mug on the side table, taking hers when she emptied it and placing it beside his.

"How do you feel about the other exams?" he asked.

"That material, I do know," she told him. "It was just a question of reviewing my notes every day. But this biology was a nightmare. I never thought I'd grasp it. You have a knack for making it sound simple. It isn't."

"I use a lot of it in my breeding program," he said on a lazy stretch. He flexed his shoulders. "You can't get good beef cattle unless you breed for specific qualities."

"I guess not." Her eyes went involuntarily to his high cheekbones, his straight nose, and then down to that disciplined, very sensuous mouth. It made her tingle to look at it.

"You're staring," he murmured.

"I was just thinking," she replied absently.

"Thinking what?"

She shifted a little and lowered her eyes, smiling shyly. "I was thinking that you've never kissed me."

"That's a lie," he returned amusedly. "I kissed you last Christmas under the mistletoe."

"That was a kiss?" she drawled.

"It was the only sort of kiss I felt comfortable with,

considering that my brothers and my sister were staring at us the whole time," he said with a twinkle in his dark eye.

"I guess they'd run you ragged if you made a serious pass at someone."

"I've made several serious passes at you," he replied, and he didn't smile. "You don't seem to notice them."

She colored, and her voice felt choked. "I notice them, all right."

"You run," he corrected. His gaze fell to her soft mouth and lingered there. "I'd enjoy kissing you, Nat," he added quietly. "But a kiss is a stepping-stone. It leads down a road you may not want to walk right away."

She frowned, puzzled. "What sort of road?"

"I don't want to get married," he said simply. "And you don't want to have intercourse."

"McKinzey Killain!" she exclaimed, outraged, sitting straight up.

"There's another word for it." He grinned wickedly. "Want to hear it?"

"You say it, and I'll brain you with your own boot!" she threatened, making a grab for one of the highly polished pair lying just past his hip.

He was too quick for her. He caught her arm as it reached his abdomen and jerked her down on the other side of him, turning her under a long, powerful leg and arm with speed and grace.

She found herself flat on her back looking into his taut, somber face. She'd expected laughter, amusement, even mocking good humor. None of those emotions was evident. He was very still, and his good eye held an intimidating expression.

She could feel the powerful muscle of his thigh across hers, the pressure vaguely arousing. She could feel the hard, heavy beat of his heart against her breasts in their light covering. She could taste his breath on her mouth as he stared at her from point-blank range. She began to feel hot and swollen all over from the unfamiliar proximity. She didn't know whether to try to laugh it off or fight her way off the carpet.

He seemed to sense her internal struggle, because that long leg moved enough to pin her in a position that was just shy of intimate.

She jerked and moved her hips. He caught them with one big, lean hand and held her down hard.

"Don't do that," he said huskily, "unless you're in a reckless mood."

She stilled, curious.

He let go of her hip and slid his hand into her hair, tugging off the band that held it in place behind her ears. He smoothed her hair over the carpet and looked into her face with an expression that bordered on possession.

His fingers trailed down the side of her neck to the opening of her blouse and lingered there, tracing a deliberate pattern on the soft skin that provoked a shiver from her responsive body.

His long leg moved, just barely, and her lips parted on an audible sound as her body arched involuntarily.

His hips shifted, pinning her, and his face hardened. "Do you know what that does to me? Or are you experimenting?"

She swallowed, and her eyes searched his. "I don't know what it does," she confessed huskily. "I feel very odd."

"Odd how?"

His intent gaze made her heartbeat quicken. "I feel swollen," she whispered, as if she were telling him a secret.

His gaze dropped to her parted mouth. "Where?" he breathed. "Here?" And his hand slid under her hips and lifted her right into the blatant contours of his aroused body.

She did gasp then, but she didn't try to get away. She looked straight at him, enthralled.

"I want you," he said in a rough whisper. "And now you know what happens when I want you." His hand contracted, grinding her against him. "You'd better be sure what *you* want, before I go over the edge."

Her body seemed to dissolve under him. She made a husky little sound deep in her throat and shivered as delicious sensations rippled through her body.

He groaned. His hand moved into the thick fall of her hair and pinned her head as he bent down. "I should be shot," he ground out against her parted lips.

"Why?" she moaned, lifting her arms around his neck.

"Nat..."

The sound went into her mouth. He kissed her with a barely leashed hunger that made every secret dream of her life come true. She relaxed under him, reached up to hold him tight, moved her legs to admit the harsh downward thrust of his hips. She moaned again, a sound almost of anguish, as the kiss grew harder and slower and more insistent. He tasted of hot chocolate and pure man as he explored her soft, willing mouth. She'd been kissed, but never like this. He knew more about women than she ever expected to learn about men. She matched his hunger with enthusiasm rather than experience, and he knew immediately that she was in over her head.

He lifted his mouth, noticing with reluctant pleasure that she followed its ascent, trying to coax it back over her lips.

"No," he whispered tenderly, holding her down with a gentle arm right across her hard-tipped breasts.

"Why not?" she asked miserably. "Don't you like kissing me?"

He drew in an unsteady breath and ground his hips against hers. "Does that feel as if I like it?" he asked with black humor.

She just looked at him, a little shy but totally without understanding.

He shifted so that he was beside her on the carpet, arched across her yielding, taut body. "I don't keep anything in my wallet to use," he said bluntly. "If you want to make love, I have to go to town and buy something to keep you from getting pregnant. Does that make it any clearer?"

Her eyes seemed to widen impossibly for a few seconds. "You mean…have sex?"

"A man has sex with a one-night stand. You're not one."

She studied him quietly, with open curiosity. "I'm not?"

He traced her mouth with a lean forefinger, watching it open hungrily. "I want you very badly," he whispered. "But your conscience would beat you to death, with or without precautions."

She still hesitated. "Maybe..."

He put his finger across her lips. "Maybe not," he said with returning good humor. "I came over to teach you biology, not reproduction."

"You don't want babies," she said, and she sounded sad.

He grimaced. "I don't want them right now," he corrected. "One day, I'd like several." He traced her thin eyebrows lazily. "You haven't had much experience with men."

"I'm doing my best to learn," she murmured dryly.

His fingers trailed into her hair and speared into its softness. "I'll tell you what to do, when the time comes. This isn't it," he added only half humorously.

She eyed him mischievously. "Are you sure?" She moved deliberately and smiled as he shuddered.

He caught her hip and held her down. "I'm sure," he resigned.

"Okay." She sighed and relaxed into the carpet. "I guess I can live on dreams if I have to."

He pursed his lips. "Do you dream about me?"

"Emphatically," she confessed.

"Should I ask how you dream about me?"

"I'll spare you the blushes," she told him, and moved away so that she could sit up. She pushed back her disheveled hair.

"So they're that sort of dreams, are they?" he asked, chuckling.

"I don't suppose you dream about me," she fished.

He didn't say anything for a long moment. Finally,

he sat up and got to his feet gracefully. "I'm leaving while there's still time," he said, and he grinned at her.

"Craven coward," she muttered. "You'd never make a teacher. You have no patience with curious students."

"You've got enough curiosity for both of us," he told her. "Walk me to the door."

"If I must."

He paused with the door open and looked down at her with open possession. "One step at a time, Nat," he said softly. "Slow and easy."

She blushed at the tone and the soft insinuation.

He bent and brushed his mouth briefly against hers. "Get some sleep. I'll see you Friday."

"We're still going to Billings?"

"I wouldn't miss it for the world," he said gently. "Good night."

Frustrated and weak in her knees, she watched him stride to his car. She didn't know how it was going to work out, but she knew that there was no going back to the old easy friendship they'd once enjoyed. She wasn't sure if she was glad or not.

Chapter Four

There were plenty of nervous faces and anxious conversations when Natalie sat in the biology classroom to wait for the professor to hand out the written test questions. She'd assumed that the lab questions would require everyone to file into the lab with another sheet of paper and identify the labeled exhibits there. But the professor announced that the dissection questions were on a separate sheet included with the exam. Everybody was on edge. It was common knowledge that many people failed the finals in this subject and had to retake the course. Natalie prayed that she wouldn't. She couldn't graduate with her class if she flubbed it.

When the papers were handed out, the professor gave the go-ahead. Natalie read each question carefully before she began to fill in the tiny circles of the multiple

choice questions. As she studied the drawing of the dissected rat and noted the placement of the various marks,
she found that she remembered almost every single one.
She was certain that she was going to pass the course.
Mack had made sure of it. She almost whooped for joy
when she turned in her paper and pencil. There was
one more thing required—she had to fill out a rating
sheet for the professor and the course, a routine part of
finals. She loved the class and respected the professor,
so her answers were positive. She turned in that sheet,
too, and left the room. There were still fifteen people
huddled over their papers when she went out the door,
with only five minutes left for completion.

She almost danced to her car. One down, she thought
delightedly. Three to go. And then, graduation! She
could hardly wait to share her good news with Mack.

The week went by very quickly. Natalie was almost
certain to graduate, because she knew she did well on
her finals. The only real surprise would be her final
grade, and it would include the marks she received for
her practice teaching. She hoped her scores would be
good enough to satisfy the school where she would
begin her career next term.

When Friday rolled around, she breathed a sigh of
relief as she left the English classroom where she'd finished her final round of questions. It was like being
freed from jail, she reflected. Although she would miss
her classmates and her professors, it had been a long
four years. She was ready to go out into the world.

She hadn't heard from Mack all week. Vivian called

her Thursday night to ask if she was still planning to go out with them. She didn't sound very enthusiastic about the double date. Natalie tried to smooth it over, but she knew that her friend was jealous, and she didn't know what to do about it. She must discuss it with Mack, she decided.

She tried his cell phone, and he answered with a voice that held both terse authority and irritation.

"Mack?" she asked, surprised by the tone, which he never used with her.

"Nat?" The impatience was gone immediately. "I thought you'd have forgotten this number by now," he added in a slow, smooth tone that sounded amused. "What do you want?"

"I need to talk to you."

There was a pause. She heard him cover the mouthpiece and talk to someone in the tone she'd heard when he first answered the phone. Then his voice came back to her. "Okay. Go ahead."

"Not over the phone," she said uncomfortably.

"All right. I'll come over."

"But I'm ready to leave," she protested. "I have to drive to town to buy a dress for tonight."

There was a pause. "Good for you."

"It's your fault. You keep making fun of the only dress I've got."

"I'll pick you up in ten minutes," he said.

"I told you, I'm going—"

"I'm going with you," he said. "Ten minutes."

The line went dead. Oh, no, she thought, foreseeing disaster. He'd have the women in the clothing store standing on their heads, and before he was through, the security guards would probably carry him out in a net.

But she realized it wasn't going to be easy to thwart him. Even if she jumped in her car and left, he knew where she was going. He'd simply follow her. It might be better to humor him. After all, she didn't have to buy a dress today. She could wear the one he didn't like.

He drew up in front of the door exactly ten minutes later, pushing the passenger door open when she came out of the house and locked it.

His dark gaze traveled over her neat figure in gray slacks and a gray and white patterned knit top. He wasn't wearing chaps or work boots. She assumed he'd been instructing his men on how to work cattle instead of helping with roundup. He looked clean and unruffled. She was willing to bet his men didn't.

"How many of your men have quit since this morning?" she asked amusedly after she'd fastened her seat belt.

He gave her a quick glare before he pulled the big, double-cabbed truck out of her driveway and into the ranch road that led to the highway. "Why do you think anyone quit?"

"It's roundup," she pointed out. She leaned against the door and studied him with a wicked grin. "Somebody always quits. Usually," she added, "it's the man who thinks he knows more than you do about vaccinations and computer-chip ear tags."

He made an uncomfortable movement and gave her a piercing glance before his foot went down harder on the accelerator. She noticed his boots. Clean and nicely polished.

"Jones quit," he confessed after a minute. "But he was going to quit anyway," he added immediately. "He thinks he knows too much about computer technology to waste it on a cattle ranch."

"You corrected him about the way he programmed your computer," she guessed.

He glared at her. "He did it wrong," he burst out. "What the hell was I supposed to do, let him tangle my herd records so that I couldn't track weight-gain ratios at all?"

She chuckled softly. "I get the picture."

He took off his gray Stetson and stuck in into the hat carrier above the visor. Impatient fingers raked his thick, straight black hair. "He was lumping the calves with the other cattle," he muttered. "They have to be done separately, or the data's no use to me."

"Had he ever worked on a ranch?"

"He worked on a pig farm," he said, and looked absolutely disgusted.

She hid a smile. "I see."

"He said the sort of operation didn't matter, that he knew enough about spreadsheet programs that it wouldn't matter." He glanced at her. "He didn't know anything."

"Ah, now I remember," she teased. "You took the computer programming courses *last* semester."

"I passed with honors," he related. "Something *he* sure as hell didn't do!"

"I hope you never take a course in teaching," she said to herself.

"I heard that," he shot at her.

"Sorry."

He paused at the highway to make sure it was clear before he turned onto it. "How did exams go?"

"Much better than I expected," she said with a smile. "Thanks for helping me with the biology test."

He smiled. "I enjoyed it."

She wasn't sure how to take that, and when he glanced at her with a sensuous smile, she flushed.

"What sort of dress are you going to buy?" he asked.

She gave him a wary look. "I want a simple black one."

"Velvet's in this season," he said carelessly. "You'd look good in green velvet. Emerald green."

"I don't know…"

"I like the feel of it in my hands."

Her eyes narrowed and she glared at him. "Oh, does Glenna wear it?" she asked before she thought.

"No." He studied her for as long as he dared take his gaze off the highway. He smiled. "I like that."

"You like what?" she asked irritably.

"You're jealous."

Her heart skipped a beat. She stared out the window, searching for a defense.

"It wasn't a complaint," he said after a minute.

"I still don't want to be anyone's mistress, in case you were wondering," she said blatantly, hoping to distract him. She was jealous—she just didn't want to admit it.

He chuckled. "I'll keep that in mind."

It was a short drive. She told him where she wanted to go, and he pulled the truck into a parking space near the door of the small boutique.

"You don't have to come in, too," she protested when he joined her on the sidewalk.

"Left to your own devices, you'll come out carrying a black sack with shoulder straps. Where you go, I go," he said imperturbably. "Think of me as a fashion consultant."

She glared at him, but he didn't budge. "All right," she gave in. "But don't you start handing out advice to the saleslady! If you do, I'm leaving."

"Fair enough."

He followed her into the shop, where a young woman and an older one were browsing through dresses on a sale rack.

As Natalie headed in that direction, he caught her hand gently in his and maneuvered her to the designer dresses.

"But I can't..." she began.

He put his forefinger across her soft mouth. "Come on."

He gave her a considering look and moved hangers until he found a mid-calf-length velvet dress with cape sleeves and a discreet V neckline. He pulled it out, holding it up to Natalie's still body. "Yes," he said quietly. "The color does something for your eyes. It makes them change color."

"Why, yes, it does," an elderly saleslady said from behind him. "And that particular model is on sale, too," she added with a smile. "We ordered it for a young bride who became unexpectedly pregnant and had to bring it back."

Natalie looked at the dress and then at Mack with uncertainty in her face.

"It's okay," he murmured drolly. "Pregnancy isn't contagious."

The saleslady had to turn away quickly. The younger woman across the shop couldn't help herself and burst out laughing.

"Try it on," he coaxed. "Just for fun."

She clasped it to her chest, turned and followed the saleslady to the back of the store where the fitting rooms were located.

How Mack had judged the size so correctly, she didn't want to guess. But it was a perfect fit, and he was absolutely right about the way it changed her eyes. It made her look mysterious, seductive, even sexy. Despite her lack of conventional beauty, it gave her an air of sophistication. She looked pretty, she thought, surprised.

"Well?" he asked from outside the fitting room.

She hesitated. Oh, why not, she asked herself. She opened the stall door and walked into the shop.

Mack didn't say anything. He didn't have to. His whole face seemed to clench as he studied her seductive young body in the exquisite garment that fit her like a custom-made glove.

"Well?" she asked, echoing his former query.

His gaze went up to collide with hers. He didn't say a word. His hands were in his pockets, and he didn't remove them. He couldn't seem to stop looking at her.

"It was made for you, my dear," the saleslady said with a sigh.

"We'll take it," Mack said quietly.

"But, Mack, I'm not sure…" she began. There hadn't been a price tag on the garment, and even on sale, it might be more than her budget could stand.

"I am." He turned on his heel and followed the saleslady out of the fitting room.

Natalie looked after them wistfully. She could protest, but Mack and the saleslady had just formed a team that the Dallas Cowboys couldn't defeat. She gave in.

By the time Natalie changed into her slacks and shirt and tidied her hair with a small brush from her purse, Mack was signing a sales slip. He handed it to the saleslady along with the pen, and turned as Natalie emerged with the dress over her arm.

"Let me have it, dear, and I'll hang it for you."

Natalie gave it up, watching blankly as the saleslady put it on a hanger, draped a bag over it and tied the bag at the bottom.

"I hope you enjoy it," the saleslady said with a smile as she handed the hanger to Mack.

"Thank you," Natalie said, uncertain if she was thanking the saleslady or her determined escort.

Mack led her out of the store and put her in the truck after he'd hung her new dress on the hook in the back seat.

"Do you need shoes to go with it?" he asked.

"I have some nice black patent leather ones, and a purse to match," she said. "Mack, how could you pay for it? Everyone will think—"

His hand caught hers and curled into it hungrily. "Nobody will know you didn't buy it yourself unless you tell them," he said curtly. His head turned and he looked at her intently. "It really was made for you."

"Well…"

His fingers curled intimately into hers. "You can wear it to Billings," he said. "And when we go night-clubbing."

Her heart raced madly, as much from the caressing touch of his strong fingers as from what he said. "Are we going nightclubbing?"

"We're going lots of places," he said casually. "You don't start teaching until fall. That means, you'll have plenty of spare time. We can go on day trips and picnics, too."

Her body tingled from head to toe. She looked at the big, beautiful hand holding hers. "All four of us?" she asked, wondering if he wasn't taking this chaperone thing a little too seriously.

"You and me, Nat."

"Oh."

He turned off the highway onto a dirt track that led under an enormous pecan tree. He stopped and cut off the engine. The dark eye that met hers was somber and intent on her face.

"Are you serious about Markham?" he asked at once.

"I told you before, he's my friend."

"What sort of friend?" he persisted. "Do you kiss him?"

She frowned worriedly. "Well, no…"

"Why not?"

She sighed angrily. "Because I don't like kissing him. Mack…"

"You like kissing me," he continued quietly.

"You're making me nervous," she blurted. "I don't understand why you're asking so many questions all of a sudden."

He unfastened his seat belt and then hers before he pulled her across his body, her back to the steering wheel and her head resting on his left shoulder. He looked at her for a long moment before he spoke.

"I want to know if you have any long-range plans that involve your teaching colleague," he said finally.

"Not the sort you mean," she confessed.

His lean hand traced her shoulder and then slid down sensuously right onto her soft, firm breast. She gasped and caught his wrist, but he wouldn't budge.

"You don't have to pretend to be outraged," he said gently. "I've touched you like this before."

"You shouldn't," she whispered, flustered.

"Why not?" His hand spread in a slow, sensuous caress that made her nipples go immediately hard. "Your body likes it, even if your mind doesn't."

"My body is stupid," she muttered.

"No, it isn't. It has excellent taste in men," he mused, tongue in cheek.

"Will you be reasonable? It's broad daylight. What if someone drives down this way?" she asked, exasperated.

"We'll tell them a bee got in your blouse and I stopped to take it out," he murmured as his head lowered. "Now stop worrying about slim possibilities and kiss me."

She tried to tell him that it wasn't a good idea, but his mouth was already firmly on her soft lips before she could get a word out. He nibbled at her upper lip in a lazy, sensual rhythm that made it difficult for her to think. When his hand slid inside the blouse and under the strap of the flimsy lace bra, she stopped thinking altogether.

She heard the soft moan of the wind outside and the closer sound of her heartbeat in her ears. She curled a hand into Mack's cotton shirt and lifted herself closer to him.

He bit her lower lip gently while his fingers felt for buttons and moved them out of buttonholes before he coaxed her soft hand inside his shirt and against warm, hard muscle and thick black hair.

It brought back memories of the rainy night he'd come to sit with her after Carl was killed. He'd held her close in his arms that night, too, and he'd pulled her hands inside his shirt, against his bare chest. She remembered his sudden, frightening loss of control....

Her hand stilled against him as she drew her mouth from under his and looked at him with traces of apprehension in her drowsy eyes.

"What's wrong?" he asked.

She swallowed. "I don't want to...to make things difficult for you," she said finally.

"They're already difficult." He shifted her in his arms so that her head lay in the crook of his arm, and his hand went under her blouse and around her to unfasten the hooks on her bra.

"We shouldn't," she tried to protest.

He lifted his head and looked around for a few seconds before his gaze came back to her. "There isn't a car in sight," he said. "And I'm not planning to ravish you within sight of a major highway."

"I knew that."

"Tell me you don't want this and I'll let you go," he said bluntly, hesitating.

She wanted to. She really did. He looked impossibly arrogant with his shirt half unbuttoned and his mouth swollen from the long, hard contact with her lips. His hair was mussed by her fingers, and he looked somber and dangerous. She should tell him to let her go. But his fingers were tracing under her arm, and her traitorous body was writhing in an attempt to get his hand where she really wanted it. She could barely breathe as she twisted helplessly against him.

"That's what I thought," he said quietly, and he shifted her again, just enough to give him room to pull the blouse and bra up, baring her breasts to his intent scrutiny.

Natalie couldn't get enough breath to make a token protest. She loved letting him look at her. She loved the slow, gentle tracing of his fingertips on her delicate skin. She loved the way he looked at her, as if she were a work of art. It wasn't possible to be ashamed.

"Nothing to say?" he teased softly.

"Nothing at all," she whispered, her breath jerking

with the little bites of pleasure he gave her with his tender exploration of her breasts.

His thumb moved roughly over her nipple, and she bit her lower lip as pure delight arched her against him.

"I've never felt with anyone the things I feel with you," he breathed as his head lowered. "Some nights, I think I'll go stark raving mad from just the dreams."

She barely heard him. His mouth suddenly covered her breast, and he suckled her, hard.

The cry she made was audible. She trembled as he fed on her soft, smooth skin. It was cool in the cab of the truck, but she was burning all over. Her arms looped around his neck, and she hid her hot face in his neck as the pressure of his mouth increased until it almost made her weep with pleasure.

She pulled at his head, trying to get his mouth even closer, but he pulled back, his eye stormy as it met hers.

"Don't," he said gently. "You'll make me hurt you."

"It won't hurt me." She shivered. Her eyes were as turbulent as the emotions that were overwhelming her. "Don't stop," she whispered unsteadily.

His fingers traced the curve of her breast, and he looked down to watch her body lift up against them.

"Your skin is like silk," he said huskily. "I can't get enough of it." He bent again, his hard mouth smoothing over her in a caress that made her moan.

She arched up, totally without inhibitions, loving his warm lips on her body.

The sound of a car in the distance brought his head up reluctantly. He glanced at the highway, grimaced and helped her sit. "I thought we were alone on the planet," he murmured with a forced laugh. "I suppose it was wishful thinking. Need any help?" he asked as she fumbled behind her for catches.

"I can do it." She glanced at the car as it whizzed past. So much for isolation, she thought, and flushed when she realized how embarrassed she would have been if the car had pulled in behind them and stopped instead of going on its way.

He watched her loop her seat belt across her chest and fasten it. He did the same with his before he cranked the truck.

"A woman like you could make a man conceited," he said with a tender smile.

"It isn't my fault that I can't resist you," she pointed out. "And if you'd stop undressing me—"

"I can't do that," he interrupted. "I'd have nothing left to live for." He backed up until he could pull onto the highway. "Besides," he added with a grin, "how would you ever get any practical experience?"

"I think I may be getting too much," she replied. Her eyes slipped over him possessively, but she looked away before he noticed.

"Don't worry," he said. "I won't push you into doing something you don't really want."

"Do you think you could?"

"I know I could," he replied quietly. "But you'd hate me for it. Maybe I'd hate myself. Whatever happens, it has to be honest and aboveboard. No sneak attacks or seduction."

"I won't sleep with you," she said defensively.

"You would, but I'm not going to let it go that far between us. I've got as much responsibility as I can handle already." His face seemed to harden before her eyes. "The boys can take care of themselves, but Viv can't. She seems to get less mature by the day." He glanced at her. "And she's poisonously angry at you right now."

"Because Whit paid me too much attention, I gather," she said miserably.

"Exactly."

"But that wasn't my fault," she muttered.

"I know that. Vivian won't believe it. Have you forgotten how she was just after Carl was killed?" he added. "She never considered you his girlfriend. She swore he only dated you to get near her. I love my sister, but she has enough conceit for two women."

"Vivian is really beautiful," she pointed out. "I'm not."

He looked at her and smiled slowly. "You're worth any ten beauty queens, Nat," he said in a tone that was like being stroked with a velvet glove. "You have a big heart and you're kind. Too kind, sometimes. You can't refuse people, and they take advantage of you."

"Yes, I noticed," she said pointedly. "Just because I let you kiss me—"

"Stop while you're ahead," he cautioned with a bland look. "That was as mutual a passion as any two people ever shared. You love having my mouth on your body. You can't even hide it."

She crossed her legs and glared out the window with her arms folded. "I don't know beans about men, so I'm a pushover."

"Really? Then why won't you let the fellow teacher touch you?"

She gave him a hard glare, which he ignored. "You came along when I was at an impressionable age," she reminded him. "Remember what I said about baby ducks and imprinting?"

"You're no baby duck."

"I'm imprinted, just the same," she said angrily. "Seventeen years old, and spoiled for other men in the course of a night. You should never have come near me while I was in such a vulnerable state!"

"I couldn't leave you by yourself to grieve," he pointed out. "And you may have been vulnerable, but you didn't protest very much."

"You didn't leave me enough breath to protest with," she reminded him. "I may have been stupid about men, but you were no novice! I was outflanked and outgunned!"

"I'm sorry about Carl, but you were no match for him. He liked a more flighty sort of girl altogether, and he had no plans to marry until he finished college. You'd have broken your heart over him."

"It was my heart to break."

He stopped at a traffic light and turned to meet her angry eyes. "For an intelligent woman, you are unbelievably naive. Did you really think he took you out because he was in love with you?"

"He was," she said. "He told me he was!"

"He told his friends that he dated you because his brother bet him he couldn't get you to go out with him. There was more to it than that," he added somberly, "but I'll spare you the rest."

"How do you know what he was planning?" she demanded, outraged.

"His younger brother and Bob were good friends," he reminded her. "When Bob got wind of it, he came to me. That's why I had words with Carl and his parents before he tried anything with you."

She was devastated. She'd mourned Carl for months when she was seventeen, and now it turned out that he'd only dated her on a dare. He hadn't loved her. He'd been playing a game. She leaned her head against her window and bit back tears. She was a bigger fool than she'd realized. Why hadn't she guessed? And why hadn't Mack told her years ago?

Chapter Five

Mack saw the glitter of tears in her eyes and he grimaced. "I'm sorry," he said tersely. "I should never have told you."

She pushed back a wisp of hair and dug in her purse for a tissue so she could wipe her eyes. "You should have told me years ago," she corrected. "What an idiot I was!"

"You were naive," he said gently. "You saw what you wanted to see."

His face was grim, and she realized belatedly that he was angry. She wondered what else Carl had said to his brother, but she was leery of asking.

He glanced at her and tapped his fingers on the steering wheel. "You were seventeen and bent on putting him on a pedestal for life. It would have been a waste."

That note in his voice was almost defensive. She

turned in the seat and looked at him openly. She was seeing things she didn't want to see. "What you did... that night," she faltered. "It was deliberate."

"It was," he confessed quietly. "I wanted to give you something to think about, at least something to compare with what you'd already experienced." His jaw tensed. "I didn't realize how innocent you were until it was too late."

"Too late?"

He slowed for a turn and he looked so formidable that she didn't say another word. A tense silence lay between them for several long seconds.

"Maybe it really was like imprinting," he said heavily. "I should never have touched you. You were far too young for what happened."

She felt her face coloring. The hungry passion they'd shared today and the night at his house was almost as explosive as what they'd shared all those years ago. Even in memory, her body burned as she relived her first experience of Mack.

"Do you think I blame you?" she asked finally, but she didn't look at him.

"I blame myself. You've lived like a recluse ever since."

She leaned her face against the glass of the window and smiled. "You were a pretty hard act to follow," she said huskily.

His hands tightened on the steering wheel. "So were you." He sounded as if the words were dragged out of him, and she turned her head to encounter a stare that stopped her heart.

It was as if she could see right into his mind, and she ached at the images that flashed at her, memories they shared.

"I didn't really expect that you'd be inexperienced just because I warned your boyfriend off," he added after a minute. "I got the shock of my life when I realized that you'd never experienced even the mildest form of intimacy."

"Men always say they know, but how do they?" she asked irritably.

He forced his gaze to the road. "Because of the way you reacted," he said tersely. "A sophisticated woman gives as much as she gets, Nat," he told her bluntly. "You were wide-eyed and fascinated by everything I did, and I got in over my head long before I expected to. I dreamed about that night for years."

"If we're making confessions, so did I," she admitted without looking at him.

He grimaced. "I should have gone home before I gave in to temptation."

Her pale eyes touched his face like loving hands. She'd never known anyone like him. She didn't think there was anyone else like him. He'd colored her dreams, become her world, in the years since that one incredible night.

She didn't answer him. He glanced at her and laughed hollowly. "Which doesn't change the past or bring us any closer to a solution," he mused. "You're not liberated, and I'm a confirmed bachelor."

She toyed with her seat belt. "Are you really? I used to think that your father made you wary of marriage.

He and your mother were totally unsuited, from what everybody says."

"Everybody being my sister, Vivian," he guessed. "She doesn't remember our mother."

"Neither do you, really, do you?" she wondered aloud.

"She died and left him with four kids," he told her. "He wasn't up to raising even one. I've always thought that the pressure of it started him drinking, and then he couldn't stop."

His face hardened with the words, and she knew he was remembering the bad times he'd had with his father.

"Mack, do you really think you're like him?" she asked softly.

"They say abused kids become abusive parents," he replied without thinking, and then could have bitten his tongue right through for the slip.

She only nodded, as if she'd expected that answer. "So they say. But there are exceptions to every rule. If you were going to be abusive, Vivian and Bob and Charles would have been sitting in the school counselor's office years ago. They could have asked to go into foster care any time they wanted to."

"Vivian would never have given up shopping sprees," he pointed out.

She swiped gently at his sleeve. "Stop that. You know she loves you. So do the boys. You're the kindest human being I've ever known."

A ruddy color ran up his high cheekbones. He didn't look at her. "Flattery?"

"Fact," she countered. Her fingers smoothed over his sleeve lazily. "You're one of a kind."

He moved his shoulder abruptly. "Don't do that."

She pulled her fingers back. "Okay. Sorry." She laughed it off, but her face flushed.

"Don't get your feelings hurt," he said irritably, glancing at her. "I want you. Don't push your luck."

Her eyes widened.

"You still haven't got the least damned notion of what it does to me when you touch me, do you?" he asked impatiently. "This stoic exterior is a pose. Every time I look at you, I see you in that velvet dress, and I want to stop the truck and…" He ground his teeth together. "It's been a long dry spell. Don't make it worse."

"What about Glenna?" she chided.

He hesitated for a minute and then glanced at her with a what-the-hell sort of smile and said, "She can't fix what she didn't break."

Her eyebrows reached for the ceiling. "You don't look broken to me."

"You know what I mean. She's pretty and responsive, but she isn't you."

Her face brightened. "Poor Glenna."

"Poor Dave What's-his-name," he countered with a mocking smile. "Apparently he doesn't get any further with you than she does with me."

"Everyone says he's very handsome."

"Everyone says she's very pretty."

She shook her head and stared out the window, folding her arms. "Vivian is barely speaking to me," she said, desperate to change the subject. "I know she's jealous of the way Whit flirts with me. I just don't know how to stop him. It almost seems as if he's doing it deliberately."

"He is," he said, his expression changing. "It's an old ploy, but it's pretty effective."

"I don't understand."

He pulled up at a stop sign a few miles outside Medicine Ridge and looked at her. "He makes her think he isn't interested so that she'll work harder to attract his attention. By that time, she's so desperate that she'll do anything he wants her to do." His eye narrowed angrily. "She's rich, Nat. He isn't. He makes a good salary, for a teacher, but I had him investigated. He spends heavily at the gambling parlors."

She bit her lower lip. "Poor Viv."

"She'd be poor if she married him," he agreed. "That's why I object to him. He did get a girl in trouble, but that's not why I don't want him hanging around Viv. He's a compulsive gambler and he doesn't think he has a problem." He looked genuinely worried. "I haven't told her."

She whistled softly. "And if you do tell her…"

"She won't believe me. She'll think I'm being contrary and dig in her heels. She might marry him out of spite." He shrugged. "I'm between a rock and a hard place."

"Maybe I should encourage him," she began.

"No."

"But I could—"

"I said no," he repeated, his tone full of authority. "Let me handle it my way."

"All right," she said, giving in.

"I know what I'm doing," he told her as he pulled the truck onto the highway. "You just be ready at five."

"Okay, boss," she drawled, and grinned at his quick glare.

Natalie was on pins and needles waiting for five o'clock. She was dressed by four. She'd topped her short hair with a glittery green rhinestone hair clip that brought out the emerald of her eyes and made the green velvet dress look even more elegant. When the Lincoln pulled up in her front yard and Mack got out to meet her on the porch, she fumbled trying to lock her door.

He took her hand in his and held it tight. "Don't start getting flustered," he chided gently, looking elegant in his dinner jacket and matching slacks. The white shirt had only the hint of ruffles down the front, with its black vest and tie. He was devastating dressed up. Apparently he found her equally devastating, because his glance swept over her from the high heels to the crown of her head. He smiled.

"You look nice, too," she said shyly.

His fingers locked into hers. "I'm rather glad we aren't going to be alone tonight," he murmured dryly as they walked toward the car. "In that dress, you'd tempt a carved statue."

"I'm not taking it off for you," she told him. "You're a confirmed bachelor."

"Change my mind," he challenged.

Her heart jumped and she laughed. "That's a first."

"Tonight is a first," he pointed out as they paused

beside the passenger door. He looked at her with slow, sensuous appraisal. "Our first date, Natalie."

She colored. "So it is."

He opened the door. In the back seat, Vivian and Whit broke apart quickly, and Vivian laughed in a high-pitched tone, pushing back her short blond hair.

"Hi, Nat!" Vivian said cheerfully, sounding totally unlike the very stressed woman who'd phoned her the day before. "You look terrific."

"So do you," Natalie said, and her friend really was a knockout in pale blue silk. Whit was wearing evening clothes, like Mack, but he managed to look slouchy just the same. Vivian didn't notice. She was clinging to Whit's arm as if he was a treasure she was fearful of losing.

"I have a black velvet dress, but I wanted something easier to move around in," Vivian said.

"Velvet's very nice," Natalie agreed.

"Very expensive, too," Vivian added, as if she knew that Natalie hadn't paid for the dress.

"They do have charge accounts, even for penniless college students," Natalie pointed out in a tone she rarely used.

Vivian flushed. "Oh. Of course."

"We aren't all wealthy, Vivian," Whit added in a cooler tone. "It's nice for you, if you can pay cash for things, but we lesser mortals have to make do with time payments."

"I said I'm sorry," Vivian said tightly.

"Did you? It didn't sound very much like it," Whit said and moved away from her.

Vivian's teeth clamped shut almost audibly, and she grasped her evening bag as if she'd like to rip it apart.

"Which play are we going to see?" Natalie asked quickly, trying to recover what was left of the evening.

"Arsenic and Old Lace," Mack said. "The Billings community college drama classes are presenting it. I've heard that they are pretty good."

"Medicine Ridge College has a strong drama department of its own, doesn't it, Natalie?" Whit asked conversationally. "I took a class in dramatic arts, but I was always nervous in front of an audience."

"So was I," Natalie agreed. "It takes someone with less inhibitions than I have."

"I had the lead in my senior play," Vivian said coldly.

"And you were wonderful," Natalie said with a smile. "Even old Professor Blake raved about your portrayal of Stella."

"Stella?" Whit asked.

"In Williams's play *A Streetcar Named Desire,*" Natalie offered.

"One of my favorites," Whit said, turning to Vivian. "And you played the lead. You never told me that!"

Vivian's face lit up magically, and for the next few minutes, she regaled Whit with memories of her one stellar performance. In the front seat, Natalie and Mack exchanged sly smiles. With any luck, Natalie's inspiration could have saved the evening.

The play was hilarious, even if Natalie did find herself involuntarily comparing the performances with those of Cary Grant and Raymond Massey in the old motion picture. She chided herself for that. The actors in the play might be amateurs, but they were very good and the audience reacted to them with hysterical laughter.

Afterward, they went to a nightclub for a late supper. Natalie and Mack ordered steak and a salad, while Whit and Vivian managed to pick the most expensive dishes on the menu.

There was dancing on the small floor with a live band, a Friday night special performance, and Natalie found herself in Mack's arms as soon as she finished the last spoonful of her dessert.

"This is worth waiting all day for," he murmured in her ear as he held her close on the dance floor. "I knew this dress would feel wonderful under my hands."

She snuggled closer. "I thought Viv was going to ask how I could afford it," she said with a sigh. She closed her eyes and smiled. "You really shouldn't have paid for it, you know."

"Yes, I should have." He made a turn, and her body was pushed even closer to his. She felt his body react with stunning urgency to the brush of hers. She faltered and almost fell.

"Sorry," she said shakily.

He only laughed, the sound rueful and faintly amused as they continued across the floor. "It's an unavoidable consequence lately with you," he murmured. "Don't worry. No one will notice. We're alone here."

She glanced past his chest at the dozen or so other couples moving lazily to the music and she laughed, too. "So I see."

"Just don't do anything reckless," he said softly.

"With very little effort, we could become the scandal of the county."

She felt his lips at her forehead and smiled. "Think so?"

One lean hand was at the back of her head, teasing around her nape and her ears in a sensual exploration that made her tingle all over. "Do you remember what I told you the night of the wreck?" he asked huskily.

"You told me a lot of things," she hedged.

"I told you that, when you were old enough, I'd teach you everything you need to know about men." His hand slid to her waist and pulled her gently closer. "You're old enough, Nat."

She stiffened. "You stop that," she whispered urgently, embarrassed by his blatant capability.

"Sorry. It doesn't work that way. I'd need a cold shower, and that isn't going to happen here." His cheek brushed against hers and his lips touched just the corner of her mouth. "We could drop Vivian and the professor off at my house first," he said under his breath.

Her heart ran wild. "And then what?"

His lips traced her earlobe. "We could do what we did that night. I've spent years dreaming about how it felt."

Her knees threatened to collapse. "Mack Killain," she groaned. "Will you please stop?"

"You can't stop an avalanche with words," he whispered roughly. "You burn in me like a fever. I can't eat, sleep, think, work, because you're between me and every single thing I do."

She swallowed. "It's just an ache," she said firmly. "Once you satisfied it, where would we be?"

He drew back a little and looked into her eyes evenly. "I don't think it can be satisfied," he said through his teeth.

She stood very still, like a doe in the glare of bright headlights, looking at him.

"And you still don't know what it feels like," he said gruffly, in a tone that was just short of accusation. "You like being kissed and touched, but you don't know what desire is."

She averted her eyes. "You're the one who always pulls back," she said huskily.

His arm contracted roughly, pinning her to him. "I have to," he said impatiently. "You have no idea what it would be like if I didn't."

"I'm twenty-two," she reminded him. "Almost twenty-three. No woman reaches that age today, even in a small town, without knowing something about relationships."

"I'm talking about physical relationships. They aren't something you have and walk away from. They're addictive." He drew in a harsh breath as the music began to wind down. "They're dangerous. A little light lovemaking is one thing. What I'd do to you in a bed is something else entirely."

The tone, as much as the content, made her uneasy. She stared at him, frowning. "I don't understand."

He groaned. "I know. That's what's killing me!"

"You're not being rational," she murmured.

The hand at her waist contracted and moved her in

a rough, quick motion against the rock-solid thrust of his body. He watched her blush with malicious pleasure. "How rational does that feel to you?" he asked outrageously.

She forced her eyes to his drawn face. "It isn't rational at all. But you keep trying to save me from anything deep and intimate. It has to happen someday," she said.

His jaw tautened even more. "Maybe it does. But I told you, I'm not a marrying man. That being the case, I'd have to be out of my mind before I'd take you to bed, Natalie."

"Dave wouldn't," she taunted. "In fact, Whit wouldn't," she added, glancing at Vivian's partner, who was watching her as much as he was watching his partner.

His hand tightened on her waist until it hurt. "Don't start anything with him," he said coldly. "Vivian would never forgive you. Neither would I."

"I was just kidding."

"I'm not laughing," he told her, and his face was solemn.

"You treat me like a child half the time," she accused, on fire with new needs. She felt reckless, out of control. His body, pressed so close to hers, was making her ache. "And then you accuse me of tempting you, when you're the one with the experience."

He let her go abruptly and moved back. "You aren't old enough for me," he said flatly.

"I'm six years younger than you are, not twenty," she pointed out.

His eye narrowed, glittering at her. "What do you want from me?"

In his customary blunt way, he'd thrown the ball into her court and stood there arrogantly waiting for an answer she couldn't give.

"I want you to be my friend," she said finally, compromising with her secret desires.

"I am."

"Then where's the problem?"

"You just felt it."

"Mack!"

He caught her hand and tugged her toward their table. "What's that song—one step forward and two steps back? That's how I feel lately."

She felt churned up, frustrated, hot with desire and furious that he was playing some sort of game with her hormones. She knew she was flushed and she couldn't quite meet Vivian's eyes when they went to the table.

"Don't sit down," Whit drawled, catching Natalie by the wrist before she could be seated. "This one's mine."

He drew her on the dance floor to the chagrin of brother and sister and wrapped her tight as the slow dance began.

"If you want to keep that arm, loosen it," Natalie told Whit with barely contained rage.

He did, at once, and grinned at her. "Sorry. That's the way big brother was holding you, though. But, then, he's almost family, isn't he? Vivian says the two of you went through high school together."

"Yes, we did. We've been friends for a long time."

"She's jealous of you," he said.

"That's a hoot," she replied, laughing. "She's a beauty queen and I'm plain."

"That isn't what I mean," he corrected. "She envies you your kind heart and intelligence. She has neither."

"That's a strange way to talk about a girl you care for," she chided.

"I like Vivian a lot," he said. "But she's like so many others, self-centered and spoiled, waiting for life to serve up whatever she wants. I'll bet there hasn't been a man in years who's said no to her."

"I don't think anyone's ever said no to her," she replied with a smile. "She's pretty and sweet, whatever else she is."

He shrugged. "Pretty and rich. I guess that's enough for most men. When do you start teaching?"

"In the fall, if I passed my exams. If I don't graduate, it will be another year before I can get a teaching job around here."

"You could go farther afield," he told her. "I was surfing the internet the other night, browsing for teachers' jobs. There are lots of openings in north Texas, especially in Dallas. I always thought I'd like to live in Texas."

"I don't really want to live that far from home," she said.

"But you don't have a home, really, do you?" he asked. "Vivian said you were orphaned when you were very young."

"My mother was born here," she said. "So was her mother, and her mother's mother. I have roots."

"They can be a trap as much as a safety cushion,"

he cautioned. "Do you really want to spend the rest of your life out here in the middle of nowhere?"

"That's an odd question for someone who came here from Los Angeles," she pointed out.

He averted his gaze. "Nevada, actually," he said. "I got tired of the rat race. I wanted someplace quiet. But it's just a little too quiet here. A year of it is more than I expected to do."

"Do you like teaching?"

He made a face. "Not really. I wanted to do great things. I had all these dreams about building exotic houses and making barrels of money, but I couldn't get into architecture. They said I had no talent for it."

"That's a shame."

"So I teach," he added with a cold smile. "English, of all things."

"Viv says you're very good at it."

"It doesn't pay enough to keep me in decent suits," he said in a vicious tone. "When I think of how I used to live, how much I had, it makes me sick."

"What did you do before you were a teacher?" she asked, fishing delicately.

"I was in real estate," he said, but he didn't meet her eyes. "It was a very lucrative business."

"Couldn't you get a license here in Montana and go back into it?"

"Nobody wants to buy land in Montana these days," he muttered. "It's not exactly hot real estate."

"I suppose not."

The music ended and he escorted her to the table, where Mack and Vivian sat fuming.

Vivian got to her feet at once. "And now it's my turn," she said pertly and with a smile that didn't quite reach her eyes.

"Sure," Whit said easily, and smiled as he led her onto the dance floor.

"What was all the conversation about?" Mack wanted to know.

"I was trying to draw him out about his former profession. He said he was in real estate in Nevada," she said, with a wary glance toward Viv and Whit, who were totally involved with each other for the moment.

"And I'm the tooth fairy," Mack said absently.

Natalie laughed helplessly.

"What?" he demanded.

"I was picturing you in a pink tutu."

That eye narrowed. "You'll pay for that one."

"Okay. A white tutu."

He shook his head. "Finish your drink. We have to leave pretty soon. I have an early appointment in town tomorrow."

"Okay, boss," she drawled, and ignored his stormy expression.

As it turned out, Mack took Natalie home first and walked her to her front door.

"Try to stay out of trouble," he cautioned. "I may see you at the grocery store tomorrow."

"Sadie shops. You don't."

"I can shop if I want to," he said. He searched her bright face. "Just for the record, I wanted to take them home first."

She smiled. "Thanks."

One shoulder lifted and fell. "It isn't the right time. Not yet." He bent and brushed a soft kiss against her forehead. "This is to throw them off the track," he whispered as he stood straight again. "A little brotherly peck should do the trick."

"Yes, it should."

His gaze fell to her soft mouth for an instant. "Next time, I'll make sure I take you home last. Good night, angel."

"Good night."

He winked and walked to the car, whistling an off-key tune on the way. Natalie waved before she went into the house. She'd wanted Mack to kiss her again, but maybe he'd had enough kissing that afternoon. She hadn't. Not by a long shot. She didn't want to feel this way about Mack, but she couldn't help herself. She wondered how it would eventually work out between them, but it was too disturbing to torture herself like that. She cleaned her face, got into her gown and went to bed. And she dreamed of Mack all night long.

Chapter Six

The phone rang on the one morning during the week when Natalie could sleep late. It was Mack, and he sounded worried.

"It's Viv," he said at once, not bothering with a greeting. "I had to take her to the emergency room early this morning. She's got the flu and it's complicated with pneumonia. She refused to let me put her in the hospital, and I've got to fly out to Dallas this morning on business. My plane leaves in less than an hour and a half. The boys are off on a hunting trip. I hate to ask you, but can you come over and stay with her until I get home?"

"Of course I can," she replied. "How long are you going to be away?"

"With luck, I'll be back by midnight. If not, first thing tomorrow."

"I don't have to go in to the grocery store to work until tomorrow afternoon. I'll be glad to stay with her. Did the doctor give you prescriptions for her, and have you been to the pharmacy to pick up her medicine?"

"No," he said gruffly. "I'll have to do that—"

"I'll pick them up on my way over," she said. "You go ahead and catch your flight. I'll be there in thirty minutes if they have her prescriptions ready."

"They should be," he said. "I dropped them off before I brought her home. I'll phone and give them my credit card number, so they'll already be paid for."

"Thanks."

"Thank *you,*" he added. "She feels pretty bad, so she shouldn't give you much trouble. Oh, and there's a little complication," he said irritably. "Whit's here."

"That should cheer her up," she reminded him.

"It will, as long as you don't look at him."

She laughed. "No problem there."

"I know you don't like him, but she won't believe it. If there was anybody else I could ask, I wouldn't bother you. I just don't like the idea of leaving her alone with him, even if she does have pneumonia."

"I don't mind. Honest. You be careful."

"The plane wouldn't dare crash," he chuckled. "I've got too much work to do."

"Keep that in mind. I'll see you when you get back."

"You be careful, too," he said. "And wear your raincoat. It's already sprinkling outside."

"I'll wear mine if you wear yours."

He chuckled again. "Okay. You win. I'll be home as soon as I can."

She said goodbye and hung up, rushing to get her bag packed so that she could get over to the ranch.

She walked into Viv's bedroom with a bag of medicine, a cold soft drink that she knew her friend liked and some cough drops.

Viv looked washed out and sick, but she managed a wan smile as Natalie approached the bed. Whit was sprawled in an armchair by the bed, looking out of sorts until he saw Natalie. His eyes ran over her trim figure in jeans and a button-up gray knit sweater with a jaunty gray and green scarf.

"Don't you look cute," he said with a smile.

Viv glared at him. So did Natalie.

"Why don't you make some coffee, Whit?" Viv asked angrily. "I could do with a cup."

He got out of the chair. "My pleasure. What do you take in yours, Nat?" he asked smoothly.

She turned and looked him right in the eye. "Nobody calls me Nat except Mack," she pointed out. "It isn't a nickname I tolerate from anyone else."

His cheekbones colored briefly. "Sorry," he said with a nervous laugh. "I'll just make that coffee. Be back as soon as I can."

Viv watched him go and then turned cold eyes on her friend. "You don't have to snap at him," she said curtly. "He was only being polite."

Natalie's eyebrows went up. "Was he?"

"Mack shouldn't have called you," she said tersely. "I'd have been just fine here with Whit."

Natalie felt uncomfortable and unwelcome. "He thought you needed nursing."

"He thought I needed a chaperone, you mean," she said angrily. "And I don't! Whit would manage just fine."

"All right, then," Natalie said with a forced smile. "I'll go home. There's your medicine and some cough drops. I guess Whit can pick up anything else you need. Sorry I bothered you."

She turned and walked to the door, almost in tears.

"Oh, Nat, don't go," Viv said miserably. "I'm sorry. You came all this way and even brought my medicine and I'm being horrible. Please come back."

Natalie had the door open. "You've got Whit...."

"Come back," Viv pleaded.

Natalie closed the door and went to the armchair by the bed, but her eyes were wounded and faintly accusing as she sat.

"Listen, Whit doesn't like me," Natalie told Viv. "He's only flirting with me to make you jealous. Why can't you see that? What in the world could he see in me? I'm not pretty and I don't have any money."

"In other words, he wouldn't like me if I didn't have a wealthy background?" Viv asked pointedly.

"I said you were pretty, too," she replied. "I know you feel bad, Viv, but you're being unreasonable. We've been friends for a long time. I don't know you lately, you're so different."

Viv shifted against her pillows. "He talks about you, too, even when you aren't here."

"It isn't what you think," Natalie said, exasperated. "He's never said or done a thing out of line."

"He's very good-looking," Viv persisted.

"So are you," Natalie said. "But right now you're sick and you don't need to upset yourself like this. Mack asked me to take care of you, and that's what I'm going to do."

Viv studied her through fever-bright eyes. "Did you know that Glenna was going with him to Dallas?" she asked with undeniable venom.

Natalie forced herself not to react. "Why?" she asked carelessly.

"Beats me. I suppose she had something to do there, too. Anyway, I don't think he'll come back tonight. Do you?"

Natalie glared at her. "You really are a horror," she said through her teeth.

Viv flushed. "Yes, I guess I am," she agreed after a minute. "Mack said he wouldn't wish the boys and me on a wife. He said it wouldn't be fair to expect anyone to have to take us on, as well as him. I know Glenna wouldn't. She hates me."

"Your brother loves all three of you very much," Natalie said, disquieted by what Viv had said.

"Well, he's not my father. Bob and Charles are in their last two years of high school and then Bob wants to go into the Army. Charles wants to study law at Harvard. That will get them out of the way, and if I marry Whit, which I want to do, Mack will have the house to himself." Her voice was terse and cool. She didn't quite meet Natalie's eyes. "Would you marry him, if he asked you?"

"That won't happen," Natalie said quietly.

"Are you sure of that?"

"Yes," came the soft reply. "I'm sure. Mack's self-sufficient and he doesn't want to be tied down. He's said often enough that marriage wasn't for him. Probably he and Glenna will go on together for years," she added, aching inside but not letting it show, "since they both like being uncommitted."

"Maybe you're right." Viv studied her friend curiously. "But he's very protective of you."

Natalie averted her eyes. "Why shouldn't he be? I'm like a second sister to him."

Vivian frowned. She didn't say anything. After a few seconds, she started coughing violently. Natalie handed her some tissues and helped her sit up with a pillow held to her chest to keep the pain at bay.

"Does that help?" Natalie asked gently when the spasm passed.

"Yes. Where did you learn that?" she asked.

"At the orphanage. One of the matrons had pneumonia frequently. She taught me."

Viv dropped her eyes. Occasionally in her jealousy, she forgot how deprived Natalie's life had been until the Killains had come along. She knew how Nat felt about Mack, and she didn't understand her sudden need to hurt a woman who'd been nothing but kind to her ever since their friendship began. She was fiercely jealous that Whit seemed to prefer Natalie, which didn't help her burgeoning resentment toward her best friend. She was confused and envious and so miserable that she could hardly stand herself. She didn't know what she was going to do if Whit made a serious pass at Natalie. She was sure that she'd do something desperate, and that it would be the end of her long friendship with the other woman.

The hours dragged after that tense exchange. Natalie kept out of Vivian's bedroom as much as she could, busying herself with tidying up around the living room. Whit paused to flirt with her from time to time, but she managed to keep him away by reminding him of Viv's condition. He was getting on her nerves, and Viv was getting more unbearable by the minute.

When eight o'clock rolled around, it was all Natalie could do to keep from running for her life. Whit was still around, and for the past fifteen minutes, he'd been coming on to Natalie. She was on the verge of assault when Mack walked in unexpectedly.

He gave Natalie and Whit a speaking glance. They were standing close together and Whit was leaning over her. It looked as if he'd just broken up something, and his eye flashed angrily.

"Why don't you make another pot of coffee, Whit?" she asked quickly.

"As soon as I get back," he promised. "I need to run to the convenience store and get some cigarettes. I'm dying for a smoke."

"Okay," Natalie said.

Mack didn't say a word. With bridled fury, he watched the other man go. But when he shook off his raincoat, he smiled at Natalie as she took it and hung it on the rack for him.

"Did it rain all the way home?" she asked.

"Just about. How's Viv?"

"She's doing fine."

"Good." He caught her hand, pulled her into the study with him and closed the door. "You can sit with me while I get these papers sorted. Then we'll go up and see Viv."

"Whit won't know where we are when he comes back."

He lifted an eyebrow. "It's my house."

"Point taken." She sat in the chair across from his big desk and watched him sort through a briefcase before he sat down with several stacks of papers and began putting them into files.

As she watched his hands, she thought back to the night Carl had been killed in the wreck...

It was a stormy night, with lightning flashes illuminating everything inside and outside the house where Natalie was living with her aunt, old Mrs. Barnes. It was her seventeenth birthday, and she was spending it alone, in tears, mourning the death of the only boy she'd ever loved. His death that night in a wreck, driving home from an out-of-town weekend fishing and camping trip with a cousin was announced on the late news. The cousin lived. Carl had died instantly, because he wasn't wearing a seat belt. The official cause of the one-car accident was driving too fast for conditions in a blinding rain. The car had veered off the highway at a high speed and crashed down a hill. One of her friends from school had called, almost distraught with grief, to tell Natalie before she had to find out from the news.

Carl Barkley had been the star quarterback of their high school football team. Natalie had been his date, and the envy of the girls in the senior class, for the Christmas dance. She was to be his date for the senior prom, as well. Handsome, blond, blue-eyed Carl, who was president of the Key Club, vice president of the student council, an honor student with a facility for physics that had gained him a place at MIT after graduation. Carl, dead at eighteen. Natalie couldn't stop crying.

At times like these, she ached for a family to console her. Old Mrs. Barnes, who'd given her a home during her junior year of high school and with whom she would live while she attended the local community college, was away for the weekend. She wasn't due back until the next morning. There was Vivian Killain, of course, her best friend. But Vivian had also been a friend of Carl, and she was too upset to drive. The only fight Natalie and Vivian had ever had was over Carl, because Vivian had started dating him first. Carl had only gone out with her once before he and Natalie ended up in English class together. It had been love at first sight for both of them, but Vivian only saw it as Natalie tempting her boyfriend away. It wasn't like that at all.

The thunder shook the whole house, and it wasn't until the rumble died down that Natalie heard someone knocking on the front door. Slipping a matching robe over a thin pink satin nightgown with spaghetti straps, she went to see who it was.

A tall, lean man in a raincoat and broad-brimmed Stetson stared at her.

"Vivian said your aunt was out of town and you were alone," Mack Killain said quietly, surveying her pale, drenched face. "I'm sorry about your boyfriend."

Natalie didn't say a word. She simply lifted her arms. He picked her up with a rough sound and kicked the door shut behind him. With her wet face buried in his throat, he carried her easily down the hall to the open door that was obviously her bedroom. He kicked that door shut, too, and sat her gently on the armchair beside the bed.

He took off his raincoat, draping it over the straight chair by the window, and placed his hat over it. He was wearing work clothes, she saw through her tears. He hadn't even stopped long enough to change out of his chaps and boots and spurs. His blue-checked long-sleeve shirt was open halfway down his chest, disclosing a feathery pattern of thick, black curling hair. His broad forehead showed the hat mark. A lock of raven-black straight hair fell over the thin black elastic of the eye patch over his left eye.

He stared at Natalie for a few seconds, taking in her swollen eyes and flushed cheeks, the paleness of the rest of her oval face.

"I didn't even get to say goodbye, Mack," she managed huskily.

"Who does?" he replied. He bent and lifted her so that he could drop down into the armchair with her in his lap. He curled her into his strong, warm body and held her while she struggled through a new round of tears. She clung to him, grateful for his presence.

She'd always been a little afraid of him, although she was careful not to let it show. She'd been the one who nursed him, over the objections of the orphanage, when he was gored in the face by one of his own bulls. His sister, Vivian, was no good at all with anyone who was hurt or sick—she simply went to pieces. And his brothers, Bob and Charles, were terrified of their big brother. Natalie had known that he stood to lose his sight in both eyes instead of just one, and she'd held him tight and told him over and over again that he mustn't give up. She'd stayed out of classes for a whole week while the doctors fought to save that one eye, and she hadn't left him day or night until he was able to go home.

Even then, she'd stopped by every day to check on him, having presumed that he'd have his family standing on its ear trying to keep him in bed for the prescribed amount of time. Sure enough, the boys had walked wide around him and Vivian just left him alone. Natalie had made sure that he did what the doctor told him to. It amused and amazed his siblings that he'd let her boss him around. Killain gave orders. He didn't take them from anybody—well, except from Natalie, when it suited him.

"We were going to the senior prom together," she said huskily, wiping her eyes with the back of her hand. "This morning, I was deciding what sort of dress to wear and how I was going to fix my hair…and he's dead."

"People die, Nat," he said, his voice deep and quiet and comforting at her ear. "But I'm sorry he did."

"You didn't know him, did you?"

"I'd spoken to him a time or two," he said with deliberate carelessness.

"He was so handsome," she said with a ragged sigh. "He was smart and brave and everybody loved him."

"Of course."

She shifted into a more comfortable position on his lap, and as she did, her hand accidentally slid under the fabric of his cotton shirt, to lie half buried in thick hair. Odd, how his powerful body tensed when it happened, she thought with confusion. She was aware of other things, too. He smelled of horses and soap and leather. His breath pulsed out just above her nose, and she could smell coffee on it. Her robe was open, and the tiny straps that held her gown up had slipped in her relaxed position. One of her breasts was pressed against Mack's chest, and she could feel warm muscle and prickly hair against it just above the nipple. Her body felt funny. She wanted to pull the gown away and press herself closer, so that his skin and hers would touch. She frowned, shocked by the longing she felt to be held hungrily by him.

She tensed a little. "You're still wearing your work clothes," she said. Her voice sounded as odd as she felt. "Why?"

"We had a fence down and we didn't know it until the sheriff called and said we had cattle strung up and down the highway," he told her. "It's taken two hours to get them back in and fix the fence. That's why it took me so long to get here. Vivian had been calling me on my cell phone since dark, but I was out of the truck."

"Don't you have a flip phone as well as the one in-stalled in your truck?" she wondered aloud.

He chuckled. "Sure. It's at home recharging."

She smiled drowsily. "Thank you for coming over. I'm sure you didn't feel like it after all that."

His broad shoulders lifted and fell. "I couldn't leave you here alone," he said simply. "And Vivian was in no sort of shape to come." His lean hand smoothed her wavy dark hair. "She thinks you cut her out with Carl, but that's just the way she is."

"I know." She sighed. "She's so pretty that she takes it for granted that the boys all want her. Most of them do, too."

"She's spoiled," he replied. "I was hard on Bob and Charles, but I've made a lot of allowances for Viv, sim-ply because she was the only girl in the family. Maybe that was a mistake."

"It's not a mistake to care for people," she pointed out.

"So they say." His fingers tangled in her soft hair. "Want something to drink?"

"No, thanks," she replied. Her fingers spread invol-untarily in the thick hair over his breastbone, and his intake of breath was sharp and audible.

His body tensed again. She and Carl had kissed, but she'd been careful not to let things go very far. In fact, she hadn't felt any sort of strong physical attraction to the football star, which was strange, considering how much he meant to her. With Mack, she experienced sen-sations she'd never felt before. She felt hot and swol-len in the most unusual places, and it puzzled her. The sudden tension she noticed in the man holding her puzzled her, as well. Mack didn't say a word, but she could feel his heartbeat increase, hear the rough sound of his breathing.

She let her face slide down his muscular arm, and her curious eyes met his good one. It was narrow and unblinking and vaguely intimidating. Even as she watched, his gaze went to where her robe was open and one of her breasts in its lace-trimmed satin lay soft and warm against his chest.

Involuntarily, she followed his intense scrutiny and saw what she hadn't realized before—the gown had slipped so far down that her nipple, hard and tight, was visibly pressing into the thick hair over his chest.

He looked into her stunned eyes, and the hand in her hair tightened. "Didn't you do this with your boyfriend?" he asked bluntly.

"No," she said shakily.

"Why not, if you loved him?" he persisted.

She frowned worriedly. It was becoming increasingly hard to think at all. "I didn't feel like this with him," she confessed in a whisper.

Mack's face changed. His hand in her hair arched her face to his and tugged it into the crook of his arm. He shifted, so that the bodice came completely away from one pert little breast, and his arm tightened, moving her skin sensuously against him.

She gasped. Her nails bit into his chest, and her lips parted in shock and delight. Involuntarily, she arched closer, so that her breast dragged roughly against his skin.

The hand in her hair began to hurt. His body tensed, and a faint shudder rippled through him.

His jaw clenched, and he fought his hunger. She realized that he wanted to feel her against him without the fabric between them, and it was what she wanted, as well. She forgot about wrong and right, about decency, about everything except the pleasure they were giving each other here, in the quiet room with the silence only broken by the sound of the rain outside the window and their breathing.

"I should be shot for doing this, and you should be shot for letting me," he said through his teeth. But even as he spoke, his free hand was stripping the robe and gown to her waist. His gaze fell to her naked breasts, and he shuddered again, violently, as his arm suddenly tightened and dragged her breasts against his hair-roughened chest in a feverish caress.

She moaned harshly. Her nails bit into the hard muscles of his upper arms as he crushed her against him and buried his face in the thick hair at her ear. He held her, rocked her, in an aching excess of desire.

Both arms were around her now. She slid her arms around his neck and clung for dear life. She couldn't catch her breath at all. It was the most intense pleasure she'd ever known. She trembled with desire.

The embrace was fierce. They held each other in a tense silence that seemed to throb with need. Her fingers tangled in the hair at the nape of his strong neck, and her eyes closed as she lay against him, unafraid and unashamed of the growing intimacy of the embrace.

He could feel his body growing harder by the second. If he moved her any closer, she'd be able to feel it. He didn't want that. It was years too soon for the sort of intimacy they were leading up to. He could barely think at all, but the part of his brain that still worked was flashing with red warning lights. She was seventeen, just barely, and he was twenty-three. She wasn't old enough or experienced enough to know what was about to happen. He was. He couldn't take advantage of her like this. He had to pull away and stop while he still could.

Abruptly, he shot to his feet, taking her with him. He held her, swaying on her feet, just in front of him. For one long, tense moment, his gaze went to her taut, bare breasts and his face seemed to clench. Then he pulled the straps up and replaced them on her shoulders, easing the robe into place. He tied it with swift, sharp movements of his big hands.

She stared at him, too overwhelmed by the intimacy and its abrupt end to think clearly. "Why did you stop?" she asked softly. "Did I do something wrong?"

Her pale green eyes made him ache as they searched his face. He caught her by the waist and took a slow, deliberate breath before he spoke. "Didn't they teach sex education at the orphanage?" he asked bluntly.

Her face flamed scarlet. Her eyes, like saucers, seemed to widen endlessly.

He shook his head. She was so deliciously naive. He felt a generation apart from her instead of only six years. "A man can't take much of that without doing something about it, Nat," he said gently. "Looking isn't enough."

She was embarrassed, but she didn't drop her eyes.

"I never could have done that with Carl," she said, feeling vaguely guilty about it. "I enjoyed kissing him, but I never wanted him to do anything else. I didn't like it when he tried to."

He ached to his boots. His hands contracted on her shoulders. "You're only seventeen," he reminded her. "I know Carl was special to you, but you aren't really old enough for a physical relationship with anyone."

"My mother was just eighteen when she had me," she pointed out.

"This is a different world than hers," he countered. "And even for an innocent woman, you're remarkably backward."

"Weren't you, at my age?" she asked in a driven tone.

He pursed his lips and studied her face. "At your age, I'd already had my first woman. She was two years my senior and pretty experienced for a place like Medicine Ridge. She taught me."

She felt her heartbeat racing madly in her chest. She hadn't expected him to be innocent, but it was shocking to have him speak about it so bluntly.

His lean fingers brushed over her cheek. "And when you're old enough," he said in a strange, caressing tone, "I'll teach you."

Those shocking words from the past resonated in her mind as she looked at him in the dimly lit study. *I'll teach you. I'll teach you.*

While she was reliving the past, he'd gotten out of his chair and moved around the desk. He was propped against it, his jacket and tie off, his arms folded, watching her.

"Oh," she said, blinking. "Sorry. I was lost in thought. Literally." She laughed softly.

He didn't smile. "Come here, Nat."

She measured the distance to the door and then laughed inwardly at her cowardice. She'd adored this man for so many years that she couldn't imagine letting anyone else touch her, ever. Besides, she assured herself, he had Glenna to satisfy those infrequent urges he'd once spoken of so bluntly. He wanted to talk without being overheard by Whit in case he came back unexpectedly, that was why he wanted her closer.

With a self-mocking smile she came to a stop less than arm's length away and looked at him.

He let his gaze encompass her, from her flat moccasins to the thrust of her breasts against the thin sweater. The top two buttons were undone, hinting at the cleavage below.

"I shouldn't leave Viv alone too long," she began.

He ignored the hint. His fingers spread along her cheek and his gaze dropped to her soft mouth. "Viv can wait," he replied quietly. His thumb abruptly moved roughly across her lips, sensitizing them in a shock of desire.

His good eye narrowed. "Go and lock the door," he said in a tone he hadn't used with her since the night Carl had died.

She wasn't going to be dictated to, she told herself. Even Mack wasn't going to be allowed to tell her what to do!

So it came as a surprise that she closed the door and locked it, her back to him. She was almost shaking with desire. She leaned her hot forehead against the cold wood of the door, hearing the jerk of her breath in her throat.

She didn't hear him approach, because the thick carpet muffled the sound of his footsteps. But she felt him at her back, felt the heat of his powerful body as both arms went past her to the door. He moved deliberately close, so that his body made contact with hers from her shoulders to her thighs. The contours of his body changed instantly, and she knew, even in her innocence, that what they shared was something rare.

"And now you know why I put you away so quickly that night, don't you?" he asked quietly.

She swallowed, her body involuntarily responding to his need by arching toward him. "Yes. I do now."

His hands slid to her flat belly and pulled her closer to him.

"You felt this way all those years ago?" she said, realizing.

"Yes." His hands smoothed to her rib cage and hesitated. "I accumulated a fair share of experience when I was younger," he continued. "But in recent years, sex has become a more serious matter to me. I've gone hungry. You were innocent and curious, and I almost lost control with you. I didn't feel comfortable letting you see how tempted I was—especially under the circumstances."

"I'm still innocent," she reminded him without turning.

"And just as curious," he concluded for her. His

Chapter Seven

Natalie caught her breath at the look on Mack's face. The naked hunger in that one beautiful dark eye was almost frightening.

His big, lean hands framed her face as he searched her eyes. "Don't be afraid of me," he said softly. "I'd cut off my arm before I'd ever hurt you."

"I know that." She studied him worriedly. "But I can't—"

His lips caught the words and stopped them. She felt his hands drop to her throat and then to her shoulders, smoothing up and down the skin left bare by her short-sleeve sweater. He was slow and tender and sensual. It was like a dance in slow motion, a poem, a symphony.

The door was hard at her back as he moved closer, trapping her between his body and the wood. One long leg inserted itself confidently between both of hers with a lazy movement that was as arousing as the kiss they were sharing.

She gasped, and his mouth lifted away. He looked at her, breathing a little jerkily. "This is perfectly natural," he said quietly. "Don't fight it."

Her eyes were wild and a little frightened by the overwhelming desire she felt. "You went away…with Glenna," she whispered.

"She went on the plane," he corrected. "She didn't go with me." His mouth traced her eyelids and closed them. His hands were under her arms, lifting her closer. They moved slowly, gently, onto her breasts and caressed them with lazy delight.

She felt her legs go weak underneath her. It was unlike any other time she'd been in his arms. He handled her as if she belonged to him, as if she were precious to him, cherished by him.

Her eyes opened when he lifted his head, and they were full of wonder, wide with breathless hunger and delight. Her heart was in them.

He searched them quietly, and a faint smile touched his hard mouth. "I've waited years for that expression," he said under his breath. "Years."

He bent again, and this time her arms lifted slowly around his neck, cradling his head as his mouth covered her parted lips. They clung to each other, letting the kiss build, feeling its power. She moaned when it became fierce and hungry, but she didn't try to get away. Involuntarily, her body pressed hard against his.

She felt him shiver. He pushed down, his hands lifting her suddenly into the hard thrust of him and holding her there with a slow, sensual rhythm that made her tremble and gasp into his mouth.

"Sweetheart!" he whispered roughly.

The kiss grew harder. She felt him move and lift her clear off the floor in his arms. He walked to the sofa and spread her lengthwise on the leather, easing his body down to cover hers in a silence that was heated and tense.

He was fiercely aroused, and she wanted him at that moment more than she'd ever wanted anything in her life. She followed where he led, even when she felt him shifting her so that his lean hips were pressed squarely against hers, between her legs, in an intimacy that was suddenly urgent and feverish with dark pleasure. She couldn't have pushed him away if her survival had depended on it. Presumably he felt the same, because his arms held her relentlessly as he began to move against her.

She shuddered with the riptide of pleasure the movement produced, and her eyes flew open, locking with his dark, passionate gaze as he lifted his head to look at her.

With his hands at her head, taking most of his weight, he moved deliberately, watching her as she lifted to meet him and gasped at the sensations the contact produced. Her nails bit into his hard arms, but she wasn't fighting. She was melting into the leather, flying up into the sky, burning, burning!

The intimacy became so torturous, so fierce, that it was almost too late to draw back when he realized what was happening to them. His hands caught her hips in a bruising clasp and he pulled her over him, holding her still, with her cheek on his pounding chest as he fought to breathe and stop all at the same time.

"No!" She choked, trying to return to the intimacy of their former embrace.

His hands forced her to be still. His breath at her forehead was hot and shaky, audible in the stillness of the study. "Don't," he bit off. "Don't move. For God's sake, don't!"

Her mouth pressed into the cotton of his shirt, hot and hungry. "I want to," she choked.

"God, don't you think I want to?" he demanded huskily. His hands hurt in their fight to keep her still. "I want you to the point of madness. But not like this, Natalie!"

Belatedly, she realized that he was trying to save her from her own hunger for him. It wasn't a thought she cherished at the moment, when her whole body was burning with a passion she'd never felt before. But slowly, the trembling eased and she began to breathe normally, if a little fast.

His hands smoothed over her hair, bunching it at her nape as he held her cheek to his chest.

"Why?" she whispered miserably when she was able to speak.

"Because I can't marry you," he explained. "And because you can't live with sleeping with me if I don't."

All her dreams vanished in a haze. As the room came into focus across his broad chest, she realized just how far gone they were and how intimate their position on the sofa had become. If he hadn't stopped, they'd be lovers already. She hadn't even protested. But he'd had the presence of mind to stop.

So much for her willpower and her principles, she thought sadly. It seemed that her body had a will of its own, and it was much stronger than her mind.

Tears poured from her eyes, and she didn't even notice until she felt his shirt become damp under her cheek.

His hand laced into her hair and soothed her scalp. "If I thought it would help matters, I'd cry, too," he murmured dryly.

She hit his shoulder with her fist. "How could you do that to me?" she demanded.

"How could you do it to me?" he shot back. "You know how I feel about commitment. I've said so often enough."

"You started it," she raged.

He sighed. "Yes, I did," he admitted after a minute. "This is all I've been able to think about since we went nightclubbing," he confessed. "That was probably the most misguided thing I've done in recent years. It's hard to put out a brushfire once it's started. Or didn't you notice?"

She moved experimentally and felt him help her move away to a healthy distance, lying beside him on the long leather couch with her cheek on his shoulder. She looked at him quietly, curiously. His face was a little flushed, and his mouth was swollen from the hard, hungry kisses they'd shared. His shirt was open at the throat. His hair was disheveled. He looked as though he'd been making love, and probably so did she. She didn't really mind. He looked sensual like that.

"You'd better leave town," he suggested with a wry smile. "You just went on the endangered list."

Her fingers spread on his shirt, but he caught and stilled them. "Stop that. I'm barely a step away from ravishment."

"How exciting," she murmured.

"You wouldn't think so for the first few minutes," he murmured skeptically. "And you wouldn't be able to live with your conscience even if you did enjoy it eventually."

She grimaced. "I guess not. I'm not really cut out for passionate affairs."

"And I'm not cut out for happily ever after," he said without looking at her.

"Because of your family?" she asked.

He drew in a long breath. She felt his chest rise and fall under her hand. "We could make a list. It wouldn't change anything." He looked at her rapt, soft face, and his hardened. "Despite everything," he whispered huskily, "I would give everything I own to have you, just once."

She managed a faint smile. "Maybe you'd be disappointed."

He traced her mouth with a lazy finger. "Maybe you would, too."

"So it's just as well, isn't it?"

"That's what my mind says," he agreed.

She nuzzled against his shoulder and closed her eyes. "Isn't there a poem about hopeless attraction?"

"Hundreds," he said.

She felt his hand smoothing her hair, almost in a comforting gesture. She smiled. "That feels nice."

"You feel nice, lying against me like this," he whispered. He bent and kissed her closed eyelids with breathless tenderness. "It was like this, the night of the wreck," he added in a hushed tone. "I held you and comforted you, and wanted you until I ached."

"But I was seventeen."

"But you were seventeen." He pressed a kiss on her forehead and put her aside so that he could get to his feet. "You haven't changed much," he added as he helped her up.

"I'm older," she pointed out.

He laughed, and it had a hollow sound. "If you were a modern woman, we'd have fewer problems."

"But I'm not modern," she replied sadly. "And that says it all."

A door opened and shut, and he glanced toward the closed door of the study. "That'll be Romeo, I reckon," he drawled with a glittery look at Natalie. "I don't like the way he hangs around you."

"He likes me," she said carelessly. "I like him, too. What's wrong with that?"

"He belongs to Vivian," he returned, and he didn't smile.

She searched his hard face. "You can't own people."

The eyebrow that wasn't under the string of the eye patch lifted sardonically. "She won't thank you for making a play for him."

She ached all over with frustration and misery, and

she hated him for arousing her and pushing her away
at the same time. It wasn't logical, but then, she wasn't
thinking clearly. She didn't mean what she said next,
but she was so angry she couldn't help herself. "What
would you care if I did? You don't like him. Maybe it
would open her eyes."

"Don't do it," he warned in a low, threatening tone.

"Or you'll do what?" she challenged icily.

He didn't answer. They were enemies in the blink of
an eye. He was furious, and it showed. He went to the
door and opened it with a jerk, waiting for her to leave.

She hesitated, but only for an instant. If that was the
way he wanted it, all right! She went out the door without looking at him, without speaking, without knowing that she'd just altered the whole pattern of her life.

Mack closed the door sharply behind her, and she
grimaced before she went to the kitchen to see if Whit
was there. He was. He'd just made coffee, in one of the
expensive modern coffee machines that did it in seconds. He'd poured two cups, one for himself and one
for Vivian.

"Where's the tray?" he asked, looking around.

"I haven't got a clue," she admitted. She looked in
cupboards, but she couldn't find one.

"Never mind," he said. "I take mine black and she
takes hers with cream. I can carry both cups if you'll
bring the cream, and we'll forget the tray."

"Okay," she said.

He was gazing at her with an experienced eye, and
it suddenly occurred to her that she must look pretty

disheveled. She thought about taking a minute to repair her makeup before she went upstairs, but Whit was already out the door.

She followed him up the staircase and into Vivian's room. It hadn't dawned on her, either, that Whit had been out in the wind and his hair was disheveled. When the two of them entered the room, Vivian put together Natalie's swollen mouth and mussed hair and Whit's mussed hair and came up with infidelity.

"Go home," she told Natalie in a vicious tone. "Go right now and don't ever come back!"

"Viv! What's wrong?" she asked.

"As if you don't know!"

Whit didn't say anything, but he had a very strange look in his eyes. "You'd better go," he said gently. "I'll look after Viv."

Natalie looked at Vivian, but she turned her face away and refused to say another word. With resignation and bitter sadness, Natalie put down the cream and left the room.

Nobody was around when she went out the front door. She'd made a clean sweep tonight. Mack and Vivian were both furious at her over Whit when she hadn't meant to cause trouble. She hoped it would all blow over.

For the moment, all she could think about was the close call she'd had in Mack's arms on the sofa, and she wished with all her heart that things had been different between them. For better or worse, she loved him with her whole heart. But he had nothing to offer her.

She went home and fell, exhausted, into bed.

* * *

Whit was left alone with Vivian, who was in tears. "You were making love to her!" she accused, her blue eyes shooting sparks at him. "My boyfriend and my best friend! How could you?"

He hesitated before he spoke, with both hands in his pockets. He'd seen Vivian as a nice, biddable little source of gambling money and light lovemaking. But she'd become jealous and possessive of him, and he was getting tired of it. There were other women.

"So what?" he asked, not denying her charge. "She's not as pretty or rich as you are, but she's sweet and she doesn't question every move I make."

Vivian stared at him, almost purple with rage and frustration and hurt pride. "Then go with her," she spat at him. "Get out. And don't come back!"

"That," he replied, "will actually be a pleasure. You're no man's idea of the perfect woman, Viv. In fact, you're a spoiled little rich girl who wants to own people. It's not worth it."

"Worth what?" she choked.

He looked at her with world-weary cynicism and contempt. "I like to gamble. You had money. We made a handsome couple. I thought we'd be a match made in heaven. But there are other rich girls, honey."

He laughed mockingly and walked out, closing the door behind him. Vivian went wild, throwing things and weeping horribly until Mack came into the room minutes later and helped her off the floor and into bed.

"What in God's name is wrong with you?" he demanded, surveying the destruction of her bedroom.

"Whit and Natalie," she choked. "They were... making love.... Whit said she was everything I'm not." Sobs choked the words for several seconds while her brother stood by the bed, frozen. "Oh, I hate them so. I hate them both! My boyfriend and my best friend! How could they do this to me?"

"How do you know they were making love?" he asked in a hollow tone.

"I saw them," she lied viciously. "And Whit admitted it. He even laughed about it!"

Mack's face became a mask. He drew the covers over Vivian with a strange, frightening silence.

Vivian wasn't making connections. She was just short of hysteria. "They won't come here again. I told them not to. I'm through with them!"

"Yes." His voice sounded strained. "Try to calm down. You'll make yourself sicker."

"If either of them call," Vivian added coldly, "I won't speak to them."

"Don't worry about that," he told her. "I'll handle it."

"I already handled it," she shot back. "And don't tell Bob and Charles. Nobody else needs to know!"

"All right, Viv. Try to get some sleep. I'll have Sadie come in tomorrow and clean up in here."

"Thanks, Mack," she managed through her tears. "You really are a dear."

He didn't answer her. He went out and closed the door quietly, and the life seemed to drain out of him. Natalie, with Vivian's boyfriend. He'd told her not to flirt with the man, and she'd been angry with him. Was that why? Did it explain why she'd go from his arms into another man's in less than ten minutes?

Well, if her idea was to make him jealous, it had failed. He had nothing but contempt for her. Like Vivian, he didn't want her in the house, in his life. He went downstairs to his study and immersed himself in paperwork, trying not to see that long leather couch where they'd lain together in the sweetest interlude of his life.

Maybe it was just as well. He couldn't marry her. There were too many strikes against them. But he didn't like the idea of her with that gambler. Or any other man…

He cursed his hateful memory and put the pencil down. Natalie ran like a golden thread through so much of his life. In recent years, she'd been involved in just about everything that went on at the ranch. She rode with him and Vivian, she came to parties, barbecues, cattle sales. She was always around. Now he wouldn't see her come running up the steps, laughing in that unaffected way she had. She wouldn't flirt with him, chide him, lecture him. He was going to be alone.

He got up and went to the liquor cabinet. He seldom drank, but he kept a bottle of aged Scotch whiskey for guests. He poured himself a shot and threw it down, enjoying the hot sting of it as it washed down his throat. He couldn't remember a time when he'd felt so powerless. He looked at the bottle and carried it to the desk. As an afterthought, he locked the door.

Vivian couldn't sleep. She got up and washed her face, careful of the broken objects she'd dashed against walls in her rage. She kept remembering Mack's face when she'd told him about Natalie and Whit. She'd never seen such an expression.

It bothered her enough to go looking for him. He wasn't in his room or anywhere upstairs. Walking slowly, because it was difficult to walk and breathe at the same time despite the antibiotic, she made it to the door of his study. She tried to open the door, but it was locked. Mack never locked the door.

She hesitated, but only for a moment. She combined the look on his face with his strange behavior and the way he'd held Natalie when they'd danced at the night-club, and with trembling hands she went to the inter-com panel and called the foreman.

"I want you to come up here right now," she said after identifying herself. "Haven't we got a man who does locksmithing part-time?"

"Yes, ma'am," he said.

"Bring him, too. And hurry!"

"Yes, ma'am!"

She sat down in the hall chair, biting her lip. It had been a lie that she'd seen Natalie and Whit together, but they both looked as if they'd been kissing. And Whit hadn't denied it. But if Mack was in love with Natalie, which was becoming a disturbing possibility, she might have caused a disaster. Despite Glenna's persistence, Mack had never behaved as if he couldn't live without her. But the way he watched Natalie, the way he'd held her on the dance floor, the way his gaze followed her... oh, God, let those men hurry!

It seemed like an eternity before the doorbell sounded. She went as quickly as she could to answer it.

"I want you to unlock this door," she told the man beside the foreman.

"Can't you use the key?" he asked, clearly hesitant.

"I don't have the key. Mack does, and he's locked himself in there." She wrapped her arms over her thick bathrobe. "Please," she said in an uncharacteristic request for help. Gone was the autocratic manner. "There's been some…some trouble. He's in there. He won't answer me."

Without a word, the locksmith took out his leather packet of tools and went to work. In short order, he had the door unlocked.

"Wait," she said when they started to open it. "Wait here. I'll call you if I need you." She didn't want to expose her brother to gossip if there was no need.

She went inside and closed the door. The sight that met her eyes was staggering. It made her shiver with guilt. Mack was lying facedown on the desk, a nearly empty whiskey bottle overturned at his hand. Mack never drank to excess; the memory of his father's alcoholism stopped him.

She went to the door and opened it just a crack. "He's just asleep. Thank you for your trouble. You can go."

"Are you sure, Miss Killain?" the foreman asked.

"Yes," she said confidently. "I'm sure."

"Then, good night. We'll come back if you need us."

Both men left. Vivian curled up in the big chair beside the desk and sat there all night with her brother. For the first time in her life, she realized how self-absorbed she'd become.

In the morning, very early, he woke up. He sat, dizzy, and scowled when he saw his sister curled in her robe in the big chair by the desk. He swept back his hair and surveyed the remains of the whiskey.

"Viv?" he called roughly. "What the hell do you think you're doing down here?"

She opened her eyes, still very sick. "I was worried about you," she said. "You never drink."

He held his head. "I never will again, I can promise you," he said wryly.

She uncurled and got slowly to her feet. "Are you all right?"

His shoulder moved jerkily. "I'm fine. How about you?"

She managed a smile. "I'll get by."

His face locked up tight. "We were both bad judges of character," he said.

"About what I said last night," she began earnestly. "I ought to tell you—"

He held up a big hand, and his face was hard with distaste. "They deserve each other," he said flatly. "You know I go around with Glenna," he added. "I don't want a long-term relationship, least of all with a penniless, fickle, two-timing orphan!"

She felt two inches high. She did blame Natalie, but she had a terrible feeling that Mack would never recover. It would take her a while to get over Whit's betrayal, as well. But she felt guilty and ashamed for making matters worse.

"Maybe they couldn't help it," she said heavily.

"Maybe they didn't want to," he returned. He got to his feet. "And that's all I'll ever say on the matter. I don't want to hear her name mentioned in this house ever again."

"All right, Mack."

He looked at the whiskey bottle with cold distaste before he dropped it into the trash can by the desk.

"Let's get you back upstairs," he told Viv with a smile. "I'm supposed to be taking care of you."

She slid her arm around his waist. "You're my brother. I love you."

He kissed her forehead and hugged her close. "Thanks."

She shrugged. "We're Killains. We're survivors."

"You bet we are. Come on."

He put her back to bed and went to see about the animals in the barn. He didn't think about the night before. And when Bob and Charles came home, nothing of what had happened was mentioned. But Vivian managed to get them alone long enough to warn them not to talk about Natalie at all in front of Mack.

"Why not?" Bob wanted to know, puzzled. "She's like family."

"Sure she is," Charles emphasized. "We all love her."

Vivian couldn't meet their eyes. "It's a long story. She's done something to hurt me and Mack. We don't want to talk about it, okay?"

They were reluctant, but she persuaded them. If she could only persuade her conscience that she was the wronged party. She couldn't forget what Whit had said to her. Natalie had been her only best friend for years.

Was it realistic that Natalie would make a play for her boyfriend? She had for Carl, all those years ago, Vivian thought bitterly, and then she remembered that Carl had only been dating Natalie for a bet. She'd known, and she hadn't told Natalie because she was jealous of her relationship with Carl. In hindsight, she began to see how painfully unfair she'd been. Her whole life had been one of pampered security. Natalie hadn't had the advantages Vivian had, but she'd never been envious or jealous of Vivian. Remembering that made Vivian feel even more guilty. But it was too late to undo the damage. If Whit was telling the truth, everyone would know it soon, because Natalie would be seen going around with him. Then, Vivian told herself, she'd be vindicated.

But it didn't happen. In fact, Whit was seen with the daughter of a local contractor who had plenty of money and liked to gamble. They were the talk of the town, so soon after Whit's visible break with Vivian.

As for Natalie, she'd gone home the night of the uproar and, surprisingly, slept all night and most of the morning after she cried herself to sleep. She barely made it to the grocery store in time to work her shift. She was grateful for the job, because it took her mind off the painful argument with Mack and the vicious tongue-lashing Vivian had given her. For the first time in years, she really did feel like an orphan. She was worried about how her exams would be graded, as well, and about graduation. It seemed that the weight of the

Chapter Eight

Natalie received her grades from the registrar the following week, and she laughed out loud with relief when she saw that she'd passed all her subjects. She would graduate, after all.

But as her classmates placed their orders for tickets to the baccalaureate service and the graduation exercises, Natalie realized with a start that she had no one to get tickets for. None of the Killains were speaking to her, and she had no family. She would have nobody to watch her graduate.

It was a painful realization. She went through the rehearsals and picked up her cap and gown, but without much enthusiasm. No one would have known from her bright exterior that she was unhappy. Even at work, she pretended that she was on top of the world.

She saw Dave Markham briefly before her big day. They hadn't had much contact since her student teaching stint had been over, and she'd missed his pleasant company.

"I hear through the grapevine that you're graduating," he told her, tongue in cheek, as he waited at the grocery store for her to check out his groceries.

She grinned. "So they say. It's really a relief. I wondered during exams if I was going to pass everything."

"Everyone goes through that," he assured her. "Finals in your senior year are enough to cause a nervous breakdown." He studied her quietly as she bent over the computer keyboard after she'd scanned his purchases into the machine. "There's another rumor going around."

She stopped, her head lifting. "Which is?"

He grimaced. "That you've had a split with the Killains," he continued. "I didn't believe it, though. You and Vivian have been friends for years."

"Sadly," she said, "it's true." She drew in a long breath as she gave him his total, then waited for him to count out the amount and give it to her.

He waited while she finalized the transaction before he spoke again, taking the sales slip automatically. "What happened? Can you tell me?"

She called for one of the grocery boys to come and help her bag his purchases before she turned to him. "I'd rather not, Dave," she said honestly. "It hurts to talk about it."

"That's why it hurts, because you haven't opened up." His eyes narrowed. "I hear Whit Moore's going around with a new girl and Vivian's quit taking classes at the vocational school."

That was news. "Did she?" She couldn't really blame her former best friend for that decision, of course. It wouldn't have been easy for her to go back into one of Whit's classes after they'd broken up in such a terrible way. She wondered if he'd ever been honest with Vivian about what had happened that night and decided that he probably hadn't. It was a major misunderstanding that might never be cleared up, and Natalie missed not only her former friend, but the boys, as well. She missed Mack most of all. She supposed that he'd heard all about it from Vivian. She'd hoped that he wouldn't believe his sister, but that was a forlorn hope. Natalie had never, in her acquaintance with the other girl, known her to tell Mack a deliberate lie.

"Mrs. Ringgold asks about you all the time," Dave added, trying to cheer her up. "She said she hopes you'll come and teach at our school in the fall, if there's an opening. So do I. I miss having you to talk to."

She remembered his hopeless love and smiled with fellow feeling. "Maybe I'll do just that," she said.

The bag boy came to sack his groceries, another customer pushed a cart up behind him, and the brief conversation was over. He left with a promise to call her and she went back to work, trying to put what she'd learned out of her mind. She wished Mack would call, at least, to give her a chance to explain the misunderstanding. But he didn't. And after Vivian's fierce hostility, she was nervous about phoning the house at all. She hoped that things would work themselves out, if she was patient.

* * *

Late afternoon on the Thursday before baccalaureate exercises Friday night, she walked out of the bank after depositing her paycheck and ran right into Mack Killain.

It was the first time she'd seen him since the day she'd had the falling out with Vivian. He moved away from her, and the look he gave her was so contemptuous, so full of distaste, that she felt dirty. That was when she realized that Vivian must have told Mack what she thought Natalie and Whit had done. It was painfully obvious that Mack wasn't going to listen to an excuse. She'd never imagined that he would look at her like that. The pain went all the way to her soul.

"How could you do that to Vivian, to your best friend?" he asked coldly.

"Do...what?" she faltered.

"You know what!" he thundered. "You two-timing, lying, cheating little flirt. He must be crazy. No man in his right mind would look twice at you."

Her mouth fell open. Her heart raced. Her mouth was dry as cotton. "Mack..."

"You had us all fooled," he continued, raising his voice and not minding who heard. Several people did. "Vivian trusted you! And while she was in bed with pneumonia, you were making out with the man she loved!"

Natalie wanted to go through the sidewalk. Her eyes brimmed over with tears. "I didn't!" she tried to defend herself, almost choking on the words.

"There's no use denying it. Vivian saw you," he said with magnificent contempt. "She told me."

It was a lie, but he believed it. Maybe he wanted to believe it. He'd said that they had no future together, and this would make the perfect excuse for him to push her out of his life. Nothing she said was going to make any difference. He simply did not want her, and he was making it clear.

She'd thought the pain was bad before. Now it was unbearable.

"All of us trusted you, made you part of our family. And this is how you repaid us, by betraying Vivian, who never did anything to hurt you." His tone was vicious, furious. "Not only that, Natalie, you didn't even try to apologize for it."

She lifted her face defiantly. "I have nothing to apologize for," she said in a husky, hoarse tone.

"Then we have nothing to say to each other, ever again," he replied harshly.

"Mack, if you'd just let me try to explain," she said, hoping for a miracle. "Calm down and talk to me."

"I am calm," he said in an icy tone. "What did you expect, anyway? A proposal of marriage?" He laughed bitterly. "You know where I stand on that issue. And even if I were in the mood for it, it wouldn't be with a woman who'd sell me out the minute the ring was on her finger. You went to him afterward," he gritted, "and you as much as told me you were going to. But if you think I'm jealous, honey, you're dead wrong. You were Vivian's friend, but I never wanted you hanging around my house. I tolerated you for Vivian's sake."

"I see." Her face was white and she was aware of pitying, embarrassed looks around her, because he was eloquent.

He hardened his heart, bristling with wounded pride as he looked at her, furious at his own weakness. Well, never again. "Which reminds me, Natalie," he added coldly, "I suppose it goes without saying that you're not welcome at the ranch anymore."

She lifted her eyes to his hard face and nodded slowly. "Yes, Mack," she said in a subdued tone. "It does go without saying."

Her heart was breaking. She turned away from that accusing, contemptuous gaze and walked briskly down the street to get away from him. She didn't know how she was going to bear this latest outrage of Vivian's. It had cost her Mack, whom she loved more than her own life. And he hated her. He hated her!

The bystanders were still staring at Mack when she was out of sight, but he didn't say a word. He stalked into the bank, noticing that people almost fell over trying to get out of his way. He was furious. After going right out of his arms into Whit's, she'd had the gall to try and deny it, even when Vivian had seen her with Whit! He would never trust his instincts about women again, he decided. If he could be fooled that easily, for that long, he was safer going around with Glenna. She might not be virtuous, but at least she was loyal—in her fashion.

Natalie went home with her heart around her knees. She made supper but couldn't eat it. She'd assumed that Mack was making assumptions. It hadn't occurred to her that Vivian would tell such a lie, or that Mack would believe it. But she'd helped things along by making those remarks to Mack in frustration when he'd put her out of the office after their tempestuous interlude. She hadn't wanted Whit, ever. But nobody would believe that now. She'd lost not only Mack, but the only family she'd known for years. She went to bed and lay awake most of the night, wretched and alone.

She wondered how she could go on living in the same town with the Killains and see Mack and Vivian and the boys week after week. Did Bob and Charles hate her, too? Was it a wholesale contempt? Vivian had lied. That a woman she'd considered her best friend could treat her so callously hurt tremendously. Perhaps she was doomed to a life without affection. God knew that her aunt, old Mrs. Barnes, had only brought her from the orphanage to be a housekeeper and part-time nurse until the old lady died. No one had ever loved her. She'd wanted Mack to. She'd even thought at odd moments that he did, somehow. But the hatred in his eyes was damning. If he'd loved her, he'd have at least given her the benefit of the doubt.

But he hadn't. He'd believed Vivian without hesitation. So all her dreams of love eternal had gone up in smoke. There was nothing left except to make a decision about what she was going to do with the rest of her life. She knew immediately that she couldn't stay in Medicine Ridge. She would have to leave. Next week, after graduation, she was going to talk to one of her instructors who'd told her she knew of a job opening in a Dallas school where a relative was principal. Dallas sounded like a nice place to live.

Natalie marched in with her class to the baccalaureate service, trying not to notice how many of her classmates' whole families had come to see them in their caps and gowns. It was a brief service, held in the college chapel with a guest speaker who was some sort of well-known political figure. Natalie barely heard what went on around her because she was so heartbroken.

When the service was over, she greeted classmates she knew and drove herself home. The next morning, she got up early to go to the college with her gown for the graduation exercises. She felt very proud of her accomplishment as she marched into the chapel along with her class and waited for her name to be called, for her diploma to be handed out. It would have been one of the best days of her life, if the Killains hadn't been angry with her. As it was, she went through the motions like a zombie, smiling, looking happy for the cameras. But inside, she was so miserable that she only wanted to be alone. The minute the service was over, she went to look for the teacher who'd offered to help her get the Dallas job. And she told her she was interested.

The Killains were somber at the dinner table on Sunday. It was the first time in days they'd all been together, with the boys home, as well. It was more like a wake than a meal.

"Natalie graduated yesterday," Bob said coolly, glaring at Mack and Vivian, who wouldn't look at him. "My friend Gig's sister was in her class. She said that Natalie didn't have one single person of her own in the crowd for baccalaureate or graduation. Viv?"

Vivian had burst into tears. She pushed away from the table and went upstairs as fast as her healing lungs would allow.

Mack threw down his napkin, leaving his supper untouched, and stalked out of the room, as grim as death itself.

Bob looked at his brother and grimaced. "I guess I should have kept my mouth shut."

"I don't see why," Charles replied irritably. "Natalie belongs to us, to all of us. But the two of them behave as if she's at the top of the FBI's most-wanted list. It's that damned Whit, you mark my words. He did something or said something that caused this. He's going around with old Murcheson's daughter now, and she's grubstaking his gambling habit. Everybody knows it. He even said that our sister was only a means to an end, so if Natalie was the cause of that breakup, good for her! She saved Viv from something a lot worse than pneumonia. Not that anybody but us cares, I guess," he muttered as he attacked his steak.

In the hall, Mack overheard and scowled. He'd thought Whit had left Vivian for Natalie, so why was he going around with the Murcheson girl? First Natalie's impassioned denial, now Viv's hysterical retreat. Something was wrong here.

He followed Vivian upstairs to her room. She was sitting in the chair by her bed, tears rolling down her pale cheeks. He sank down on the bed facing her.

"Why don't you tell me why you're crying, Viv," he invited gently.

She wiped at her red eyes with a tissue to catch the tears. "I lied," she whispered.

His whole body stiffened. "I beg your pardon?"

"I mean, Natalie was pretty disheveled and Whit's hair was ruffled. They looked like they'd been making out," she said defensively. "I didn't actually see them, though. But there was nobody else in the house except the two of them and they were down there for almost an hour." Her face hardened as she said it, so she missed the sudden pallor of her brother's face.

"I was down there," he snapped. "Whit went out to get cigarettes. He'd just come back and made coffee when he and Natalie went up to your room."

She gaped at him. Her jaw fell. Horror claimed her face. "Oh, no," she whispered. "Oh, dear God, no!"

"She did nothing. With Whit," he added, averting his gaze to the window. He looked, at that moment, as if he'd never smiled in his life. He was hearing himself accuse Natalie on the street in front of half a dozen bystanders of being a faithless tease.

Now it made sense. Mack had gotten drunk because he thought Natalie had gone straight from his arms to Whit's. Vivian had told him so, believing that Natalie and Whit had been alone for that hour. Whit had admitted it. And all the time…

"I'll go to her," Vivian said at once. "I'll apologize, on my knees if I have to!"

"Don't bother," he said, getting to his feet. "She won't let you past the porch. I told her she wasn't welcome here ever again." His fists clenched at his hips. "And several other things that were…overheard," he added through his teeth. "She went to her graduation all alone." He had to stop because he was too choked to say another word. He went out without looking at Vivian, and the door closed with a jerk behind him.

Vivian put her face in her hands and bawled. Out of her own selfishness, she'd destroyed two lives. Mack loved Natalie. And she knew—she *knew*—that Natalie loved Mack, had always loved him! It wasn't Natalie who'd betrayed them. It was Vivian herself. Her pride had been hurt because Whit preferred Natalie, but she'd been done a huge favor. She was besotted enough with the man to have given him all the money he'd asked for. She'd had a narrow escape, for which she had Natalie to thank. But they weren't friends anymore. They'd pushed Natalie out of their lives. It was wishful thinking to suppose she'd forgive them or ever give them a chance to hurt her again. She'd never really been loved, unless it was by the parents who'd been so tragically killed in her childhood. She was alone in the world, and she must feel it now more than ever before. Vivian took a deep breath and dried her eyes. Surely there was some way, something she could do, to make amends. She had to.

Mack went off on a prolonged business trip the next day. He barely spoke to Vivian on his way out, and he looked like death warmed over. She could only imagine how he felt, after the way he'd behaved. Natalie might forgive him one day, but she'd probably never be able to forget.

It took her two days to get up enough courage to drive over to Natalie's house and knock on the door. She got a real shock when the door was opened, because there were two suitcases sitting on the floor, and Natalie was dressed for travel.

"Natalie, could I speak to you for a minute?" Vivian asked hesitantly.

"A minute is all I have," came the cool, distant reply. "I thought you were my cab. I have to get to the airport. One of my college professors is letting me fly with her to Dallas."

"What's in Dallas?" Vivian asked, shocked.

"My new job." Natalie looked past her at a cab that was just pulling into the driveway. She checked to make sure she had her purse and all the documents she needed before she lifted her suitcases and put them on the porch. She locked the door while Vivian stood nearby, speechless.

"I've put the house on the market," she continued. "I won't be coming back."

"Oh, Nat," Vivian whispered miserably. "I lied. I lied to Mack. I thought… You were downstairs and so was Whit, for an hour or more. Whit didn't deny what I accused him of doing with you. But I didn't know Mack had come home."

Natalie looked straight at her. In that instant she looked as formidable as Vivian's taciturn brother. "Mack believed you," she said. That was all. But it was more than a statement of fact. It meant that he didn't even suspect that Natalie might be innocent. She was tarred and feathered and put on a rail without qualm.

"I'm his sister. I've never lied to him before," she added. "Nat, I have to tell you something. You have to listen!"

"Are you the lady who wants to go to the airport?" the cabdriver asked.

"Yes, I am," Natalie said, carrying her bags down the steps without another word to Vivian.

"Don't go!" Vivian cried. "Please don't go!"

"There's nothing left in Medicine Ridge for me, and we both know it, Vivian," she told the other woman without meeting her eyes as the cabdriver put both her bags in the trunk and then went to open the back door for Natalie to get into the cab. "You've finally got what you wanted. Aren't you happy? I'll never be even an imagined potential rival for any of your boyfriends again."

"I didn't know," Vivian moaned. "I jumped to conclusions and hurt everybody. But please, Natalie, at least let me apologize! And don't blame Mack for it. It's not his fault."

"Mack doesn't want me," Natalie said heavily. "I suppose I knew it from the beginning, but he made it very clear the last time I saw him. He'll date Glenna and be very happy. Maybe you will, too. But I'm tired of being the scapegoat. I'm going to find a new life for myself in Dallas. Goodbye, Vivian," she said tersely, still without looking in Vivian's direction.

Vivian had never felt so terrible in all her life. She stood on the steps, alone, and watched the best friend she'd ever had leave town because of her.

"I'm sorry," she whispered to the retreating cab. "Oh, Natalie, I'm so very sorry!"

She had to tell Mack that Natalie had gone, of course. That was almost as hard as watching Natalie leave. She found him in his study, at the computer, making decisions about restocking. He looked up when he saw her at the door.

"Well?" he asked.

She went into the room and closed the door behind her. She looked washed out, miserable, defeated.

"I went to apologize to Natalie," she began.

His face tautened, and he looked a little paler. But he gathered himself together quickly and only lifted an eyebrow as he dropped his gaze to the computer screen. "I gather that it didn't go well?"

She fingered her wristwatch nervously. This was harder than she'd dreamed. "I was just in time to see her leave."

He frowned as he lifted his head. "Leave?"

She nodded. She sat in the chair beside the desk, where she'd sat and watched him the night he got drunk. She hated telling him what happened. He'd had so much responsibility in his life, so much pain. He'd never really had anyone to love, either, except for his siblings. He'd loved Natalie. Vivian had cost him the only woman who could have made him happy.

"Leave for where?" he demanded shortly.

She swallowed. "Dallas."

"Dallas, Texas? Who the hell does she know in

Texas?" he persisted, still not understanding what Vivian was saying.

"She's got a job there," she said reluctantly. "She's... selling her house. She said she wouldn't be coming back."

For a few seconds, Mack didn't speak. He stared at his sister as though he hadn't understood her. Then, all at once, the life seemed to drain out of him. He stared at the dark paneling of the wall blindly while the truth hit him squarely in the gut. Natalie had left town. They'd hurt her so badly that she couldn't even stay in the same community. Probably the gossip had been hard on her, too, because Mack had made harsh accusations in front of everyone. And how did you stop gossip, when it was never spoken in public?

He sank down into his chair without a word.

"I tried to explain," she continued. "To apologize." She swallowed hard. "She wouldn't even look at me. I don't blame her. I've ruined her life because I was selfish and conceited and obsessed with jealousy. Now that I look back, I realize that it wasn't the first time I saw Nat as a rival and treated her accordingly. I've been an idiot. And I'm sorry, Mack. I really am."

His chest rose and fell. He toyed with the pencil on the desk, trying to adjust to a world without at least the occasional glimpse of Natalie. Now that he'd lost her for good, he knew how desperately he loved her. It was a hell of an irony.

"I could go to Dallas and try to make her listen," Vivian persisted, because he looked so defeated. Her brother, the steel man, was melting in front of her.

His shoulders seemed to slump a little. He shook his head. "Let her go," he said heavily. "We've done enough harm."

"But you love her!"

His eyes closed briefly and then opened. He turned to the computer and moved the mouse to reopen his file, his face drawn and remote. He didn't say another word.

After a minute of painful silence, Vivian got up and left him there. She loved her brother. It devastated her to realize how much she'd hurt him lately. And that was nothing to what she'd done to Natalie. She could never make up for what she'd cost Natalie and her brother. But she wished she had the chance to try.

Natalie, meanwhile, had settled into a small apartment near the school. She'd interviewed for the position and after a few days, she was notified that she had the job. The teaching roster had been filled for the year, but one of the teachers had come down with hepatitis and couldn't continue, so there was a vacancy. Natalie was just what they wanted for the third graders, a bilingual teacher who could understand and communicate with the Hispanic students. She was glad she'd opted for Spanish for her language sequence instead of German, which had been her first choice. It had been one of only a few good moves she'd made in her life.

She thought about Vivian's painful visit and the admission that she'd lied to Mack about Natalie and Whit. So Mack knew, but he hadn't tried to stop her. He hadn't phoned or written. Apparently she didn't even mean that much to him. He must have meant all the terrible things he'd said to her on the street, where everyone could hear him.

Part of her realized that it was for the best. He'd said that he didn't want marriage or an affair, which could only have led to more misery for both of them. It was just as well that the bond was broken abruptly. But their history went back so far that she couldn't even conceive of life without Mack. And when Vivian was herself, they'd had such wonderful times together, along with Bob and Charles. Natalie had felt as if she belonged to the Killains, and they to her. Now she was cut adrift again, without roots or ties. She had to adjust to being alone.

At least she had a job and a place to live. She'd found work with a temporary agency for the summer so that she could save up for a few additions to her meager wardrobe for the beginning of school in August. She would survive, she promised herself. In fact, she would thrive!

But she didn't. The days turned to weeks, and although she adjusted to her new surroundings, she still felt like an outsider. When she began teaching, she was nervous and uncertain of herself, and the children knew it and took advantage of her tentative style. Her classroom was a madhouse. It wasn't until one of the other teachers, a veteran of first days on the job, came to restore order that she could manage to teach.

She was taken gently aside and taught how to handle her exuberant students. The next day was a different story. She kept order and began to learn the children's names. She learned to recognize other members of the staff, and she enjoyed her work. But at night, she lay awake remembering the feel of Mack Killain's strong arms around her, and she ached for him.

By the second week of school, she was beginning to fit in. But on the way home she passed a small basketball court and noticed two boys who looked barely high-school age pushing and shoving each other and raging at each other in language that was appalling even in a modern culture. On a whim, she went toward them.

"Okay, guys, knock it off," she said, pushing her way between them. Unfortunately she did it just as the hand of one boy went inside his denim shirt and came out with a knife. She saw a flash of metal and felt a pain in her chest so intense that it made her fall to the ground.

"You've killed her, you fool!" one of them cried.

"It was your fault! She just got in the way!"

They ran away, still arguing. She lay there, feeling a wetness on the concrete around her chest. She couldn't get air into her lungs. She heard voices. She heard traffic. She saw the blue sky turn a blinding, painful white....

Mack Killain was downloading a new package of software into his computer when the phone rang. It had been a busy summer, and the unwelcome bull roundup was under way, along with getting fattened calves ready for market and pulling out herd members that were unproductive. He'd worked himself half to death trying not to think about Natalie. He still did. She haunted him, waking and sleeping.

He picked up the receiver absently on impulse, instead of letting the answering machine take over, still loading his program while he said, "Hello?"

"Mack Killain?"

"Yes?"

"This is Dr. Hayes at the Dallas Medical Center," came a voice from the other end of the line.

Mack's heart stopped. "Natalie!" he exploded with a sense of premonition.

There was a pause. "Well, yes, I am calling about a Miss Natalie Brock. Your name and number were on an accident card in her purse. I'm trying to locate a member of her family."

"What happened? Is she hurt?" Mack demanded.

"She needs immediate surgery or she's going to die," the doctor said frankly, "but I have to have written authorization for it, and she can't sign anything. She's unconscious. I have to have a member of her family."

Mack felt his heart stop. He gripped the receiver tightly. "I'm her cousin," Mack lied glibly. "I'm the only relative she has. I'll sign for her. I can be there in two hours."

"She'll be dead in two hours," came the sharp reply.

Mack closed his eyes, praying silently. "I've got a fax machine," he said. "I can write out a permission slip on my letterhead and sign it and fax it to you. Will that do?"

"Yes. But quickly, please. Here's our fax number."

Mack jotted it down. "I'll have it there in two minutes," he promised. "Don't let her die," he added in a tone as cold as ice before he hung up.

His hands shook as he stopped the loading process

and pulled up his word processor instead. He typed a quick permission note, printed it out on ranch letterhead, whipped out two pens before he found one with ink, signed it, and rushed it into the fax machine. In the time he'd promised, he had it on the way.

He cut off the computer and picked up the phone, calling a charter service in a nearby city. "I want a Learjet over here in ten minutes to take me to Dallas. Don't tell me you can't do it," he added shortly. "I'll be waiting at the local airport." He gave the location and hung up.

There was no time to pack. He went barreling out of the office just as Bob and Charles came in behind a stunned Vivian.

"What's going on?" Vivian asked in concern, because Mack's face was white.

"I have no idea. But Natalie's in a Dallas hospital about to undergo emergency surgery. I had to sign for her, so if anybody calls here and asks, we're her cousins."

"Where are you going?" Bob asked.

"To Dallas, of course," Mack said impatiently, pushing past them.

"Not without us, you aren't," Charles told him bluntly. "Natalie belongs to all of us. I'm not staying here."

"Neither am I," Bob seconded.

"Where one goes, we all go," Vivian added. "I'm the one who caused all this in the first place. Natalie needs me, and I'm going. I'll make her listen to my apology when she's well."

"I don't have time to argue with you. Get in the car. I'll lock the door."

"How are we going to get there?" Vivian asked as she herded her tall brothers outside.

"I've got a charter jet on the way."

"Flying," Bob told his sibling. "That's cool."

"Yeah, I like flying," Charles agreed.

"Well, I don't," Vivian muttered. "But it's quicker than driving."

She piled into the front seat with Mack while the two boys got in back. All the way to the airport, Mack drove like a maniac. By the time they arrived, the three passengers had held their collective breaths long enough to qualify as deep-sea divers.

They spilled out in the parking lot at the small airport. The jet was already there, as the charter service had promised, gassed up and ready, with its door open and the ladder down.

Mack didn't say a word until he shook hands with the pilot and copilot and got into the back with his sister and brothers. Until now, he'd had the organization of the trip to keep his mind off the danger of the situation.

Now, with hours with nothing to do but think during the flight, he recalled what the surgeon had said to him—that Natalie could die. He had no idea what had happened. He had to know. He pulled the cell phone he always carried from his pocket and, after checking with the pilot that it was safe to use once they were in the air, he got the number of the Dallas hospital and bullied his way verbally to a resident in the emergency room. He explained who he was, asked if the fax had been received and was told that Miss Brock was in surgery. They had no report on her condition, except that there was at least one stab wound and one of her lungs had collapsed. The resident was sorry, but he had no further information. Mack told him an approximate arrival time and hung up.

"A knife wound?" Bob exclaimed. "Our Nat?"

"She's a teacher," Vivian said miserably. "Some students are very dangerous these days."

"She teaches grammar school," Mack said disgustedly. "How could a little kid stab her?"

"It might have been someone related to one of the little kids," Charles offered.

Vivian brushed back her blond hair. "It's my fault if she dies," she said quietly.

"She's not going to die," Mack said firmly. "Don't talk like that!"

She glanced at him, saw his expression and put her hand over his. "Okay. I'm sorry."

He averted his face, but he didn't shake off her hand. He was terrified. He'd never been so frightened in all his life. If he lost Natalie, there was nothing in the world to live for. It would be the end, the absolute end of everything.

Chapter Nine

When Natalie regained consciousness, there was a smell of antiseptic. Her side ached. Her lung hurt. She had a tube up her nose, and it was irritating her nasal passages. She felt bruised and broken and sick. Her eyes opened slowly to a white room with people in green gowns, moving around a room that only she seemed to occupy.

She blinked hard, trying to get her eyes to focus. Obviously, she was in a recovery room. She couldn't remember how she got there.

A deep voice, raised and urgent, was demanding access to her, and a nurse was threatening to call security. It didn't do any good. He was finally gowned and masked and let in, because a riot was about to ensue in the corridor.

There was a breeze and then a familiar face with a black eye patch hovered just above her. She couldn't quite focus. Her mind was foggy.

A big, warm hand spread against her cheek, and the one eye above her was much brighter than she remembered it. It seemed to be wet. Impossible, of course. She was simply dreaming.

"Don't you die, damn it!" he choked huskily. "Do you hear me, Natalie? Don't you dare!"

"Mr. Killain," one of the nurses was trying to intervene.

He ignored her. "Natalie, can you hear me?" he demanded. "Wake up!"

She blinked again. Her eyes barely focused. She was drifting in and out. "Mack," she whispered, and her eyes closed again.

He was raving mad. She heard him tossing orders around as if he were in charge, and she heard running feet in response. She would have smiled if she'd been able. Every woman's dream until he opened his mouth…

She didn't know that she'd spoken aloud, or that the smile had been visible.

Mack had one of her small hands in his with a death grip. Now that he could see her, touch her, he was breathing normally again. But she looked white, and her chest was barely moving. He was scared to death, and it displayed itself in venomous bad temper. Somebody would probably run him out any minute, maybe arrest him for causing a disturbance. But he'd have gone through an armed camp to get to her, just to see her, to make sure that she was alive. He couldn't have imagined himself like this not so long ago.

Neither could his siblings, who stood in awe of him as he broke hospital rules right and left and sent veteran health-care workers running. This was a Mack they'd never seen before. It was obvious that he was in love with the woman lying so still and quiet in the recovery room. All of them looked at each other, wondering why they hadn't realized it a long time ago.

The surgeon—presumably the one who'd spoken to him on the telephone—came into the recovery room still wearing his operating clothes. He looked like a fire-eater himself, tall and dark-eyed and taciturn.

"Killain?" he asked.

"Yes." Killain let go of Natalie's limp hand long enough to shake the surgeon's. "How is she?"

"Lost a lower lobe of her lung," he said. "There was some internal bleeding and we'll have to keep her here for a while. The danger now is complications. But she'll make it," he added confidently.

Mack felt himself relax for the first time in hours. "I want to stay with her," he said bluntly.

The doctor raised an eyebrow and chuckled. "I think that's fairly obvious to the staff," he mused. "Since you're a relative, I don't have an objection. But we would prefer to have you wait until we can get her out of recovery and into a room. Meanwhile, it would help if you'd go to the business office and fill out some papers for her. She was brought in unconscious."

Mack hesitated, but Natalie was asleep. Perhaps it

wouldn't hurt to leave her, just briefly. "All right," he said finally.

The surgeon didn't dare look as relieved as he felt. He pointed Mack toward the business office, noticing that three younger people fell in step behind him. The victim apparently had plenty of family to look after her. That lightened his step as he went toward the operating theater to start the next case.

Several hours later, Natalie opened her eyes again, groggy from the anesthetic and hurting. She groaned and touched her side, which was heavily bandaged.

A big, warm hand caught hers and lifted it away. "Be careful. You'll pull out the IV," a familiar voice said tenderly. It sounded like Mack. It couldn't be, of course.

She turned her head and there he was. She managed a smile. "I thought I was dreaming," she murmured drowsily.

"The nurses don't. They think they're having a nightmare," Bob said with a wicked glance at his brother.

"I saw an orderly run right out the front door," Charles added dryly.

"Shut up," Mack said impatiently.

"He just wants to make sure you're properly looked after, Nat," Vivian said, coming close enough to brush back Natalie's hair. "You poor baby," she added softly. "We're all going to take care of you."

"That's right," Bob agreed.

"You belong to us," Charles added firmly.

Mack didn't say anything.

Too groggy to understand much of what was going

on, Natalie managed another weak smile and then grimaced. But after a minute she relaxed and went back to sleep.

Vivian studied the apparatus she was hooked to. "I think this has a painkiller unit that automatically injects her every few minutes. I'm going to ask someone."

Without another word, she went into the hall.

Bob and Charles shared a speaking glance and announced that they were going after coffee, offering to bring back a cup for their big brother.

Mack just nodded. He only had eyes for Natalie. It was like coming home after a long journey. He didn't want to do anything except sit there and look at her. Even in her weak, wan condition, she was beautiful to him. His hand curled closer around hers and gripped it securely.

All the things he'd said came back to haunt him. How could he ever have doubted her? She wouldn't lie to him. Somewhere deep inside he knew that. So only one reason for his immediate assumption of her guilt was left. He'd been fighting a rearguard action against her gentle presence with the last bit of willpower he possessed. He was blind in one eye. Someday, he might lose his sight in the other, as well. He had the responsibility for his two brothers and his sister until they could stand on their own. He hadn't felt that it was fair to inflict all that on a young woman like Natalie.

But ever since the crisis had developed, his family had been united behind him and shared his concern for Natalie. They loved her, too. He knew that there would inevitably be conflicts, hopefully small ones, but he'd seen what life without her would be like, and anything was preferable. He'd do whatever he could to make her happy, to keep her safe. Of course, when she was her old self again, she was going to want to knock him over the head with a baseball bat. He was resigned to even that.

The first order of business was to get her well. He was going to take her back to Montana if he had to wrap her in sheets tied at both ends. She might not like it, but she'd have to go. She didn't have anyplace else to recuperate, and she couldn't work. At the ranch, the four of them could take turns sitting with her.

While he was considering possibilities, Vivian came back. "It automatically injects painkillers," she announced with a smile. "I spoke with the duty nurses at their station. They have computers everywhere with records and charts...." She glanced at her brother with a self-conscious smile. "It fascinates me. I didn't realize nursing was so challenging, or so complicated."

"I haven't seen a lot of nurses in here," he remarked darkly.

She grinned at him. "You will when you leave," she said, tongue in cheek.

"Don't you start," he muttered.

She hugged him and sat in the chair on the other side of the bed. "Why don't you go and get something to eat? I'll sit with Nat."

He shook his head. He had her hand firmly in his and he wasn't letting go until he knew for certain that she wasn't trying to give up.

"Want some coffee?" she persisted.

"The boys went to bring some back."

"Okay. In that case, I think I'll walk down to the canteen and get a bag of potato chips and a soft drink."

"Good idea."

She smiled to herself as she went out. He hadn't spared her a glance. She could read him like a book. He was afraid that if he left, Natalie might not recover. He was going to keep her alive by sheer will, if he had to. Vivian couldn't blame him for being concerned. Natalie did look so white and thin lying there. Vivian blamed herself for Natalie's condition. If she hadn't been so horrible, none of this would have happened. She had yet to make her own apologies. But it was nice to know that Nat would be around to hear them.

She wandered down the corridor. Back in the room, Mack leaned forward to study Natalie's sleeping face. "Poor little scrap," he murmured softly, touching her cheek with a touch light enough not to disturb her. "How did I ever think I could manage without you?"

At some level, she was aware that he was speaking to her. But she was fighting the pain and the drugs, and her mind was foggy. She felt his touch, first on her cheek and then lightly brushing her mouth. He was whispering in her ear, words that sounded like the softest kind of endearments. At that point, she was sure she was dreaming. Mack never used endearments....

It was late that night before she returned to something approaching consciousness. She looked around the room with surprised amusement. Vivian was asleep in the chair by the radiator. Mack was sprawled, snoring faintly, in the chair beside her bed, with her hand still gripped in his. Beside him, on the floor, Bob and Charles were asleep sharing a blanket on the cold linoleum. She could only imagine the nursing staff's frustration trying to work around them. And wasn't there some rule about the number of visitors and how long they could stay? Then she remembered the uproar Mack had caused on his arrival, and she imagined he'd broken every rule they had already.

"Mack?" she whispered. Her voice barely carried. She tried again. "Mack?"

He stirred sleepily, and his eye opened at once. He sat up, increasing his firm hold on her hand. "What is it, sweetheart?"

The endearment was disconcerting. He stood and came closer, bending over her with evident concern. "Tell me," he asked softly. "What do you want?"

She searched his face with hungry eyes. It had been weeks since she'd seen him. There was something different....

"You've lost weight," she whispered.

His gaze fell to her hand in his. "So have you."

She wanted to tell him that she'd been only half alive without him, that it was the lack of him in her life that had aged her. But she couldn't say that. She'd been hurt and someone had called him. Probably her serious condition had caused Vivian to finally tell him the truth. He'd come out of guilt. Perhaps they all had.

She pulled her hand out of his and laid it across her chest. "I don't need anything," she said, averting her face. "Thank you," she added politely.

The effect of that cool, polite reply hit him hard. She

was conscious again, and she'd be remembering their last meeting and what he'd said to her. He put his hands deep in his pockets and studied her for a long minute before he went to the chair and sat down. The breath he let out was audible.

She was still groggy enough that she went back to sleep at once. Mack didn't. He sat brooding, watching her, until the first rays of dawn filtered through the venetian blinds. Around him, the boys and Vivian began to stir.

Vivian got up and looked out the door, noticing the bustle of early-morning duty shifts. "Why don't you three go get us a nice hotel suite and have a bath. I'll stay here with Natalie while they get her bathed and fed. By the time you come back, she'll be ready for visitors."

Mack was reluctant. Vivian pulled him out of the chair. "You're absolutely dead on your feet, and you look fifty," she said. "You're not going to be any good to anybody until you get some rest. Have you slept at all?"

He grimaced. "She woke up in the night," he said, as if that explained it all. His face was drawn with worry and guilt. "She remembered what I said to her. It was in her eyes."

"She'll remember what I said, too," Vivian replied. "We'll get through it. She's not a person who holds grudges. It will be all right."

He hesitated. "She isn't going to want to go home with us," he realized. His face began to tauten. "But she will, if I have to put her in a sack! If she wakes up before I come back, you tell her that!"

The loud tones woke Natalie. She winced as she

moved, and her chest hurt, but her eyes lifted to Mack's hard face, and they began to sparkle. She struggled to sit up. "I'm not going…anywhere with you, Mack Killain," she told him in as strong a tone as she could manage in her depleted condition. "I wouldn't walk to the…elevator with you!"

"Calm down," Vivian said firmly, easing her down on the pillows. "When you've gotten your strength back, I'll get you a frying pan and you can lay about him with it. In fact, I'll even bend over and give you a shot at me. But for now," she added softly, "you have to get well. You can only stay in the hospital until you're back on your feet. But full recuperation takes longer—and you can't stay by yourself."

Bob and Charles were awake and crowding around the bed with their siblings.

"Right," Charles said firmly, looking so much like his older brother that it was uncanny. "We'll all take care of you."

"I'll hook up my game system and teach you how to play arcade games," Bob offered.

"I'll teach you chess," Charles seconded.

"I'll teach you how to be a real pain in the neck," Vivian added, tongue in cheek. "I think I wrote the book on it."

Natalie wavered as her eyes went to Mack. His gaze was steady on her face, quiet, and he looked almost vulnerable. Maybe it was a trick of the light.

"You could teach her how to jump to conclusions," Vivian murmured dryly.

"I learned that from you," he shot right back. He

turned to Natalie. "I'm not coaxing. You're coming back with us, one way or the other, and that's the end of it."

Natalie's eyes started flashing. "You listen here, Mack Killain!"

"No, you listen," he interrupted firmly. "I'm going to talk to the surgeon and find out what sort of care you need. I'll hire a private nurse and get a hospital bed moved in. Whatever it takes."

Natalie's small fist hit the bedcovers in frustration. That hurt her chest, and she grimaced.

"Temper, temper," Mack said mockingly. "That won't get you anywhere."

"I am not a parcel to be picked up and carried off," she raged. "I don't belong to you!"

He lifted one eyebrow. "In one way or another," he said very quietly, "you've belonged to me since you were seventeen." He turned to Vivian. "I'll take the boys to a hotel and come back in a couple of hours. I'll phone you as soon as we're settled and you can get in touch with us if you need to."

"Okay," Vivian said with a smile. "Don't worry," she added when he hesitated at the door. "I'll take good care of her."

He still hesitated, but after a minute he shot a last, worried look at a furious Natalie and followed the boys into the hall.

"I won't go!" Natalie choked out.

Vivian went close to the bed and gently smoothed Natalie's hair from her forehead. "Yes, you will," she said gently. "Mack and I have a lot to make up to you. I was so jealous of you that I couldn't stand it. I thought

I'd die if I couldn't have Whit." She shook her head sorrowfully. "You know, he even lied to me that he'd been making out with you. You were both downstairs for almost an hour and I didn't have a clue that Mack had come home in the meantime," she added ruefully, watching Natalie blush as she recalled what she and Mack had been doing during that time. "Whit said he'd found you more receptive than I'd ever been. It was a major misunderstanding all around, and the lie I told Mack, that I'd seen you and Whit together, didn't do anything to help matters." Her worried blue eyes met Natalie's green ones. "Can you forgive me, do you think?"

Natalie let out the anger in a slow breath. "Of course," she said. "We've been friends far too long for me to hold a grudge."

Vivian bent and kissed her cheek. "I haven't been much of a friend up until this point," she said. "But I'm going to do a better job from now on. And the first matter of business is to get you a sponge bath and some breakfast."

"Mack believed you," Natalie said.

Vivian paused on her way to the door. She came back and put a gentle hand over Natalie's where it lay on her stomach over the covers. "The night I told Mack that lie, he went into the office and locked the door and drank half a bottle of Scotch whiskey. I had to get the foreman and a locksmith to open it for me. When I finally got in, he'd passed out."

Her eyes were troubled. "He never loses control like that. That was when I knew how much I'd hurt him.

And after your graduation, when Bob and Charles lit into us about not being there, he went off by himself and wouldn't even talk to us for days. I know what we did hurt you, Natalie," she concluded. "But it hurt us just as badly. I'm sorry. Mack was right about Whit all along. He's going around with another rich girl, but one who likes to gamble herself, and he's got all the money he wants for the time being. I was an idiot."

"You were in love," Natalie excused her. "It doesn't exactly make people lucid."

"Doesn't it?" Vivian asked pointedly, and with a curious smile.

"Don't ask me," the other woman replied, averting her face. "I was only seventeen when I had my first and last taste of it."

"I know," Vivian said disconcertingly. She smiled gently. "It was always Mack. And I knew it, and used it to hurt you. I regret that more than anything."

"That wasn't what I meant," Natalie ground out.

Vivian didn't press the issue. She patted her hand gently. "Everything's going to be all right. Believe that, if you don't believe another word I say."

Natalie shifted to a more comfortable position. "Did all of you come down here together?" she asked.

"Yes. Your surgeon phoned and told us you were fighting for your life and that somebody had to give permission for him to operate." She grimaced. "Mack had to fax a permission slip to him as next of kin, so if anyone asks, we're your cousins." She held up a hand when Natalie started to speak. "If he hadn't, you might have died, Nat."

"I had that accident card in my purse, the one you made me fill out with Mack's name and phone number on it," Natalie recalled. "I guess they found it when I was brought in."

Vivian hesitated. "Do you remember what happened?"

"Yes. I saw two boys fighting on a basketball court. Like an idiot, I went in to stop it." She smiled wryly. "One of them had a knife, and I was just in time to catch it in my chest. Fortunately it only cost me a little bit of one lung instead of my life."

"Next time, call the police," Vivian said firmly. "That's their job, and they do it very well."

"Next time, if there ever is one, I will." Natalie caught Vivian's hand as she moved it. "Thank you for coming all the way here. I never dreamed that any of you would—especially Mack."

"When the boys heard, the first thing they said was that you belonged to us," Vivian told her. "And you do. Whether you like it or not."

"I like it very much." Her lower lip became briefly unsteady. "I'm glad we're still friends," she managed shakily.

"Oh, Nat!" Vivian leaned down to hug her as gently as she could. "I'm sorry, I'm so sorry! I'll never, never be so selfish and horrible again, ever!"

Natalie hugged her with her good arm and sighed as the tears poured out of her, therapeutic and comforting, hot on her pale face.

Vivian drew back and found tissues for both of them

to wipe their wet eyes with, and they laughed while they did it.

"Mack still has his apologies to make," Vivian added. "I think he'll welcome the opportunity. But it's going to be hard for him, so meet him halfway, would you?"

Natalie looked worried. "He looks bad."

"He should. He's been driving himself for weeks. I won't even try to tell you how hard he's been to live with."

"That isn't anything unusual," Natalie said with her first glint of humor.

"This has been much worse than usual. If you don't believe it, try looking into the hall when he comes back. You'll see medical people running for the exits in droves." She chuckled. "We just stood and gaped at him when he walked into the recovery room and started throwing orders around. The army sure lost a great leader when he was mustered out after his tour of duty. He made captain, at that."

"Did… Glenna come, too?" she had to ask.

"He hasn't seen Glenna since you left town," Vivian said quietly. "He doesn't talk about her, either."

Natalie didn't comment. She was sure that Mack was trying to heal a guilt complex, although he had no reason to feel guilty. He'd made a wrong assumption and accused her of something she hadn't done, but he hadn't caused her to be stabbed. That had been her own lack of foresight in stepping into a situation she wasn't trained to handle. It could have happened anywhere.

For the moment, she nodded and lay back. Vivian left her to find the nurses.

* * *

Mack came back with the boys just after lunch. He looked rested. They all did. She supposed they'd taken the opportunity to catch a little sleep in a real bed.

The boys only stayed for a few minutes, having discovered a mall near the hospital where they could look over the video games. Vivian went to the hospital cafeteria to get herself a salad for lunch. Mack sat in the chair beside the bed and looked at Natalie, who was much more animated than she had been the night before.

He reached out and caught her fingers in his, sending a wicked tingle of sensation through her, and he smiled at her gently. "You look better. How do you feel?"

"Like I've been buffaloed," she said. She was shy with him, as she'd never been. Amazing, considering their history. They knew each other so well, almost intimately, but she couldn't find anything to say to him.

He seemed to realize that. His fingers curled closer into hers and he leaned forward. "The surgeon says you can leave Friday," he told her. "I can take you back on the Learjet if you're not showing any bronchial symptoms."

"The Learjet?"

"I chartered one to bring us down here. The pilot and copilot are staying at my hotel until we're ready to leave."

"That must be costing a fortune," she blurted.

He smiled cynically. "What do you think I'm worth? In addition to a very successful cattle ranch and interests in several businesses, I own shares in half a dozen stocks that skyrocketed since I bought my first shares."

She averted her eyes. "I've got an apartment here," she began.

"You *had* an apartment here."

She stared at him, confused. "What?"

"I told your landlady you weren't coming back," he said flatly. "I had your stuff packed up, carefully, and shipped to Medicine Ridge. I even had your mail collected and filled out a form for it to be forwarded on to you back home."

"You can't!" she exclaimed. "Mack, I have a job here!"

"Oh, yes, I spoke to the principal about that," he continued, maddeningly calm. "They're sorry to lose you, but considering the length of your recovery, they have to have someone come in to replace you. You can reapply if you want to come back. But you won't want to."

"Of course I'll want to come back!" she exclaimed, stunned at the changes he'd created, the havoc he'd created in her nice new life. "You can't do this!"

"I've already done it, Nat," he replied, standing to loom over her, still holding her hand. "And when you have time to think about it, you'll realize that it was the only thing I could do," he added somberly. "Leaving you here alone was never an option, not even if I'd hated you."

She dropped her eyes to his big, lean hand holding hers. It was tanned, like his face, from the long hours he spent working on the ranch. "I thought you did hate me, when I left."

He laughed with pure self-contempt. "I know you did. Viv was right, I could sure teach you how to jump to conclusions." His eye narrowed. He put a hand on the pillow beside her head and leaned close. "But there are a lot of other things I'd rather teach you."

"What things?" she asked breathlessly.

"What I promised I would, when you were seventeen." His mouth brushed her lips as gently as a breath, lingering, tasting, arousing. "Don't you remember, Natalie? I said that, when the time came, I was going to teach you how to make love."

Chapter Ten

Natalie couldn't believe she'd actually heard him say that, and in a tone so tender that she hardly recognized it. It was difficult to think, anyway, with his hard mouth making little tingles of excitement everywhere it touched her face.

"Do you think I'm joking?" he asked when she didn't answer him. He bent, his breath whispering against her parted lips. "All the teasing stopped when Dr. Hayes called me and said you were at the point of death," he added tautly. His head lifted, and he looked into her eyes. "From now on, it's totally serious."

She didn't understand. Her expression told him so.

He brushed his mouth softly over her lips, careful not to take advantage of the situation or cause her even more pain. "I should never have let you leave Medicine Ridge in the first place," he said gruffly.

"You told me I wasn't welcome at the ranch ever again," she admonished, her lower lip trembling.

He actually groaned. He kissed her with something that felt like utter desperation and visibly had to force himself to stop. His hand was faintly unsteady as it pushed back her disheveled hair and traced her oval face. "I thought you went from me to him," he confessed huskily. "I couldn't bear the thought."

Her expression lightened. Her heart seemed to lift. For the first time, she reached to touch his hard mouth. "As if I could," she said with wistful sadness.

He brought her palm to his lips and kissed it hungrily. "Weeks of misery," he said heavily, "all because Vivian and I jumped to conclusions."

"It's hard to trust people. I ought to know." She searched his one beautiful eye slowly. She was uncertain with him, hesitant. The medicine was still affecting her, and she was wary of his sudden affection. She didn't trust it. Worse, she was remembering her past. There had never been a person she loved that she didn't lose. First her parents and then Carl; even if Carl hadn't been in love with her, he'd been her first real taste of it.

"Such a somber expression," he said gently. "What are you thinking?"

"That I've lost everybody I ever loved," she whispered involuntarily, shivering.

His head lifted and he looked straight into her wide, worried eyes. "You won't lose me," he said quietly.

Her heart ran wild. Now she was certain that she

was hearing things. She opened her mouth to ask him to say it again, but just as she did, the nurse came in to check her vitals. Mack only smiled at her frustration and went in the hall to stretch his legs.

When he came back, it was as if he hadn't said anything outrageous at all. He started outlining travel plans, and by the time he finished, Vivian and the boys were back and conversation remained general.

Natalie's lungs were clear by Friday morning, and the surgeon, Dr. Hayes, released her for travel home in the Learjet. Mack lifted her out of the wheelchair at the hospital entrance and into the hired car, which they took to the airport. Less than an hour later, they were airborne, and by late afternoon, they were landing in Medicine Ridge.

The foreman had driven the Lincoln to the airport and had another ranch hand follow him in one of the ranch trucks. That made enough room for the Learjet's weary passengers to ride in the car to the ranch house. There, Mack picked Natalie up in his arms and, holding her just a little too close, he mounted the front steps and carried her over the threshold.

He glanced at her with a faintly possessive smile as he stopped just briefly in the vestibule to search her soft eyes.

"You don't have to carry me," she whispered, aware that the boys had headed straight for the kitchen and Vivian had gone ahead of them upstairs to open the guest room door for them.

"Why not?" he mused, bending to brush her mouth lazily with his. "It's good practice."

Practice for what, she wondered wearily, but she didn't question the odd remark. She moved her arm and grimaced as her whole side protested. The wound was still painful.

"Sorry," he said gently. "I keep forgetting the condition you're in. We'll go right on up."

He carried her easily up the long, graceful staircase to the guest room that adjoined his bedroom. She gave him a worried look.

"I'm not having you at the other end of the house in this condition," he told her as he passed Vivian and went into the airy room with its canopied double bed, where he gently put her down. "I'm going to leave the connecting door open, as well. If you need me in the night, all you have to do is call me. I'm a light sleeper." He glanced at his sister with a speaking glance. "Something I can't say for anybody else in this family."

Vivian grimaced. "I do eventually wake up," she said defensively.

"I've got your pain medication in my pocket," he added. "If you need it at bedtime, I'll make sure you get it. Vivian can help you into a gown."

"Something nice and modest," Vivian murmured, tongue in cheek, with a wicked glance at her brother.

"Good idea," he said imperturbably. He paused at the door and that good eye twinkled. "And I'll wear pajamas for a change."

Vivian chuckled at Natalie's flushed cheeks as Mack left them alone. "You're in no condition for any hanky-panky," she reminded her friend. "So stop worrying and just concentrate on getting well. You'll never convince me that you won't feel safer with Mack a few yards away in the night."

"I will," Natalie had to admit. "But I still feel like I'm imposing."

"Family doesn't impose," her friend shot right back. "Now let's get you into something light and comfortable, and then I'll go and see what's on the menu for supper. I don't know about you, but I'm starved!"

It came as a surprise when Mack brought a tray to her room and sat down to have his supper with her. But other surprises followed. Instead of going to work in the study, as was his habit, he read her a selection of first-person accounts of life in Montana before the turn of the century. History was her favorite subject, and she loved it. She closed her eyes and listened to his deep voice until she fell asleep.

She'd been heavily sedated in the hospital and she hadn't had nightmares. But her first night in a comfortable bed, she relived the stabbing. She was lifted close to a warm, comforting chest and held very gently while soothing endearments were whispered into her ear. At first it felt like a dream. But the heat and muscle of the chest felt very real, like the thick hair that covered it. Her hand moved experimentally in the darkness.

"Mack?" she whispered hesitantly.

"I hope you don't expect to wake up and find any other man in your bed from now on," he murmured sleepily. His big hand smoothed her hair gently. "You had a nightmare, sweetheart. Just a nightmare. Try to go back to sleep."

She blinked and lifted her face just enough to look around. It was her bedroom, but Mack was under the covers with her and had apparently been there for some time.

He pulled her down and held her as close as he dared. "Did you really think I meant to leave you alone in here after what you've been through?" he asked somberly.

"But what will the family think?" she asked worriedly.

"That I love you, probably."

She was so drowsy that she couldn't make sense of the words. "Oh."

"Which is why we're getting married, as soon as you're back on your feet."

She wondered if painkillers could make people hallucinate. "Now I know I'm still asleep," she murmured to herself.

"No such luck. Try to sleep before I do something stupid. And for the record, my sister's idea of a modest nightgown is sick. Really sick. I can feel your skin through that damned thing!"

He probably could. She could certainly feel his chest against her breasts much better than she was comfortable doing. But she still wasn't quite awake. Her fingers curved into the thicket of hair that covered his breastbone. "What sort of stupid thing were you thinking of trying?" she asked conversationally.

"This." His hand found the tiny buttons that held the

bodice together and efficiently slipped them so that she was lying skin to skin against his chest.

She felt her nipples go hard at once, and she gasped with the heated rush of sensation that made her heart race.

"That's exactly how I feel," he murmured dryly, "a few inches lower."

It took her a few seconds to realize what he was saying, and she was glad that the darkness hid her face. "You pig!" she exclaimed.

He chuckled. "I can't resist it. You do rise to the bait like a trophy fish," he commented. "You'll get used to it. I've been blinder than I look, but a lot of things became clear when that surgeon phoned me. The main one was that you belong to me. I'm not a perfect physical specimen, and I've cornered the market on dependents, but you could do worse."

"There's nothing wrong with you," she said quietly. "You have a slight disability."

"We both know I could go blind eventually, Natalie," he said, speaking to her as he never had before. "But I think we could cope with that, if we had to."

"Of course we could," she replied.

His hand smoothed her hair. "The boys and Vivian love you, and you love them. We may have disagreements, but we'll be a family, just the same. A big family, if we all have children," he added, chuckling. "But children will be a bonus."

Her hand flattened on his chest. "I'd like to have a child with you," she said daringly. She felt his heart jump when she said it. "Would you like a son or a daughter?" she added.

"I'd like anything we get," he said quietly. "And so would you."

That sounded permanent. She smiled and couldn't stop smiling. Children meant a commitment.

"Yes. So would I," she said, closing her eyes with a long, heartfelt sigh of contentment.

His hand tensed on her hair. "I wouldn't do too much of that," he cautioned.

"What?"

"I can feel every cell of your body from the waist up, Nat," he said in a strained tone. "And I've gone hungry for a while. You aren't up to a passionate night. Not yet."

"That last bit sounds promising," she murmured.

"I'll make you a promise," he replied. "When you're in a condition to appreciate it, I'll make you glad you waited for me."

"I already am, Mack," she whispered. "I love you more than the air I breathe."

For a few seconds, he didn't say anything. Then he turned, and his mouth found hers in the darkness in a kiss that was hard and hungry and passionate but so tender that it touched her heart. But after a few seconds, when one of his legs slid against hers almost involuntarily, he stiffened and abruptly rolled over onto his back beside her, groaning as he laughed.

"I knew this was a bad idea," he sighed.

Her body was tingling with delicious sensations. She pulled herself into a sitting position, grimacing with discomfort. "Well, there goes that brilliant idea," she murmured, holding her rib cage as she eased back down.

"What brilliant idea?" he asked.

"I was going to see if I could—" She stopped dead when she realized what she was about to say. "I mean, I..."

There was a highly amused sound from beside her. "If you got on top, Nat, I'd still have to hold you there, and after the first few seconds, I wouldn't be gentle. We'd reopen that wound and the pain would be vicious."

She swallowed. "Just a thought. Forget I mentioned it."

He laughed tenderly, bending to kiss her briefly. "I'll try," he said softly. "Thanks for the thought, anyway. But this isn't the time or the place. First we get married," he continued. "And then we can make all sorts of discoveries about each other."

Her heart was still racing. "It's exciting to think about that."

"For both of us," he admitted. "But we'd better quit right now, while we're ahead." He bent and brushed his mouth softly over a hard nipple, lingering to taste it with his tongue.

She caught her breath and he lifted his head to look at her in the soft glow of the small night-light.

"I like that," she whispered.

"Me, too." He was hesitating. This was a bad idea. One of the worst he'd ever had. But he was bending to her body while he was thinking it. His mouth covered her breast again, very gently, and one lean hand smoothed down her body to ease her gown up. He traced her upper thigh with slow, expert movements, making lazy and exciting forays inside it under the gown.

She started trembling. Her hands hesitated on his shoulders while she let her mind go blank except for the pleasure he was giving her. It had been so long. While she was thinking it, she said it.

"So long," he breathed urgently. "Yes, Nat. Too long!"

Her hands went between them to his broad chest and caressed him with delight, enjoying the thickness of hair and the warm muscles under it.

She felt his body tense and his hand move to a much more intimate exploration. She tried to catch his wrist, but it was too sweet to deny. She gave in, moaning as she felt the most exquisite sensations pulse through her.

She was drowning in pleasure. It was so intense that she barely felt him take her hand and guide it down his body. He'd unsnapped his pajamas and she was inside them, discovering the major difference between men and women with a fascination that was going to make her die of embarrassment sooner or later. For the moment, though, it was exciting to touch him that way. She couldn't have dreamed of doing that with anyone else.

He shifted restlessly, enticing her slow tracing to grow in confidence as he groaned aloud at her breast.

"It won't hurt you, will it?" she whispered shakily.

"What you're doing?" He shivered and his mouth grew hungry at her breast, making her moan, as well. "I'm in agony. No, don't stop!" he said quickly, catching her hand before it withdrew. "Don't stop, baby," he whispered, moving to cover her mouth with his. "I love feeling you touch me! I love it!"

She opened her lips to speak, and he invaded them as his hand moved into a more intimate exploration, one that caused her whole body to spin off into a realm she'd never known existed.

She was moving in a helpless rhythm, helping him, enticing him to continue. Her eyes opened and his was there, seeing her pleasure, watching.

"This is how it feels when a man and a woman go all the way," he whispered huskily, and before she could question the blunt statement, his touch became urgent and invasive, and she seemed to explode into a thousand pulsating, white-hot fragments under his fascinated scrutiny.

She clutched his shoulders, shivering in the aftermath, her open mouth against his bare shoulder. Seconds later, she was crying. Her chest hurt again, but her whole body felt as if it had been caressed to heaven.

"Mack," she whimpered. "Oh, Mack!"

He was kissing her, soft, undemanding caresses all over her face and throat, down to her still taut breasts and back up again. She could feel his body against her without a stitch of clothing in the way. And only then did she realize that her gown was lying on the floor somewhere.

She didn't remember the clothes being removed. She only remembered the throbbing pleasure that even in memory made her tremble.

"When we have each other, we're going to set fires," he whispered into her ear.

"I want to," she breathed into his lips. Her hands smoothed his cheeks as she looked at him with caressing eyes. "I want to right now." Her hips moved against his, feeling the hard thrust of him that he made no effort to hide.

"So do I. More than you realize," he replied tersely. "But we're not going one step further than this until you're completely healed and we're married."

"Mack!" she groaned.

"You can't take my weight," he said. "Even if you lie over me, it would be more violent than this when I went into you. And once I started, I'd lose control."

Her gasp was audible. Word pictures formed in her mind and made her flush in the dim light.

"You're still a virgin," he continued huskily. "No matter how much I arouse you, it's probably going to be uncomfortable. But I want you to know what it's going to feel like when you adjust to me. I don't want you afraid of me on our wedding night."

"As if I could be…after that," she whispered, pushing her face into his throat. "Oh, it was…glorious!"

"Watching you was glorious," he said roughly. "But we have to stop. I won't take my pleasure at the expense of your pain."

He got up abruptly, pausing to help her into her gown before he picked up his pajama trousers. He turned toward her deliberately, watching her avert her eyes.

"Are you afraid to look at me?" he asked gently.

She grimaced. "I'm sorry. It's…difficult."

He laughed, but it wasn't mocking laughter. "All right, chicken." She heard his pajama trousers snap, unusually loud in the room, before he climbed into bed beside her and drew her demurely to his side.

"You're going to stay with me all night?" she whispered breathlessly.

"All night, every night, if I have to put a chastity belt on you to protect you until we're married," he said wickedly. "And I may. I want you excessively."

She nuzzled her face against his shoulder. "I felt like that, too. I didn't expect to. I've never known what it was to want someone until you started making passes at me."

"I couldn't help it," he sighed. "I'd reached the end of my patience."

"What do you mean?"

He kissed the tip of her nose. "Later. I've got work to do tomorrow. We both have to get some sleep. Okay?"

She sighed, as close to heaven as she'd ever dreamed of being. "Okay, Mack."

She let her sated body relax and curled into him, closing her eyes. He gathered her as close as he dared and pulled the covers up.

"And don't brood over what I just did to you," he murmured firmly. "It's part of the courtship ritual. We'll restrain ourselves until it's legal. In the meantime, you and Vivian can plan the wedding."

She moved drowsily. "Are you really serious?"

"Deadly," he said, and he wasn't laughing. "I wanted you when you were seventeen and I want you now. Somewhere in the middle, I fell in love without realizing it. These past few weeks have been the purest hell I've ever known. I don't want to go through them again."

"Neither do I." She touched his face in the darkness.

"I'll be the best wife in the world, I promise I will. I'll take care of you until we die."

He swallowed hard. "I'll take care of you, too, Natalie," he whispered. "And I'll never stop loving you. Not even when they lay me down in the dark."

She pressed her mouth against his bare shoulder and her hands clung to him. "Not without me, you don't. Where you go, I go. No matter where."

He couldn't manage another word. He kissed her forehead with breathless tenderness and wrapped her close in the darkness.

The wedding took a lot of planning. It had to be small, because Natalie didn't recover as fast as she'd hoped to. But it had to be big enough to accommodate everyone who wanted to see them married, and that meant having it at church. They settled on the local Presbyterian church, and Natalie decided to have a traditional white wedding gown and to let Vivian be maid of honor. Mack decided to have two best men so that both his brothers could stand up with them. It was unconventional, but very much a family affair.

With Mack in a dark suit and Natalie in her elegant puffy-sleeved white silk dress with a long veil and a bouquet of white roses, they were married. They exchanged rings and when Mack lifted the veil to look at her for the first time as his wife, tears rained down her face as he bent and kissed her more tenderly than he ever had before. They looked at each other with expressions that brought tears to the eyes of some of the matrons in the congregation. Afterward, there was the mad dash out the door—done leisurely to accommodate Natalie's still slow pace—and the rice and ribbons. It was traditional in that respect, at least, and in the reception in the fellowship hall with the cakes and punch.

"You made the most beautiful bride in the world, Nat," Vivian said as she kissed her warmly after the ceremony. "I'm so glad things worked out, in spite of me."

Natalie laughed warmly. "We both have a lot to learn about life. Besides," she added, "every bad experience has a silver lining. Look at what mine has produced. And not only for me," she added wryly.

Vivian wrinkled her nose as she smiled. "Imagine me, in nursing school," she chuckled. "But the nurses in Dallas said I was a natural, and I think I am. I love the work, the equipment, everything. I daresay if I study hard, I'll make a decent nurse."

"You could make a decent doctor, if you wanted to," Mack added as he joined them to slip a possessive arm around his new wife. "We can afford medical school."

"I know that," Vivian said. "But I'm not really keen on spending ten years in school, just the same. Besides," she said with a grin, "everyone knows that the nurses are the real power in hospitals!"

Natalie laughed. "You certainly would be."

Mack kissed his sister's cheek. "You've changed a lot in the past few months," he pointed out. "I'm very proud of you."

Vivian flushed with pleasure. "I'm proud of you, too, big brother. Even though it took you so long to realize that marriage isn't a trap."

He searched her face quietly. "I was afraid that it

might be too much responsibility for Natalie to take on. But uncertainty is part of life. Families band together and get through the bad times."

"Indeed they do," Vivian seconded. "I'm so glad we all had a second chance. Look what wonderful things we've done with it!"

"And the most wonderful is only a few hours away," Mack whispered in Natalie's ear a few minutes later as they were preparing to leave on their brief honeymoon to Cancún.

Natalie pressed her hand against his cheek and felt him lift and turn it to press his lips to the palm. "I've waited a long time for you," she said cheekily. "You said you'd be worth it."

He chuckled. "Wait and see."

They had Vivian and the boys drive them to the Medicine Ridge airport, where they took the Learjet to Cancún. They were booked into a luxury hotel on the long island just off the mainland, with one of the most beautiful sugary white beaches in the world. It looked like paradise to Natalie.

"It's so beautiful," she kept repeating after they'd checked in and were standing on their private balcony. "It looks like a picture postcard!"

"You can't swim just yet," he reminded her. "But would you like to go and walk on the beach?"

She turned to him and smiled softly. "Would you?"

He pursed his lips and gave her lithe body in the peach silk dress a long and ardent scrutiny. "I think we both know what *I'd* like to do," he mused. "But I'll humor you."

"It would be nice to look for shells," she said. "And besides, it's not dark yet."

He blinked. "I beg your pardon?"

"It's not dark. I mean, it's broad daylight." She hesitated, because he wasn't getting it at all. She flushed a little. "I couldn't possibly take off my clothes in the light and do...that...in bed with you looking at me!"

Chapter Eleven

He stared at her with utter astonishment. "My God!"

He looked as if she'd thrown a pie in his face. She put her hands on her hips. "My God, what?" she demanded. He sure was acting funny.

He took the tourist booklet out of her hands and put it on the round table inside the sliding door. He pulled her to him, very gently, and bent to her mouth.

It was the first time he'd kissed her with intent, as a lover instead of a fiancé. Despite their intimacy her first night back at the Killain house, she hadn't dreamed there were such deep levels of intimacy in a simple kiss, until she felt her knees buckle and her body begin to burn with sensations she'd never felt.

She held on to his arms as his big, warm hands began a slow, teasing exploration of her figure that rose to just under her breasts, and around them, without touching them at all. After a few seconds, her body began to follow them, to entice them and finally to plead for the teasing touch that he denied her. When it came, when she felt his hands close around them, she moaned harshly and caught his wrists to hold his hands there.

It was like that night he'd touched her so intimately and taught her the sensations her untried body could feel with him. He'd taken her to heights that she'd dreamed about and moaned hungrily over in the time before the wedding. He hadn't come very close to her in the meantime, apparently dead serious about abstaining until the rings were in place. He had continued to share her bed, but with the hall door cracked open and a resistance to all her flirting that made her reel. He was affectionate, gentle, even tender—but there was nothing indiscreet or urgent. Until now.

She never felt him ease her down on the bed. Each caress was followed by one that was more enticing, more teasing, more provocative. Her world narrowed to the needs of her body. She'd gone hungry for him in recent days. She ached to have him against her. She wanted his hands on her bare skin. She wanted his eyes on her. She wanted utter, absolute possession. She arched her back and ground her mouth into his, her hands trembling as they locked behind his head and guided those expert lips to her breasts. They were bare, although she didn't realize it until his mouth fastened hard onto a taut nipple and began to suckle it. She made a sound that she didn't recognize and twisted up to prolong the sweet agony of the contact. It had been so long. Too long. Ages too long!

In the tense, lazy minutes that followed, she was all too eager to shed her clothing, because her body was hungry for his mouth and his hands. They felt warm in the faint chill of the air conditioner, but she was blind to the light that flowed in through the venetian blinds as he ripped the cover off the bed and pushed the pillows after it. His body moved lazily against hers between urgent unfastening and unbuttoning. He managed to get the fabric out of the way and follow it with two pairs of shoes in a blind, throbbing heat that had both of them out of their minds with desire.

"I thought I'd go mad before the ceremony," he said against her breasts. "I ached like a boy before his first time. All I could think about was that night we lay naked together in your bed, and you let me satisfy you!"

"I thought about it, too," she groaned, clinging to him. "I want it again. I want you!"

"I want you, too," he said huskily, suckling her a little roughly in his ardor. "More than you realize!"

He lifted away from her for a minute, his expression barely controlled, tense. He looked at her nudity with raging desire while he gauged her readiness for what was to come. He traced a torturous path down her taut body and touched her blatantly, his eye narrow and glittery.

"Yes, you're ready," he breathed.

She wondered how he knew, but before she could ask, he was moving her closer to him with an expertise she couldn't begin to match.

He rolled onto his side, pulling her between his long, powerful legs. His hands settled on her slender hips, moving her against the hard thrust of him in an arousing rhythm as he played hungrily with her soft, parted lips.

One of his long legs eased between both of hers in a teasing motion that was even more arousing than the play of his warm hands on her bare skin. She shivered and tried to get closer.

"Don't rush it," he said tenderly. "I have to be slow, so that I don't hurt you too much. Let me show you what I want you to do."

He guided her with his hips until she was right up against him in an intimacy they'd never shared unclothed. Her eyes widened as she felt him in the most intimate place of all. She jerked a little at the unfamiliar closeness.

"That's it, sweetheart," he coaxed, both hands on her hips, drawing her over him tenderly so that he moved slowly against the faint barrier she could feel.

Her hands bit into his hard arms. She stared at him, fascinated at the play of expressions on his taut features as his body began to invade hers with the advent of a sharp, unexpected pain. He hesitated, and his hand went between them, working magic on her tense muscles.

She began to shiver with the onrush of pleasure, diverted from the pain. He was so blatant with his ardor that she lost the last vestiges of fear and began to move with him, hungry, greedy for more of the fierce pleasure he was teaching her.

"It won't hurt for long," he promised as he began to move closer. "I'll be careful with you."

"I don't care," she choked, pushing against him in an agony of need. Her eyes closed on a sob. "Oh, please, Mack! It aches so!"

"Natalie," he groaned, losing his patience in the heated brushing of her thighs against his. He brought her against him hard while his mouth ground into hers. He felt her body open to him completely, hesitate, flinch briefly.

His eye opened and looked into both of hers, but she wasn't hesitating, she wasn't protesting. Her eyes were blind with passion, her face flushed with desire.

His hands contracted while he watched her face. She gasped at the slow, deep, sweet invasion and moaned sharply as her body adjusted to this new and wonderful intimacy.

"Don't tense," he whispered.

"I'm not!" she whispered back, swallowing hard. "It feels…" Her eyes closed and she gasped. "So good, Mack! So…good! So good!"

She was sobbing with every fierce movement of his hips, her hands clutching at him, her body following the quick, hard dance of his in the silence of the room. Spirals of pleasure were running through her like flames, lifting her, turning her against him. She felt him inside her and the pleasure began to pulse, like the quick, sharp beat of her heart as he moved in a deep, throbbing rhythm. She had a glimpse of his face going taut, and she heard his breath become torturous as the movement increased in fury and insistence.

She was reaching for some incredibly sweet peak of pleasure. It was there, it was…there. If only she could find the right position, the right movement, the right… yes! She lifted to him in an arch, gasping.

"There?" he whispered. "All right. Here we go. Don't fight it…don't fight it…don't… Natalie!"

His voice throbbed like her body, like the pulse that was beating in her eyes, her brain, her body, a heat that was as close to pain as it was to pleasure. And all at once, it became an unbearably wonderful tension that pulled and pulled and suddenly snapped, throwing her against him in an agony of pleasure. She shivered and felt him shiver as they clung together in the most delicious ecstasy she'd ever experienced in her life.

She heard his voice at her ear, harsh and deep, as his body clenched one last time and finally relaxed, pressing her into the mattress with the weight of him. Her arms curled around his long back and her eyes closed and she smiled, achingly content as she held him like that, heavy and damp and warm, vulnerable in his satiation, on her heart.

All too soon, he leaned up, his gaze holding on her rapt face. He smiled gently. "Well?"

She knew what he was asking. She smiled shyly and hid her face in his warm, damp throat.

He rolled over, still joined to her, holding her close. "How's the rib cage?"

"It's fine," she whispered.

"And what do you think about lovemaking, Mrs. Killain?" he whispered wickedly.

"I think it's wonderful," she blurted. "I never would have believed it could be so sweet. And I was afraid!" she added, laughing.

"I noticed." He kissed her nose. "Are you ready for a shock?"

She looked at him, puzzled. "A shock?"

"Uh-huh."

While she was trying to work it out, he lifted her away from him, and she looked down. Her face went scarlet.

"Now you know, don't you?" he asked with a worldly wisdom she couldn't match. He put her down and got out of bed, magnificently naked and not a bit inhibited. He went to the small icebox and pulled out a bottle of beer, which he took to bed, sprawling on top of the sheets against the headboard.

"Come on," he coaxed, opening his arm to gather her beside him. "You'll get used to it. Marriage is an adventure. You have to expect startling discoveries."

"This is one," she murmured, still shy of him like this.

He chuckled. "I'm just flesh and blood. The mystery will get less mysterious as we go along. We're through the worst of the honeymoon shocks, though."

"Think so?" she mused. "You haven't seen me with my hair in curlers and no makeup yet."

He bent and kissed the tip of her nose. "You're beautiful to me. It won't matter what you wear. Or how you look. I love you. Now more than ever."

He opened the beer and took a sip, putting the bottle to her lips. She made a face.

"It isn't good beer," he agreed. "But it's cold and good for the sort of thirst we've worked up." He took another sip and let his eyes run down the length of her soft body, lingering on the places he'd touched and kissed until she flushed. "You really are a knockout," he murmured. "I knew you were nicely shaped, Mrs. Killain, but you're more than I ever expected."

"That goes for me, too," she said.

He kissed her lips tenderly. "Feel like doing that again?" he whispered. "Or is it going to be uncomfortable?"

She rolled onto her side and slid one of her legs to the inside of his. "It won't be uncomfortable," she whispered. She rubbed her body against him and felt him tense with a sense of pride and accomplishment. "I want you."

The beer bottle barely made it to the table without overturning as he pulled her to him and kissed her with renewed passion. He really shouldn't have been capable of this much desire this soon, but he wasn't going to question a nice miracle. His mouth opened on her eager one, and he forgot the rest of his questions.

That evening, they sat on the balcony after a light supper, drinking cola and watching the moon rise over the Gulf of Mexico. They sat side by side, holding hands and glancing at each other every few seconds to make sure that it was all real.

"In all my dreams, it was never like this," she confessed softly.

"Not in mine, either," he replied gently. "I don't like to leave you even long enough to take a shower." His gaze went hungrily to her face. "I never thought it could be like this, Natalie," he breathed. "Not so that I feel as if we're sewn together by invisible threads."

She drew the back of his big hand to her lips. "This is what they say marriage should be," she said dreamily. "But it's more than I hoped for."

His fingers curled into hers. "I know." He glanced at her hungrily. "You'll never know how I felt when Vivian confessed that she'd lied. I couldn't bear the thought that I'd almost lost you."

"It's all in the past," she said tenderly. "Speaking of your sister, Vivian phoned while you were showering," she said suddenly. "She said that Bob and Charles have gone hunting with that Marlowe man and she was going to spend the weekend cramming for her first test."

"I told the boys not to go off and leave her alone," he said grimly.

"Stop that," she chided. "Vivian's grown, and the boys practically are. You have to stop dictating every move they make."

He glared at her. "Wait until we have kids that age, and tell me that then!" he chided.

She sighed over him, her eyes full of wonderful dreams. "I'd like one of each," she mused. "A boy to look like you, and a girl who'll spend time with me when I'm working in the kitchen or the garden, or who'll be old enough for school when I go back to teaching."

"Planning to?" he asked comfortably.

"Not until the children are old enough to go, too," she said. "We can afford for me to stay home with them while they're small, and I will. When they're old enough to go to school, I'll go back to work."

He brought her hand to his mouth and smiled. "Sensible," he agreed. "And I'll change diapers and give bottles and teach them how to ride."

She studied his handsome face and thought back over all the long years they'd known each other, and the trials they'd faced together. "It's the bad times that bring us close," she commented softly.

"Yes," he said. "Like fire tempering steel. We've seen the best and worst of each other, and we have enough in common that even if we didn't have the best sex on two continents, we'd still make a good marriage."

She pursed her lips. "As it is," she said, "we'll make an extraordinary one."

"I couldn't agree more." He lifted his can of soda and she lifted hers, and they made a toast.

Out on the bay, a cruise ship was just coming into port, its lights making a fiesta of the darkness, a jeweled portrait in the night. Natalie felt like that inside, like a holiday ship making its way to a safe harbor. The orphan finally had a home where she belonged. She clasped her husband's hand tight in her own and sighed with pure joy.

* * * * *

SPECIAL EXCERPT FROM

HQN

*Texas Ranger Colter Banks has renounced true love—
but the one woman he never expected to draw him in,
Clancey Lang, might just catch his heart forever.*

Read on for a sneak preview of
Unleashed,
part of the Long, Tall Texans series
from New York Times *bestselling author Diana Palmer.*

"Even a doctor couldn't read this handwriting," Clancey muttered to herself as she tried to decrypt a note jotted in the margin of a photocopied arrest record.

"What are you muttering about now?" Colter Banks asked from the doorway.

Colter was her boss, a Texas Ranger who worked cold cases for the San Antonio office of the Department of Public Safety. He was gorgeous—tall, narrow hipped, with powerful long legs and broad shoulders. He had dark brown hair and liquid black eyes. Those eyes were glaring at her.

She looked up with a disgusted expression on her oval face. She brushed away a strand of dark, wavy hair from her forehead. Pale gray eyes glared at him. "I can't read this." She waved the sheet at him.

"If you'd like to resign…" he offered, and looked hopeful.

"I can't resign. This was the only job available and I have to eat," she grumbled.

He took the sheet from her and frowned as he studied the note he'd placed next to a certain charge on the rap sheet.

"Ha!" she exclaimed.

He glanced at her. "What do you mean, ha?"

"You can't read it, either, can you?" she accused.

He lifted his chin. "Of course I can read it," he scoffed. "I wrote it."

"So, what does it say?"

He stared at it again. He had to puzzle it out or she was never going to let him forget this. While he stared at the scribble and tried to make sense of it, the phone rang.

He tossed the sheet back on her desk. "Phone."

"Excuse," she said under her breath.

He glared at her as he pulled his cell phone out of its holder. "Banks," he said.

He listened. His face grew harder. He glanced at Clancey, who was waving the sheet at him again, and turned his back. "Yes, I can do that," he replied. "Sure. I'll stop by on my way home. No problem. See you."

He put his phone back and looked pointedly at his watch. "I've got to see the assistant DA on a case I'm working, that Reed case from five years ago. We heard that Morris Duffy, who was suspected in his disappearance, may be getting out of prison a year early for good behavior, and soon," he remarked, missing the sudden worried expression on his assistant's face. "We could sure use a break in the case." He glanced again at his watch. "I'd better go on. Almost quitting time."

Clancey got her composure back before his eyes fell on her face. "You still haven't translated this for me," she said pointedly, indicating the sheet.

He glared at her.

Don't miss Unleashed *by Diana Palmer,
available May 2020 wherever HQN books
and ebooks are sold.*

HQNBooks.com

PHDPEXP0519

HARLEQUIN
SPECIAL EDITION

**Believe in love. Overcome obstacles.
Find happiness.**

Save **$1.00**

off the purchase of ANY

Harlequin Special Edition book.

Available wherever books are sold,
including most bookstores, supermarkets,
drugstores and discount stores.

- ✂

Save $1.00

off the purchase of ANY Harlequin Special Edition book.

Coupon valid until September 30, 2020.
Redeemable at participating outlets in U.S. and Canada only.
Limit one coupon per customer.

52616684

5 65373 00076 2 (8100)0 12454

DPCOUP0320